"THIS IS PANDORA'S BOX. READ BEYOND THIS POINT AND YOU UNLOCK IT; READ ALL OF IT AND YOU RENOUNCE YOUR RIGHT TO CHOOSE A COURSE OF ACTION."

So begins this most gripping novel of terror by the author of *Sleeping Dogs*. And Lucas Garfield, having read the shocking deathbed confession of his most trusted friend and colleague, John Roper Anson, is indeed set on a relentless course of search-and-destroy actions that will leave many dead and the American power structure shaken to its roots.

The secret revealed is the existence of a Watergate tape of which Nixon himself was not aware. Its message is a terrifying recital of political murder, corruption and abuse of power at the highest levels. Knowledge of the contents of this tape— the sixty-fifth—carries with it the power to destroy the fabric of American government.

THE 65TH TAPE
FRANK ROSS'S THIRD THRILLER IS EVEN BETTER THAN HIS OTHERS. ALISTAIR MacLEAN SAID ABOUT ROSS'S FIRST THRILLER: "IT CANNOT FAIL TO BE A SUCCESS . . . A MASTERPIECE OF SUSTAINED PYRO-TECHNICS."

Bantam Books by Frank Ross

THE 65th TAPE
SLEEPING DOGS

THE 65th TAPE

Frank Ross

To PAT and JUDY
with gratitude and affection

*This low-priced Bantam Book
has been completely reset in a type face
designed for easy reading, and was printed
from new plates. It contains the complete
text of the original hard-cover edition.*
NOT ONE WORD HAS BEEN OMITTED.

THE 65th TAPE
*A Bantam Book / published by arrangement with
Atheneum Publishers, Inc.*

PRINTING HISTORY
Atheneum edition published July 1979
2nd printing .... October 1979
Bantam edition / October 1980

ISBN 0-553-13747-6

Published simultaneously in the United States and Canada

PRINTED IN THE UNITED STATES OF AMERICA
0 9 8 7 6 5 4 3 2 1

CONTENTS

BOOK ONE **NUMBERS**

*Whoso killeth any person, the
murderer shall be put to death
by the mouth of witnesses.*

NUMBERS 35:30

"This is Pandora's box. Read beyond this point and you unlock it; read all of it and you renounce your right to choose a course of action."

He had written on pale yellow paper with an irregular deckled edge. Lucas Garfield raised his eyes to the window and ran his fingers, hesitant as detectors in a suspected minefield, over the grainy surface. Had this been written by any other man, he reflected abstractly, he would have read on with impunity. After a lifetime in government service and fifteen years in the mainstream of national security, his cynicism was honed to perfection; it was his experience that no performance ever matched the promise made for it, good or bad. The trouble with modern man was that his ideals and aspirations were dwarfed by his vocabulary. Communication, person to person, was now a form of graphic shorthand; bold outlines with simple, recognizable shapes, colored brightly and animated like TV cartoon characters. Language, the precise handcuffing of words to meaning, had become an arcane disease of the throat.

He touched the grain of the paper again, left to right, top to bottom, his eyes still on the window. The man who had written the words had suffered no verbal deficiencies. At Yale they had read ethics together, dissected Latin, Greek, German, French and Italian for moral definitions. The class of '32. Life had blessed them, thrice blessed them, and they had set out to repay the debt.

"Read beyond this point and you unlock it."

Lucas Garfield unlocked it. The writing was clear, generous, elegant but the hand that formed it had shaken irresistibly; pain punctuated every word.

"I have been to Walter Reed today and Randall was honest enough to tell me he can do nothing more. He will not venture an opinion on the time I may have left, so I must presume there is no time at all. In that event, this letter will be in your hands within days. I am instructing my lawyers to send it to you (privately, of course) the moment they are informed of my death."

The door of the library squeaked and Garfield's golden retriever, Cornball, pattered in and came to rest its muzzle on Garfield's lap. He roughed the hair on the dog's skull and

3

back and looked down at his hand. It was old, baby-smooth old. He went back to the letter.

"You once defined morality—in a moment of depression, admittedly—as one of two conscious states: a state of grace, in which a man may codify his link with God, or a condition of expedient benevolence in which man deifies himself to justify his ends. I must say to you now that I have clung throughout my life to a belief in the first. In doing so, I have been guilty of the second.

"I will not embarrass you by making this a deathbed confession: I am not anxious to reveal to my oldest friend the full extent of my inadequacy. However, after long and painful consideration, I recognize I have certain responsibilities to myself, to my country and to my family (by no means my least consideration). I would have been prepared to die with the knowledge of my infidelity to a philosophy, but I cannot do so knowing that the nation itself is a potential victim.

"For good or ill, I gave my support in the late fifties to a group of men who shared my zeal for a return to what would be dismissed out of hand today as 'the old values.' Our aims, essentially, were secular; socially conservative, perhaps, and therefore by contemporary standards reactionary, but the membership was such that any doubts I might have had were put to rest. It would not be an exaggeration to say that my confreres were academically, industrially, culturally and politically the best and the brightest. I never had cause to doubt their ideals, their motivation, their remarkable intensity of purpose. They met and communicated in secret and, in that sense, you may say any cause they espoused must be subject to suspicion. But that was not my experience.

"The group has a name. The Matrix. The definition of the word, in the sense they prefer, is 'a womb' and 'a rock enclosing a diamond.' The child of the womb or the diamond within the rock is the Constitution. Their minds, their ingenuity, their influence are directed to the protection and advancement of that coda.

"My total commitment to The Matrix ethic came to an end on April 14, 1973. You will recognize the relevance of that date, if your memory serves you. I had been recalled to Washington from London two days earlier for a special State Department briefing. We were engulfed in the Watergate affair and its ripples had spread throughout the world.

"At around 8:00 A.M. on the 14th, I received a call from one of Haldeman's people. The President wanted to talk to me. Would I present myself at the White House at ten o'clock. We were to talk in the Executive Office Building but, when I arrived, I was forced to wait more than an hour. Sometime after 11:30 I was shown into the office. Nixon wasn't there, but Haldeman was.

"He told me the President was busy just then, apologized for the continued delay. At that moment, two more summoned guests were escorted into the office and Haldeman introduced us formally before he left. The introductions were unnecessary. We not only knew each other, we were mutually identifiable. All three of us were members of The Matrix. The shock of meeting, of discovering that we had all been summoned by the President at precisely the same time for palpably confidential meetings, temporarily threw us off balance. I'm afraid we forgot the fundamental principles of our association. We talked.

"As I have told you earlier in this letter, that moment saw the termination of my commitment. Our concern, our consternation, led to questioning and cross-questioning and, finally, one of my two colleagues revealed a series of facts, inklings, speculations, circumstantial scraps of evidence that horrified me, stunned me. I will not tell you his name, but you must accept that he was supremely qualified to acquire secret information about virtually anyone. He had made it his business to investigate the genetic code of The Matrix and in doing so had isolated the fact that the group had no soul of its own—God forgive us our supreme stupidity. Innocent members had supplied funds, influence, connections, knowledge, intelligence to advance legitimate aims. Their goodwill had been grossly used. No, abused. The Matrix had been manipulated like a class of unformed toddlers.

"The Investigator then tied his researches to specific members of the group—myself included. Information I had supplied had been used for blatant political and commercial maneuvering. One man, he discovered, had become the repository of our corporate power. He was, like many in the group, a politician, and I must say one in whom I had invested total confidence and respect. He had been singled out for public and political prominence.

"I can scarcely commit this to paper. I could scarcely give credence to what I heard that day.

"The Investigator began slowly to piece together cause and effect; he set out to tie specific members of the group, including himself, to actual cases of abuse. Remember, he did not at first see the significance of his discoveries beyond a possible power-broking situation, and his interest lay in the security aspect and the likelihood of widespread fraud and corruption. For instance, he discovered that certain commercial and political maneuverings in Europe had occurred as a result of information revealed—in good faith—by me. Bad enough, but nothing compared with what he was to unearth later.

"He persisted over many months, working in secret, but using the resources of the great intelligence-gathering organization of which he was a senior executive. The breakthrough came when he read a report submitted by his New Orleans office on a deathbed 'confession' by the inmate of a local institution for the criminally insane. It was what his organization described as 'a kook file,' one of many in which people on the point of death lay claim to appalling (and in his view, self-inflating) actions. Names were mentioned, those of men with whom a third-rate criminal could never be expected to associate. Much of the confession was so fantastic that it was formally dismissed. My colleague, however, knew those names; they were fellow members of The Matrix. They were also men of stature and impeccable record.

"He continued his long and laborious investigation. Every twist and turn revealed deeper, more sinister connections linking The Matrix, as a force, with underworld activities and outright political corruption. He found gross injustice and, finally, deliberate unpardonable murder. Two things became clear: The members of the group were, generally speaking, unwilling and unwitting dupes, links in a chain. More important, someone, some person or caucus, was using them for blatant self-seeking gain. Eventually, this odious trail of circumstantial evidence connected this person, this force, to people, places, times, events—the assassinations of John Kennedy, Robert Kennedy and Martin Luther King.

"You have the right to doubt *my* own sanity at this point. Only the reputation and character of the speaker, a man I had known for more than twenty years, cautioned me against instant rejection of what he related that morning. His final words were that this force behind The Matrix appeared, again circumstantially, to be channeled toward acquiring ultimate political power 'legitimately.'

"He then named the selected candidate. This man, he said, would, in due course, be launched on a path to the White House. We, the members of The Matrix, had, in our innocence, made that possible.

"At that point Nixon came in. He talked to us for half an hour about the implications of Watergate and how he viewed its effects on foreign policy and our commitments around the world. I confess I heard little of what he said. He requested that I stay on after this briefing and we talked for another fifteen minutes. When I left the Executive Office Building my two colleagues had already gone. That evening, I tried to reach them both without success and five days later, on my return to London, I learned that one of them had died of a heart attack at his home in Colorado.

"Some time later, the Investigator—I am bound not to reveal his name—called me and arranged a meeting. He flew over a week later and we talked for two days during an ostensible fishing weekend in Hampshire. It had just been revealed publicly that conversations in the President's offices at the White House had been taped throughout the course of his administration. The implication was that our conversation in the hideaway office was also on tape. There were two courses open to us: to reveal its existence to the President or to acquire that tape. The first option we rejected on the grounds that, if it had not already been discovered, the existence of the tape, once revealed, would unquestionably be used to divert attention from Watergate and would initiate an infinitely more damning witchhunt. We seized on the second alternative.

"The details of how we went about this are irrelevant in the sense that they are best withheld. The Investigator used the confusion and the prolonged attempts by the courts to secure documentary evidence against Nixon, to plan his own 'plumbers' break-in. It was successful. That portion of the tape containing our conversation was pinpointed and edited from the original reel. The investigations continued and he kept me informed, although a continuous flow of information was ruled out by its very nature. Two years ago, in March, I learned from the newspapers that my colleague was missing, believed drowned in a sailing accident off the California coast. I have no doubt in my mind whatsoever that his death was no accident. He was within weeks, he claimed in his last call, of pinpointing the power behind The Matrix.

"I had been ill, at that time, for several months and it became clear that I should, in all conscience, resign my post as Ambassador to England. My illness, as you now know, was terminal, and it drained me of strength and the power to act. In the course of the last two years, I have allowed myself to believe that Fate, in its way, ultimately chose the correct path for me.

"However, over the past few months I have been reading with growing concern reports on the progress of the man

7

who, the *Washington Post* suggests, will wrest the Democratic nomination from the President this year. The Harris Poll, I see in today's *Post*, gives him a popularity rating eight point above the incumbent. That man is Senator Ambrose Bradley of Arizona. The candidate named by my colleague, the Investigator, in that taped conversation at the White House in 1973 was Senator Ambrose Bradley.

"It is painful that both you and I should know Bradley and count him, possibly, as a friend—certainly of our student days. He was a founder member of The Matrix. I must record that I have always respected and admired him and still find it difficult to associate him with criminal intent. If he is implicated in the terrible things revealed to me, he deserves no sympathy, no quarter. He must be neutered or destroyed, whatever is expedient. If, on the other hand, he is involved in the sense that I am involved, as a pawn, a dupe, then he must be given an opportunity to redeem himself. God knows, my own naiveté in this was absolute. My awakening came by sheer chance.

"I said at the beginning of this letter that it was a Pandora's box and intimated that you could turn away from it if you chose. But if you have read this far, Luke, there is no longer any turning back. My death will set in motion a chain of circumstance that cannot be stopped. You are wholly committed, I'm afraid. I will explain.

"Before his death, the Investigator and I decided the tape must be secure. He lodged it, therefore, in a safe-deposit box in the Clasunard Security and Trust Company vault in Atlanta, Georgia, a city with which he had no personal or obvious professional connections. I retained the key and a passcard registered in the depositor's name—an assumed name, of course, but one for which the Investigator had identifying documents. On my death, my lawyers were required to dispatch a number of letters, this one included among them. Another was hand-delivered to Stephen Quinn Faber, a former CIA agent who was a senior assistant to the Investigator and a close family friend. In his letter is a request that he go to Atlanta at once and, with the enclosed key and documents, withdraw from the vault a black brief-case. It contains the tape. His instructions are to carry it with the greatest precautions to the Statler Hotel in Washingon where, at exactly 0815 hours on the second morning after my death, he will register. A reservation will have been made in his name (by you, of course); it will be for room 421. My letter tells him that the room will have been intensively prepared to avoid any possibility of mistakes. (I enclose a list of the measures he expects.) The handover will take place in that room at 0820. Also in the deposit box is a wallet containing $20,000. This, Faber has been told, is to cover his expenses and any inconvenience arising from the immediacy of the journey.

"Cautions: I cannot guarantee Faber's safety totally, nor the secrecy of the Clasunard box. The Investigator, having probed almost to the heart of The Matrix power structure, was aware that he was being watched. It is not impossible that he was followed to Atlanta and that Faber's arrival, even two years later, will be noted and acted upon. We are dealing, no matter how melodramatic this may appear to you, with highly organized and precise people. Don't underestimate them.

"In addition, the Investigator's widow—a fine woman who knows nothing about any of this—informed me not too long ago that she had been approached at her home in New York on at least three occasions by perfectly documented CIA officers who produced warrants permitting them to take away her late husband's personal papers. Three times, Luke! My contact with The Matrix since '73 has been nonexistent, but I credit them with the intelligence to see the importance of recruiting genuine CIA personnel. They—he, this manipulator—were, as I've said, responsible, to my mind, for the Investigator's death. They must assume that his inquiries are based on documentary evidence of some kind. They might also assume that this evidence lies in the Clasunard vault.

"I am guilty of many things, Luke, and I am sickened by my spiritual weakness in clutching at expediency in situations where moral courage was the real key. I bequeath you my responsibility. You cannot permit Bradley to reach the White House if there is even the faintest suggestion that he is being controlled. You must also seek out his controller. How you do it is your affair, but it must be done. The tape may help—although I pray to God you won't find it necessary to make it public. Not for my own reputation, I hasten to add, but for the country's sake. Once started, this thing could become an avalanche. It would rip holes in the very fabric of American society."

Lucas Garfield pushed the dog's head gently to one side and got to his feet. The sky was weeping snow and the lawns ran white from the house to the belt of willow beside the river. He held the last page of the letter up to the light.

"It's a great comfort to me that Helen was taken first. She would have had no part in this, would have permitted me no

9

craven concealment, whatever the cost. My only cause for rejoicing now is the knowledge that we will soon be reunited before God.

"I can do no more—or, if I can, I am too weak, too ill equipped. You hold forty-five years of service to America in your hands; you hold my family, my honor. Do whatever you feel is necessary but, if you can, spare me one thing.

"Try to see that the sins of the father are not visited on the son."

He had signed it: "Your affectionate and genuine friend— John Roper Anson."

Cornball whimpered from the door. He had been trying to edge it open with snout and paws, but the old brass hinges proved too much for him. Garfield let him out and the dog skidded eagerly across the hallway to the front door. Garfield folded the letter carefully and wedged it in the pocket of his gray herringbone gardening coat.

Outside, he watched Cornball thrash and roll in the new snow. The dog leaped to its feet, shook off a cloud of powdery flakes and bounded away to his favorite tree, the tall old beech by the driveway.

Garfield pulled the coat tight around him. Habit and practice and professional conviction told him to apply the first principle of tradecraft: disbelief. But he knew that was beyond him. Throughout their lives, he and John Roper Anson had been bound by a totality of trust. Essential truth was the greater part of that trust. Besides, his own part in this had already been engineered; there was only one course open to him.

He had no personal feelings in the matter, beyond the faint weariness of spirit that attends an old man confronted with the death of someone his own age. He could believe anything, anything at all, emanating from the Watergate mess—or nothing at all. Ambrose Bradley, on the other hand, was more than just a political cardboard cutout. He'd started as a freshman at Yale the year Garfield and John Roper Anson graduated. Good family, shrewd legal mind, solid career on the bench; he would have reached the Supreme Court if he hadn't turned to politics, and that proved a wise choice. A year ago, local newspapers and TV stations in his home state of Arizona had begun banging the drum for him as a White House candidate. Nobody listened at first, but the message spread.

Ambrose Bradley maintained the stance of the perfect

gentleman. No, he was not an official candidate. No, he was not conducting an undeclared campaign. Yes, he had made over 300 speeches at critical electoral points around the country in the past six months, but strictly by invitation. Whose invitation? Governors, fellow Senators, Party officials—and a lot of ordinary people. Why? The nation was restless; it was looking for a decisive Party line. And then there was the crack that made him famous: "If the President's looked behind him lately and not seen anyone following, I think I ought to tell him it's because nobody can be sure what direction he's traveling." It was a line that gave him national TV exposure and a reputation, ill deserved, as a wit; but he managed to cling to his respectability, to his integrity and his fire; he was an impassioned man at the microphone. Now, just a few days into January, Ambrose Bradley was still not admitting his candidacy, but the Party managers were already convinced. Bradley was going to carry the Iowa caucus by a mile and beat the hell out of the front-runners in the New Hampshire primary next month. It wouldn't be a broker's convention this year, they said, even this far off. The President could start the countdown on his tenancy at 1600 Pennsylvania Avenue.

Garfield took the stick Cornball had found and volleyed it out over the snow. The dog yelped to the chase.

Two certainties. One, he could not ignore any warning uttered by John Roper Anson. Two, Bradley was too old at sixty-three to be a natural Presidential runner. Presidential candidates, like all Presidents, reflect their times—but not their backers. Bradley's sincere insistence that he was not campaigning was an obvious lie, which suggested that his promoters were seasoned players who considered the timing of his entry absolutely essential. Nothing a manager liked more than to have his leading man drafted from the floor.

Ambrose Bradley had also, coincidentally, majored in ethics. In the past year, he appeared to have rediscovered the vocabulary of his student days: His speeches were studded with morality. To be perfectly fair, in his mouth it sounded good: the concept of human invincibility in the cause of justice; goodness, mercy, truth, purity; the perfect clarity of honor.

The word made him smile. Ralph Waldo Emerson's truism came to him: "The more he spoke of honor, the faster we counted the spoons."

Unfair to Bradley.

Unfair to The Matrix? Unfair to the man—any man—who might be manipulating it?

Cornball flurried to a halt with the stick in his mouth. Garfield swept it away, high and wide. It came to rest in the branches of the old beech. Cornball raced off to the end of the world in pursuit.

Garfield trudged after him. The existence of The Matrix itself was hardly earth-shattering. Every democracy spawned its bastards. He'd heard of it, though not by name. Touched it, but less often and less firmly than he had made contact with many other ostensibly "committed" organizations. Like the Council on Foreign Relations, Inc., for instance. Headquarters: Harold Pratt House, a four story mansion on the corner of Park Avenue and 68th Street in New York. Membership; 1650. Every lawyer, banker, professor, general, journalist and bureaucrat with any influence on the foreign policy objectives of every President since Roosevelt had been either courted or recruited by CFR. The Rockefellers were its Olympus; its policy was liberal, bipartisan, devoted to foreign aid and NATO. Power was its glory. When John Kennedy staffed his White House he was handed a list of eighty-two possible names; sixty-three were CFR members. Most of the President's current foreign policy advisers were CFR men. So Bradley was making ground under the auspices of a new power; right or left of the Established order, better or worse. In the end all that mattered to Garfield was that he should know who they were, where and how they peddled their influence, and for what paymaster.

"The more he spoke of honor . . ."

John Roper Anson was right. Bradley was an honorable man. He could win an election on an honor platform because he was a natural media star—from his sterling silver hair to his Rock of Ages cut and build; it made him a prize specimen for manipulation. If half of what John Roper Anson claimed in his letter was true . . .

"The faster we counted the spoons." He said it aloud, firmly. So begin counting a few spoons.

Stage One was to "receive" the tape. Leo McCullen could arrange that. He could also check out Stephen Quinn Faber.

Garfield pressed one foot experimentally into a patch of virgin snow and lifted it carefully, preserving the perfect indentation of the herringboned rubber sole. The weakness, of course, lay in John Roper Anson himself. Had he really understood what he'd gotten himself into? Had he been used? He had been incapable of cynical manipulation while he lived, but his innocence would have been a useful tool in a power broker's hands.

Garfield raised his head and sniffed the breeze. He couldn't afford to take that kind of a chance. Before he accepted that tape he had to be sure it was genuine. Someone was going to have to go back to April 14, 1973, and doublecheck every conversation recorded that morning.

MONDAY: 1030—McCULLEN

Garfield hovered over the phone in his study for a full hour before he picked it up. The chronic indecision of old age, he told himself, although he didn't care to believe it. Slowing down, softening up, making concessions that shouldn't be made to sentiment and personal friendships. How many miles to senility?

He was sixty-eight years old but only his wife and close friends and the informed knew that; the rest might have guessed him to be in his mid-fifties. He had been blessed with a baby face that belied his age treacherously for the first forty-five years of his life and then carried him into a puppy-fat old age. It was a face still without lines; it wasn't in his character to overindulge himself with smiles, scowls or anxiety. The eyes were clear and the skin around them untrammeled by crow's-feet; the mouth and jaw held their line and, when exposed, the small square teeth were uneven enough to be obviously his own. The light gold half glasses he automatically slipped on his nose when reading merely heightened the effect of a young man camouflaging his age.

It had, nevertheless, been a long life, crammed. Diplomacy was the family trade and Garfield had been inducted into his calling before he was ten years old by a father who, in his turn, had been primed for the foreign service. At twenty-five, Luke was a lowly secretary in Addis Ababa and they left him there just long enough to witness the Italian invasion of Abyssinia. Then came Manila and Shanghai and Brussels and Oslo—another perfect piece of timing; Oslo, the Nazi invasion. State somehow seemed to catch the flavor; a man who was always in the right place at the right time had to have a taste for it. They gave him the London liaison role in September 1940, and Goering sent in the Luftwaffe in droves three days after he arrived to prove his built-in sense of history still worked. He was still there when Eisenhower flew

13

in to preside over the D-Day landings, then they dragged him, protesting, to Washington to help draw up the blueprints that finally converted OSS into the CIA.

From that moment on, he liked to tell himself, he was the bartered bride, the unidentified chattel of an unholy marriage between the Presidency and State. Any dreams he had of a valid, respectable—more important, visible—career as a diplomat, rose like steam, condensed and dried without a trace. John Roper Anson, his friend and confidant at Yale, one by one took all the laurels Garfield had promised himself and succeeded finally to the glittering prize: Ambassador to London. By 1974, Lucas Garfield was a monolith, still invisible, still without credit in his own calling, but more powerful than any of his contemporaries. He had survived five Presidents and received the blessings of their henchmen. He was also ready to retire. Watergate changed any hope of that. Ford and Kissinger had put it to him personally over dinner at the White House, and there was no way he could have said no.

The last lap, Kissinger had promised. He was to recruit two good men from within the Intelligence community—and it would take time because they had to be reflections of himself. Together they would establish the framework of an Intelligence overlord committee. Their brief: to assess the major agencies, monitor their activities and clip their wings when they showed signs of going over the top. Garfield would be responsible only to the President; his recommendations and requirements would be channeled through the President. The committee—Three Men in a Boat, Kissinger called them—would have no official status but they would be expected to function at street level when required. They would have the divine right to spy on the spymasters by any means at their disposal, including the Oval Office.

Garfield had found his men. In four years, their effect on political intelligence-gathering had been explosive. Their effect on the agencies themselves was seismic; the world of dirty tricks and proscribed eavesdropping, burglary, subversion of citizens' rights, the deliberate progressive assassinations of foreign political figures—all of it had come crashing down as Garfield's committee chipped away at the decaying foundations of the national security system. In those four years, Garfield had hardened beyond redemption, sensed it happening to himself and let it go on. Last summer, horrified at his wife Polly's sudden illness and the realization that their time together was almost at its natural end, he protested his determination to retire, but again the President had prevailed. One more year. Just one more year.

The House Assassinations Committee had turned a lot of soil and the worms were wriggling in the unwelcome light of day. It was the wrong time, said the President, to go swing in an old man's hammock. But Garfield's threat of resignation had been little more than a bid to assuage the guilt he felt over his neglect of Polly. The President was right; things were moving at last. The Central Intelligence Agency was again giving up its secrets, in spite of massive attempts to plug the leaks. It was more than mismanagement, or the idiotic overstepping of limits this time. The cancer was rooted deep; the corruption was rife. An auditor, a discontented little ledger jockey who had worked for the Company most of his professional life, had cast the first stone, painstakingly charting the system by which the Company siphoned funds to Heaven knew where; so far they had uncovered only the route, not the destination. Other revelations followed: Organizations had been approached with vague overtures of "cooperation." At the least sign of hostility, the promises were left undefined and unfulfilled. The operation was cool, discreet, almost watertight. But Garfield had no names, as yet; no incontestable proof. On the other hand, he had shrunk from challenging the Company head on.

Much more to the point, its new Director, Donald Rattray Petersen, had drawn the shutters and switched off the lights in an attempt to preserve what was left of his empire. In a speech to a small group of congressmen a few weeks back he'd rejected the proposition that the CIA could be both the nation's babysitter and its punching bag at one and the same time. From now on, he'd said, the punches would be thrown back . . . and he had the muscle to punch hard.

How much Petersen knew about the worm-ridden heap he was sitting on was anyone's guess. He was a pro, a Company man from way back; a timeserver. So far, his arrival had not been marked by a wave of resignations or major reshuffles, so either he was playing a waiting game or he was ignorant, as yet, of his real problem.

Garfield was jolted back to the question of John Roper Anson by Cornball, who planted front paws on his knees and reared up to lick his face. He pushed the dog away and stared at the telephone on his desk. He had only to lift it and dial and the bandwagon would roll. His committee's structure was that good. In four years he had also recruited—at arm's length—his own personal Praetorian Guard: agents, controllers, executives from the service agencies, CIA, FBI and the technical corps. They worked for him at one remove, Mafia style; sometimes for money, more often for the reward of favor, occasionally to relieve personal frustrations or out of downright boredom. A few worked for reasons that could be cataloged as genuine patriotic concern (dear God, how the passage of time had rendered that phrase meaningless).

Leo McCullen was such a man.

Leo (Leon) Ian McCullen practiced the virtue of unquestioning obedience to almost religious extremes. Garfield had observed him for a year; analyzed his childhood, education, family, friends, persuasions, hobbies, predilections and career; disinterred, touched, tasted and x-rayed his thirty-eight years. When he was satisfied, Garfield had him approached, tested, dallied with, tempted, nudged, plagued, confounded. Leo came through. In time he earned the right to meet his Maker and look upon his face, a concept diametrically opposed to the rules Garfield had established from the beginning. But every rule needed an exception, and there was no quarreling with the fact that Leo was exceptional. For the past year and a half he had, from his vantage point inside the Company, been burrowing quietly away to trace the source of the cancer Garfield knew was burning there. The dangers were immense, the practical rewards nil, the demands constant. Leo had shrugged them all off, recruited his own little band and dug, dug, dug. It was only a matter of time. Leo was that kind of man. Whether they *had* time now was another question.

McCullen answered at once; he was incapable of letting a phone ring more than twice. Garfield didn't identify himself.

"I've got something for you. Can you call me?"

"Ten minutes," said McCullen.

Garfield put down the receiver and stared at it. Something was going round in his head, a thought, a scrap of half-forgotten information, the embryo of a hunch. It involved the Company, Roper Anson, Leo, but it wouldn't come together. He shook his head and stared across the room. Cornball stared back, disapproving.

Garfield could follow the geography in his mind's eye. Leo's office at Langley was on the third floor. A fifty-yard walk to the farthest elevator, because that brought him out closer to the parking space occupied by his dark blue Ford. Out onto the service road that led to the George Washington Memorial Parkway; a left turn and a mile and a half to the

16

turnoff. He would probably use the pay phone in the gas station.

"Sorry about that, sir." Eleven minutes, forty-five seconds. McCullen was apologizing for the extra minute and three-quarters.

"This is sensitive, Leo. I want some information relating to a White House meet—April 14, 1973."

"Classified, sir?"

"Maybe yes, maybe no. I'm not trying to be difficult. It could go either way. Have you got someone you can run?"

"You don't want me involved personally?"

"No."

"Right. Is it information of record or verbal?"

"Both." Garfield closed his eyes. "I'm saying it's a meet I want checked first. Around 11:30, April 14, 1973. Morning. Executive Office Building, White House. President Nixon met with three men. American, probably government."

"You have any of their names, sir?"

"I do." Gruffly. "But I'd prefer you to initiate without advance information. I want to be sure of this. Names, dates, everything."

"Right. You said it was verbal *and* on record. What else do you need, sir?"

"I said the date was April '73."

"Nixon. You think it's on tape?"

"Could be. If it's not, I want to know why. Was it recorded—that's one. Two—does the tape exist. Three—is there a copy. And Leo—check an hour or so on each side of that time."

"Can do, I think."

Garfield dropped the papers on his desk and took the base of the telephone in his hand. "Don't think, Leo. Be sure! 110 percent sure."

McCullen gave no hint that the implication had stung him. "Understood, sir. Affirmative. How long have I got?"

"Twenty-four hours. Can't let it go any longer than that. Who can you use?"

"Margolis, sir. Walt Margolis. He's been doing some stuff for me on the other matter. Useful. He's researching now on his memoirs. I have responsibility for clearing his requests for files and any liaison work with State and Justice. He's doing a lot of reading over at State and Justice."

"Good. What's he writing up?"

"He was the Company's Chief of Liaison to the Warren Commission in '64, sir. Most of his research is directed to the

17

conspiracy theory on the assassination of Kennedy. It means he can turn over a lot of stuff too dangerous for me to show interest in."

Garfield lowered the phone to his lap and stared down at Anson's letter on his desk. Conspiracy.

"How are they playing him?"

"He's not the first, sir; I guess he won't be the last. The Kennedy thing gets to a lot of them. At least he's not bucking the Company and looking for a publisher. Abrams put out the usual memo to Head of Records. Any file Margolis wants, there's a twenty-four hour suspension order on it first, while Abrams has someone check it out for sensitivity."

Garfield pondered. The memoir option was a good one. But vulnerable. At the end of their formal careers, Agency officers of Margolis's rank and status were granted the privilege of a well-paid breathing space between active service and official retirement. They were permitted to write their autobiographies, ball-by-ball accounts of their ungodly careers in the service of the State. The work was never published for public consumption, but it provided the Agency with a piquant and useful ongoing history of itself, and the retiring veterans with a psychic enema that purged them of their professional hang-ups and private griefs. In the course of their writing, officers had the right to consult records and files pertinent to their careers or tangential to their work. As former Chief of Liaison to Warren, Margolis would be in a position to cut a swathe through a whole range of classified information.

"Wartime OSS," McCullen was saying. "Experienced trade-craftsman. Case Officer rank in the late fifties, then Controller on a series of penetration exercises in Eastern Europe. A good man. I've taken him into my confidence, sir."

Garfield winced. "How far?"

"Oh, don't worry, sir. He didn't need any persuasion. From what he's seen of the Company over the last few years there's no love lost in that direction."

"Maybe."

"He's safe, sir," stressed McCullen. "I told him just enough to make him useful to me." Pause. "He already knew something was beginning to smell. He was way ahead of us."

Garfield grunted noncommittally. "All right, use him as you think fit. But one thing, Leo . . ."

"Sir?"

"Play the Kennedy thing low. Tell him to cool it in that area."

18

"He's a pro, sir. The old breed. Point him and he goes, like a good gun dog. He won't ask questions."

Garfield looked down at Cornball, prostrate at his feet, and sniffed. "All right, Leo. Wind him up and send him in."

TUESDAY: 0900—McCULLEN

Leo McCullen dressed with the precision of a royal equerry, image and impact uppermost in his mind. His shirts were always blue, his suits always dark, his shoes always laced, and polished to a dazzling luminosity. His hair was conservatively short and perfectly styled at the ears and neck, and his strong open features permanently tanned. The effect of healthy efficiency was magnified by the sterling silver spectacles he wore and strengthened by their tinted, smoky brown lenses.

He slipped into the back seat of the car alongside Garfield, removed his black hat, adjusted his black coat and took the brown folder from his case.

"You were right." He flashed a sidelong glance of admiration at Garfield. "7:12, April 14, 1973. The President's appointments secretary logged an early morning call to . . ."

Garfield gripped his forearm. "Forget the names unless I ask for them."

"Okay. So—the visitor arrived at ten o'clock. He had to wait over an hour. He wasn't the only one. Most of the arranged meetings that day never met schedule. The Watergate thing dominated most of the day. Anyway, I'll come to that. Nixon told Haldeman to run as many meetings together as he could and to postpone any that weren't important. There were two other men waiting to see Nixon. You want me to name them?"

"No. Just their jobs."

"Well, sir, the two other guys were . . . heavy armament. One was Agency, and if you don't want to talk about his name I can't talk about his job either, because that would crack it. He was very big. The other man was . . ." He looked anxiously at Garfield again. "Look, sir, I can't lay this one out, either. He was practically the biggest thing in State short of the Secretary."

"Very well. Just tell me what happened, Leo. I'll read the file later."

"Well, Margolis had no trouble pinning down what Nixon was doing at that time. It's a matter of public record."

McCullen drew a paperback book from his neat black and silver dispatch case. He held it up: *The White House Transcripts,* with an introduction by R. W. Apple, Jr., of the *New York Times.* "All in here. Page 283." He found the page and held it out to Garfield who pointedly ignored it. McCullen read, "Appendix 14. Meeting: The President, Haldeman and Ehrlichman, EOB Office, April 14, 1973. Brackets, 8:55–11:31 A.M." He leaned back in his seat. Garfield raised a hand to wave him on.

"That was the day Nixon got his first report on Watergate from Haldeman and Ehrlichman based on a three-day inquiry. John Mitchell, John Dean and Jeb Magruder were on the hot seat. You can imagine why the President didn't have much time to talk to anyone else."

Garfield nodded. "So what happened?"

"Well, like I've said, Nixon, being tied up, asked Haldeman to do the glad-handing. So after the briefing with Nixon ended Haldeman rounds up the three guys who are waiting, apologizes for the President's nonappearance and bundles them all into Nixon's office at EOB at about 11:40. Then he went off. Nixon didn't return to his office right away. The three guys were in there for about half an hour before Nixon turned up sometime after 12:00 P.M. There's nothing we've got says what they talked about while they were waiting."

"No tape?"

McCullen's smoked glasses flashed. "I'm getting to that, sir. The Nixon-Haldeman-Ehrlichman meeting was one of four meetings and three telephone conversations on that day that Nixon released under pressure from Jaworski. But he only released edited transcripts. Not the tapes."

"So the Nixon-Haldeman-Ehrlichman meeting immediately preceded Nixon's talk with these three men?"

"It did. Now, Margolis did some contact work with a case officer he worked with a couple of times over at Justice. He's retired now and he wants to stay clean, but he told Margolis he'd played with some stuff for the White House when they got around to editing the tapes for transcribing. He says there'd been some pretty sloppy work done—you know, erasing, junking up tracks, that kind of thing—and it was too late to do anything by the time it reached him, but he said nobody knew what the hell was really on all those tapes, not even Nixon. His guess is that when Jaworski started calling for evidence, the White House staff checked the tapes against the appointment book and diaries. Anything extraneous—like unscheduled meetings—was most likely cut off tapes that were submitted, and they probably had that stuff rewound onto new reels. A lot of it never saw the light, but sure as hell they never threw anything away, that much Margolis's contact says he'll put his pension on."

"Conclusion?"

"Margolis says there has to be only one. Any conversation recorded around this time will be part of a set of tapes Jaworski asked for in April '74. On April 16 he petitioned Judge Sirica to subpoena tapes and documents on sixty-four Presidential conversations. The sequence ties in and Margolis has pinned them down.

"In that sequence, this three-way conversation you asked me to find out about should have been part of the tape of the April 14th meeting between Nixon, Haldeman and Ehrlichman—the 64th. It's not. Either it was edited off the main tape and rewound separately, or it was erased. If it was rewound, Margolis says that would make it the sixty-fifth tape. Exactly where it is now is anybody's guess."

Garfield pressed the button that lowered the glass partition between himself and his elderly driver, Nick Montero. "Pull over in the next couple of hundred yards, will you?" He raised the glass again and turned to McCullen. "Let me have that file, Leo."

McCullen handed it over. The question showed on his face for several seconds before he gave voice to it. "Is that all you wanted to know?"

"That's all."

The car stopped and McCullen gathered up his briefcase and coat. Garfield took a green file from his own slim zipcase and held it out. "Read this," he said. "You'll need a carpenter, a wire man and a good preventive security engineer. I want something picked up from the Statler. Don't move in yourself. Get someone outside the Company to do the pickup."

"Pickup?"

"It's all in there, Leo."

"Any connection between this and . . ."

"Read it, Leo. Just read it and act on it. Call me and we'll run over any last-minute snags." He checked his fob watch. "At around one o'clock. Call me then."

Garfield emerged with relief into the brightness of the White House basement and turned to thank his escort. The Marine sergeant snapped up a salute and pulled the door shut behind him. He would return along the secret tunnel to the Treasury Department a block away and await further instructions.

Garfield removed his hat and checked his fob watch. The Secret Service had been told to expect him at 0945; he was three minutes early. It wouldn't do to walk up to the first floor alone; the Duty Officer would make a point of remembering his name, the security officer would be materially embarrassed and the President might be asked questions he could not answer about elderly visitors who insisted on walking the tunnel. Wait.

At 0944 the officer strode around a corner from the East Wing. He checked his stride when he saw Garfield and a flicker of irritation crossed his face; the Marine sergeant would feel the sharp edge of somebody's tongue this day.

"Sir." The word was barely a politeness. Garfield fell into step behind the agent's angrily squared shoulders. He would have liked to tell the man, "I don't like this any more than you do," but that would have been an expression of humanity—and humanity was an exclusively reserved Executive Privilege in these corridors. Mere functionaries had no right to it.

They avoided the staff and service elevators, as usual. Garfield could appreciate the wisdom of this in protecting his identity, but his legs were no longer capable of mounting stairs at a young man's pace and he privately resented the need for this cloak-and-dagger mountaineering exercise every time he met with the President. That damned tunnel, these stairs—*and* the return journey—for ten minutes of conversation; habitually unsatisfactory conversation, because Garfield never came visiting with good news.

The Secret Service man waited with ill-concealed impatience at the head of the stairs on the first floor of the West Wing as Garfield toiled upward, pausing from time to time to allow his heart its due. He leaned on the banister for a few seconds when he achieved the summit and glanced along the corridor. The Executive Protective Service officer was on his feet beside the small monitoring device which kept track of the President's movements. The machine, he noted when they came closer, indicated that the President was *in situ*.

The escort flashed a yellow message sheet enclosed in a dark blue folder. The EPS man consulted a clipboard, checked the time and noted it in his report book. He unclipped the velvet rope guarding the door to the Oval Office, knocked and spoke to someone inside. He stood back and beckoned Garfield.

The President's Press Secretary was over by a door on the far side, a blue leather folder bunched with papers under his arm. As he slipped out, his eyes turned on Garfield for a fraction of a second, registered curiosity, glazed professionally, turned away.

The President was in jeans, a blue work shirt and moccasins. He looked relaxed, unworried, unreasonably fit. If the opinion polls were correct, mused Garfield, all three qualities could be regarded as electoral strikes against him. The people now pandering to Ambrose Bradley preferred their Presidents dogfaced, remote, old and lined, if only as an indication that the job was taking them seriously.

"Hi, Luke." The President came around the huge old desk and they shook hands warmly. The President led his visitor to a chair facing the desk, but instead of returning to his rightful position behind it, dropped easily into a chair that matched Garfield's. It was a characteristic gesture but it unsettled the old man. Proximity and good fellowship were not going to help this time.

"Mr. President . . ."

The host stretched himself in his chair. "I apologize for the work clothes, Luke. Been trying to get a few things tied down before the day's official schedule begins. I've got the French foreign minister coming by in twenty minutes, so I'll need a little time after this to change." He raised his eyebrows.

Garfield ducked his head appreciatively at the implied restriction. "Thank you, sir. I'll keep it short."

"Knowing you, Luke, that'll make it even harder to take. O.K.—let's have it." He stretched his mouth without showing his teeth; it was a gesture of understanding, not humor.

Garfield related his story; the letter, the preliminary investigation, his reactions. He honored his promise to keep it short. The President's expression didn't change, but when Garfield reached the suggestion of a Kennedy assassination conspiracy, his fist rose and he gnawed gently on the bared knuckle of his index finger. When Garfield finished talking, the President got out of his chair, paced across the room, then back again. He returned to the chair and this time sat upright, edge-of-the-seat style.

"Why're you telling me this, Luke?"

Garfield pretended a puzzled stare. "I thought that would be obvious, Mr. President."

The man shook his head sadly. "I need you to level with me, Luke. I mean, really level. If you thought this was just another sideshow you wouldn't be here. I'm not asking you the rights and wrongs of the thing. I want to know if we're vulnerable."

The royal we. Garfield paused.

"There's nothing in any of this that could be construed to connect you and the . . . ," he began carefully.

"God help me, Luke. . . ." The President seemed on the point of losing control; in anyone else the moment would have spawned a profanity. He sighed out his disappointment. "I'm asking you for help, man. Do you think there's anything *in* that letter? Confide in me. How much of the story are you ready to go along with?"

Garfield looked down at his hands. "You know the man concerned, sir. We'll know for sure tomorrow morning when I get the tape."

He got no response, but he was prepared for that. The President rocked his head back and forth, his eyes on the far wall. He said at last, "I was just thinking, Luke; John Roper Anson was as clean and decent a human being as any I could name. Straight as a die, honest, clear-thinking, one of the finest brains in the country." He raised his hands helplessly and dropped them on his knees. "So what in the Lord's name could have persuaded him to join up with these . . . these *. . . lunatics?"*

Garfield ran his tongue around his teeth; time was short. "He was a pragmatist, sir, but never a politician. He couldn't swallow the idea of spiritual and moral decay as a national inevitability. That's what he believed was happening. And it's what he *believed* that drove him. He's not the first old man to think he could change the world by turning the clock back. But the fact is, that's what he thought and that's what he joined The Matrix to do."

"So we accept he's telling the truth. All the way."

Garfield was aching to fill a pipe and light it but the President's widely advertised hatred of tobacco had hardened during his term in office into a formal rule—no smoking in his presence.

24

"We have to. Provisionally. We know the tape exists. I couldn't point to any good reason why John Roper Anson should say it's dynamite if it isn't. We're committed, as I see it. That means we have to consider a course of action. And Bradley's position."

The name hung like cordite in the air between them. The President wrinkled his nose. "Action?"

Garfield leaned forward, elbows on knees. "Yes, sir. Action." He summoned up the blood. "Unless you feel there's no threat to democracy involved in handing the White House over to a puppet. There's someone behind Bradley with an appetite for Presidential power; a man already up to his neck in conspiracy and murder."

The President's eyes clouded, then a grin raised the portcullis on his teeth. "Like I said, Luke; you make it hard to take sometimes." He leaned deep into his chair and swung a foot up on to the corner of the big desk. "What's your private view of Bradley?"

"Good man, I'd have said—before this. I know him. Not the typical Arizona lawyer. First-class record in public service. Made a good governor. I'd say he earned his seat in the Senate—although you'd know more about that." He locked eyes with the President. "His FBI file is clean as they come. The *official* CIA file is a litany to virtuous living. Family, friends, business. Clean, clean, clean."

"And Roper Anson's letter overrides all that?"

"Everyone in the country's on file. Computer cards, microfilm, credit ratings, more files. If you want to get to know a man, all you have to do is punch a key and he's yours. If the record says he's got green hair and five eyes, he's got green hair and five eyes. We don't allow for records that lie." The bulge of the pipe in his pocket was an unbearable temptation. "Trouble is, we invest too much faith in the system. A little know-how, a pinch of influence and you can make the record read any way you like. It's been done. Scandal, malpractice, sexual peccadilloes—you can wipe them all clean overnight."

"And Bradley's wiped the slate?"

Garfield shook his head. "I didn't say that."

The President balanced a letterknife embossed with the official seal on the end of a finger. "Come to the point, Luke."

"I have to know two things. One—is Bradley a dupe or is he actively involved in a conspiracy? Two—who's pulling the strings? It's the man in back of him I need most. Bradley himself won't pose problems. I can neutralize him very . . ."

"Neutralize?" The President let the paperknife fall to the desk blotter.

"What I mean is . . ." Garfield began, but the President checked him.

"I didn't hear that. Understand? You didn't say that, Luke. I wouldn't like to think you believed you had the moral right or the power to *neutralize* any American citizen, let alone Ambrose Bradley. This isn't some two-bit banana republic."

"The word was intended as a figure of speech, sir. Just . . ."

"I don't like figures of speech. You have something to say to me, say it loud and clear." He flashed a glance at his watch. "You've got five minutes."

Garfield closed his fingers round the bulge of the pipe. "Very well, sir. There's only one man I'd trust to tell me the truth about Bradley. Bradley himself. And the only way to do that is to confront him with what we know."

The President's eyes flicked over his face. He nodded, lips pursed. "You could make a damn fool of yourself."

"If he's innocent, he'll back out of the race right away. If he's a willing party to the conspiracy, he'll understand that he's finished as a candidate. He can go with honor or he can go with a lifetime's reputation in ruins. Whatever way, it's pretty clear he can't be allowed to run in the primaries."

The President swung his foot off the desk and laced his fingers across his chest. "I'll say this once, Luke, and I won't refer to it again, so remember every word." He breathed deeply; an athlete under the gun. "First, I'm not going to intervene personally to make Bradley withdraw. Neither are you." He closed his eyes to Garfield's attempted interruption. "No—hear me out. This is absolutely on the record and if you give me any reason in the future to recall what I said today, I'll quote it chapter and verse. Ambrose Bradley will be allowed to declare his candidacy. He'll run in the primaries. That's his right under the Constitution, and if you think I'm going to be the first president to blackmail an opposition front-runner, you're out of your mind. Second: there's no way I'm going to let you confront him with this . . . conspiracy stuff. You admit you know him. He's going to want to know by what right you approach him . . . and that leads right up to this desk, Luke."

Garfield discovered he had his pipe in his hands. He stuffed it back into his pocket. "Then I suggest you disband the Cleaners and accept my resignation."

"Now that's blackmail." The President bounced forward in his chair. "Look, Luke—think like a politician for a minute. Confronting Bradley, we'll have to unmask the Cleaners. How d'you think Bradley's going to react—in an election year—to the discovery that we have an unofficial, clandestine, all-powerful Intelligence network operating in this country without the knowledge or blessing of Congress? Monitoring the regular Intelligence services at will. No restraints on it. Unlimited power to investigate." He picked up the paperknife again. "Secret police. State spies. You want to tell me what he'd make out of *that* in political capital?"

"There are ways of . . ."

"I'll be frank with you, Luke. I inherited you but I could learn to live without you. Your job is to work in secret. You keep things that way, you hear?"

"With respect, sir, we can't afford to ignore Anson's letter that easily."

"*Moonshine.* What are you going to prove if you get your hand on that tape? Three men shooting the breeze. Gossip. Slander. You know *anyone* who believes in tapes any more?"

"You don't have to be involved, sir."

"Don't have to be involved! Would you like to ask my campaign managers how they react to that?"

Garfield rose stiffly to his feet. The climb from the basement had cramped the muscles of his calves and thighs. "You want me then—officially—to drop the investigation?"

"I want you—*officially*," the President echoed Garfield's emphasis on the word, "to understand that I don't want to know about taped conversations, conspiracies and lunatic killers." His voice modulated subtly and he folded his arms across his chest, drawing inviolability around him like a cloak. "I don't want to be associated with withdrawals from Presidential campaigns or mudslinging or any other fairy tales you have up your sleeve. This election is going to run straight and clean—and if I end up the loser, that's the way it'll be."

Garfield waited. Then: "And if the nation is the loser?"

The President spun the paperknife in his fingers adroitly. "Protecting the national interest is your job, Luke," he said quietly. "Your *privilege.* Your committee has overall responsibility for monitoring security. I'm not taking that away from you. All I'm saying is I won't have any truck with your people crossing the line into party politics." The gray eyes fixed unflinching on Garfield's face. "I don't have to tell you your job. If you see a breach of security you're obliged to investigate it. If you're satisfied it's a threat, correct it. Do I make myself clear?"

"I think so, yes."

"I hope so. I wouldn't want you to leave here with the wrong idea. We each have our duty. I see mine pretty clearly. How do you see yours?"

"Very clearly indeed, Mr. President."

"No messing with politics?"

"No, sir."

"No . . . compromising circumstances?"

"There'll be no embarrassments. You have my word on it."

The President stood up and offered his hand. They shook. They walked to a side door together, the President's arm on Garfield's shoulder.

"Sorry I have to push you out, Luke. You understand. Bear in mind what I've said, right?"

"I'll do *exactly* as you say. No more, no less."

"No direct attempt to force anyone out of the race?"

Garfield opened the door and managed a grin. "No direct intervention, of course, Mr. President. On reflection, perhaps the more candidates we have in this race the better."

"What d'you mean?"

Garfield shook his head and clamped his hand comfortingly on the pipe in his pocket. "Nothing, sir. Just a thought."

TUESDAY: 2045—GARFIELD

Beyond the doors, above the racket of disconnected voices and laughter and clinking glass, a tape-recorded baritone inveighed against the days of wine and roses. Garfield turned the key in the lock as if to drown out the noise and set his back to the double doors.

He was in dinner clothes, although the version he wore bore no resemblance to those of his companions. Alfred Goldman's giant inflated figure was sheathed in superbly flared black silk trousers, a shirt of frothy white lace and a green velvet jacket with braided collar. Munro Fletcher's classic black double-breasted suit and plain shirt breathed the discreet conservatism of London's Savile Row. Garfield's debt to antiquity was evident in his flyaway collar and black bow as well as the ravenswing shine on the seat of his pants. He patted his ample paunch.

"Hate this monkey suit, but I'll be damned if I'll buy another one. Drink?" He moved to the side table and an outcropping of crystal glasses and decanters.

"Let's get on with it," Fletcher protested. He levered himself into a deep, velvet-covered armchair and folded one leg carefully across the other. He had a long, conspicuously unemotional face and white hair slicked straight back over his skull. His skin was the color of polished pine, his eyes palely colorless. Garfield had sought many times for an outward imperfection in Fletcher's physical cast or his dress but had never found one. He had recruited Munro Fletcher himself in 1975 after a year of most persistent and intensive investigation. It was Munro Fletcher who had given their group—officially the National Security Advisory Committee—its innocent little sobriquet: the Cleaners.

Goldman threw himself into a couch. "Scotch for me. If there's any of that twelve-year-old malt around, I'll take a slug." He lounged back, his wild black curls bubbling over his forehead and ears and collar. Garfield passed him a liberal whiskey, poured himself a brandy and sat down beside Goldman.

Fletcher spoke again. "I don't like this. Not here. Why couldn't it wait?"

Garfield raised a glass to him. "We won't be interrupted. We're as safe here as anywhere—particularly at this stage of the party. It was important we meet tonight."

"Well, I don't see . . . ," began Fletcher.

Goldman broke in. "Why the sweat, Luke? I told you when we spoke before lunch today I'd pull out all the stops on Bradley at my end. But that needs time."

Garfield held the brandy balloon under his nose and breathed deeply. He closed his eyes, sniffed again, drank. "I was reacting off the top of my head when I talked to you both. I still had the President's voice in my ears. It was nudging my judgment."

"Our judgment is supposed to be above Presidential nudging," Fletcher drawled.

Garfield whirled the brandy in its glass. "I hope you won't broadcast that, Fletch. Nothing is *above* Presidential privilege. I like to think of us as standing to one side of it—not too far removed to lose touch but far enough to achieve a perspective. Sensitive to executive thinking but not brain-

29

washed by it. No, distance is useful. I've put some distance between our talks this morning and I've come up with a set of decisions."

Fletcher stirred anxiously. "Decisions? You mean proposals."

Garfield sipped his brandy. "No, Fletch, I truly don't mean proposals and if you want to debate the command decision structure you've chosen the wrong time. I've never hidden it from either of you: If the time ever came when I felt an exercise of supreme authority was essential to the proper handling of a situation, I'd exercise it. Well, I'm doing you the courtesy of informing you in advance what I intend should happen. If you're opposed, you can exercise the escape clause. Either way, I assume full responsibility for anything that happens."

Beyond the double doors, the baritone died in a titter of applause and a sugar-coated contralto edged into a sentimentalized rendition of "I Love Paris." Garfield finished his brandy and crossed the room to refill his glass. A log fire sputtered in the grate and four tall lamps radiated dampened light under royal blue shades. Garfield returned to his seat beside Goldman.

"Well?"

Goldman drained his glass, grunted up and went to refill it. He said from the table, "If that's what you decided, Luke, I'd say you were probably justified. You knew Anson. You saw the President. Go ahead. I'll play."

"Fletch?"

"It seems I'm outvoted." His ego bruised easily.

"Good. All right, this is the situation. Bradley must be on the point of declaring himself formally for the race. That's the word on the Hill and it makes sense. He can't hold out much longer. Now, I've considered a personal approach to him . . ." Goldman winced visibly, ". . . but the President's right; it's too risky. Bound to reflect straight back on him."

"I don't see why," said Fletcher. "No President can show a cleaner pair of hands."

"Bear with me, Fletch. So . . . if the tape exists, who's heard it?"

Goldman answered hesitantly. "Anson. The Investigator. Can't be anyone else."

"How about Richard Nixon?"

"Of course not!" Fletcher snapped at once. He slipped a slim gold cigarette case from an inner pocket, selected a long

30

filtered cigarette and lit it. Garfield waited for the performance to end. "If Nixon knew that tape existed," Fletcher went on seriously, "he'd have blown it higher than a kite. Perfect smokescreen for Watergate. He's not a fool. He wouldn't have cast that lifeline aside."

"Right. So either he hasn't heard it or he doesn't know it exists." Garfield lit his pipe. "So what could we predict of him if he *had* found it, given Fletch's general outline?"

Goldman balanced his glass on the palm of his hand. "He'd have a ball. He'd tie the GOP campaign managers in knots first, then he'd release the dirt—piece by piece. He'd blow the election inside out."

"You agree with that, Fletch?"

Munro Fletcher scowled through the pale blue smoke of his hand-rolled cigarette. "That's the way a politician would play it. I'd say Nixon was all politician."

"I wouldn't disagree with that." Garfield sipped his brandy. "All right. Let me take you back a step. Hypothesis. Let's assume Nixon comes into possession of the tape, and consider for a moment what he might do if he didn't blow it as Fred suggests. Suppose he approaches Bradley personally. No—hold it, Fred; let me finish. He confronts Bradley with the contents tells him he intends to use the information publicly unless Bradley backs out of the election. If Bradley's innocent, he'll check out what Nixon tells him and discover he's been manipulated. Reaction? He'd step down. If he's guilty, he'll recognize the value of what Nixon holds. Outcome: again, he'd step down."

"Just a minute, Luke," Fletcher leaned lazily in his chair, his thin white hands caressing the long cigarette. "Aren't you getting a little ahead of yourself? This *hypothesis* of yours is beginning to sound like a proposition. Just for the record, tell me straight out, will you, that it's still hypothetical."

Garfield turned in his seat to face him. "Let me ask you a question, Fletch: short of public exposure, which we can't afford, do you know of any other way to stop Bradley from walking off with the Presidency?" He rode over Fletcher's attempt at a reply. "I'll tell you: there isn't. We either resolve this quietly and quickly, before the primaries, or we resign ourselves to Bradley's winning the White House. You want that?"

They stared into the fire. Fletcher stirred at last.

"All right. Tell me this, then: Bradley's a pragmatist and a tough in-fighter. He must know that in a public confrontation, Nixon's word against his, he'd have to win hands down. So why wouldn't he call Nixon's bluff, tell him to blow his horn and wait for the laughter?"

Garfield twinkled. He was enjoying the game.

"Point taken. It would take something more..." He nursed the brandy to his chest. "Something to convince Bradley that Nixon really has something and isn't afraid to use it."

"And what might that be, Luke?" asked Goldman. He was grinning.

"I said that Nixon would need something else. So he would. Something even Bradley would be impressed by. Nixon will tell Bradley that if he doesn't back out, he'll seek the Republican nomination for President himself."

Fletcher and Goldman sat stock-still, their expressions hovering between ridicule and disbelief. Garfield pressed on. "His platform would be an unprecedented once-and-for-all crusade to get to the truth behind the Kennedy assassination. And he'll name names. By God, he'll name names."

"Garbage!" Goldman spat. "That's pure garbage."

"I agree," Garfield retorted swiftly. "But he'd be holding two aces no one can ignore, Bradley particularly. One, the tape of the conversation. Two, a national guilt complex about Dallas. There isn't a voter in the country who wouldn't listen. More important, by declaring his intention to run, Nixon lays it on the line unequivocally that he has what he says he has. That's the clincher."

Goldman tipped the last of the malt scotch into his throat. "And you think Nixon's going to stand still for that? 'Sure, I'll put my head on a block for you guys. Anything for a buddy.' Come on, Luke!"

"You think he won't cooperate?"

"Not with Las Vegas, Fort Knox and the World Bank as guarantees."

"Why not?"

Fletcher stabbed the air with a long bony finger. "Simply because he has nothing to gain and everything to lose. Use your head, Luke. This is absurd."

"Wrong."

"Care to explain that?" prompted Goldman.

Garfield nodded slowly. "Very well. No more games. There isn't a President in history who left office with a clean slate. It's an administrational impossibility. Richard Nixon left a lot of scars behind and the big ones we know about; everyone does. But I'm telling you: I could release—tonight if necessary—a piece of information that would rock this nation to its roots. It's not just damaging; it's unthinkable. Curiously enough, it's something over which Richard Nixon exercised no personal control at the time. That's why they'd tear him to pieces. Executive culpability. The evil men do in the name of the President. He couldn't survive it, believe me."

Munro Fletcher ground out his cigarette in the ashtray. "And in whose name do you justify *your* evil, Luke? I'll tell you what'd happen if you hung your piece of information under Richard Nixon's nose. He'd go for your throat."

Garfield puffed at his pipe in silence for a while. Then, "Everything you say is true, both of you. What I have in mind is undemocratic, devious, immoral and improbable. But that's what we're going to do because it's the lesser of two evils— and if you don't think that's justification enough, I won't waste my time trying to convince you. I want the man behind Bradley because I think he just might be someone I've been looking for a long time, without even knowing he was there."

Fletcher's long ascetic face was lined with weariness. "You're forgetting a couple of things. First, the President warned you to stay clear of Bradley and . . ."

"He told me to keep *my* hands off Bradley," Garfield interrupted. "He also took pains to point out that Bradley was *my* responsibility; *our* responsibility. He doesn't want to see it or hear it or smell it. He won't. What's your other point, Fletch?"

"How do you intend playing Richard Nixon—if you really believe this ridiculous charade is ever going to get off the ground? I offer you a sizeable stake, Luke, here and now, that he won't. . . ."

Garfield took the pipe from his mouth. "He already has. You'd be throwing your money away."

"Agreed? He said yes?" Fletcher refused to accept the evidence of his ears.

"I called him this afternoon in San Clemente. We were very frank with each other. He has some admirable practical qualities. Great resilience. Called me back an hour later. Said he'd talked it over with his staff and they thought he was crazy but he could see where his duty lay."

"I bet," growled Alfred Goldman.

Abe Lincoln was alone. He slouched in his hollowed stone, glowering over the cold, snow-dusted landscape with benevolent frustration. Harry Anson let his eyes caress the chiseled record of Abe's ideal enshrined in rhetoric. He stuffed gloved hands deep into the pockets of his inadequate tan raincoat. His father had lived with that rhetoric nailed to his conscience: He would have died with it. Come back here, John Roper Anson had told him when he was still in high school. When the road ahead divides and the signposts are hard to read, come back and take a look at Abe. And think. There'll be reasons for coming back; life won't give you the Pennant and the World Series every year. Poor John Roper—he had been a living parody; he actually believed all that stuff.

The statue stared imperiously over Anson's head into the whirling snowflakes, like a bored guest at a dull party looking for someone more interesting to talk to. Anson turned away. The crazy thing was he had actually come here. Straight from the airport. When he picked up the Porsche at the Hertz office—a ridiculous extravagance, that car, and one he still couldn't explain to himself—he had programmed the drive in his mind. Destination: John Roper's apartment in Foggy Bottom. Somehow, the car had taken over. He'd parked it short of the Ericsson Memorial on Ohio Drive. The guiding hands of dead men.

At the far end of the Reflecting Pool a black man bent strenuously behind a four-wheeled cart and urged it across the crunching snow. He was thinly clothed but for a fake-fur cossack hat and a bright red muffler that writhed and fluttered in the wind behind him. Anson shivered in sympathy, for the black and for the ghost of his father who cherished the notion of universal warmth and compassion with such innocence that he could invoke the virtues of communing with stone. John Roper had always been quick to invoke virtue.

"What's the first thing a boy does on entering the Kingdom of Heaven?" was his all-time favorite, delivered with sonorous resonance over dinner on Sundays when it was his pleasure to invite friends and their families to eat with him after church.

"Pray to Jesus for the souls of loved ones left behind, sir," was the required response. The "sir" was their private seal of conspiracy.

34

"I want you to understand, boy, that it doesn't signify foolishness on my part or servility on yours. It's just a sign to strangers that we maintain a proper respect in this house for the status quo. There's nothing sacred about the status quo except your right to change it by the quality of your cause. Right now, you have no cause not to refer to me as 'sir' in front of company and I have no right to deny you that discipline."

And his mother would smuggle him a secret smile.

She had died in 1958, before the young Kennedys imposed their New Frontiers, before the Beatles redefined sound, before the rise of hash and speed and juvenile ODs; before The Fall. She too had died a parody of Old America, although sweet Providence and her family had kept her in blissful ignorance during the last years.

A few weeks after her death, thirteen-year-old Harry had received a special delivery package at the door of their house in Georgetown. It was addressed to him personally. Inside was a letter from Norman Rockwell. It said: "This doesn't belong to me anymore. I guess it never did. Your mother inspired it and told me it wasn't half bad. You should be the best judge of that."

The painting was one of Rockwell's wartime covers for the *Saturday Evening Post*. It showed a somber but richly furnished office with a globe of the world in one corner and a draped flag in the other. There was a wide desk, and in the pool of light spilled by a brass-stemmed, green-cowled lamp lay a scatter of State papers and a signed photograph of FDR. Behind the desk, a handsome man with graying hair had removed his spectacles and was rubbing tired eyes. But the ghost of a grin curled on his lips. Just appearing at the left of the frame was a tall woman in a superb blue evening gown. Her hair was coiffed to show off a diamond tiara. Over her gown was tied a businesslike checked apron and she carried a plate of cookies and a glass of milk. The man behind the desk was John Roper Anson. The woman was his wife, Helen. She was that close to the Great American Dream.

Twenty-one years later and John Roper was where he'd wanted to be. With her. At least, if there was any justice in heaven he would be. Friday at Arlington. The White House had cabled him at the Rome Embassy—the President's name was on the cable but that didn't necessarily mean he'd sent it—and they'd decided it had to be Arlington. Before he left his apartment near the Spanish Steps, he'd called Grazia out of her weekly beauty class at Fabrizi's and told her he was going back to Washington to bury his father. She played the scene with the same strangulated vibrato she used on yelping puppies, wailing kids and uncooperative headwaiters. It shocked him until he remembered she had no data to react to; he'd told her nothing about John Roper, shared not one family memory with her. He'd cut her off in the end because the embassy pool car was bleating from the street below and because he was suddenly sick of her and sick of himself. The memory still left a taste in his mouth twelve hours later. John Roper, who mattered, was dead and wrenched from his life. Grazia, who had no value to anyone, was the closest thing left, if a relationship was to be judged by the mutual proximity of flesh and flesh. The comparison was odious; the rate of exchange grotesque. Halfway to London he'd vowed never to see her again. She could have the apartment, the car, the clothes, everything. Halfway to Washington he'd caught a ghost of her body musk. Felt one long finger descend his spine. Tasted . . .

There would be plenty of time to make permanent decisions. Two or three days at least.

The black worker pushed his cart level with Anson, sensed the presence of another human being and flashed an uncertain glance. Anson inclined his head in the little shrug of recognition John Roper had taught him. "You'd be surprised what a difference it can make to know that someone cares enough to notice," he used to say. "Doesn't call for words, speeches, handouts, prayers on the sidewalk. Just eyes meeting. God striking matches on the soul."

The black man hurried on and Anson turned away and made for the Porsche. In Rome, the ambassador had taken him aside and paid his respects. His own phrase. John Roper, he said, had been a giant; there would never be another like him. On Friday at Arlington, said the ambassador, there would be at least a dozen heads of state walking behind the bier with the President, better than 500 members of the Washington diplomatic corps, a whole army of wary-eyed mandarins from State and Justice and the Pentagon, and a representative of the English royal family.

All of that, thought Anson, and more: the shrinking band of creaking old men and sable-trimmed dowagers who were John Roper's contemporaries and who still clung stubbornly to life. The half dozen oddballs in full morning rig who had served John R. in wartime outposts and toasted FDR at their reunion every year.

36

A string of five cars faded from left to right along Ohio Drive, blowing snow clouds. The grating of their chained tires came to him shrill as dentists' drills on chipped bone. Anson kicked out at a wedge of compacted snow. What all of this was working up to was his own absence of grief. No tears, no catch in the throat, no corrosive memories. Not even a sense of guilt. Thanks to John Roper, there was no need. But it didn't seem right.

He reached the car and scraped iced slush from the door lock before he could insert the key. He switched on the ignition and gunned the engine until the heater blew warm air.

Down by the river in East Potomac Park, the bare black arms of the flowering cherry trees swore blindly that there would never be another spring.

WEDNESDAY: 0800—FABER

The man with the black briefcase strode aggressively against the surging sidewalk mainstream, but no one challenged his progress. He parted the eight o'clock crowds like a scythe; pale faces shrunk from his, shoulders twisted aside to avoid even a glancing blow.

He had class, thought the watcher. Presence. Too much of it for the job he was doing. At least he was on time. That was something.

The watcher backed deeper into the sheltering doorway, collar upturned against a curtain of windblown snow. It was building up to be another terrible winter; three in a row. Everyone sensed it. In the eyes of the shop assistants and office workers there had settled the fixed glaze of resignation; another two months of this was the least they could expect.

The man with the briefcase crossed the intersection. He would reach the entrance to the Statler in thirty seconds. As scheduled. He would be at the desk in one minute, fifteen seconds. There would be no holdup at reception. The bell captain would have an elevator poised to whisk him to the fourth floor. He would reach his room exactly four minutes from now.

At a fourth floor window across the street from the Statler, five pairs of eyes had swept the area for more than an hour. Every car lingering too long at the curb, every arrival at the door of the lobby, every delivery van and truck had been

37

examined, photographed and logged. If doubts or suspicions were aroused, a mobile picture transmitter was on hand to wire Polaroid prints across the city to Fairfax County. At the other end a handpicked team of Army Intelligence technicians was ready to feed the wireprint into a scanning device linked to the FBI's criminal intelligence records computer on Pennsylvania Avenue.

Only one print had been fed into the system so far and, by coincidence, it had been a positive "make." Benny Colquhoun, a three-state auto rustler from Idaho, would never know it was his lucky day. His portrait, having been identified as "Crime—auto," was scrapped. Benny was an irrelevancy today.

At the entrance, the man with the briefcase hesitated momentarily and glanced back in disgust at the flakes of snow on his shoulder. He brushed at them with an impatient hand and entered the lobby. For the watchers it was a gesture of confirmation.

At the desk, the aging clerk performed his party piece, running his eye down the list of expected arrivals, finding the reservation card, processing it. The room had been reserved by a man who had spoken to the general manager in his private office. The Statler was not unused to mystery, to clandestine requests for cooperation, but this one had certain unusual elements. All of Tuesday, work had been in progress in the reserved room on the fourth floor. An outside carpenter, plumber and telephone engineer had each come and gone, working in silence, disappearing when they had finished as discreetly as they appeared. No staff members had been allowed near the room.

"Mr. Faber?" The clerk slid the registration slip across the desk. The man nodded curtly and signed the card with his left hand. The right, held rigid at his side, clasped the black case. The clerk snapped his fingers and the bell captain homed in; he reached for the black case. The man's left hand came up quickly. "That won't be necessary," he said coolly. He waited for the captain to back off before allowing his hand to fall. He picked up the keys, followed the bell captain to the elevator and stepped in. The captain made to follow him, but he blocked the way. "I'll find my way," he said flatly. The doors closed.

Third floor. Faber held the elevator doors on Open and checked the corridor, listening to the silence. He allowed the doors to close and went up to the fifth. Same corridor. Same silence. He pressed the button for the fourth floor. The doors opened and he took one step into the corridor. And froze.

At the far end, where a large window overlooked the hotel's central well, a man in white overalls was hunched over an open electrical panel. His shoulders and arms were trembling with sustained effort as he bore down with all his weight on a monkey wrench held chest high. With a final heave and a shower of flaking paint, a nut gave and the workman sank down gratefully on the wrench with a gasp of escaping air.

Faber walked slowly toward him but the workman seemed to be unaware of his approach. The man swung open the window, leaned out and called instructions to someone below. Faber reached into his waistband and curled his fingers around the butt of the Smith and Wesson.

The workman turned. For a second his expression changed and he darted a glance at his watch. Then he nodded at Faber and turned away to the inspection panel. It was a nod of recognition. Unmistakable.

Faber released his grip on the gun butt but did not remove his hand entirely. He should have guessed they would have someone inside the hotel, he thought. But it made him uneasy. Any departure from schedule was cause for concern. There was no place in an operation like this for wild cards, last-minute touches; the letter had stressed that.

He moved quickly to the door marked 421, turned the key and slipped inside. He closed the door at once, rammed the double bolts in place, top and bottom, and latched the security chain.

A fringe of perspiration clung to his brow and he flicked at it with a silk handkerchief. He placed the black case on the table, bending at the knees as he did so to ensure that his arm didn't bend or his grip weaken. He opened his clenched hand with great care, then withdrew his forefinger from the loop of a metal pin protruding from the top of the case. The pin was the only external evidence of the specially adapted Belgian PRB 413 antipersonnel mine he had built into the case. It was four and a half inches long and its thermoplastic casing contained cast Composition B explosive and a prefragmented, spirally wound steel wire sleeve. On detonation, the sleeve would separate into 600 high-velocity fragments. The loop through which Faber had threaded his forefinger would have to travel just one-quarter of an inch from its root to detonate the mine, destroy Faber, the tape and anyone foolish enough to try to snatch it from him.

The mine had been his own idea. Now he disconnected it, massaged his knuckles and made a quick survey of the room. Functional. The windows had been sealed and an inner skin of armored glass inserted behind the frames. He tapped it. Shatterproof. Bulletproof, hopefully. A tight-fitting rubber cap had been stretched over the air-conditioning vent and a strip of plastic material fitted flush around the door. If anyone tried to blast his way in, Faber reflected, he would have time to activate the alarm system built into the phone. The letter had detailed the time lapse to be expected. This was what the Company would term "a virgin job." Safe and secure. Protected from all possible violation.

He shrugged off his jacket, slid the Smith and Wesson from its clip holster, released the safety catch and put the gun on the table. It was a wise virgin who took precautions where none were needed. He pressed two buttons positioned at either end of the case and the top swung wide open. The circular tape canister nestled in a bed of green baize, a single leather strap anchoring it to avoid contact with the bottle-shaped shrapnel mine beside it. He disengaged the mine, lifted it out and set it squarely in the middle of the bed in the far corner of the room. He snapped the case shut.

A soft purring sound came from the telephone. He looked at his watch and picked up the receiver. It was a two-way radio. The voice was sibilant in his ear. A hand-held transceiver was operating at the other end on ultrahigh frequency. "Hotel One. Timed 0815. Clean sweep. A-OK. I'm moving to you now."

Faber's eyes never left the Rolex Oyster on his wrist. "No!" he said. "Five minutes yet. Stick to the schedule."

Again the voice hissed, but he shook his head. "I don't give a damn if you're drowning, baby. That's the way it's gonna be. By the book!"

He dropped the phone on its cradle and moved back to the case. Before he could reach it, the phone purred again. He turned angrily, then realized the sound was not coming from the telephone. He stared at the door as the muted buzzer sounded again. Insistent. Demanding.

He picked up the Smith and Wesson and weighed it in his hand, automatically estimating its potency through the wood of the door. The buzzer sounded again. Longer, then a bunch of short staccato stabs.

"Christ, what is this!"

A flush of anger charged his cheeks with crimson. He curled his finger around the trigger of the Smith and Wesson and approached the door in an arc, flattening himself along the wall beside it, the muzzle of the gun held awkwardly, but efficiently, stomach-high against the wood.

In the center of the door a recessed spy-hole had been cut, no bigger than a nickel. Faber turned to face the wall and bent sideways from the waist, twisting his trunk like a matador to crane his head across the door without exposing the mass of his body. He drew in breath and, by standing on tiptoe, managed to slide his cheek across until his eye made contact with the peephole. He slid the cover to one side. An eye stared back at him.

The man in the white boiler suit jerked his head back immediately. In his right hand was a small steel mallet; in his left, a steel-tipped bolt. In one fluid movement he jammed the bolt into the spy-hole and drew back the mallet. Faber saw the eye disappear, saw a blur of white and steely black, and the nerves in his neck stiffened to the message from the brain: "Pull back! Pull back!" He began to die even as the mallet smashed down on the head of the bolt. His pupil contracted to a microdot as the steel shaft began its journey down the short black tunnel. The bolt rammed viciously through space into membrane and fiber and ligament, through muscle and tissue and nerve, into the electrified jelly of the brain. Faber's body trembled, spastic with shock, timid as a butterfly impaled to a board by a schoolboy's pin.

He was dying when the man pressed plastic explosive strips onto five fixed points around the door. He was dead when the flashlight battery instigated the explosion that sent the door and Faber spinning back to the window.

The workman stepped confidently into the room and picked up the black case. Faber's body lay spread-eagled under the door. He gave it only a cursory glance before turning his back. He began to run along the corridor toward the emergency stairway.

At the far end, the elevator shuddered to a halt and the doors hissed open. A young woman stepped out, her head bowed over a big shoulderbag, a wet headscarf clutched between her teeth. She had moved a few steps from the elevator before she looked up and her face registered shock as she took in the smashed and gutted door and the cloud of gray blue smoke.

Her mouth yawned wide to scream. The white-suited workman sprinted across the space between them and slammed his hand over her open mouth.

"Be good, lady. Be very good and you'll be okay. You

understand what I'm telling you?" She nodded under his grip. "Okay. I'm gonna take my hand away and you're gonna hold it down. Right?" She nodded again. He withdrew his hand. The girl shook uncontrollably. She tried to speak but the product was a whispered stutter.

He said again, "You saw nothing, lady. You weren't here. You know from nothing." He glared at her.

She swallowed on her terror, brown eyes wide with hysteria. She pressed herself into the wall and held out her handbag to him. "Take whatever you want," she blabbed. "Please leave me al . . ." She fumbled in the bag. "I've got fifty dollars in my purse."

He grasped her by the shoulder and shook her. "I don't want your goddamn money," he hissed hoarsely. "For chrissakes, are you some kind of a crazy woman? Listen to me." He raised his arm and the fist bunched for a blow. The girl cowered back against the wall, one hand buried in her bag almost to the elbow.

The blow never fell. The Berretta coughed twice through the handbag's soft brown leather and the white boiler suit grew a scarlet rose over the left-hand breast pocket. The man swallowed one last cupful of air, reeled and fell to the floor.

The girl stooped quickly, tugged the case from his hand and started for the blasted doorway. She paused momentarily and looked in. She could see one arm and a leg under the fallen door. For two seconds she hesitated, then headed briskly back to the emergency stairs. If only he had let her come in when she'd asked. Faber had been so determined to live by the book, he'd died by it.

She pushed determinedly through the glass-topped door into the stairwell. The Cleaners would take care of the Faber mess. It would need a power of cleaning.

WEDNESDAY: 1215—GARFIELD

The female courier placed the flat film can respectfully at the center of the table and cast a brief glance at the room's occupants through deep brown eyes.

There was little more than a rumor of light in the room; the ill-tempered January wind had brought sleet and snow and, finally, low black clouds. It was past midday but the

42

faculty buildings were already iridescent with a rash of fluorescent glare. The woman left without a word and they waited until the door clicked shut. But even then they found it painful to look at the object before them.

Two men were already dead. The blood spilled at the Statler left no doubt as to what might lie ahead.

It was not Garfield's practice to use artificial light at these meetings unless absolutely necessary; it was part of an unspoken, unwritten contract of faith, one of their articles of association. It crystallized the nature of their profession, their qualifications for membership. What brought them at least once a week to the Chapter House at Georgetown, to this book-lined cell with the high windows that rationed sunlight on the best of days, was a passion for anonymity. Today its gloom was a fitting reflection of their mood.

Alfred Goldman looked at the can of tape. "My God," he muttered, half to himself. "For that!"

Lucas Garfield tried to shake them out of their depression with an air of brisk efficiency. He pulled the can toward him across the polished rosewood, unscrewed the twin halves, took out the spool and threaded it onto a compact recording deck in front of him. He looked up. "I share your feelings, gentlemen. But what happened today is a measure of why we have to see this through." He stabbed a key and the voice leaped into the room.

For Garfield, the first words of John Roper Anson were painful. He trapped his lower lip in his teeth and bit on it for comfort. The other two voices were immediately recognizable and he noted that both Fletcher and Goldman knew them, too. The conversation had overtones of a dormitory council of war, whispers at first as the conspirators tried to wring reason from the curious fact of their being called to the White House on the same day; then clamor, then restraint. What reason? What motivation? Had The Matrix link been pinned to them?

As the conversation developed and their fears coalesced, the deeper voice of the Investigator overwhelmed the other two. Fletcher and Goldman kept their eyes on Garfield, as though his expression would confirm or deny what they were hearing. His face remained impassive.

At the end of the run, as the spool grew narrow on its rotating arm, there came the click of an opening door and the voice of Richard Nixon. "Ah, gentlemen. Sorry you've been kept waiting," and the sound died. Garfield switched off the tape deck and fell back into his chair. He found his pipe and packed it with unnecessary attention to detail. "Well?" he said at last.

"What the hell am I expected to say after *that?*" Goldman pointed at arm's length to the tape.

"Fletch?"

Munro Fletcher bent his long thin hands into a Gothic arch and cracked his knuckles with spectacular effect. "That's not a tape you've got there, Luke," he said. "That's a neutron bomb."

"You think it'd carry weight?"

"I think it'd carry the nation." Fletcher ran a hand back over his hair. "The beautiful thing about that is not what it claims to be fact, but the manner in which it got itself made. It *has* to be fact—anyone hearing it will think that immediately. Why else would grown men, important men, whisper and shiver in fear for their necks? My God, Luke, you could settle the hash of half the population with that damn thing."

"Are you advising me on a course of action?"

"Yes, I am. Kill it. Burn it. Lose it. That kind of pig swill kills. It'll contaminate this country for a generation."

Garfield turned to Goldman. "Fred?"

Goldman flashed sympathy at his colleague. "I know how he feels, but I think he's wrong. You've got yourself a bomb there, all right. I don't think any of us have doubts about the Anson thing now. Not anymore. I don't anyway. Anson was right, too, about not turning this into a goddamn witch-hunt and Fletch just about said the same thing. We can't afford to have that kind of mud slung around any more. So, what've we got? We've got the *means* to stop Bradley but we're agreed we couldn't use it publicly even if we're pushed. That's the crunch point. We'd back down if Bradley told us: Go fly a kite. Okay, you outlined a pretty fancy scenario last night, Luke. You said Nixon'd play. If you think you can *control* him— and I mean keep him secure and going in the direction you tell him—then, okay, I'll buy that. But that tape can only be used as a threat." He palmed a long black cheroot from behind the silk handkerchief in his breast pocket and lit it.

"Fletch?"

The old man turned away coldly. "You know my view. It won't deteriorate for being repeated. I won't take your escape clause, Luke. I'm too damned concerned about what that thing might do—what you might use it for—to turn my back on it now. All right, count me in, but I want some guarantees on where we're going with this and where we draw the line."

"Any other recommendations?" Garfield looked from face to face, eyebrows climbing his forehead. "Right. Then we have a phone call to make, don't we?" His round face was wrinkle-free and, in good light, as rosy-cheeked as a nursery-rhyme milkmaid's, but the set of his jaw belied the benevolent image and his eyes had lost all color.

He stretched up from the chair, produced a chain from his trouser pocket and inserted a small brass key into a box wedged between the books on the lowest of the shelves. He reached in, brought out a black telephone and placed it in front of him on the table. He lifted the receiver and a voice answered at once.

Garfield said, "I want to talk to Richard Nixon. Direct, please, and keep the line open so I can hear the intermediaries. Quickly."

They waited. They saw Garfield stiffen, smile. He removed the pipe from his teeth and said, "Good morning to you, Mr. President. I thought you'd want to know the—er—delivery was made."

Nixon's voice had a grating quality, an almost bronchic rasp; it was the only discernible surviving evidence of the mild stroke he had suffered the previous fall. "You got it?" he asked quickly.

"Yes," said Garfield.

"Did everything go—you have any trouble?"

"A little trouble, yes." Garfield stared into the faces of his companions, indicating that his response was an attempt to convey to them the ex-President's question.

"What kind of trouble? Spell it out for me."

Garfield held the burning bowl of his pipe to his nose and sniffed it. "Well, Mr. President, the courier met with an accident. He's dead, I'm afraid. We got the fellow responsible but we shan't be able to count on him for any information. Bad news, Mr. President."

Garfield touched his upper lip with the tip of his tongue. Goldman was spread so far across the table he was almost lying flat.

"But you took delivery?"

"Yes, we did. The merchandise is—as advertised." Garfield uttered a grotesquely humorless chuckle. "You'll be glad to hear that, Mr. President."

"Uh-huh." Garfield was aware of Nixon's breathing: short

labored bursts with a perceptible whistling undertone at the tail of each inhalation. "When do I get to hear it?"

"I can't be sure about that yet."

"What d'you mean, you can't be sure? You're not saying you expect me to front this . . . operation . . . without knowing the facts of the case? Because if you are, we've got nothing to talk about. You didn't give me any choice about whether I got into this or not, but this is where I say Finish."

"I don't think this is the time for analysis," said Garfield tactfully. Goldman and Fletcher eyed him suspiciously. Garfield scowled. "But of course you'll hear the tape. We have to trust each other in this. I'll admit, initially, I pressured you, but . . ."

Nixon closed in on him quickly. "I've had my share of pressure and I've had my share of screwing it down on other men, and as God is my witness I swear I've never been responsible for pushing a man into a corner for less—understand this—for *less* than the good of the country."

"I think I can match that criteria," said Garfield. "That's precisely . . ."

"I'm not finished on this yet," Nixon snapped. "You threatened me. Yes, I'm going to be absolutely forthright with you as I hope you'll be with me from now on. They were threats you made. You knew you couldn't break me . . ."

"Mr. President," said Garfield patiently. "We both agree it's for the good of the country. I accept that . . ."

"I want you to get something straight here. What I have to say to you is this: You didn't have to threaten me. You just had to come right out and say: Mr. President, this is what you—and *only* you—can do for your country. You think I'd back away from an honest responsibility?"

"We're not in disagreement at any point," Garfield said firmly.

"That includes protection, right?"

"You'll have all the protection you need, sir."

"You say this courier was killed. That implies Bradley's people are onto the tape?"

"The implication is they've been waiting for something to happen. In this case, they've been watching a safe-deposit vault for something like two years. That's a lot of patience, Mr. President. They're telling us they have a lot to lose."

"Are we talking on the same level here? They'd try getting to me to protect Bradley?"

"It's possible," Garfield said carefully. "But not very likely.

46

The one thing we both want, us and them, is to make no waves. They can't afford scandal. They have to keep Bradley clean or he's finished as a possible candidate. *We* have to make sure he's finished—but without fuss. I don't have to draw pictures, do I, sir?" He fidgeted in his chair. "Perhaps I can call you later today to discuss the next stage."

"Make it after four this afternoon, California time. I'm playing a round of golf. Not as fast on my feet as I was."

"None of us are, sir," Garfield said gently. "We all have a cross to bear."

Nixon's laughter was brittle. "So we do. But you keep this in mind for me, as a special favor, okay? I've carried crosses all my life and I don't have any lack of experience learning how to bear them. That's all a President does, you know. He bears crosses. All I want you to do is make damn sure I don't get myself crucified on this one." He was still laughing when he cut the call dead.

"What'd he say?" Goldman growled pugnaciously.

Garfield stuffed the dead pipe into his coat pocket and got to his feet. "Mr. Nixon looks forward to the pleasure of our company, Fred. He's in." He pulled on his gloves. "You know—I have the strangest feeling he's enjoying every damned minute of this."

THURSDAY: 0920—ANSON

The State Department's Bureau of Intelligence and Research, INR, is the runt of the Intelligence community litter. Its budget, at eight million dollars a year, is the smallest and it has no collection capacity of its own. It relies entirely on State Department diplomatic cables and other community data and its 350 employees are essentially desk men. INR represents State on all United States Intelligence Board and other inter-agency panels and coordinates the departmental work within State, and the Under Secretary's staff work for forty committees. Henry Kissinger's assumption of the role of Secretary of State had given INR a decisive boost and they were not about to lose that status.

George Hyman's office at INR had the ambience of a secluded reading room at a good club. His job specification was vague, as befitted a fringe Intelligence functionary and he carried a personality to match. He was a small, round, good-humored man in his mid-fifties; neat and mannered, precise and fluent. He came out to meet Anson with both arms extended.

"Harry! Harry, my boy. Come right on in." He ushered Anson into the room. "Sit down, son. Sit you down."

Hyman's hand-delivered note had been in the mailbox at John Roper's apartment when Anson arrived. George had written a million letters of condolence and it showed. Anson found it genuinely moving. "Come see me tomorrow if you feel like it. Nine-thirty would be fine," it ended.

"You'd like some tea, I bet," Hyman said hopefully. He took lemon tea three times a day as part of his weight-watching regime.

"Thanks."

"Joan! Mr. Anson's joining me for tea." He flipped up the key on his desk communicator. His face became serious. "I won't harp on it, Harry, but I have to say my piece. John Roper and I were close, you know that. I won't compare my sense of loss with yours but accept it when I tell you I was devastated to hear of his death." He made a little shrugging motion with his hands. "You know about the funeral? 10:30 at Arlington."

Anson nodded. "I got a telegram from the White House before I left Rome. They're doing him proud."

"No man deserves better."

The matronly secretary brought in two fine bone china cups and saucers and a tall Delft teapot on a tray. Hyman slipped gratefully into the tea ceremony, checking the pot for "nose," placing thinly sliced lemon in each cup with tiny silver tongs, pouring the pale golden liquid. "I'm afraid this is one of my non-cookie days," he said apologetically, as if the omission were a flagrant breach of etiquette. They sipped experimentally. Hyman breathed a satisfied "aaaaah!" sound and leaned back into his swivel chair. "I wanted to see you *personally*, Harry and—er—professionally too, since we had to meet. You mind my talking shop just now?"

Anson shook his head. "John Roper's dead, George. He'd have been prepared for it. Anyway, he thought mourning was a contradiction in terms."

"Hmmmm." Hyman sipped again at his tea. "All right. Then let's get on with it. You've been doing a lot of work on the Italian extremist groups, I hear."

"Nothing sensational. Clipping newspapers mostly. I met a few people on the inside. Then we had a memo from State last month to drop it. I guess the Company decided to infiltrate and didn't want amateurs like me fouling up their viper's nest."

Hyman stretched out a thin grin. "Do I detect an element of professional antagonism in there somewhere?"

Anson lifted his shoulders noncommittally. "They have their way of doing things. It's not ours. My job out there is security, not covert activity. I don't care much either way."

"But you don't find yourself in love with the Company—professionally speaking?"

"If what I read about Petersen comes near the whole truth, I'd say he's doing the country a favor. The CIA needed its wings clipped. I like the way he's been doing it. I hope it stays fine for him."

"But you don't believe the twain should meet—Intelligence and diplomacy, I mean?"

Anson emptied his cup and leaned forward to replace it on the tray. Hyman poured him another at once. Anson watched him. "Impossible to separate them, nowadays. But every time they meet, we come out of it with blood on our nose. We're left to clear up the debris. You don't buy back diplomatic trust cheaply after the Company's been caught with its hand in the cookie jar." He returned to the back of his chair with the lemon tea. "Why? Is it important?"

Hyman poured himself more tea, drawing out the process with elaborate attention to detail. "It could be," he said reflectively. "Yes, it could very well be important. I think . . ." He tailed off into round-eyed contemplation of space. "We may be doing a little exercise here on some of those groups. Academic stuff. Paper warriors." He stretched the grin again. "I'll report back to Political Intelligence, see what they say. Anyhow . . ." He leaned forward, as if breaking a spell. "Since you're here, you might as well hang around a few days. They'll come back to me if they need your help."

Anson said blankly, "George, I'm no expert, believe me. If they've gotten some idea that I'm the last word in . . ."

Hyman raised a hand. "Harry, just relax. The mills of State . . . who knows what goes on in the collective bureaucratic mind?"

"What do you mean by a few days?"

"Well," Hyman flattened out his hands and rotated one over the other like a paddle wheel. "A week, two weeks, if they come up with something in that time."

Anson clattered the cup back on the tray. "Are you trying to tell me I'm on transfer or something? What is this, George?"

Hyman shook his head sadly. "My fault. I should've waited till you had time to find your feet, get over the . . ." He left it unsaid. "Let's talk about it some other time, Harry. You're taking this completely the wrong way."

"All right, George. Whatever you say." Anson waved a hand carelessly. "I guess maybe I'm still strung out a little."

Hyman beamed with pleasure. "I thought you'd be *pleased*. Truly, I thought you would. There must be things you have to take care of here in Washington—John Roper's affairs. The estate. The apartment. . . . I imagine you'll keep that on—at least for the time being?" He pressed the question hard.

"I'll need somewhere to live if I'm going to stick around. Yes, I guess I'll keep it for the time being." He watched Hyman's face closely. It was ripe with good humor, tinged with an obvious relief. But the long slope of his forehead was faintly glazed with perspiration and his hands were finding it difficult to settle. Anson experienced the heart-tug of career concern. What had he done? Failed to do? Who was carpeting him? Goddamn their eyes for choosing this as the time and place. No wonder they'd singled out George Hyman to plunge in the shiv.

He said, "What do I have to do?"

Hyman came out of the chair and around his desk. He propped an elegant haunch on one corner and surveyed his victim. "Nothing much, son. Just make yourself available. Be around."

"How can I be around? I've got no . . ."

Hyman leaned across his desk and thumbed the communicator. "Joan? Would you like to show Mr. Anson that office we spoke of this morning?"

"Be glad to, sir." She cleared her throat. "I have Mr. Margolis waiting out here. He was wondering if . . ."

A hard-voweled snarl bulldozed across her formality. "What the hell you got in there, Hyman? The inflatable version of Miss America?"

Hyman chuckled and flicked off the switch. He looked down at Anson, still amused, but the strain was not far behind his eyes. "Come meet a friend of mine." He hooked a finger.

"Well, well, well. Caught you in the act, Hyman."

Anson's first impression was of sheer bulk, then he adjusted to the man's lack of stature. Five-eight, but the meat was packed tight, muscle to hairline. The face was the cut, color and texture of hewn sandstone, its tone magnified by a wild thatch of white hair. His arms were too long for his legs, his shoulders too wide for his head.

George Hyman took the outstretched hand and winced at the shake. "Harry," he said with mock resignation, "this is Walt Margolis."

Anson stuck out a hand and Margolis encased it enthusiastically. Hyman added, "For my sins, we're friends. Long time."

"We go back to the Ark," grinned Margolis.

"And now he's back to haunt me," mocked Hyman. He was still harboring perspiration on his brow.

"Back to haunt *him!* You wanna know the effect seeing this guy every day has on me, kid?"

Anson felt out of place. "Look George—maybe your secretary can take me along to the . . ." he began.

Hyman's small hand locked on his arm. "And let you off the hook? No, sir! Walt's working on a project here, among other places. Mostly, he just wants someone to talk to . . ."

"Like hell he does!" roared Margolis happily.

". . . but sometimes," persisted Hyman, "he has to shuffle paper to keep up the pretense and he comes up here to find a desk and a few cubic feet of peace and quiet. Well . . ." His eyelids flickered repeatedly. "He couldn't have turned up at a better time. If you two both want space, from here on in you'll have to share it." He looked quickly from one to the other.

Walt Margolis came to his rescue. He swung on Anson, face stern, eyes keen. "You got any bad habits, kid?"

"What do you mea . . . ?" Anson began innocently.

They roared with laughter as he fell into the trap.

"Give me a coupla days, son," Margolis said cheerfully, "and I'll teach you enough of 'em for a seat in Congress. Come on."

He swung Anson around by the shoulder and marched him away. George Hyman watched them uncertainly until they turned at right angles and disappeared into a corridor. He went back to his office, checked the teapot, poured a cup of cold liquid, sipped it and picked up an old-fashioned black phone. The line clicked into life. A voice said, "Yes?"

Hyman said, "Don't ever ask me to do that again. Just don't bother to even *ask* next time."

Lucas Garfield displayed no remorse. "Everything go as it should?"

"I've just packed him off with Margolis."

"Good. That's fine."

Hyman patted a handkerchief to his face and forehead. "It may be fine for you, although I fail to see how. He's John Roper's son, Luke. That actually means something to me."

"*You* made it happen."

"You left me no choice."

"Sometimes none of us have choices, George. But don't get frazzled about a situation that may never amount to anything. I've told you already, the boy probably knows nothing."

"He's still John Roper's son."

"That's not your headache, George. I promised you'd be out of it before you knew you were in. Well, your part's over for the moment."

"For the moment!"

"Relax, George, please. Favors earn favors. Your call next time. Just leave things to Margolis, will you?"

At the elevator, Margolis said confidentially, "Did he feed you that tea crap in there?"

Anson grinned. There was no malice in the sandstone face. "Yes." The doors parted and they stepped in. Margolis's hand hovered over the panel of buttons on the wall. He winked.

"You really wanna go see this office?"

"Not much."

"Good boy. I'll tell you something about this town. If you wanna exercise your tongue around here, exercise your legs, too. I wouldn't give a goddamn 'hello' to anyone in this dump I didn't know." He nudged Anson in the ribs. "Think I'm crazy, do you?" His face split to reveal huge white teeth.

They came out of the building and fell naturally into step as Margolis crossed C Street to the Academy of Sciences. Two things Anson had taken for granted when they happened now came back to disturb his peace of mind. The first was irrational, inconclusive and unproven but it was damned persistent: Margolis had deliberately broken in on his meeting with George Hyman. A nagging suspicion—a hunch—that's all it was. There was something odd too about the way Hyman had reacted to the interruption; he was relieved, as if he'd been waiting for the old man to come along and take Anson off his hands.

The second thing was more concrete. When they came out of the elevator, Margolis had handed Anson his coat. He'd had it over his arm. Now, when he thought about it, the implications were legion. The coat, a tan Burberry, had been draped from a hanger and deposited in a wall closet ten yards to the left of George Hyman's office door when he arrived. When Anson and Hyman emerged, Margolis must have had it on his arm, which meant he had already been to the closet and removed it. And that meant he and Hyman must have had it all worked out in advance.

Margolis walked with his hands deep in the pockets of his shapeless black coat. They turned the corner of 21st Street into Constitution. Margolis paused on the curb. "Whaddaya say?" He nodded across the snow-girded sweep of West Potomac Park to the Lincoln Memorial and stepped into the street without waiting for a response. Beyond the shelter of the buildings, the wind raged off the icy breast of the Potomac, scourging the bared flesh of face and hands with perfect cruelty, but it seemed to have no effect on the old man. He led the way along a cleared path and they stopped in the protection of the Memorial's wall.

Anson shivered and buttoned his coat at the collar. "Why here?"

Margolis flipped a Philip Morris out of its pack and lit it expertly in cupped hands. The book of matches was royal blue with an impressive gold crest in one corner. Across the middle was the name: Teddy's. Margolis peeled the dead match to its core and flicked it away. "John Roper never tell you this was the place to be when you had some thinking to do?" He spoke with remarkable gentleness.

Anson watched his own breath spin away on the racing air. More rhapsodies. Another bleeding heart full of compassion. "What do you want, Mr. Margolis?" he said flatly. "Just tell me what you want and we can get the hell out of this icebox."

The white head bent to the cigarette, drew smoke and came up puckered with real amusement. "Not buying it, huh?" He slapped Anson on the shoulder. "Me neither. To hell with George Hyman. Let's walk. I'm getting arthritis of the brain."

They paralleled the Reflecting Pool in silence and turned left to avoid crossing 17th. The White House, a specter in misted gray, sat shivering beyond the Ellipse. Anson said at last, "What was that scenario back there all about?"

Margolis cleared his throat. "Setup, kid. The whole thing. George is a nice guy and he liked your pa. I had to bend his fender some to persuade him to get you there."

"Why bother? If *you* wanted to talk to me you could have phoned. Or is that too simpleminded a proposition for this town?"

"Yeah, I guess you're right." Margolis stopped walking.

"Okay, level. They bury your old man at Arlington tomorrow. 10:30, right?"

"Well?"

"Two Presidents gonna be there. Half of Congress. The whole of State. Anyone who amounts to anything. They're running shuttles from New York."

"Look, I don't know what you're . . ."

"I wanna be there." The jaw snapped shut. "They could sell tickets to that thing tomorrow and fill Arlington from end to end and they still wouldn't take my money. I never was much good at buying favors, but this is one I'd swing for, kid. I guess a lot of people are on your back for the same thing, and I wouldn't blame you for feeling riled up the way I conned you into this, but . . ." He leveled a glare into Anson's face. "I *need* to be there. I have to see that man go to his rest."

Anson was so relieved he grinned openly. All this—all *this!*—so that a superannuated nonentity could rise above the social tideline. "Why the hell didn't George ask me that straight out?"

Margolis hung his head. "George is a bureaucrat. They breathe pure protocol. Protocol don't cover my situation."

Anson sighed. "Well, Mr. Margolis . . ."

"Walt. I was Walt to your old man."

"Walt. There're invitations. State is handling that side of it. I suppose I could ask them . . ."

"George'll fix it if it comes from you, son."

"Okay. I'll tell George to fix it."

Margolis slapped horny hands on Anson's arms. It was uncomfortably close to an embrace. His face relaxed. "You have a right to know why," he said.

"My father had a lot of friends I never knew."

"You bet he did." The white head bobbed. He took Anson's elbow and they moved off again. "First time I met him was in '62. He was on a mission for Kennedy in Southeast Asia; 'Nam, Laos, Cambodia, Thailand. I was working Phnom Penh at the time for the Company." He glanced quickly at Anson. "The CIA," he explained seriously.

"Yeah, I've heard of it." Anson tried not to smile.

"Sure. Well, I was assigned to your old man. Adviser. Every GI in Southeast Asia around that time was called an adviser. In my case—muscle. Bodyguard. The White House rated him three bodyguards but your old man, he wouldn't have it. One was too many, he told 'em. So he took me. We

54

had a swell time. Well—tough for him, swell for me. Then he went on up to Prague to meet with the Chinese and I didn't see him again for years. Next time was Bonn. I was based there, controlling a feedback circuit into East Germany. On the road a lot. I got back one day and they told me my wife was dying."

He flapped an arm despairingly.

"Two weeks! You know what cancer of the bone marrow is?" He shivered in his coat. "John Roper Anson was ambassador and he heard about Rowena. That was her name, Rowena. Pretty name." He stopped abruptly and stared back at the John Paul Jones Memorial as if it held some precious relic of his past. "Rowena," he said faintly. He turned again and they trudged on through the snow. "I was on my knees, Harry. I mean, on my knees. Nothing I could do. Just watch her die. Then—one day—your old man calls me up. Never met a man I took to so fast. Never met one since. He . . . well, he said a lot of things and I listened and we had a coupla drinks and the time got around to five in the afternoon and we were still talking. Then this guy comes into the room and whispers in his ear and John Roper looks me in the eye. 'She's gone, Walt,' he says."

He kicked savagely at the snow. "You know, for a few seconds there I didn't know what he meant. Then it clicked and . . . I could have slugged him. Then I upped and bawled like a kid and he just waited. Lucky for the both of us. When I got through he told me why. The doctors'd told him she was going and what that'd do to her. Knew what it'd do to me watching her go. Said a guy had to be protected from some memories. Hold on to the good ones."

Anson said uncomfortably, "I don't think I'd have the guts to do it. I'm sorry—about your wife."

Margolis laid a hand on his shoulder. "Don't ever apologize to me, kid. For anything. Your old man earned more gratitude than you could use up in a coupla lifetimes."

They turned right on Constitution and passed the rails of the White House fence on their way into the Mall. There was a lot more about Bonn, about Rowena and their daughter, Alice, about John Roper's saintliness. The way Walt talked, there was no other word that fitted. He moved on to less inspired areas. His job.

"I go back over thirty-eight years in this job, kid—before Langley; wartime OSS. You get to an age when you need reassurance. You want to look over your shoulder and see something you're proud of. Well, I couldn't point to one thing and say: That makes it all worthwhile." He scuffed his wide flat feet in the snow. "I'm sixty-two years old. I would have been out to pasture in '77 . . ." He laughed. "Year of the stab in the back, they call it at DDO. 820 men in Clandestine Services. Out in one day. You know what they said? 'Intelligence is 95 percent technology now.' They brought in the computer brains—Foreign Assessment Center, Intelligence Tasking Center—and they said human resources—that's what they call people at Langley these days—human resources are dead. I was about on pension myself but Cambodia began running a temperature again and this particular human resource got to be useful. For a time."

"You're retired?"

Margolis chuckled. "They took me off the operational list last Fall. But we have this cute little retirement plan for beat-up warhorses out at Langley. Certain types of rank and service give you certain rights. My rights include putting my career down on paper."

"You mean like . . . memoirs?"

"They call it supplementary debriefing. You like that? You get to write it all down if you want. Make a bit of history for yourself. Dick Helms got the idea when he was director. Strictly not for outsiders. Nobody reads the stuff except guys like me who're writing their own. I also get to see any classified files I need, long as they relate to my career. That's why George Hyman gave me space at INR, so I can dig into their record section."

"Thirty-eight years is a lot of words."

"I told you, Harry, I couldn't finger anything worth writing down. To my credit, that is. No, what I'm doing isn't to my credit or anyone else's. That's why I'm doing it. Whatever happens, they'll remember Walt Margolis."

"What do you mean?"

"I'll tell you. Back in '63–'64 I ran the Company liaison team to the Warren Commission. The Kennedy killing. I'm putting a few things together the Company kinda 'lost' when they were submitting testimony to the Commission. And you know something else? The more I turn over, the more I tail on to the conspiracy angle. . . . Crazy! They have me on full pay for a year to rub shit in their faces. That's democracy for you, Harry boy."

"I thought democracy worked both ways."

"Hah!" The wind snatched the sound and whirled it away. "Wrong, boy. Democracy works along the line of least resistance. Only way it can go because there's a deadweight of muscle pushing on it. Believe me, I know."

Anson's cheeks flushed hot. "Maybe Langley has views on democracy, too. Do they know what you're doing?"

"Sure they know. I told you, it's my right to put it down on paper. Restricted right, in some ways, but I'm cute enough to stay inside the guidelines. While I do that they're stuck with me."

"What happens if you find yourself on the wrong end of *their* line of least resistance?" Anson felt his irritation bounding ahead of him.

Margolis plumped a hand on his arm, bridging the gulf opening between them. "Son—they're way ahead of me. They check out every file I call before I get to it. They have eyes and ears at State, Justice, Supreme Court, wherever I go, reporting back. They know what I'm seeing, but what they don't know is what I'm thinking." He tapped the white hair at his temple. "Combination of what I *read* and what I *know*. They can't know that." He waved both arms, windmill fashion. "So what the hell. Come the day it's all on paper—then they can start to feel worried."

"I'd be worried now, if I were in your shoes."

"You wouldn't. You're your old man's son. You're clean. The Company's clean in some ways. Not many. Mostly it's full of guys who've got nasty habits they want to forget. Oh, they believe they've done a good job, fair and square. Gave their lives to Langley. They feel sore the way things have gone. Suddenly the game isn't so fashionable anymore and people who wanna stay in business need to make sure they haven't left any trails. A few people left trails out of Dallas. A lot of bad conscience walked away from Kennedy."

Anson pulled a face to cover his disbelief, but it was difficult to be contentious for long with a man like Walt Margolis. "I thought the Assassinations Committee had gone over all that. If you think you have something they don't know . . ."

Margolis spat expertly two yards ahead of him. "The trouble with this country is we clean house too often in public. The way I see it, the Company has a right to put its own affairs in order. Do no one any good to go back over that ground in the newspapers. That's the way I see it."

Anson said sharply, "I don't think my father would."

"Wrong!" Margolis slammed fist into palm. "Your old man put country before everything. Out of date, him and me, but that's the way we were brought up. Country first."

"He told you that? About . . . this Kennedy thing?"

"Face to face." His tone changed slightly. "He didn't say anything to you about it?"

"We didn't see much of each other in the last three or four years." And if they had, thought Anson, John Roper wouldn't have wasted time reciting other people's fantasies—particularly if it involved breaking a confidence to do so.

"You must have communicated. John Roper was a man who wrote letters. I had a few myself," persisted Margolis.

"Some. But he never talked politics."

Margolis waved his arms. "He was a big man in this country. He must have had *opinions*. He knew every President since FDR. He had more connections than Bernard Baruch. You can't hold back that kind of muscle. I'd say he had to be on the inside track of every major group in America, one way or another."

Anson came to a halt, genuinely bewildered. "I don't know what you mean by that."

Margolis shrugged vaguely. "People come together to make things happen. You know—politics, business, science, the arts, education—yeah, and diplomacy too. That's the way influential men influence things. You heard of the Council on Foreign Relations? Power brokers, kid. They don't all have a clubhouse or headed notepaper or annual conventions but, believe me, guys get together and they make things happen. Presidents get elected that way. That's what I mean."

Anson shook his head firmly. "Maybe they do, but John Roper wasn't that kind of groupie. In fact, I'd say he made a point of steering clear of anything that smelled of collusion. He wouldn't want to know. He believed in due process, all along the line. Genuinely."

They had drawn level with the Natural History Building. Without warning, Margolis stepped off the curb and flagged down a cab. "Jesus, Harry," he said apologetically. "I'm fifteen minutes over the top for a meet at La Salle. I tell you what we'll do. You go back and take a looksee at that office. I'll see you there for coffee if I can make it back in time." He ducked into the cab and stuck his head out of the window. "We'll go to Arlington together tomorrow, okay?"

Once again he left Anson no time to reply.

Garfield took the call in the library. "Who is that?"

"Leo. I'm at home. Margolis just called."

"That was quick."

"He says the Anson kid's out of the picture."

"He *thinks* he's out. How could he tell? He left Hyman's office with Anson at 9:45. It's now 10:22. How sure can he be about anything in that time?"

McCullen stonewalled stoically. "His track record's good, this far. If he says Anson doesn't know anything . . ."

Garfield lurched into a handy chair. "He asked Anson straight out if his father had told him anything about The Matrix? Written anything?"

"Pretty much. Answer is no. Margolis wouldn't foul that up. He's got a lot of jungle shrewd."

"Margolis could be fooling himself. Maybe he didn't reach the boy."

McCullen made a noise in his throat. "He says he had him halfway to tears."

"I can imagine." Dryly. "What did he tell him?"

The caller coughed discreetly. "He told him about his wife dying in Bonn when Anson's father was ambassador there." Another cough. "John Roper stepped in and saved Margolis from being in on the deathbed scene. Cancer."

Garfield pinched the bridge of his nose. "What is he in private, some kind of a poet?"

"I don't think he'd have put it as badly as that."

"I hope not. Are they making contact again?"

"The funeral at Arlington, definitely. Margolis plans to ask him to dinner Friday night. Get him relaxed, help him open up. Sounds about right to me."

Long sigh from Garfield. "Very well. I want that contact maintained. Anson may know something without knowing he knows it."

"Er—that again, sir?"

"Subliminal record. People hear facts in isolation. They record them in their memory banks in isolation. Needs an outside stimulus to thread those facts together to make sense, to make a whole."

Garfield paused. "How much did he feed the boy?"

"Everything."

"Including the usual diatribe on his Kennedy theory, I suppose," Garfield said caustically.

"I'd say, with respect, that part's in our favor. No one would doubt Margolis had a genuine bee in his britches about Kennedy. Anson'll maybe write him off as some kind of kook but he'll remember the stuff about the memoirs. If he knows anything, it'll trigger his memory. That's why I'm inclined to

59

accept Walt's record that Anson doesn't know a thing. If Anson's father told him a tenth of what he put in that letter to you, the kid would've jumped out of his skin the second Walt opened up."

Garfield clenched his teeth to hold back his temper. "All right, Leo," he said stiffly. "So we'll have to try a little harder. I'll think about it. Tell Margolis to stay with him."

McCullen's pause bristled with uncertainty. "That could be a headache. I think we may have domestic problems with Margolis."

"What kind?"

"Milt Abrams called an hour ago. He asked me what Margolis was doing. Told me to run a domestic check on him."

"Well?"

"Abrams has lines out on Margolis everywhere he goes. I told you he'd ordered a twenty-four-hour suspension on all files Margolis requisitioned on the Warren Commission evidence."

Garfield sighed. "And I told you then that was no worse than Margolis should expect. Abrams is the responsible officer. Margolis is his problem. He'd be a fool to let Margolis run wild."

"Abrams will bust a gut to show the brass he's the boy wonder, and there's a surefire way of doing that: Prove that Walt has been handling files way over his classification status."

"Then keep Margolis in line, Leo. I mean that. Tell him to keep his head down. Cool the Kennedy thing here and now. If he jeopardizes this . . ."

"We're not exactly making that easy for him, sir. And we're making it tough on Anson too. If Abrams gets to hear the two of them are spending time together . . ."

"Then make sure he doesn't."

McCullen tested the ground hesitantly. "I was wondering why it was necessary, sir. Anson, I mean. If Margolis is right and the kid knows nothing about this, why're we . . . ?"

"You're out of your depth, Leo," Garfield snapped viciously. "Just follow instructions." He had almost slammed down the receiver when he snatched it back to his ear. "Leo!"

"Sir?"

"Margolis's wife. Where *did* she die?"

The discreet cough again. "She didn't, far as I know. They were divorced in 1961. She remarried—real estate operator in

60

Santa Barbara. Margolis won custody of the daughter. She must be about twenty-eight now. Walt hasn't seen his wife since."

THURSDAY: 1100—ANSON

Anson surveyed the office again; so this was how they lived, the folks on the Hill. Little boxes of bureaucracy: sanitized, color-coded, bland and—he touched the window catch and confirmed that it was bolted shut—hermetically sealed. The bottom line of the executive pyramid; twenty levels above the clerk-infested open-plan prairies of Administration, of course, but ten levels at least below the mandarins who sat in mahogany-paneled isolation, knitting wars.

He lowered himself into one of his three regulation hospitality chairs and bounced on it speculatively. Why three? Was it computed that no one this unimportant could possibly want more than three people to talk to at once? State Department thinking worked in number groups: one bar for lieutenant or a small famine or a casual border spat between tribesmen, two for captain or a smallpox outbreak in Estonia or fighting in Guatemala, and so on up to three-star general or a cholera pandemic in South America or the failure of the SALT talks. There was nothing above a three-star general in his experience, just a brightly lit cloud of steam and a babel of sincere clichés.

It was coming up to the midmorning break. Everyone broke for elevenses here, just like the English. Shut down, minds off, cigarettes on. According to custom, even this relaxation was colored by rank and status. The mandarins took tea or liquor, the up-and-coming swallowed their uppers or downers with black coffee and the herd punched vile liquids from open-mouthed dispensers.

Still, State was being good to him, oozing sympathy. This office, an extension of leave—wrapped in crap about academic studies of Italian extremists—and Geroge Hyman trying to be a true friend of the family without descending to sentiment.

It would all be so much easier if they simply ignored him, allowed him to settle his father's affairs, talk with the family lawyers, nurse his wretchedness in the comfortable solitary confinement of John Roper's apartment.

He eyed the electric clock on the far wall. 10:57. No sign

of Walt Margolis yet. What could he possibly have to do at La Salle? He went to the desk, flipped open the day-to-day planner and checked the lined space for Thursday. Tom Pringle, his father's legal executor, had invited him for a cocktail-hour chat at the Mayflower. He wrote it down. Six-thirty was an age away. He got to his feet, fished his jacket and coat from the tiny built-in locker and strolled out.

Teddy's was less than six months old and still enjoying a vogue among executive grade bureaucrats. It served muffins and regular or Irish coffee at this time of day in a turn-of-the-century setting punctuated with fake mementos, and pictures and knickknacks commemorating the administration of Theodore Roosevelt. According to embassy gossip, it was fast developing a reputation as a pickup joint for guys on the make. Out-of-towners were directed to Teddy's by lobbyists hustling support. Bagmen checked in there to make the pass. Foreign diplomats started their evenings with overgenerous hosts at the bar. Come 7:30, they said, you could sit at a center table in Teddy's and watch an oil company bankroller paying off an Energy Department slave, a Third World trade delegation collecting payola in negotiable blondes, Congressional committee investigators pouring confidence down the throat of big corporation flunkies. The world and his mistress met at Teddy's, they said.

At 11:00 A.M. the accusation rang hollow. The place was filling fast. Anson wedged himself into a corner table with a tourist's view of the room and ordered coffee. He was sipping it tentatively when Margolis's voice rose over the chatter.

"Hey, Harry. Didn't take you long to get the habit."

Margolis swayed over to the table, agreeable as a sailor on shore leave. "I'm pooped. I was too late for that meeting at La Salle. Why don't we keep you company, whaddaya say?" He half-turned and waved a hand at the athletic-looking man in square silver spectacles behind him. "You know Leo McCullen?" Anson shook his head. Walt bowed with comic vulgarity. "Okay—so this is Leo McCullen. Leo, meet Harry Anson out of State. He's on . . ." Walt's eyes clouded briefly. ". . . He's on temporary detachment here."

McCullen came forward with sudden interest and slid into a chair, his brow furrowed. "You're not . . . ?" He looked quickly at Margolis. "You're John Anson's son, I guess." He held out his hand. "I'm proud to say I was . . . well, an acquaintance of your father's."

The hand was lean and brown and tightly muscled. Anson shook it. He said, "Did you know him well?"

"No, not well. He was very kind to me a couple of times. Helped me out when I could have made a fool of myself."

"You with State?"

Anson noted the questioning glance McCullen threw at Margolis. Walt chuckled. "We're all family here, Leo." He turned to Anson. "Leo's with the Company, Harry. My chief for the past two years. Deputy to Milt Abrams in Classification over at Langley." Margolis patted McCullen's arm paternally. "Harry's a straight, Leo. He's at the embassy in Rome. *Corps diplomatique.*" He gave the phrase a French accent that was surprisingly good.

"I should've known that," McCullen apologized.

"No need. I'm not my father's son yet." Anson tried to make it a joke but the attempt at modesty seemed to embarrass them.

"He means," said Walt, flagging down a waitress with the panache of a Parisian traffic cop, "that he knows what it takes on our side of the business, Leo." The waitress arrived and Walt flattered her with an order for two coffees, *"muy negro, por favor."* He turned back to them, "Harry's kicked around in embassy security. Surveillance, checkouts, letter drops, developing local assets. That kinda thing."

Anson looked at him in surprise. "I haven't told . . ."

Walt stabbed a finger to the side of his nose. "Schtum, Harry. I get around a lot. I get to pick up all kinds of material, here and there. Safe with me, boy."

"Your father's funeral . . . ," began McCullen.

"Tomorrow. 10:30."

Margolis swallowed a handful of nuts from the bowl in the middle of the table. The waitress arrived with the coffee.

"Is it . . . ?"

"Arlington," Margolis cut in. "Where else would they lay John Roper Anson?" He raised the cup to his lips and took a mighty draft of the hot liquid. He seemed to have a lead-sheathed gullet. He pushed back his chair. "Look, kids, I've got myself a heavy date over at Justice. See you later, okay Harry? Leo, I'll be in touch. Be good now."

They watched him go, butting through the incoming crowd like a tug in a heavy swell.

"He's quite a guy," murmured McCullen.

"That's for sure."

They devoted themselves to their coffee in silence for a full

63

minute, then McCullen ventured, "If there's anything I can do to help . . ."

"Thanks, no. Everyone's breaking their backs to help."

"Yeah."

They sat through another extended silence. McCullen tried again. "I guess you'll be glad to get back to Rome. Work's the best healer."

Anson looked at him, lowered his eyes again quickly. If only you knew. He savored the thought of unloading his troubles. Why the hell not? This guy was another bleeding heart, another "acquaintance" of John Roper's, another anxious-to-please. Everyone was burning for confidences.

"I don't think I should grind my ax, Mr. Mc . . ."

"Leo."

"Leo." Everyone wanted to be loved, invested in. He sighed to show that his reluctance had a realistic edge. "Rome is a fine posting, Leo. I like it there. But since I got back it's maybe lost a little of its . . . enticement value."

"I can understand that."

"With respect—I doubt it. I came back here with a whole pile of guilt on my shoulders. I guess it happens when parents die. You look back to what you should have been, what you should have done and said to them, and . . . well, you know what I mean."

"Sure."

"Nothing seems to be what you thought it was. Oh, I've made it so far. I do my job and I get the right noises in return. But that's all. I've traded on my father's name, I guess. I certainly used his money. I've had one hell of a good time. About twice a year I wrote home. Maybe once a year I saw him, but usually because he came to me. My father told me weeks ago he was ill. I found plenty of reasons for not letting it worry me. I was busy."

McCullen nodded gently. "The son hasn't been born yet who doesn't feel that way, Harry." He used the familiarity confidently. "You'll get things straightened out."

"Not in Rome, I won't."

"Pressures? The job?"

Anson grimaced without humor. "Pressures, yes. Not the job. Like I said, coming back to Washington changed a lot of things. I don't feel the same. I don't want to go back to being the same man, doing the same things."

"Relationship problems?" McCullen was looking down at his coffee.

Anson grinned bitterly. "I suppose you could call it a relationship. My father wouldn't."

"Girl?"

"A wave-you-good-bye-at-the-airport girl. A telephone-call-a-day girl. The kind you forget when the No Smoking sign goes off two minutes after takeoff."

"That's tough."

Anson checked himself before he went on. This was further by a mile than he had intended to go. He had never been this forthright before. What was so persuasive about this guy's silences? "I deserve it," he grated.

"She troubling you in some kind of a . . . physical way?"

"I don't understand. What do you mean physical?"

"She's not pregnant?"

Anson hissed with real amusement. "Grazia? Pregnant? You don't know too much about the Italian jet-set type, do you, Leo? They don't believe in babies by the score anymore. The old ideals don't figure nowadays. Fuck-it-and-see is for the peasants."

McCullen snatched a look at his watch. He leaned forward over the table. "Look, Harry. Walt tells me they've given you some kind of a nesting box over at INR. True?"

Anson shrugged. "Don't ask me why. I'm only here for three days, officially. They've gone to a heap of trouble. I don't need it."

McCullen gripped his arm. "Hang on to it."

"What do you mean?"

"Just do as I say. Hang on to it. Do you know George Hyman?"

"Yeah. He's exec. control. Friend of my father's." Cynically.

"Good. I said I owed your father a lot, Harry. I meant it. I never had a chance to repay him—and I don't suppose he'd have let me if I could. But I think he'd go for the idea of me helping you out. If I can."

"Now wait a minute, Leo . . ."

"No. Give a dog his day." He got to his feet and slipped around the table to face Anson. "I pull a little weight, Harry. Not too much, but I've got connections who do."

He pulled on a pair of beautifully cut black leather gloves. "Sit tight and wait for the word. It'll take a few days, maybe a couple of weeks, but George Hyman owes me a couple of favors, too. I'll call him this afternoon."

Anson stood up and they shook hands. He said, "I think

I'm going to hate myself five minutes from now. I've just been squirming about using my father's name and how I want to change all that, and now I'm . . ." He stopped.

McCullen pulled on his coat and tied a silk scarf at his throat. "Harry, I promise you something. First chance you have to do me a favor, I'll come running, okay?"

FRIDAY: 0705—GARFIELD

Lucas Garfield lay back against the wedge of pillows, the *Washington Post* in his left hand, a blue and white coffee cup in his right. His wife, Polly, put her head around the door for the third time since she'd brought in his breakfast tray.

"Drink it," she ordered.

"Hrummmm."

"It's 7:05."

"Hrumm."

"You said you had to be out of the house a half hour early today."

"Hrumm."

"You're behind schedule."

"Hrumm."

Polly Garfield smothered a smile. "I thought it might be a great idea today to draw every last cent out of the account at Chase Manhattan and elope to Guatemala with Robert Redford."

No response, but he was now bolt upright in the bed. He clattered the coffee cup to its saucer and folded the *Post* to a quarter its full size. "Get me that phone," he snapped.

His wife took the instrument from the small table on his right, removed the tray one-handed and dropped the phone into his lap. He seemed not to have noticed. His eyes were fixed on the far wall beyond the bed. "What is it, Luke?" It was a question she had asked a hundred thousand times in the course of their married life without ever expecting an adequate reply. She got none now.

"I have a call to make. Here . . ." He pulled at her free arm and raised his face to peck at her cheek. ". . . go run me a bath, will you? I need to be in town in an hour."

He waited while she closed the door, then lifted the instrument and depressed the matt black button above the dial. The operator's voice came on right away: deep, cold, morning fresh. The night shift ended at 7:00 A.M. "Sir?"

"Waterboy, please." He used the code word that he, Goldman and Fletcher had decided on after their last contact.

The operator coughed diplomatically. "California time is 4:07, sir."

"I'm aware of that. Get it."

He heard the receiver come off its rest, heard the muffled scraping sounds as if it were being dragged across sheet and pillow to a reluctant mouth.

"Yeah?"

"I'm sorry to wake you, sir. It's important."

Pause. "Who the . . . oh! Is that you . . . ?"

"I said I'm sorry to have to wake you but there's been a development."

"Development?" The voice took on a new alertness. "What's the time? It can't be more than . . ."

"We're going to have to move quickly, Mr. President. It looks like Bradley's formally declaring for the Presidency. The *Washington Post*'s running the story this morning."

"The ———— he is." The oath was involuntary. "Is it official?"

"No, it's an exclusive by their political editor. No quotes. Could be pure speculation. Could be a leak. We can't take the chance. Story says Bradley will make it official in two or three days."

"Just a minute." Garfield heard more muffled scraping sounds and a nasal grunting. Nixon was fully awake now. He came back on the line. "That's not much time. What do we do about this?"

"If you and I had been able to—er—cooperate a little earlier than we di . . ."

"Don't try that one on me, Mister. We've been over that ground. I've told you till I'm sick of hearing my own voice that I was ready and willing to do what had to be . . ."

Garfield cut him off. "No recriminations, Mr. President. Not from my side. I was merely making the point that we've lost time. Bradley's declaring and that means you're committed."

"We've got a couple of days. There must be something you could hit him with."

Garfield said encouragingly, "We none of us want this thing to go all the way. It's up to you now, sir. He's in Washington but I hear he's headed for an engagement in L.A. tonight. I can let you know his ETA and his movements. I'm afraid now . . . ," he leaned back into the pillow, "I'm afraid we have to make a direct hit. You and him."

"You have nothing else you can use?"

"Nothing outside of the tape. Nothing to make him back down."

"But surely the guy's vulnerable now. He's a candidate. Even rumor, gossip ... Jesus, he's taking on an incumbent President, isn't he? Threaten him with..." He stopped.

Garfield spoke quickly, unequivocally, "I need things to happen very quickly, Mr. President, and you have to initiate. We agreed, didn't we ... ?"

"Now, you wait just a minute ..."

"We can't afford to wait, sir." Garfield stamped all over his protests. "I want Bradley and his people to know—certainly within twenty-four hours—that you know about the tape. And what's on it. I want them to feel threatened right away. No time to settle in. I want them to keep running and I want them to sweat."

"And you want me to put my head on the block."

"For the best reasons any man will ever have to serve his country. If I weren't convinced of that we wouldn't be talking here."

The pause was a long one. Then, "You know what happens if this goes wrong?"

"Yes, sir. I know."

"Politically, I mean," Nixon insisted. "Let's suppose you were a ———— cheap hustler. No, wait a minute! You blackmail me into a position where I agree to do what you want. What am I doing? I'll tell you, Mister. I'm committing suicide. That's one. Two, I'm putting the Party machine on the spot. Three, I'm handing the Democrats a bag of shit they can throw for the rest of the campaign and, four, the President wins by default."

"And, five, Bradley is finished and, six, whatever he has behind him blows wide open."

"That's not a payoff that'll do me any good."

"But we agreed, Mr. President," purred Garfield, "that what was important was the welfare of the country. It's not a sideshow where you win a prize for shooting the ball off the water jet."

"Don't patronize me ..."

"Patronage is *your* privilege, Mr. President," Garfield interjected quickly. "That's what we're talking about. No other American is in a position to do what you can do. Your patronage is unique. I'm asking you to exercise it for reasons I know you accept as just and honorable."

68

Nixon chuckled dryly. "Which is why you approached me in the first place with threats. Blackmail."

Garfield sighed heavily. "How would you have reacted if I'd come hat in hand, sir? We're both pragmatists. We believe in practical politics: the art of the possible. I had to win your respect and that meant establishing my credibility. You wouldn't argue with that, I suspect . . ." There was steel in his tone.

Richard Nixon drew breath in a long, sibilant, thoughtful stream. "All right. You made your point. But if anything goes wrong . . ."

"If anything goes wrong, Mr. President, your salvation will be the truth. I'm in a position to reveal the truth . . . if things go wrong."

Nixon laughed loudly. "Now, that's a day I'd hope to live to see. Just ask yourself a question: Who the ——— d'you think is ever going to believe you? Go ahead—tell me." He waited, but Garfield refused to be drawn. "Sure—you know the answer to that as well as I do."

Garfield said, "Mr. President, we must . . ."

"I know. All right. When?"

"Tonight. After his speech. I'll give you the timing later. When you face him keep detail to the minimum. We've made some, ah, technical arrangements . . ."

"When do I get to hear the tape?"

"I have an edited transcript; the major points are all there. It will be enough for you to work on."

"You telling me I can't hear the tape? Is that what you're saying?"

"At the moment, sir, it would achieve nothing. And believe me, whoever is close to that tape is in considerable danger. It's better this way."

Nixon seemed about to argue, then changed his mind. He said absently, "I can handle it, I guess." His voice took on a matter-of-fact edge. "When are you going to tell the President about this?"

"When it's necessary."

"Suppose I talk to him myself?"

"He'd be—er—surprised to hear from you, I think. Perhaps it wouldn't be practical politics for him to take your call, sir."

The laughter from the other end was full enough this time to be genuine. "I'll say this for you, Mister," Nixon choked, "I'd rather have you on my side than against me. You'd beat Joe McCarthy to hell and back for goddamn cheek."

Polly Garfield put her head around the door but began to withdraw when she saw the telephone in her husband's hand. He beckoned her toward him.

"Well, that's most kind of you, sir," he said pleasantly. "I'll do my best to live up to that." Nixon began to speak again but Garfield interrupted, "It's been a pleasure, as always, sir. I'll call you later," and put down the phone.

He blinked up at Polly. "What were you saying about Robert Redford?" he asked innocently.

FRIDAY: 1200—ANSON

Harry Anson braked the Porsche under the sign Resident's Parking Space: John Roper Anson, switched off the engine and lit a cigarette. His hands were trembling. The underground parking lot was comfortingly dark. He needed the dark. Remote, infinite, enveloping darkness with no mirrors and no candles burning brightly in corners.

It had been unreal. The service, the cortege, the chain of black-bound dignitaries and their black-bound wives, the Marines in their two, stiff white-capped ranks beside the grave and the racketing fusillade as they fired three times toward heaven. Old men he couldn't remember ever having met touching his hand—not shaking it—as if sorrow were an open wound. Distinguished men who, for half an hour, devalued their importance as a mark of respect, then consulted their watches and sped away, as if death were contagious.

The President had come to shake his hand, his left clutching Anson's elbow to cushion the loneliness. He'd said something appropriate but Anson couldn't remember what it was or what he said in response. The play's the thing, John Roper used to say, particularly at the graveside. There was no answer to death, no substitute for lost love; but it was a fashion, socially speaking, to pretend that there was. Ten minutes later, Anson had looked up from his contemplation of the rectangular shaft in the earth and the box that contained his father's flesh—and found he was alone. He had dropped Margolis at the gates of Arlington when they arrived and, later, he'd seen McCullen's tinted glasses through a break in the wall of faces when the cortege emerged from the chapel. He didn't see them again. They had presumably left him to his pain.

It *was* pain. It didn't seem possible, but it was pain, sure enough. Self-induced, self-generating, self-serving punishment.

The Secretary of State had read the lesson: the Sermon on the Mount. "Blessed are the pure in heart . . ." Who would read that over the body of Harold Roper Anson when the time came? Only someone as insensitive to the truth as himself.

He got out of the Porsche and ground out his cigarette. They would probably leave him alone now for at least the weekend. Except Walt Margolis. Dear old Walt. "Come to dinner Friday night, Harry. It's important to me, you understand?" Important to *him* maybe, but why had he agreed to go? Because Walt Margolis would have cajoled and argued until he capitulated. It was simply easier to agree. He ignored the elevator and took the stairs to his father's apartment, swinging up each step on his toes, creating pain. On the second floor he saw the janitor look up from halfway along the corridor and wave commiseration, but he climbed on. The man was a cringing, patronizing Uriah Heep who had already ambushed him three times since he arrived.

The janitor had truly respected Mr. Anson for a great and wonderful man, and he had no intention of losing a potentially high-tipping asset without a fight.

At the door, Harry leaned his head on the polished wood. Maybe if he sat alone long enough the regret would come welling up in him and tears would flow as they properly should. Why, for God's sake, couldn't he feel *real* loss? Not this phony, spoiled-brat vexation. He had lost a father, dammit, not his virginity. He turned his key, swung his foot at the door behind his back—and froze. For a microscopic instant he thought he was about to see his father's ghost, then the bathroom door swung back and the shadow on it became—Grazia.

Graziella Montecorvino was wearing his blue bathrobe and her red hair hung in shining rat's tails on both sides of her face. She wore no makeup and her olive skin shone with rapturous health. She had a hair dryer in her hands and was unwinding the cord when the door slammed. Her head rose like a startled gazelle's, the wide, sloping green eyes round with shock. The dryer thudded to the carpet and she clutched her face in hands.

"Oh, *mia tesoro!*"

The tears came as swiftly, effortlessly, efficiently as spray from a first-class sprinkler system. She ran to him, arms outstretched, then crumpled to her knees at his feet, her face pressed hard into his crotch. It was so predictable, so ridiculously theatrical, he could have laughed aloud. The avenging angel of the Lord. Grazia was made for the part.

"What the hell are you doing here?"

She poured her monumental sadness onto his trousers. "Oh, *tesoro, tesoro!*"

He took a firm grip under her arms and heaved her upright. She resisted with her deadweight; her performance was far from over. He dragged her over to a chair, sat her down and lit a cigarette. He shoved it between her quivering lips and, immediately, she sucked in smoke, swallowed, exhaled and allowed a couple of well-balanced whimpers to escape her perfect mouth.

Anson saw it, recalled a dozen incidents like it and his anger boiled over. The sheer callous, stage-managed bravura of it left him speechless for a moment, then he burst out, "Don't give me that noble peasant shit, you cow. I asked you what the hell you're doing here?"

Her head snapped up, her eyes blazed and the left side of her mouth curled upward. "You unfeeling son of a bitch! I came 5,000 miles to comfort you, that's why I'm here. *Comfort* you? Hah!" She spat the word. "I should have known . . . Harry Roper Anson doesn't need comfort. He doesn't need *anyone.*" She whirled one long brown leg over the other, throwing the bathrobe wide to expose the red blonde seat of Anson's guilt.

He turned away in despair and wrestled off his coat and jacket. He took them into the bedroom and came to a halt in the doorway. The bed was littered with silken underwear and shoes and hats and neatly packed boxes of cosmetics and jewelry. On the floor, hanging from doors and window frames and the open cupboards of the dressing room, were Pucci day dresses and casual wear, elegant trouser suits and skirts by Valentino, and four perfect evening gowns that had Missoni written all over them.

He wheeled back into the sitting room. "So you rushed breathless to be at my side, did you? Without a thought for yourself? Flew to the grieving lover. . . . What exactly do you think you're going to do with all this junk?"

"It is not junk!"

"It's *junk!* And how did you get in here anyway?"

She pulled on the cigarette and let the smoke dribble from her mouth. The tears still glistened on the precipices of her cheekbones but she had switched emotions. This was a side of Harry Anson she knew she could deal with.

"You couldn't have gotten a key."

"A pretty little old man let me in. He was most sorry that Mrs. Harry Anson had missed the funeral."

"*Mrs.* Anson?"

"Oh, *tesoro*, don't be angry. How would he let me in to your father's apartment if he thought I was not your wife?"

Anson turned into the bedroom and hurled his coat and jacket with massive savagery. It was as far as he would go and he knew it. Grazia had established a bridgehead. Before the afternoon was out, she would be in his bed and he would be in her.

FRIDAY: 1215—MARGOLIS

Walt Margolis was thinking the unthinkable.

The Central Intelligence Agency was not so much a steel deposit vault as a tight-knit circle of self-interested zealots. Like a protective ring of wagons drawn up against attacking redskins, the Company prepared its defenses to face, and function, outwards. Which was to say it was most vulnerable at its core. Add to that a dogmatic code of allegiance—still remarkably intact—and you had an organization which trusted nothing and no one beyond its doors but retained a touching belief in the integrity of its staff. The idea of attack from within was bizarre.

Margolis stalked on down the corridor toward Abrams's office.

Leo McCullen had sidetracked him at a bad time, but they worked well together and Leo was good news. Whoever was pulling his strings had sound reasons for upending the Company, and a lot of muscle. No doubt of that. Yet, looking close, it raised the same old questions all over again: was he or was he not betraying an organization that had given him his *raison d'être* for a working lifetime? Answer: you bet he was. Which, again, carried him back to the other question: did he owe allegiance to the outfit or to the principles on which it ran? No question. The principles. So what was he complaining about? No complaint. Just think the unthinkable.

He banged a tattoo on Abrams's outer office door, opened up and craned his head inside. "Who's my girl?" he grinned.

"Walter!"

He bared his teeth in mock pain at this use of his full name, but Shirley Stevenson had fielded this joke too often to misinterpret the gesture.

"Hi, Shirl." He strolled in and flipped the door shut behind him. He looked around quickly and cocked a head at Abrams's inner sanctum.

"He's out," the secretary said with a sniff. Ms. Stevenson wore her hair in tight bunches, her eyes heavily outlined and her age on her sleeve. Fifty-five if she was a day, she nevertheless stubbornly refused to part with her youth, and her long flower-print dress lent substance to that determination. Shirley had bloomed when the world was young and Walt Margolis with it; they had age on their side, a fellow feeling born of regret for things past and a liking for each other that verged on sexual attraction. Shirley had never concealed her readiness to take him up on any offer.

"Wine, women or song?" asked Walt with a wink. Her distaste for Abrams was another secret they shared.

"Donald Petersen," she mouthed.

He made a little clucking noise with his teeth and levered himself into a chair; a comfortable one.

"Something wrong?" She always thought something was wrong. Few officers came in to see her unless they were in trouble.

"You still think the sun rises on me, honey?" It had to be light. She would only go so far.

"There *is* something wrong."

He raised his arms and flattened the palms upward. "There's always something wrong, Shril. But today, I've gotta admit, it's pretty damn difficult to talk about. If it weren't for you, I wouldn't know where to turn. Anyone else, I wouldn't presume to ask."

"Ask what?" Her face went taut as a rolled boxing glove.

"No." He made to rise from the chair. "You can only ask someone to trust you so far and then . . ." He shrugged.

"Trust you? You haven't done anything . . . wrong, have you?" The ridiculous young-old face showed genuine concern.

"No. Nothing like that." He leaned over the desk and squeezed her hand. She flushed prettily under his touch.

"You know if there's anything I can do . . ."

He dumped himself down on the corner of her desk. "Shirl, I'm going to level with you. Feel a damn fool, but I'll level. Milt Abrams's got my personal file in there." He jerked his head at the closed door of the inner office. "Anyhow, to put it bluntly, it's full of details I need bad right now and, goddamn it, Records say they can't ask Abrams to return it till he's good and finished. All I wanna see in it is a couple of pages of notes. My notes, Shirl. About me. You know I'm writing my memoir. I gotta have these facts. Your chief might just sit on that file for another month."

"Why don't you ask him for it?" Shirley said practically.

"I did. He said he didn't have it."

The secretary frowned. "I don't know why he'd say that. There must be some mistake. Records have it wrong, I bet."

"What d'you think I've been telling myself? But I gotta check a coupla things out, Shirl. I need it bad. Bad enough to . . ." He squeezed her hand again. ". . . ask you to let me see if it's in there."

She eyed him coolly, gauging the depth of his lies. "You know what you're asking, Walter?"

"Yup."

"What do you want to do?"

"Check to see if it's in his office. If it's there, I'll just photocopy the pages I need on the machine right over there," he pointed to the Xerox in the corner of her office, "and put the file back."

She rolled one finger into the hair bunched on her left shoulder and coiled it thoughtfully, then stood up. "I have to go to the powder room," she said decisively. "Just watch the office for me for five minutes, there's a darling." She fingered a small brass key from her purse and lay it flat on the desk.

Margolis waited for the door to close, then took the key to Abrams's inner office door and turned it in the lock. He closed it behind him. The room was cleanly, almost scientifically, furnished and tainted with the perfume of pine aerosol. He went straight to the desk and dropped on his haunches by the drawers. They were all locked.

He fanned the twiglets of hooked steel on their link and tested three, one after the other. The fourth turned accommodatingly. The drawer was compartmentalized to accept papers and memoranda of varying sizes. He flicked through them. Nothing. The next drawer was completely empty. He began to sweat. He must have had three minutes already. Shirl had said five. Five was what she'd give, no more. Next drawer down. It was wedged tight with what looked like ledgers and bulky covered reports. He ran his eyes over the titlepieces on the bindings. Nothing. He was about to push the drawer home when a slim file without title caught his attention. He plucked it out deftly and opened it on the desk.

There were thirteen pages and the typing was single-spaced, but the first few lines of the first sheet convinced him. He experienced an almost sick excitement. He pushed the drawer shut, taking care to arrange the contents as they were before he plundered it, then locked all of them. He pulled up the leg of his pants, bound the thirteen sheets around his calf and jerked up his sock to anchor them in place. He went out, placed the brass key on Shirl's desk and slipped into the corridor.

Tomorrow he'd buy her flowers.

FRIDAY: 1230—PETERSEN

Donald Petersen traveled with the speed of a *Concorde,* the ease of light and the panoply of a medieval doge. He came into Dulles aboard *Air Force Two,* safe in the knowledge that: One, he could justify such blatant hedonism if asked, and two, he wouldn't be asked. As Director of the Central Intelligence Agency, there were dizzying heights to which Donald Petersen could climb without consulting anyone. A Presidential airplane was his if it became known that he needed it. Air traffic patterns were frozen to accommodate his comings and goings. Bureaucratic activity was suspended to make him welcome. Cities were choked with traffic to ensure his smooth passage from airport to city center and back.

Another man, faced with the power to manipulate life and people that easily, would have retreated into a proper humility. Petersen was by no means a humble man, and today, every second he had been able to snatch from the clock, every action taken to clear his path to Washington, was justifiable.

He allowed them to drive him out to Langley, two cars behind his, one in front: police and Secret Service men and bureaucrats and panting acolytes. They were necessary. When the caravan arrived, he dismissed all of them but Milt Abrams and rode the personal elevator to his office. Abrams did not have to be told; he dialed Senator Ambrose Bradley's Washington number right away.

Petersen took the receiver as Bradley came on the line. "It's me," he said sharply. "I got your cable. What the hell is so goddamn urgent?" He pulled himself up short. Bradley was not a clerk. "Sorry," he went on quickly. "I had to turn New York inside out to get back here."

"No offense taken, Don." Ambrose Bradley had the slow soft tone that could stop a mob without rising above conversation level. Silk on steel. The great attorney has it. So does the judge, the mesmeric after-dinner speaker, the crusading lay preacher and the exceptional politician. Bradley was all of these. He said, "Arizona called me last night. Late, as usual. He doesn't seem to sleep anymore. He has to talk to you and it couldn't be direct, he said. Something about the Statler incident. Said you'd understand. You have any idea what he means by that?"

"Yes." Petersen snapped the word shut.

"He sounded . . . concerned. Why should he be concerned?"

"You know how he is, Senator. It's nothing you need worry about." He cleared his throat. "You flying to L.A. today?"

"In about an hour."

"You need anything?"

"It's just a speaking engagement. The Beverly Hilton. But if there's . . . a problem, I'd feel happier in my mind to know about it." The soft voice had a steely insistence.

"I said it was nothing."

"Arizona doesn't call you urgently for nothing, Don. If it concerns me in any way . . ."

Petersen bunched his lips in temper and squared a scowl at Abrams. "A piece of merchandise, that's all. It went astray at the Statler."

"The way you people use the word 'merchandise' covers a lot of ground. Was it important?"

"I don't think we can talk about this on the phone."

"Was it important?"

"I can't tell you that, Senator; simple reason I don't know. I had reason to believe it was valuable, but I don't know."

"You wouldn't play me for a fool, I hope?"

"Senator, I've got more to lose than you have, O.K.? We're on the same side. We work together. I'm here to protect your interests and so is Arizona. That's what we're doing."

"I'd like to think, then, that our interests coincide. I wouldn't like to believe Arizona was taking independent action on something without consulting me first."

"You know he wouldn't do that, Senator."

"I'm happy to hear you say so, Don. This'd be the wrong moment for arbitrary decisions."

77

"What do you mean?"

"The *Post* ran a story this morning forecasting our intention to declare formally in the next two or three days. They didn't get it from me. It didn't come from my office, I'll swear to that. I don't like leaks."

"Goddamn it!"

"Precisely." The voice was mild. "You know where I'll be if you need me . . . to confirm any decision you and Arizona have in mind."

"Thanks, Senator. I'll remember that."

"And, Don?"

"Yes."

"Just so we understand each other . . . I'm running a straight clean campaign, and I'm ahead. I intend to keep things that way. Clean and ahead. I won't welcome interference. Of any kind."

Petersen closed his eyes and jammed his teeth together hard. "Whatever you say, Senator. You're the man."

FRIDAY: 1245—MARGOLIS

Leo McCullen turned irritably to the telephone.

"Walt."

McCullen grunted noncommittally.

"Look. Something's come up. I need to see you right away. I missed you at Arlington."

"You want a meet now?"

"Sooner the better." Real excitement trembled in the old man's voice.

"Pay dirt?"

"Mother lode. Suddenly it begins to fit. Some names come into it, other things, too. One name in particular. New one to me: an outsider."

"That's fine, Walt. Hold it there."

"Sure. This could be the big one."

"Are you certain?"

"See for yourself. A few details don't fit, but maybe you can come up with some ideas. The more heads the better now."

McCullen consulted his watch. He had promised Garfield he would stand by his phone for the next twelve hours. Garfield wouldn't accept a visit to Margolis as a valid diversion.

"Look, why not get on over here, Walt? I'm kinda tied down just now. Can you make it?"

"No can do. Heavy day—and I got Anson coming by the apartment tonight. Look, it'll hold. Tomorrow. Come over here tomorrow morning. But I'm telling you, this one will blow your mind."

"Okay, tomorrow. Now stay cool and let it simmer. If it's as good as it sounds . . ."

"It's good."

"And Walt?"

"Yeah?"

"Do me a favor."

"Sure."

"Watch your back."

In the apartment immediately below Walt Margolis's, the technician straightened up from the control console as Walt replaced his telephone with a terminal squeak. The man took off his padded earphones, found a ballpoint pen and wrote on the notepad beside him the time and the date. Then, beneath it:

"Tape sequence numbers 326 to 391. Caller: Margolis. Recipient: unrevealed. Subject: discovery of name. Remarks: Meeting planned Saturday earliest, Margolis apartment."

He reached for a pack of Camels and lit one, studied his neat, well-rounded handwriting, then checked the time again. He ran the tape back to 326 and listened once more.

Something different. Not in the message; in the voice. Excitement. A guy who'd made a hit. Maybe this one wouldn't wait. He reached for a phone, dialed. When the subscriber answered, he said, "I think you ought to hear this. It'll only take a coupla minutes." He let the tape run, this time with the phone plugged into it. When it finished he slid out the plug and brought the receiver back to his ear. "That tell you anything?"

The reply left him in no doubt.

"That's all right," he said eagerly. "Any time. I've been sitting here for two months and this is the first time any damn thing came up worth whistling at. Who's this guy on the other end? First time he's been contacted through here."

The staccato reply brought a flush to his cheeks.

"Hey, look—forget I asked, will you? Yeah, sure, I understand. Hear no evil, right?"

He replaced the phone. Ungrateful bastards! His fingers danced over a series of switches on the console, flicking them dead. He stretched to his feet, rubbing circulation back into his stiff neck, and reached for his coat. He reckoned he deserved a fat tuna on rye and some scalding coffee.

FRIDAY: 1315—LaCROIX

Beyond the green blinds the Arizona sun bleached the sky, staining it with watercolor ochers and golds and bronze and cerulean blue. The desert was shadow-pocked, rippling in its self-generated heat haze.

The house was perfectly still, perfectly quiet, perfectly in tune with the primitive miracle outside: in tune with Creation's divine simplicity, in tune with God. Aaron LaCroix brought his hands together, fingers straight and aimed, like antennae, to heaven; he bent his shaven head and closed his eyes.

Dear God, return again this day to the heart of Thy servant and renew and bless and sustain him in Thy cause. If it be Thy will, cut him down and cast him to hell's flames and let his soul writhe in eternal damnation. That will be the Sign of Thy displeasure, the symbolic breaking of the Covenant which Thou hast forged with this, Thy servant. But if in Thy glorious wisdom, Thou are well pleased in Thy servant and would arm him again this day to pledge himself in Thy Holy Name, then let him know the warmth of Thy love, the restless power of the Holy Spirit, the blessed strength of Thy only begotten son, Jesus Christ, Our Lord.

He crossed himself, the inner edge of his right hand turned to his face. This twisting of the hand and forearm lent an almost theatrical flourish to the act. He repeated it three times. When he had finished, he prayed again silently for ten minutes, then raised his head to the blind-hung sweep of windows looking out on the desert.

The phone rang. He reached into the folds of his black-edged green silk robe and produced a small pocket watch. He replaced it and touched a button on the control panel under his right hand. The wheelchair moved forward noiselessly. He turned it right, skirted the Heikfaert harpsichord and brought the chair to a halt behind his desk. He took up the telephone.

"This is Petersen"

LaCroix raised a hand to the blanched white skin at his temple. "I hoped you might call earlier."

80

"The way I read Bradley's cable, you wanted me back in Washington before I called."

"Never mind. You're alone?"

"Naturally."

"You can talk freely?"

"The phone is safe."

"Good." He let his long, bony-fingered hand fall to the green silk of his robe and splayed it out. "There are complications. I shall need your assistance."

"The tape?"

"Yes. I took the precaution of sending Javallo to California on the afternoon of the Statler . . . confusion."

Petersen flared. "You should have told me . . ."

"Communication between us is not easy, my dear Donald. Particularly when you're traveling. Besides, Javallo has a watching brief, nothing else. It occurred to me that, if we couldn't have the tape, we should at least take account of the man responsible for making it."

"I don't get this."

"Consider. Whoever has that tape—and we have to assume it's Government or parties hostile to Bradley politically—whoever has it will need to confirm its importance. Whatever it reveals must be quantified, evaluated and proved genuine. If it's one of the White House tapes, as we believe, then there will be an attempt to ratify its contents—if only to determine when and where it was recorded and in what circumstances. Does that sound reasonable?"

"Who the hell can confirm that?"

"Openly, no one. Indirectly, Richard Nixon."

Petersen spluttered. "For chrissakes, you're . . ."

LaCroix straightened electrically. "Keep your profanities to youself!"

"I'm sorry." Petersen was fighting to keep his temper. "You haven't approached Nixon?"

"Don't be ridiculous. Of course I haven't. As I said, it seemed obvious to me that Nixon would be drawn into this if there was any doubt about the tape and its legitimacy. If not Nixon, someone near or around him who could validate it."

"That would be a lousy move. If he thought . . ."

LaCroix lowered his lids; the muted sun beat in through the disphanous skin and glowed pinkly. "My instruction to Javallo was to talk with your contact on Nixon's staff at San Clemente. Henry . . . ?"

"Jake Henry."

"Yes."

"What happened?"

"A great deal more than I expected. Nixon has already been approached—that much Javallo was able to report yesterday."

"Have they played him the tape?"

LaCroix sighed. "Javallo doesn't know that. Henry doesn't know. We hope he'll be able to find out. Rather more to the point, he doesn't know who has the tape or what they intend to do with it."

"If it concerns us—The Matrix . . ."

"We've been over that ground. Quite clearly it does. There's no comfort to be had in benign optimism. If Bradley is threatened by this, we must acquire that tape—and as quickly as possible."

"I just talked to Bradley. He has an idea we should leave him to run his own campaign. If he gets to hear something nasty scratching away behind the woodwork . . ."

LaCroix shook his head. "Leave the Senator to me, Donald. We have an . . . understanding."

"You'll need it. I don't like the way things are going. Bradley's developing a taste for immortality. He's losing his sense of perspective."

"He's doing what he's required to do."

"Tell *him* that and watch his reaction. He's getting too damned cocky for my liking. I think he can see the Holy Grail up there, just in reach. If he wins the nomination . . ."

"*When* he wins the nomination. No doubts on that score, please. *When* he wins."

Petersen's weariness sighed down the line. "You given any thought to the possibility he may scoop the nomination and then take off on his own?"

"I'm prepared for all eventualities. Even that. But I wouldn't consider it a major hazard."

"You consider the Nixon thing a major hazard?"

LaCroix took the instrument from his ear and weighed it in his hand, his eyes remote, his tongue traveling the harsh dry skin of his lower lip. He said at last, "I do. I consider it worthy of your most . . . *energetic* consideration."

Petersen's chuckle was tinderbox dry. "Getting too hot for you, Aaron?"

LaCroix stiffened, but controlled the automatic reflex to anger. He was too old to react to mindless provocation, particularly the delinquent variety. Petersen was one of a handful of men privileged to know that Aaron LaCroix survived as a human organism only so long as he avoided the direct rays of the sun. Exposure to the subtle infrared and ultraviolet bands of the light spectrum was a guarantee of death; not instant, but measurable in tormenting minutes. The phenomenon was known as photosensitivity; it was rare and it was incurable. It had struck him down—an act of God as he interpreted it himself—at the pinnacle of his powers. He had been fifty-four years old when the doctors came to him in 1959: six years after his embryo movement had taken shape, just one year after it had begun to coalesce into The Matrix. It had begun with a seizure which radiated cerebral and spinal complications—ripples that crossed the pool of life and distorted it beyond recognition. In the first weeks of his prostration, his paralysis, the fine, strong muscles of legs and arms and back and shoulders withered and sagged; he lost his hair, his eyebrows and lashes; his mind hung suspended in a time-space vacuum. Drug after drug had coursed its way through his system, but the doctors could do nothing. They shipped him to California, New York and, finally, to Switzerland. He survived, as he knew he must, but he survived only as a mind, a compulsive force.

In that too he saw the hand of God.

In 1962 he returned to America. There was nothing more the doctors could do. He was crippled and the drugs he was given during the long illness had sensitized his skin. He could neither walk nor step outside, except into the night. Four months, the doctors had said; if he was lucky, a year.

It was then that Aaron LaCroix had decided to "die," knowing the doctors were fools.

Over a period of six months, with the help of his confidants in The Matrix, he had planned his own demise. When it came it was total. The funeral was lavish, his will generous. All record of Aaron LaCroix ended on that day. Silently he had moved to Arizona. And despite the doctors' predictions he had lived there for seventeen years now: a recluse, untouched, uncontaminated, unknown. He had built his house on the desert, at the core of the fiery furnace, as one final insurance that he would never be found; for even if his "death" in some impossible way were revealed as a fraud, who would think of looking for him in such a place?

His contacts with mankind were limited to his immediate acolytes, men who had been with him from the very first: Donald Petersen, Ambrose Bradley, Tony Javallo and his house staff of three enigmatic Filipinos. There were others who, as they grew closer to The Matrix, were allowed to know of the force that lay at the core; some knew only a name, others not even that. But the *presence* was felt always.

The Matrix was indeed the rock enclosing the gem, and LaCroix sat alone and commanding at its epicenter.

He sighed heavily. "What is it that binds us together, Donald?" he asked slowly.

Petersen paused. "Give me that again?"

"You ask me what happens if Bradley decides to turn his back on us. Why have you never chosen to turn *your* back on me?"

"Look, Aaron . . . ," Petersen began lightly, "I was just trying to make my position clear. I'm not about to pull out."

"Why not, Donald? You assumed my responsibilities to The Matrix when I was on the point of death. You held the group together, breathed strength and purpose into it. You could have rejected me on my return."

"We work together. We have a team here, right?"

"We have ambitions. That's all. Different, selfish, but identifiably linked. Our problems as a *team* will begin when Bradley is in the White House. You envisage certain rewards. You'll have them. I shall be concerned with a more universal purpose. When that time comes, it will be important to both of us that our ambitions take the same line. We both know that and we always have. Certain things are important to you; they can be realized if you contribute to what is important to me. What is . . . ," he gave dramatic pause to the word, *"hot"* for me is bound to be equally uncomfortable for you."

"What do you want me to do?"

"That's better. I want you to take over the San Clemente situation. Javallo is at the Douglas Port Motel in Newport Beach. I suggest you call him. I leave it to you to muster any additional manpower you think necessary."

"Leave it to me."

LaCroix smiled. "Of course, Donald. I'm happy to."

You bet your arse you are, thought Petersen as the line clicked dead in his ear.

He picked up the sheet torn from the message pad: "Tape sequence numbers 326 to 391. Caller: Margolis. Recipient: unrevealed. Subject: discovery of name. Remarks: Meeting planned Saturday earliest, Margolis apartment."

He checked his watch: 0130.

He rolled the sheet into a ball and slipped it into his

pocket. Margolis was Abrams's baby, Abrams's problem. He paused in the middle of the room. No. He'd sweat Abrams later. This one he'd control himself. Right away.

FRIDAY: 2240—BRADLEY

It was a poor speech but they gave him a standing ovation that lasted a full five minutes. It would have gone on even longer if the comedian in the red velvet dinner jacket hadn't seized the bottle of champagne and shaken and sprayed it like a fountain over his delighted fellow guests. Hysteria. The reaction wasn't new to him. A year earlier he could have been at a loss to understand why, but he'd won his master's degree in crowd psychology on the speaking circuits. He had learned that when 650 politically motivated citizens were persuaded to pay $1000 a plate to eat with him, the ultimate emotional reaction was guaranteed because that was the prize they expected, the interest on their investment. In the beginning he'd found it difficult to maintain a decent modesty about this effect he had on people, but experience had denied him that pleasure, too. Every sit-down function, he'd learned, was sown beforehand with "pulse raisers"—Petersen's description. Their role was to create pockets of emotional response, drop the pebble in the pool. Tony Javallo organized the pulse raisers. Bradley had never met Javallo and he hoped he never would.

They broke up at 10:15 and he took a brandy with Hank Tyson and the West Coast committeemen, then pleaded exhaustion and a tight schedule next day to extricate himself.

He walked alone to the desk and asked for his key. Halfway across the lobby to the elevator a powerfully built man in a gray silk suit strode over to him, hand outstretched. Ambrose Bradley groaned inwardly.

"Good evening, sir. Hotel security. Thought you might need an escort . . . er—after the dinner."

Bradley shook his head. "I think they've had enough of me for one evening, son," he smiled. "Thanks anyway."

"My privilege, sir." The young man showed no intention of leaving. He pressed the elevator button and ushered Bradley inside. He touched the sixth floor key and retired respectfully to the rear of the car, hands folded across his stomach. Bradley shrugged. Would he ever be permitted to do anything for himself again?

They got out and the young man led the way to Bradley's suite. At the door he turned and held out his palm expectantly. Bradley handed him the key. How far, he thought with amusement, was the boy programmed to go? Would he put him to bed, tuck him in?

"Well, thanks, son . . . ," he began, but the man swung wide the door, stepped inside and waited for Bradley to enter. He sighed and walked reluctantly into the room.

The five standard lamps were on. In the deep armchair by the window an older, swarthier man of impressive height sat impassively. A third man in a dark blue, military-style raincoat half-leaned, half-sat on the table edge. He came forward.

"Sorry about this, Senator," he said. "I don't want to worry you, but . . ."

Bradley exhibited the first sign of impatience. "Look—I'm all for hotel security, gentlemen, but I don't need protective custody. So, if you'll just fade away, I'll get myself to bed. I've got an early plane."

The young man who had met him in the lobby closed the door and set his back to it, arms folded resolutely. The blue raincoat gestured Bradley to an armchair in the middle of the room. "Why don't you sit here, Senator," he said.

"I said I'm tired and . . ."

"This'll only take a coupla minutes, Senator." The blue raincoat beckoned to the large man in the chair. "Get the camera focused."

Bradley turned. Against the wall, facing the chair he had been directed to, was a small black cinecamera on a three-legged stand. On the floor beside it were three black cabinets engineered in matt steel. The big man threw a switch and consulted a display of dials on one of them. He turned his head and nodded. The blue raincoat dropped on one knee in front of the television set and switched it on. He tuned it; the carrier wave rasped noisily, then died. "Sound O.K.?"

The big man said, "Testing. One, two, three, four. You register?"

"Register," snapped a voice from the TV screen. Bradley, bewildered, craned to look at the screen, but the kneeling man obscured it.

The big man bent over the camera. "You mind sitting square to the camera, Senator?" he growled.

Bradley obeyed without thinking, his mind racing.

"That's good." The big man straightened. "Whenever you want," he said to the blue raincoat.

"Fine. That's fine." The blue raincoat got to his feet and beckoned the big man to join him. They left the room. The TV screen hissed, bright but empty. Then it blinked, fluttered nervously and gelled.

The face of Richard Nixon appeared in perfect close-up on the screen. Bradley jerked forward involuntarily in his chair.

"Just sit back in the chair, Senator," said Nixon easily. "That way I can see your face."

Bradley pulled himself together quickly. "I suppose you have a reasonable explanation for this . . . sir?"

"We're both reasonable men, Senator, so it seemed to me you wouldn't be too happy about it if I came visiting personally. Might complicate things for both of us."

"Off the cuff, I can't think of any reason we have to visit each other." Bradley plaited his fingers in his lap, relaxed the muscles of his face and neck.

"Maybe you haven't given the idea enough thought." Nixon's face creased in a shallow attempt at good humor but it didn't come off; the tension lines ran deep across his brow and on either side of his mouth.

"It's a little late for analysis," Bradley said coolly. "I can't imagine you've set all of this up for no good reason, so why don't we get down to cases."

Nixon nodded eagerly. The vertical hold slipped and his face disappeared upward, to be followed swiftly by a procession of faces. The picture readjusted itself.

"I have a proposition for you, Senator," Nixon said steadily.

"You'd be wasting your breath."

"Now that's unfair. You haven't heard it yet."

Bradley shook his head and chuckled softly. "I don't have to hear it, Mr. President. I don't want to hear it. Now or later. When I tell the press about this . . ."

Nixon scowled. "Okay. We'll get down to cases." He looked down as though studying something on his knees. When his face came up again it was set aggressively. Bradley thought speculatively, *He isn't enjoying this. It isn't his idea.* "Senator, you and I have something in common."

"I challenge that."

Nixon ignored him doggedly. "We both know the value of a media image. We've seen it work from opposite ends of the scale but we know how it works—for and against."

"I'll bow to your experience on that," Bradley interrupted comfortably.

"Good. So tell me something. The *Washington Post* says you'll declare in the next few days. Is that right?"

"I don't confide in the *Washington Post* or any other newspaper."

"But they got it right?"

"I don't confide in you either."

"I'll take that as affirmative."

"Take it any way you like."

Nixon's face worked angrily. His mouth tightened. "I'm going to make this easy for you, Bradley. I've got some names and some dates written down in front of me here, and I'm going to read them out. Anytime you want me to stop, just tell me." He looked down again. "John Roper Anson." His face came up and he studied a monitor screen slightly to his left. He clearly saw nothing in Bradley's face to confirm the impact of the name on his victim. "The Matrix."

This time Bradley could not conceal a flicker of reaction. Nixon looked full into the camera. "Good, Senator. That's good." He looked down again. "John Kennedy. Robert Kennedy. Martin Luther King." He checked the monitor and found no response. "Okay, Senator. How about the killing at the Statler Wednesday morning?"

A nerve jumped in Bradley's cheek and, as he fought to control it, jumped again and again. Nixon nodded to himself. "That reached you, huh? I guess that's good enough for me."

Bradley said huskily, "Good enough for what?" The Statler incident, LaCroix had said. And Petersen had confirmed it; a piece of merchandise went astray at the Statler. A *killing* at the Statler? He reached a hand to his forehead. It was sweating profusely. The Kennedys. King. Assassinations. What in the name of heaven was he talking about?

Nixon was saying, "... used to the idea that it won't do you any good. You can't cover up."

"I have nothing to cover up," he filled in quickly. "If this charade is over now . . ."

"Not just yet." Nixon looked down again. When his face rose this time it was full of confidence. "Let's say we have a hypothetical situation, Senator. Let's say an organization started in business in the late fifties and recruited a whole squad of influential men. The Matrix—let's call it that. Big ideas, this organization, but the people behind it—they've got even bigger ideas. Political ambitions. In the beginning they have to use muscle to make things happen because they don't have the political background they need yet. They see a

88

situation needs resolving—bang!—they use a sniper bullet to resolve it. They resolve the Kennedys that way. And King. Maybe others, too, but we're not concerned with numbers right now. Okay—time passes and they have all the organizational equipment they need to go for the big one—the White House. They have the man, too: a man they've been building slow and easy over the years, a man with a fine legal standing, ex-judge, ex-Governor, seat in the Senate."

"Is this . . . ?"

"You'll have your chance in a minute, Senator." Nixon smiled, eyes narrowed. "I guess they're real careful, these people. They create their candidate, run him around the circuit a whole year before the primaries—but they hold him down. Come January in election year and he still isn't saying . . ."

Bradley spoke quietly. "I assume there's a point to this?"

"Sure there is, Senator. The point is you just won't be making it official, this year or any year."

"I see. Will you take my word or do you want it in writing?"

"Don't smart-ass me, Bradley. You don't have that kind of leeway."

Bradley forced a smile. "I've always taken it for granted you were a born poker player," he said lightly. "But I never thought you were mad. I've just changed my opinion."

"You admit you're running for The Matrix?"

"I think you're talking about someone else, sir."

"And the Kennedys, King, the Statler killing—you don't know anything about those."

"I genuinely believe you're unbalanced. You must be."

"Since you put it that way, Senator, you leave me no choice. All right. This is the way I'm calling it. That Statler thing you maybe know nothing about. There was a tape involved. Very interesting piece of tape. Recorded April 14, 1973. Think about it. Conversation involved John Roper Anson—please! I know you had connections with him—and two others. Subject: you and The Matrix. That tape, my friend, pins you and your outfit to three assassinations. So listen. I have the tape and if I hear that you've declared officially for the Presidency, I'm going to play it to anyone and everyone who'll listen. And let me tell you this, Bradley. They'll listen. They'll listen fit to bust a gut. You know why? Because they love you, that's why. Because they've put you on a pedestal. They've raised you up above their heads and made a hero out of you. The only pleasure they've got left now is to tear you down and trample on your reputation. And they'll love it, every minute of it. I told you we had something in common. We were both raised up."

"And you expect me to accept this ... insanity and drop everything?"

"Health grounds," Nixon said harshly. "You developed a heart murmur in '75, they tell me. Use it."

"And suppose I don't?"

Nixon smirked. "I think we've covered that, don't you, Senator?"

Bradley stroked his jaw. "Let's continue the hypothesis. Suppose I said no. Did nothing. That leaves you high and dry. You'd have to play your tape, assuming there is a tape, which I don't believe for a second. Two little words. Nixon and tape. Do you really believe anyone in this nation would believe you? Do you think any sane, levelheaded man, woman or child could associate those words, Nixon and tape, and come up with a belief in either of them? No sir. Whatever you have amounts to nothing. In your hands, it amounts to nothing. You couldn't do anything that would materially encourage—er—shall we say, the *Washington Post?*—to believe you were telling the truth."

"Wrong. You're not thinking, Senator. There's one way."

"Not even a deathbed confession."

"Better than that. If you declare, I'll declare."

Bradley's disbelief came out as an explosive burst of air. "Run for the Presidency? You!"

"Not far, maybe. But, yes—I'd declare. One reason. One platform. The truth behind the Kennedy assassination. The tape. One press call, one playing of the tape; that's all I'd need."

"They'd laugh you out of the country."

"You think so? Figure it out yourself. What d'you think they'd ask themselves? First reaction: He wouldn't dare! Right? Second reaction: He's for real. Third reaction: He believes it—he must believe it to put his head on the block this way. Fourth reaction: Okay—let's see what this tape adds up to. Let's take another look at Ambrose Bradley and The Matrix. You with me so far?"

Bradley sat in fixed contemplation of the TV screen. He said slowly, "Would it do any good if I swore to you on my honor that I have no idea what you're talking about?"

"I watched your face, Bradley. You know what I'm talking about."

"I could explain ..."

90

"Not to me. I don't want explanations."

"You just want my hide."

"I just want that look on your face that says you're finished."

"I can't give you that. You know I can't."

Nixon's head bobbed backward and forward as he swung on his chair. "You just did. Good night, Senator."

The screen flashed brightly, then presented a pattern of leaping horizontal lines. As if summoned, the big man came into the room. The young man joined him and they began to dismantle the equipment. The blue raincoat went to the bedroom and came back with three black leather cases; the equipment was lowered into them. In less than five minutes there was no evidence left of the telelink. The big man and the youngster shouldered the black cases; the blue raincoat braced the camera tripod over his shoulder.

"Leave you now, Senator," he said.

Bradley said nothing.

"I don't suppose anyone downstairs'll bother you, but if they do, you were doing an interview for CBS. I told the desk, just in case."

Bradley tried to gauge LaCroix's reaction but the phone gave no clues. "Did you hear what I said?" he hissed.

"Yes. I heard you, Senator."

"Is that all you have to say?"

"What *should* I say?"

"The Kennedys. King. For God's sake, Aaron."

"For *your* sake, not God's. For our sake. For the country's sake."

"You mean . . . you *did?*"

"I mean nothing, Senator."

"You're lying. Dear God, you're *lying!*"

"What is it I have to say to you, Ambrose, to make you feel cleansed? That I know nothing or that I know everything?"

"Just tell me you—we—The Matrix have nothing to do with this."

"Very well. We have nothing to do with this. Does that make it easier?"

Bradley cushioned his head in one hand.

"Ambrose?" LaCroix waited. "Ambrose!"

There was still no sound. "Ambrose!"

"Yes?"

"I want you to leave tomorrow as planned. You're returning to Washington?"

"Yes."

"We'll talk then."

Bradley let his breath escape loudly. "We'll talk now, Aaron. You—you and Petersen; you . . ."

"Is this an open line?"

"It's a private line. Direct."

"We can't talk now. Later. This is madness, Ambrose. I won't talk anymore. Get some sleep and . . ."

"You think I'll ever sleep *again!*"

LaCroix's voice dropped an octave. "Sleep in your *innocence*, Senator. As you've always done! And when you get back to Washington tomorrow, do nothing." He stopped. "Now, see here, Ambrose. This is nonsense. You have nothing to fear. Perhaps it would be as well if you left Washington tomorrow evening. Come down to Phoenix. A week, say. Stay at The Springs. I'll get this thing sorted out. Leave it to me. Just leave it to me."

SATURDAY: 1200—ANSON

Twenty years earlier, the apartment building had been at the heart of one of the better residential areas in downtown Washington. It now lay stranded like a cavalry fort in Indian territory, a victim of inner-city decay and black poverty, flanked on either side by greasy diners and menacing flophouses, forlorn and embattled walk-ups and street vandalism. By the front door, a group of young blacks idly hammered a baseball at its walls, marking out their stamping ground.

Margolis had had an apartment here for fifteen years, he told Anson, ever since his wife died. He had kept on the family farmhouse in Virginia, but rented the apartment to be nearer the job. Perhaps he had other reasons, reflected Anson. Perhaps he couldn't easily forget the manner of his wife's death in Bonn.

He took the bare concrete steps two at a time to the fourth floor. He had phoned the old man half a dozen times yesterday to cancel the dinner date because of Grazia's arrival, and he had twice put on his coat and prepared to walk out on her. Her opening gestures had led to the full works; Grazia had stormed and raged, battered him with clichéd ravings about the kind of woman who could drag him out on such a night. He had, as usual, settled for a strategic withdrawal; he had sat himself before the television while she took her grief to bed.

He sniffed experimentally, manufacturing sound. A fabricated cold Margolis would understand; Grazia was too much to ask any man to believe. After the call to Margolis at 7:30, he had gone to sleep in a chair. This morning he had left silently.

Now he felt better. The physical exertion of climbing the stairs refreshed him. He pressed the bell. Again. Once more. There was no sound from within. Maybe the old man had taken off for the weekend. His daughter Alice was in Seattle, a singer of sorts, he had said, who hit the highway to imagined stardom when she was in her teens and ended up on the low road to obscurity.

"Hey, Louie!"

Anson had reached the second floor on his way down.

"You!"

He craned his head around the metal balustrade and looked up the stairwell.

"Yeah, you, Louie." The face hanging over the rail was attached to a sphere of flesh wrapped in a vast patterned robe with black silk lapels. "You looking for Walt?"

"That's right," Anson threw back. "Walt Margolis."

"He ain't here."

"I kind of got that message," said Anson. "Thanks for the confirmation." He turned to leave.

"Hey, Louie!" The sphere rolled off the landing and bounced down the stairs. Anson waited. The robe, he could see now, was a boxer's wrap and laced boots showed beneath its folds. Despite the awesome dumpling of flesh in which they were set, the eyes that eventually appraised him in a swift up-and-down motion were wide and friendly. He rubbed a hand the size of a pitcher's glove down the front of the wrap and held it out. "Buffalo Morgan. Formerly of Kansas City. You probably heard of me."

Anson retrieved his hand and adopted the mask of the disciple who racks his brain for a vital memory just out of reach.

"No?" said the fat man, disappointed. "Well, maybe not. You're a kid. All you hear about nowadays are pussyfoot punks, the glitter guys. All footwork and no punch. Fighters? They wouldn't have lasted three rounds with Marciano." He sniffed disdainfully.

"The name is Anson. Harry Anson. I'm a friend of Walt's."

"Which is to say, Louie, a friend of mine. I was working out on the barbells when I heard you hitting Walt's bell. I keep in trim, see. Always remember that. Stay trim. Not that I'm so fast on my feet anymore, but what the hell, none of us is getting any younger." He grinned. "Hear the bell, take a break."

Anson warmed to the outrageous little man. "You know where Walt is?"

Morgan drew a huge breath and exhaled slowly, arms braced chest high, elbows out. "Can't say. Walt don't go away much weekends. Up there with his books and the rest. I keep telling him, 'Get some exercise,' but he don't listen. Bad for a man, books. Wastes away the tissues. Cramps up the muscles." He grabbed another ten cubic meters of air. "You work with Walt, Louie?"

"Sort of. We're in the same business, you might say."

"You a spy, huh?"

Buffalo Morgan smirked at Anson's shocked reaction. "Oh, I know Walt was with the CIA up at Langley. Spooks, they call 'em. You a spook?"

Anson shook his head affably. "Walt was in Administration before he retired. Files, that kind of thing. Me too. We don't get to see the glamour side of the business. Spooks are something else."

"Couple of 'em came looking for Walt yesterday. Late afternoon," said Buffalo.

"Looking? Who came looking?"

"Coupla guys. Spooks. I could tell. They smell wrong. They came ringing for Walt, like you. I was just going out for a jog. Always do; gets the sinuses clear. They passed me bottom of the stairs. Asked Walt's apartment number like they thought they oughta say something. I figure they work with him."

Anson laid a hand on the mountainous shoulder. "What then?"

Buffalo screwed up his eyes until they disappeared behind folds of fat. "Nothing happened, Louie. They went on up and rang the bell."

Anson felt a quite inexplicable sense of discomfort. He brushed past Buffalo Morgan and climbed the stairs to Margolis's door. The fat man followed. Anson turned the handle. Locked.

"What's eating you, Louie? Walt in some kinda trouble?"

"I don't know, Buffalo. But I want you to do something for me."

94

"Any friend of Walt's . . . ," began Morgan but Anson cut him short.

"Buffalo," he said, "I want you to lean on that door. Break it down."

The door splintered around the old lock at the first charge of Morgan's shoulder and spat rusty screws and antique sawdust across the gray carpet inside. The room was undisturbed. Everything in its place. Neat. Too neat for a man like Walt Margolis. In the kitchen not a single cup lay unwashed. Anson returned to the living room as Buffalo Morgan opened the bedroom door.

"Louie!"

Walt Margolis was sitting up in bed, propped between two large pillows. An open book lay under his hands, as if sleep had overtaken him in the middle of a sentence, and his forehead was wrinkled with some profound conclusion. What Walt Margolis had been thinking they would never know. His eyes were half-open. He was peacefully, professionally, dead.

"Christ, Louie!"

Anson pushed into the room, went to the bed and bent to stare into the dead face. The bedclothes were smooth. There was no sign of struggle. He'd died without knowing it was the last time he would sleep.

"Is he . . . ?" Morgan bit off the unnecessary question.

Anson ignored him. The poor old bastard. Well, he was also a Company man and there were carefully prescribed regulations that covered the death of Company men. It made no difference if it happened in Rome or Tokyo or New Jersey, the priority always applied. In the event of death, contact with civil police agencies shall be regarded as secondary until it has been established that no breach of security is involved. The first call must go to Special Operations. He called Langley's general number from the pay phone on the stairs, then went back to the bedroom to wait. The hooded eyes of Walt Margolis fixed him from infinity until Buffalo moved across and closed them. He looked down at the peaceful figure of his friend. "I told him," he said. He shook his head violently until the jowls trembled with a life of their own. "I told him he oughta exercise. He wouldn't listen."

They arrived inside fifteen minutes. Buffalo was ushered from the room by one of the two young officers, escorted back to his own apartment and questioned.

The second checked the room without touching anything.

It didn't take long. He swung on Anson and took a small notepad from his pocket.

"Anson?"

"Harry Anson. State Department. Margolis was a friend."

The man scribbled on the pad and slipped it into an inside pocket as if dispensing with further formalities.

"How do you read it?" Anson asked.

"He's dead," the young man said blandly. "No sign of disturbance. No break-in apart from yours. But we can take care of that." He shrugged. "Heart attack, my guess. But I'm no doctor. Leave it to the path, boys. Maybe fatso was right: too little exercise." He patted his nonexistent stomach. "Gets to us all in the end."

"Now what, Mr.—er . . . ?"

"Dill. Clarence H. Dill."

"Dill. I'm not familiar with . . ."

"Not many people are, Mr. Anson. This looks straightforward. No problems. Next of kin will have to be informed. Meantime, we sweep the place, and if everyone's happy we hand over to the civil police. I don't see anything might worry the State Department."

"No." Anson was developing an irrational dislike for the man. "Tell me just so's I know next time. When I called you now, I gave nothing except Walt's name. I forgot to give an address. I was going to phone back. But you were already here . . ."

Dill's expression of boredom did not change. "We know who and where our people are, Mr. Anson. We have to." Two white-suited medics entered the room, opened a folding stretcher and swung Margolis's body onto it. Dill watched them intently.

Anson allowed the bitterness an outlet. "I'd like to compliment you on your efficiency, Mr. Dill," he rasped.

"That's what we like to hear, Mr. Anson."

On the way down to the lobby, Buffalo Morgan said, "He had a kid, you know. A daughter."

Anson nodded but didn't look at him. "I know."

"Somebody gotta tell her."

"It'll be done."

Buffalo stopped and grabbed his elbow insistently. "I'm not saying it won't be done, Louie. I'm saying a friend should do it, is all. The kid deserves a little sympathy the way she hears her old man is dead."

"I'll do what I can." Anson was pinned to the wall by Buffalo's vast stomach. Until he moved, Anson couldn't.

"Like finding the kid and telling her yourself?"

"I don't know. She's no kid, the way I hear it. She's a traveling lady."

"She's Walt's kid," Buffalo growled warningly. "We got no call to judge her. Where's she at?"

They moved on downstairs, Buffalo clomping on Anson's heels, hanging over him like spectral guilt. Anson turned the corner on to a landing. "She's in show business, I think. A singer or maybe a dancer, I don't know. These people come and go, here and there. They don't leave forwarding addresses."

"But you'll find her, right?"

Anson stopped abruptly and Morgan walked slap into him from behind. "Okay, Buffalo. You win. I'll find her myself. I'll talk to her myself. I guess we owe Walt that much."

"You bet your . . ." The emotive *f* shaped itself on Buffalo's lips but never emerged. He stooped and swept up a black kitten from Anson's toe caps. It was a pathetic little animal, skinny, bony, its fur worn and matted. Around its neck was a slim black collar with a small brass name tag suspended under its throat. Buffalo warmed it against his blue sandpaper jowl and the kitten mewed its pleasure.

"This one I'll tell myself, seeing as how it's half mine anyway." He held out the bundle to Anson who retreated a step. "This is—hell—this is Cat. He kinda walked in here one day and took over. Sometimes he'd sit on Walt's floor, waiting for food and milk, and sometimes he'd come down to my floor and I'd do the right thing."

Anson eyed the cat suspiciously. It looked capable of anything, including a rictal twitch of effluent all over its host.

Buffalo Morgan said, "You know what they say about cats—no love, no respect, no pride. They'll screw anyone for what they can get. This one, lemme tell you—never once been in my place and never once set foot in Walt's neither. Just sits on the landing outside till one of us gets the message he ain't going away till he's fed. So we feed him, me and Walt. See this?" He flicked the brass tag on the cat's collar. "Walt's idea. Give a cat a bad name, he says." He stared at Anson's stony face. "You get it? Give a cat a bad name? Name tag?" He shook his head. "He just got it a few days ago. Cat never had no name. We never got around to it. Now he's only got half a home." His face clouded. He lowered the kitten gently to the floor. They went on downstairs.

The sky was threatening snow again when they came into the street. The group of young blacks had been augmented by Saturday afternoon strollers and professional rubbernecks. Anson crossed the sidewalk to the Porsche. Buffalo ambled after him. At the car Anson started to speak but thought better of it and swung inside. He closed the door and rolled down the window. Tearing apart a cigarette pack, he scribbled his telephone numbers on it and handed it to Buffalo. "Call me if . . . if anything."

Buffalo stared at it, then, with a grunt, stuffed it into a pocket. "You won't forget Walt's girl, huh?" The fat man dropped his paw on Anson's shoulder and tensed his fingers.

"I said I wouldn't."

"I'd do the same for you, Louie," said Buffalo Morgan. He straightened and looked back at the small crowd at the door of the apartment house. "You need *me* anytime, you just come looking, hear?" He moved away to the discreet gray truck in which Walt's body was being loaded. Anson watched the ceremony in the rearview mirror.

Curious, the way there was always a professional gag to cover a Company death. Margolis's last ride in the Company hearse was a "slay" ride in the jargon; his frail body, no more than a gentle undulation now beneath a white sheet, was "confetti."

Anson lit a cigarette. They had allowed him a last look at Walt's body before they took it away, standing back like stage magicians, confident that none of their props could be discerned by the naked eye. He felt helpless and a little guilty. He could have driven over last night, maybe even got here in time. He remembered the two "spooks" Buffalo had met on their way to Walt's door. Who were they? Maybe they could have helped, too, if they'd had the sense to break in.

The Company hearse pulled away and passed him, spraying the Porsche with mud-colored slush. Its barred double doors mocked him. Out of nowhere the idea thudded home: How do you induce a heart attack artificially? Or reproduce the symptoms? The Senate hearings on the CIA campaign against Castro, something about . . . Yes. Lyophilized snake venom, when carried in a skin-penetrating fluid, could trigger a seizure in minutes. The venom would be absorbed in seconds by the carrier fluid, which in turn would melt into the body fluids. No trace. Heart attack was the obvious diagnosis. One way. There would be others and the Company would know about all of them. He strangled the rim of the steering wheel. That was Clarence H. Dill getting under his skin. No—that was stupid. Walt had nothing to fear from his own kind. Had he?

"They know what I'm reading, kid, but they can't know what I'm thinking."

They didn't kill people to stop them from reading files. Not their own kind. Unless he really had been getting too close to a perfect truth. It was crazy. No, it was emotional crap. It was the way this whole thing was getting to him. Coincidences, phony ploys, weak excuses—the way George Hyman had brought Walt into his life. Maybe that was 99 parts imagination, too.

He turned the ignition key and checked the road behind him in his side mirror. A dark blue Ford had stopped short of the entrance to the apartment building and the kids pooled around it. The tall man's silver-framed spectacles glinted as he crossed the sidewalk and entered the building.

Anson kicked the Porsche into the traffic and hit 45 mph in first gear before he changed down.

What the hell was Leo McCullen doing there? And who called him?

Coincidences . . .

BOOK TWO JUDGES

*Why asketh thou thus after
my name, seeing it is secret?*
JUDGES, 13:18

The huge cross burned in the desert, proclaiming it a place of deliverance. Twinkling red beacons shone into infinity, a man-made reflection of the awesome constellations they faced in the clear night sky. A beam of light should have no end. Long after man's perceptions have failed him and life has guttered and died in his eye, the light goes on, visible to those with the power to see.

The power to see.

LaCroix drove the wheelchair to the open window and the cool air, a balm and a benediction at the end of a sweltering day. It was not technological chance that the airstrip had been built in the shape of a cross. It was a sign for all who came there: a welcome for those who recognized its power, a warning for those who didn't. The man who would arrive shortly fell somewhere between the two.

He turned the wheelchair from the window to a small table, spartan and bare under the tapestry-draped walls of the huge room, and placed his palms flat on the unfinished surface. He sat still, his shaven skull bent.

"Richard Milhous Nixon." He spoke the words softly, his rich baritone caressing every syllable. A half smile fluttered across his face. So, they had set a rabbit to catch a . . . what? A fox? No, he could not see himself as a hunted animal. An eagle. An American eagle. Yes. They would never understand the difference. They were earthbound. Ungodly. Talk was their greatest currency. Nixon had talked of assassinations, of conspiracy; he'd quoted names. Who was using him? Who had set this rabbit loose? Of course, it was a crass attempt to force his own hand, a measure that hinted at the fear he could generate. Yes, they feared him. Somewhere there existed a man who needed him to fail. Someone who knew that Bradley was the chosen instrument. That man had been told, therefore; facts secret to The Matrix had been conveyed to him. And he had devised his own secret movement. He had pushed Richard Nixon into this incredible performance. He would presumably go much further. It was now important to match that intent—and demonstrate his own tenacity.

He heard the aircraft engine and propelled the wheelchair to the window. The plane was flattening against the backdrop of distant mountains, its lights stabbing from wing tips, nose and belly. He watched it bank and straighten, cutting the moon's beams into flashing slices. It whined as it checked its approach on the cross of lights and feathered to a perfect landing in a ghostly cloud of moonlit dust. The plane taxied down to the reception hut and came to rest under the glare of the floodlights. LaCroix watched the man squeeze onto the extending ladder and walk toward the house, his shadow bounding gigantically ahead of him. LaCroix automatically fussed his gown into place, snatched up a book from the table and opened it on the ledge between the arms of the wheelchair. One of the Filipinos opened the door and introduced the visitor with a narrowing motion of the eyes.

Tony Javallo came through the door, his eyes darting from side to side. He never entered a room any other way; he had survived his childhood as a hunted animal, never more than inches from the outstretched arm of the law, and a sense of security was a sensation completely foreign to him. He had large, long-muscled hands, curiously out of proportion with his body; they possessed a restless energy that bulged the muscles without any apparent movement of the fingers. He rested his black irises on LaCroix, stared longer than was necessary, nodded and found a straight-backed wooden chair. He dusted the arms of his black jacket.

LaCroix said formally, "I hope the journey was comfortable."

Javallo eyed him silently, then returned to his brushing.

LaCroix brought the wheelchair head-on to face the visitor. He prided himself that few men could return his stare for long, that few men could overwhelm his personality or sustain a long-drawn-out intellectual exchange with him, but Javallo was an exception. He could not be drawn into wordplay. He had no intellect. He accepted no challenges. But his eyes could stare the devil down, and his arrogance and aggressiveness were absolute. Each confrontation with him was an invitation to combat; LaCroix could never ignore it and he could never win. He cleared his throat. A nervous cough.

"I have a very sensitive job I want you to take care of."

Javallo's eyes hooded lazily. "You telling me San Clemente ain't sensitive?" He spoke in a conversational whisper, a grudging concession to speech, sparingly, as a sufferer from acute laryngitis would ration the use of a painful throat.

"San Clemente is a secondary consideration at this stage. Petersen's people can handle it. You were there to find Nixon's connection with the tape. The connection has taken matters into another area entirely."

104

"You wanna tell me in English?" The tone was threateningly arrogant.

"Nixon approached Bradley personally last night in Los Angeles."

"He never left the compound. I know—I was there."

LaCroix smiled icily. "He confronted Bradley on a closed circuit TV hookup. Very . . . scientific."

"Jake Henry didn't say anything about a TV hookup." The implication suggested LaCroix was lying.

"Mr. Henry has been less than helpful in this situation. Nevertheless, you can take my word for it; it happened. Nixon made his position clear. He threatened Bradley and The Matrix with public exposure if Bradley declares formally for the Presidency. He says he has the tape—although I think that was probably a lie. On the other hand, he knows . . . a great deal."

Javallo's hands pulsed with muscular energy. "Whaddaya mean—he knows?"

"He recited to Bradley a list of names. The Kennedys. King. He was aware of the Statler incident."

Javallo's eyes widened. "You saying he put the finger on *me?*" The whisper was barely a hiss of escaping air.

LaCroix paused, enjoying the spectacle of Javallo under threat. He shook his head. "No. I said he was probably lying about the tape. He has been fed a few crumbs of information. That's all. You're . . . quite safe."

Javallo aimed a death ray into his face with the black irises. "Where we go from here?"

LaCroix stabbed the control panel on the chair and wheeled it to the wall-length window. Outside, under the arcs of the dispersal area, the pilot and two of the Filipinos were refueling the Cessna. He said, "You leave now for Washington. Tomorrow I want you to refresh your contacts within the Party. Can you do that?"

"Why would I do that?"

LaCroix spun the chair expertly to face him across the room. "It's my opinion Nixon is bluffing. He's being *used* as a bluff. He threatened Bradley with what he clearly regards as the ultimate deterrent. If Bradley declares, Nixon would also declare."

"The guy's a nut."

"Not exactly. He suggests he would be prepared to weather the public vituperation this would bring down on him in the interests of turning the eyes of the media on Bradley and The Matrix."

"He could do that?"

"It would follow if he carried out his threat absolutely. But I don't think he has that kind of courage. Nor the necessary commitment. He *is* being manipulated, after all. Why should he feel morally bound to engineer his own execution?"

The word switched on an electric current in Javallo's hands. "You saying we waste him?"

LaCroix brought hands to mouth, fingertips steepled. "I'm saying we call his bluff. We bring him to the edge, show him how far he has to fall. Tomorrow you talk to committee workers in both Parties. *Selected* workers. Not the managers; they'd be too slow to act—if they'd act at all. No—you will contact second- or third-level activists, people you can trust to talk. Men and woman who will find it impossible to contain their sense of outrage. If they also have links with newspapermen, so much the better."

"You want it out?" Javallo was as close to displaying disbelief as his personality permitted.

"I want it broadcast as widely as possible."

"He'll cream us. You're crazy."

LaCroix turned back to the window and studied the long shadows of the men working around the plane. "He'll do nothing of the kind. He'll be more than occupied with saving his own skin."

"You told Petersen about this?"

LaCroix suppressed a volcanic surge of anger. "Petersen will know in good time."

Javallo got to his feet; his hands hung low at his sides, gun-fighter nervous. "You better get it together. It's my neck you're sticking out there." He looked down at his hands. "Petersen told you he had to stiff a guy in Washington last night?"

LaCroix betrayed his ignorance blatantly. He tried to cover up; too late. Javallo's lip curled.

"I thought so. Call him now, padre, or I don't move a step." He leaned across the back of the chair. "We do this together or we don't do anything. You can work out the pecking order later."

SATURDAY: 2130—ANSON

Anson stabbed at the button and the TV screen dissolved in a kaleidoscope of collapsing color. He jabbed again and again. It flashed back to life, fed him snatches of news, football, sitcoms and old movies. The watery stew of entertainment. He held it momentarily on the deep cleavage of a black girl singer, then cut her dead. He gulped at the can of beer balanced on the arm of his chair. Bread and circuses. He stood up and stretched his arms.

"Dear viewers," he proclaimed to the room. "In a preemptive dawn raid, the U.S. Air Force bombed Peking, Hanoi, Moscow and East Berlin using high-yield nuclear weapons. Consequently, the world has shifted on its axis and is now plummeting through eternity at a speed approaching that of light. Well, so much for the world news. Back home, the weather is terrible and you can book that ski weekend in Florida in the certainty that snow conditions will be excellent. Now, over to the Muppets."

"A moment, only!" Grazia called from the kitchen. For the past hour she had been juggling pots and pans in a noisy attempt to impress him. Another hour and he knew they would be checking out for a meal at Maxwell's or Ronnie's.

"No rush," he muttered. "The end of the world is nigh. Make it a minute steak." He split the top of another can and switched on an Aznavour tape.

The velvet smoothness massaged his half-drunk brain. He opened the denim shirt another two buttons and rubbed his chest. He was thirty-three. Five-eleven, 180 pounds on a good day. Check. No disfiguring scars. Physically A-O.K. and certified by the U.S. government. Check. He was of sound mind and had no hang-ups.

Tilt.

He stared at the ceiling and reran across its screen the images of Margolis and McCullen at Teddy's. Aznavour advanced the theory that every day was what you made it. That either you have a love for life or . . .

From the kitchen came an odor like burning leather. Anson groaned softly and sqatted on the floor. He had killed five cans of Schlitz. He had always prided himself on his analytical mind, his ability to assess quickly, discard the fluff, extract the essentials. Now his head was behaving like a plate of spaghetti.

Aznavour invited him to watch as he wove the web of his illusions. He sat down very suddenly on the arm of the chair, a picture of Walt's apartment floating fuzzily on the screen of his mind. Clean, neat. Too neat, he'd thought at the time. But something else . . . what else? Leo McCullen's arrival. Something . . . something . . .

"Tesoro!" Grazia was standing at the door of the kitchen, a plate in her hand, her mouth curved down like a suicidal Pierrot's. "The stove! It is a *shit* stove!"

He inspected the damage. A small black tablet of what might once have been some kind of fowl lay on the dish like a victim of Pompeii. Anson sank back to the carpet. "I reserved a table," he said lightly.

"You what?" Eyes flashing.

He nodded.

"Fuck you, mister!" The plate landed heavily on the carpet and she flounced into the bedroom. The door crashed shut behind her.

Something . . . something. Think.

Too neat.

Yes.

Tidy. Yes, all right.

He struggled to his feet, not daring to let it go. That was it! The apartment. No files. No memoirs. Nothing. Where were they? Is *that* why Leo McCullen went visiting?

"Tesoro?"

She leaned in from the bedroom door, the silky black of her dress clinging to her breasts, hips and long legs. A mink wrap swung casually across her shoulders. She looked down at him for approval, then approached, stepping carefully over the ruined meal that lay like a road accident at his feet. He blinked at her vacantly. One elegant shoe came to rest gently in his crotch.

"Tonight, for you, *tesoro*—oysters," she breathed.

SUNDAY: 1130—GARFIELD

The book-lined room was unspeakably cold. Lucas Garfield's heavy black coat was buttoned to the throat to take full advantage of the Persian lamb collar, and he made no attempt to remove his hat as he joined Munro Fletcher and Alfred Goldman. They had been waiting for more than ten minutes and their tempers were short. The Chapter House was no place for middle-aged men on a brutal Sunday morning, and each of them had paid the penalty of presuming on their wives' tolerance. Fletcher had been the victim of two widely reported illnesses in eighteen months. Mild pleurisy, as NSA's senior civilian consultant had put it. At sixty-two he reacted instantly to extremes of temperature. He was begin-

108

ning to consider death, in his private moments, as an objective rather than a threat, but it worried him that it might compromise earthly priorities.

He noted the prayer book in Garfield's gloved hand and flushed. "I'd have thought the Lord Almighty could've waited a couple of hours, Luke," he said acidly.

Garfield shuddered and looked around as if expecting heavenly fire to spring from the bookshelves to warm him. "He probably could, Fletch, but my wife couldn't. I took her to church first. I always do. I guess I could manufacture reasons for changing that, but I've never found anything . . ." He stopped suddenly and his face showed concern. "You shouldn't be here. You're not well."

"I'm just cold, thanks all the same. You said 11:30 and I was here at 11:25 and now I'm cold. I want to get home and into a warm bed."

Goldman pulled out a chair and sat down. He wore a thick green hunting jacket with a sheepskin collar and lining and a cossack hat of sturdy curly lamb's wool. He looked even more the heathen warrior than usual but his long brown hands were shaking with cold. He said, "I guess it's about Margolis. What do we do?"

Fletcher spun on him, stopped, then grinned weakly and sat down on the chair beside him. "He's right, Luke," he said quietly. "You've played this one far too close to your doublet. What made them kill Margolis?"

A shadow of impatience swept over Garfield's face. He tapped his chin with the white prayer book. "Did anyone *kill* anyone?" He tossed the book on the table.

Fletcher brought the flat of his hand down on the polished rosewood. "No more, Luke! For God's sake, let's level with each other and get out of here." He sighed and shook his head as if dismissing his own outburst. He went on more reasonably. "The Washington P.D. report on Margolis is a pickup from Langley. The coroner's report is three times longer than any you're ever likely to find in a Natural Causes file and that comes out of Langley, too. No one in the city police department has seen the body yet, questioned neighbors or checked background. They've been told hands off. The Police Commissioner got word direct from the top."

Goldman was examining the reflection of his hands in the polished wood of the tabletop. "Donald Rattray Petersen," he said precisely. "No names, no investigation, no police coroner, no digging, no follow-up, no fuss. By order."

Garfield waved a hand at them without raising his arm

from the table. "That's hardly unusual in this case—any case where a senior officer of the Company is involved."

Fletcher stared at him hard. "You introduced Margolis into this thing, Luke, and we went along with it. We took you at your word that Margolis was clean, that he was disposed to do what we asked. That he was a man we could trust, a man who could take care of himself. You said nothing about this being a potential wet job. You held back on us, Luke, and we let you get away with it because you wanted time to work out a scenario he could fit." He sat back in his chair and scrubbed his hands together to encourage circulation. "Now I, for one, want to hear it straight. If I have to leave this room without it, Luke, I warn you—I won't be coming back."

"No one retires from this committee, Fletch," Garfield said slowly.

"Try me." The response was a whiplash.

"No. Let's talk instead." Goldman came in with heavy emphasis and a smile as warm as a sarcophagus. "I'd like to pretend I don't know what you've got to hide, Luke, but I can't, can I?" He gazed innocently at the glowering Garfield.

"Meaning?"

"Meaning that my membership on this committee runs in tandem with my responsibilities to Army Intelligence. Where do I draw the line between my identity here and my role as director of a service arm? You tell me."

"All right, you've made your point." Garfield touched the prayer book with his fingertips and slid it around the table in short stabbing movements. "When Kissinger set up this committee," he said quietly, "the goals were formidable enough: to monitor the activities of all national security agencies and restrain their—er—natural inclinations to expand. I, personally, would have chosen a less . . . *emotional* . . . moment to create such a group than immediately after Watergate. But I had no choice in that."

He looked into each of their faces in turn. "You were brought onto this committee at my behest. I was judge and jury, prosecutor and defense attorney in the trial that went on behind your backs to decide whether you were the men I needed. I make no apologies for that. That was the kind of power I was given and I exercised it.

"Very well. That power is not diminished by the fact that you sit at the same table with me. Our job is to hold our colleagues in check and we do that with a minimum of interference and fuss. We know, generally speaking, who we can trust and who we can't."

Goldman traced the name Donald Rattray Petersen in the shining wood.

"But I've never concealed from you that I'm always one pace behind and one step above you. I have to be. Our primary task is to measure the frailty of powerful secret men. My secondary responsibility is to measure *your* frailty."

Munro Fletcher took in a long noisy hiss of breath and clamped his teeth on it. Goldman was still entranced by his writing on the tabletop.

"I retain the right to use what methods I deem necessary to hold that balance. I used Margolis. I accept full responsibility for his death."

Goldman looked up curiously. "Are you going to tell us he stepped out of line? *You* had to waste him?"

"That's juvenile and provocative, Fred. You know better than that. There's no doubt in my mind who killed Margolis. They used subtler methods but the intention was unequivocal. I mean, I don't think it was a mistake, just like Faber wasn't a mistake. Those two sanctions called for a lot of nerve and nerve is the product of panic. Panic says something else, too—they haven't got the time or the resources to discriminate. If they run into an obstacle, they'll smash it down. Permanently."

Fletcher said dismissively, "I think we're capable of tracing that train of logic ourselves. The crunch now surely is Bradley. We're no nearer proving his association with an assassination conspiracy, we can't act on the tape because the President says no, and you've lost the one man who might've given you a lead into The Matrix. It strikes me, Luke, you've made one damn fine mess of this from the start. I told you a dozen times—you play things too much behind your back. We're here to collaborate, Fred and I. There's nothing in the articles of association that says we act as a wall for you to bounce your inspirations off."

Garfield shrugged unrepentantly.

Alfred Goldman raised his eyes. "Out with it, Luke."

Garfield looked at him over his half glasses. "All right, Fred." He switched his stare to Fletcher. "I welcome your collaboration, Fletch. You know that. But we don't have much time and, like I said, I reserve the right to act as the situation demands. Well, I've taken action."

"My God, here we go again," moaned Fletcher.

Garfield smothered his irritation. "Nixon confronted Bradley Friday night."

Goldman rocked forward on his elbows. *"That* we had a right to know *before* it happened."

"Right to *know!"* hissed Fletcher.

"I called this meeting," Garfield went on equably, "because I judge we can expect a reaction anytime now."

"What excuse have you got in mind when they blow Nixon's fool head off his shoulders?" taunted Fletcher.

"Your appetite for logic isn't working too well, Fletch. They won't do that. They may be indiscriminate, but whoever's running Bradley has an appetite for gamesmanship. He'll know someone switched Nixon on; no one's going to believe the man took that kind of chance independently. He's not the martyr type. Kill Nixon, and Bradley's tied in a hundred percent with no way out. No, they have to come up with something cleverer than murder this time."

"O.K." Goldman waved a hand to indicate acceptance. "That forces them to act."

"It also forces Bradley to hold off his declaration," Garfield interjected smoothly. "That's time he can ill afford at this stage of the game."

"How's that?" Fletcher asked suspiciously.

"Nixon's ultimatum. He told Bradley he'd run the tape publicly if Bradley declared."

"And that's all?"

"There's another option—a bargaining option we couldn't follow through on."

"And that is?" Fletcher's cynicism was knife-edged.

"I'll pass, Fletch," Garfield returned stonily.

Goldman intervened hurriedly. "Okay, Luke. That's your business. Your funeral. I'm ready to let you play it your way on the chessboard, but we've got practical problems in this, too. Number One: Who's handling this on the ground?"

"McCullen's still in place."

"You can't run McCullen at street level, Luke. You need another Margolis. Number Two: None of Margolis's files were in his apartment. Why won't you give me clearance to check out the house in Virginia? Number Three: Who's watching Nixon's back? Number Four . . ."

Garfield waved him into silence. "That's enough, Fred. First, I've put the Margolis house out-of-bounds for a reason. I'll come to that. Forget the Margolis files; they're at the house in Virginia, safe and sound. Anyway, they mean very little. Nixon—I've got an exercise under way to protect him."

Fletcher said sourly, "Does he know about it?"

112

"He demanded it, Fletch."

Goldman persisted. "Street level, Luke. Who's McCullen gonna run?"

Garfield rose, shuddered and dug hands deep into his pockets. He moved toward the door. "Someone'll pick up the ball, Fred. And this time—for his protection and ours—he won't know he's running. He'll run because his conscience tells him to, because it's important to him."

"If he doesn't know . . ."

"He'll pick up the vibes. That's one of the reasons I didn't want the house in Virginia disturbed. He has to start somewhere."

Goldman came out of his chair, towered head and shoulders over Garfield. "You lost Margolis because you played the game too far out of sight, Luke. I'm warning you, if this one falls under a truck . . ."

"What'll you do, Fred," Garfield snapped. "Report me to Rotary International? Tear up my Lions' membership? Do you really think I'm playing games here for the sheer idiot pleasure of exercising an appetite for convolution? Well, listen to me, both of you. I don't measure the seriousness of a situation by the corpses it creates; I rate it on what I feel *here!*" He stuck his index finger into the bulge of his gut, precisely over the point where his ulcer raged late at night. "Here! And what it's telling me I don't have any immediate remedies for. My hands are tied behind my back, officially, and any move I make has to be covert and secure. Watertight! I have to force The Matrix, Bradley, whoever, to come out from under their rock. That's why I brought Nixon into this. Anyone else—a politician—wouldn't mean a thing because all we've got—the *only* thing we've got—is a tape recorded in Nixon's White House that makes posthumous claims we can't prove. So . . ." He brushed glowing red cheeks with the sleeve of his coat. "We have a name The Matrix knows—John Roper Anson. His son came in from Rome last week for the funeral. I've arranged to have the boy held over here in Washington. I don't know how I'll use him yet. Frankly, the whole thing depends on how he reacts to a couple of . . . experiments I'm doing."

"You're going to hold him under their nose?"

"I'm trying to make it important to him to stick *his* nose into the pot. I want him to ask himself questions and look for answers."

"You think he'll find something we haven't?"

"No. Finding something isn't going to be the solution to

113

this problem, Fred. We can pin down every single member of The Matrix and what good would it do us? Think about it. They're going to be the usual diehards or the usual idealists or both. They'll be rich as Croesus because there's no percentage in recruiting paupers into a power-broking operation like this one. So they'll have status in the community, social position, influence. Influence is why they're there. If I was putting up a Presidential candidate and I'd spent twenty years or so preparing the ground, I'd make damn sure my membership covered every area likely to help the cause: politics, the public service, diplomacy, law, education, banking."

"We get the picture," Fletcher said dryly.

"Good. So we *find* these citizens and we hold 'em in the palm of our hand. What then? We accuse! We—an unknown, covert and unidentifiable committee—publicly arraign before the American people a generous selection of the most celebrated names in contemporary public life. In an election year. Against the President's instructions." He buttoned his coat. "No, gentlemen. Finding them means nothing. Provocation is how we work this out. Harry Anson may be able to do that. Nixon may be able to do that. Without them we don't have a thing to work with."

Fletcher had been staring thoughtfully into deep space for several seconds. At that moment his face came alight: the answer. He stood directly in Garfield's path. "That Nixon countermove you talked about. The bargaining option we can't follow through on. If his threat to Bradley doesn't pay off . . . are you really going to force Nixon to declare for the race himself? It *is* pure bluff, isn't it?"

Garfield raised the latch on the door. "Of course, Fletch, of course."

He was smiling as he left them.

SUNDAY: 1130—ABRAMS

There was something to be said for tackling a problem head-on when all other avenues remained stubbornly closed. There was also something to be said for running full speed, head down, against a brick wall.

Like it was crazy.

It was still better than being eaten alive with frustration. The confusion and anger Margolis's death had sown last night had flourished with sleep. By dawn, Anson knew the demons had to be exorcised. At 11:30 he phoned Milton Abrams at Langley.

"It's Sunday, Mr. Anson," said the operator heavily. "Mr. Abrams is here to catch up on paperwork. I'm afraid you'll have to make an appoint—"

"Tell him I'll be there in half an hour. Tell him I want to talk about Walt Margolis."

Milton Abrams was Head of Classification, one of twenty-nine structured departments within the CIA, all blessed with equally euphemistic labels: Office of Training, Operational Services Division, Missions and Programs Staff. They had the ring of passive legitimacy, like subsections of a giant banking conglomerate. In an underworld attuned to the concept of public relations as an art form, the creator of the Company's innocent labels was a veritable Michelangelo. In his vocabulary the department that busied itself with the chore of killing and maiming in the pursuit of foreign intelligence became the Covert Action Staff, while the group of technicians responsible for devising new horizons in burglarizing, eavesdropping and the general subversion of citizen rights was the Technical Services Division. Among their more celebrated clients were E. Howard Hunt and G. Gordon Liddy.

Classification's ostensible role was to monitor sensitive material, weigh its importance, status-code those who should receive it and channel information direct. Classification ate paper by the ton, day in, day out. Before his retirement, Margolis had been attached to the department as an executive functionary—"a glorified messenger boy," in Walt's terms. His immediate boss was Leo McCullen, Milt Abrams's deputy. If Margolis had wanted to play it the easy way, the job could have been an effortless sinecure; but Margolis would have seen it as potentially the most informative niche inside Langley. He had been in a position to test the wind over a hundred areas of sensitive policy. All he had to do was read, digest and fit the pieces into his private hobby horse. Just what part McCullen played in all this, thought Anson, was debatable. It was also another of those coincidences. McCullen's precipitous arrival at Walt's apartment suggested more than a former boss's interest in a departmental employee. If anyone could set the record straight on that it was the boss man himself, Milton Abrams.

Anson had found it necessary only twice in his career to visit the sprawling seven-story building set in the woods above the Potomac, and on neither occasion had he felt at ease in himself or in the surroundings. Long bright central corridors

115

with sentinel potted plants quickly lost their promise of clean-cut efficiency and candor. The airport modern style gave way to darker, narrower arteries, restricted areas governed by warning lights and rooms where there was no call for a window. Deceit hung heavy, like stale perfume clinging to a faithless husband's collar. It was a place designed to intimidate, outside and within.

Milton Abrams wore the casual cords and suede jacket of the vestigial Sunday worker. He seemed to have been designed by computer in accordance with a Langley patent for operational executives: tall, wide-shouldered, good-looking in a Middle-American Sunday supplement way. Intelligent. He waved a hand as if too tired to shake as Anson was shown into his office. "Take a seat," he said. "There's no shortage." There was not. The office was ringed with black leather conference chairs. He returned to a shuffle-and-deal session with a pile of multicolored paperwork.

"Look at this," he said. "Instructions, memos, forms, requisitions. More paper. Nobody reads the stuff, you know." He picked up a thick file bound in green card and flicked its pages. "418 pages. Know what it's all about? Trees. I kid you not. Trees. Somebody got it into his head we were verging on a tree crisis that would materially affect the country's economy. Render us treeless in the face of the Soviet hordes. So he called for a report." He weighed it in his hand. "Took three years to write and you can bet your ass half a forest was chopped down to print it. Net result? I don't even have to read it. No tree crisis in our time. Jesus!" He grinned, showing a perfect set of capped teeth. "Nobody knows what to do with it, so they shove it onto me along with a forecast that World War Three is imminent." He shook his head again and dropped the tome with a crash on his desk. "Anyway." The grin was still there. "So much for Milt Abrams, Super-clerk. What can I do for you, Mr. Anson?"

His delivery was good. Very good. Abrams's boyish looks and brisk, fresh manner could have made him a fortune as a stockbroker. He was over six feet tall, well muscled, but dressed down, as if natural athleticism were a virtue best concealed. He wore a knitted Fair Isle pullover with studiously baggy pockets under the jacket and on his desk lay a pair of severe horn-rims. Anson speculated whether the lenses were window glass, another attempt to hide the curse of youthfulness that so often foiled premature ambition.

Abrams was all calculation—down to the last detail. Even the opening speech had established an identity. In five or six

116

sentences he had presented his credentials as a registrar of verbiage, an amiable clerk, an archivist trapped beneath a mountain of paperwork. A man in his position needed good reasons to want to demean himself. That alone made him interesting. Self-denigration wasn't one of the universal attributes of department heads at Langley.

Anson took a chair across the desk and sat down.

"Mr. Abrams . . . ," he began.

"Milt."

"Milt. I've been temporarily detached to . . ."

"Georgie Hyman. INR."

"Right."

"My secretary told me."

"She did?"

"She knows everything." Abrams performed it in a stage whisper, implying her infallibility as a source.

"I've been back in Washington about four days, and I seem to have attracted a lot of people. Friends of my father, people he worked with . . ."

"He was a popular figure," interjected Abrams. He seemed to hate having to hear a sentence end.

"One of the guys I ran into was Walt Margolis. He worked for you."

Abrams steepled his fingers. "Margolis? Yes, of course, Walt."

"He's dead," said Anson unnecessarily.

Abrams nodded. Anson let the silence grow. Abrams made no move to fill it.

"I'd like to ask you . . . Milt. Was Walt Margolis of any particular interest to you? The Company?"

"Yes and no. He was an employee," said Abrams lightly. He picked up the horn-rims and swung them like a metronome. "Margolis could be a headache, but we learn to live with headaches."

"How much pain did Margolis cause?" Anson allowed a hostile edge into his tone. There was no percentage in letting things get too cozy. Not with a professional fence sitter like Abrams.

"Pain? That's a strong word. Too strong. No, Margolis—Walt—was an old-timer and, like most old men, he had his obsessions. You know what I mean?"

"Not exactly."

Abrams cocked his head to one side. "No? Come on, you knew Walt."

"I didn't exactly get a chance to *know* him."

117

"I did. Margolis lived in the past. He'd been a great field man in his day and he couldn't forget that. Couldn't reconcile coming in. His job with me was a sinecure, a way of working out his last couple of years in harness without the stresses. He deserved a rest. Like most of them, he didn't see it that way."

"He was writing his memoirs," pressed Anson.

"The usual deal. For the record. Some of that stuff can make damned fascinating reading. Make your hair curl."

"And Walt's?"

"Never saw any of it. I guessed what was bugging him, though."

"What was that?"

"Oh, Walt was involved in the Warren Commission thing—who wasn't?—but when the report came out, he couldn't let it ride. There must be a couple of million buffs who get a kick out of playing truth-or-dare with the conspiracy angle, but Margolis let it get obsessional. You know what I mean. He had this thing about the Kennedy evidence submission. He thought too much was held back from Warren, so he decided he was going to collate it the right way. He started out reading every damn file he could find. Millions of them. I don't know if you've seen any of that stuff, but it's dry as toast and confusing as hell. That's when he became a headache. The Company grew out of that a long time ago. We had years with the Assassinations Committee. Walt became a bore." Abrams sighed. "Guess we all get that way in the end."

He paused. Was it Anson's imagination, or was this a pause to invite agreement. If so, now was the time to hit him. Anson said quickly, "As his senior officer, you have the right to call for an investigation into the circumstances of his death. I'm here to ask you to exercise that right. I'd like you to call for an independent autopsy on Margolis. I want the best heart man in the business to find out why a perfectly healthy man dies suddenly from a coronary."

Abrams rode it well. His reaction was from the gut, not the mind. He threw his glasses on the desk. "A what? An independent . . . ? Do you realize what the hell you're saying?"

"Not saying. Asking. As far as I can find out, Walt Margolis had no history of cardiac disease or coronary trouble of any sort. He was fit as a derby winner when I saw him last. Just before he died. I want someone qualified to tell me he really died naturally."

118

"You think he was . . . ?" Abrams interrupted himself this time. "You're saying you . . ." His voice faded, his forehead creased. "Christ! Well, this I'll have to think about . . ."

"As I see it, if Margolis had enemies then, per se, they're no friends of the Company," hammered Anson. He seemed to be getting through. After all, Abrams was Company and that could mean many things, not least that he was anxious to protect his own. Only a fool would swallow the media line that the Company was staffed solely by amoral bounty hunters. Maybe Abrams had more spunk than Anson had been prepared to give him credit for.

Abrams looked genuinely alarmed.

"So will you fix that autopsy?"

Abrams got up from the desk and walked slowly to a chart on the wall. He studied its mass of colored pins. When he turned, his mouth was set hard. "I can't do it, Anson. I'm sorry. I appreciate your concern and I respect your feelings for Margolis. But take it from me, they're misplaced. Sorry, I can't do it."

Anson rose and Abrams leaned across the desk. "Don't take it the wrong way, Anson. Hear me out." The boyishness disappeared. The veteran of a hundred campaigns came out of the foxhole. "Margolis was trouble, I said that. He still could be. . . ." Abrams punched fist into palm. "O.K.—I'll level with you. Walt Margolis was more than just an obsessed old man. He was being watched. More so than many men in his position and not for a nice reason. Margolis was a security risk. A big one. Files had been taken, we knew that, but we didn't want to rush in and come up with egg all over our faces. So we waited and let him run under surveillance. For three months, we did nothing else—and for God's sake, this is in total confidence, Anson; they'd have my guts if they knew I was telling you this . . ."

"They?"

"What?"

"Nothing. Go on."

Abrams pursed his lips. "Margolis didn't have to pirate classified files to write what he was writing. He had all the facilities right here. Complete freedom. But he took files out and they came back copied. We found out. Heat tests. One day we found out why. Margolis had problems." He closed his eyes painfully. "Medical—social problems. Funny people going up to his apartment on a regular basis. We monitored them over a long period. The men—if you want to *call* them that—had one thing in common, Anson. One thing." He

119

paused as if debating with himself the wisdom of continuing the assault on a dead man's name. Anson knew he would. "What they had in common was their predilection. They were all practicing homosexuals."

Anson felt a muscle spasm in his stomach. He said tightly, "Go on."

"You can guess the rest. We bugged the apartment. The tapes don't make for family listening. Walt Margolis was a fag."

"And?"

"He was being blackmailed. One of his—ah—visitors was putting the arm on him to come across with a series of sensitive documents. I guess they were going to be used to compromise various individuals. Men with positions in government, Anson. *Respectable* people. Margolis was supplying those documents."

"Blackmail?" echoed Anson. His mouth was dry. "What kind of blackmail could any *respectable* citizen be worried about? How can you blackmail a *respectable* man, for God's sake?"

"Homosexuality isn't indictable in this state, Anson. Blackmail is. Stealing documents—classified documents—from an intelligence agency is bigger. Margolis was caught in a net he wove himself. His death—and I hate to say this, but we're being frank now—his death saved him from a formal charge. You say he had no history of heart trouble. Right. But can you imagine the strain all of this put on him?" Abrams drew a hand across his brow. It was not theatrical. "To answer your question: No, he wasn't killed. It wasn't necessary, Anson. He killed himself by doing what he did."

Anson felt a desperate need to breathe clean air. He harbored no resentment for Abrams; the poor bastard was only doing his job. He tried to complete it with a degree of dignity. He put on his old man's horn-rims. "You can see how it would be insensitive, to say the least, to reopen any investigation into his death. I'm sure you see that." He looked down at his feet. "A lot of decent people would be involved. And he had a daughter, too. Naturally she'll be told none of this. Why burden the living? Margolis served the Company well. We'll let him be remembered for that."

Anson took the open hand. There were traces of perspiration on the palm and the grip was a shadow of what it might have been. "I'm grateful to you, Mr. Abrams."

"Milt."

"Milt."

"Hasn't been easy. But promise me something, will you?
120

None of this ... nothing I've said ... Well, you know what I mean. Let the dead bury the dead, right?"

"Sure."

Milton Abrams perched on the corner of his desk and watched Anson leave. When the door was closed, he clenched his fists. "Jesus Christ! Jesus *Christ!*"

He looked like a man who had narrowly escaped a major road accident.

MONDAY: 0645—ANSON

Anson reached an arm from the scented cocoon of the bed and groped for his watch. Alongside him Grazia slept, but even in sleep she was not calm; her flesh was hot to the touch and her limbs stirred constantly, languidly, as if unable to restrain some unconscious animal instinct for seduction. A strand of her hair coiled across his cheek; its perfume was tantalizing, seductive. A leg strayed between his and his pelvis stirred.

He pulled away.

Milton Abrams, horn-rims swinging easily in his fingers, took over his mind again. Margolis a fag? Stealing documents to fend off a blackmailer? Why burden the living, Abrams had said. Why indeed? But who else was there to burden? If Walt Margolis had been blackmailed—and there was no reason why Abrams should lie—he had to know why his father's name had figured so prominently with the old man. He felt a taste of bitters in his mouth and slipped from the bed. Grazia murmured, slid a hand along the pillow like a hungry snake, but did not wake.

He took a shower, dressed and shaved and made some coffee. He checked a couple of times to be sure she was still asleep and switched on the radio, low. The weather, predictably, got top rating. Cities and towns had been crippled by the savage cold. Snowplows hissed, helicopters dropped food to stranded towns, office heating plants failed.

He let the coffee scorch his tongue, burning the taste of sleep away, the taste of bad dreams.

A commentator was voicing about some Washington scuttlebutt concerning Nixon. A story was going the rounds, fresh out of the rumor factory, that Nixon was thinking of tossing his cap into the Presidential race. Yes, thought Anson, and Batista is about to overthrow Castro at the polls.

121

"... The former President has not as yet confirmed or denied these speculations. ..."

It was pure Washington: Create some half-assed story and then get the guy involved to stick his head into the noose. Have you stopped beating your wife? Anson swallowed the last of the coffee and went down to the garage to warm up the Porsche.

"Leave your wheels in the garage and give the Reaper a day off," intoned the breezy breakfast show host. Anson took the Porsche into the soundproofed streets and across town. Constitution was practically deserted. Highway patrols were reporting multiple pileups on freeways into the city, and rescue units had a waiting list of commuters trapped nose-deep in drifts and mini-avalanches on country roads all over Maryland.

"Leave your wheels in the garage ..."

A red emergency truck wailed out of a side street and skidded across the avenue ahead of him. Its studded tires spun, bit hard, found a hold and shunted the vehicle along Constitution with a jet of snow frothing in its wake. Anson peered through the white sheet of the windshield. The Porsche's wheels spun with exasperation and he wrestled it out of a four-wheel slide. He resisted the thought of returning to the apartment. It had been 3 A.M. when his mind had churned up something Buffalo Morgan had told him the day they found Walt's body: "Why he came back to a crummy dump like this I'll never know." The big old house in Virginia. The place called Hutton's Farm.

Walt's apartment had been neat as a whistle. Too neat, too clean. That had bothered him from the start.

"... give the Reaper a day off ..." The going became really difficult beyond the suburbs and it was just short of an hour later when he spotted the sign to Hutton's Farm. It pointed along a track, hedged high on both sides and deep with driven snow. He pulled off the road, rattled over a cattle grid and forged slowly into the lane. He stopped after less than a hundred yards. The Porsche was up to its hubcaps and the track ahead was a tube of drifted snow between tall hedges. Anson broke off a few twigs and placed them behind the rear wheels of the car. He got in and reversed tentatively until the tires bit firmly on the twig mattress. Then he set off down the lane.

Hutton's Farm was a two-story white-painted clapboard structure. A fussy hand had gotten to it, probably in the mid-thirties, and added a wrought iron balustrade to the roof

122

ridge and plaster cornucopias at either end. A brick portico with wrought iron gates had been built out from the main door. From the main gates, the drive swung through wide lawns to the house. Along the way Anson could see an ornamental pond embraced by clipped box trees, a sundial, a pergola, a summerhouse and the entrance to what was possibly a walled garden. His eye recorded the details, but his attention was already fixed on the one feature he had not expected. The car stood a few yards from the portico, snow thick on its roof and hood and trunk.

Anson inched through the small wicket gate to one side of the arch and ran as quickly as the thick snow would permit across the lawns to the box tree hedge. He crouched, checked the windows for movement, then high-stepped it to the far corner of the house. Still no movement inside.

He walked to the portico. The gate swung open at his touch and he went inside. The bell was a butterfly key. He turned it several times and heard the ancient mechanism raise its voice hoarsely. He went back to the car and looked inside. There was a small tissue box on the rear seat, a folding umbrella, a copy of *New York* magazine and a yellow slicker. The car was a Ford sedan, Washington plates. He checked the license. Rented. No tracks back or front. He went back to the front door, turned the handle and pushed. It was warm inside.

The staircase rose and turned right. There was a high polished table in front of him, a small Persian carpet over the stone flags of the hall and double doors to his left. He pushed through them.

The voice was calm, persuasive and pitched low. It came from maybe a yard behind him and to his left. It said, "Lean forward on the table. In front of you. Don't turn your head. This is a Saturday Night Special and it kicks high left. If it doesn't kill you it'll maim you for life."

He stepped forward instantly, minimizing each movement to avoid surprise. He placed his hands on the table edge, angled his feet behind him and stared resolutely at the wall. He waited, but there was no stir of movement, no frisking hands, no further commands. *Oh, Jesus! Don't pull that trigger. You can't* . . . Then the timbre of the voice registered with him, and before he knew what he was doing he'd turned his head to stare.

The girl was perched on a low sideboard, the gun in her left hand, her right nursing its barrel. Her tongue reached up to moisten her top lip and he interpreted the movement as uncertainty. "Don't!" she snapped and came upright, feet apart. He swung back to face the far wall.

"The name is Anson. State Department. I'm an old friend of Walt Margolis and . . ."

"Walt Margolis has no friends. He's dead."

"I know that. I *was* a friend."

"They were *all* his friends. They all said they were his friends. After he died." Her voice dropped.

Anson held out a hand, like a blind man feeling for reassurance. "Believe me. I came because . . ."

"Don't you *dare* move!"

"All right! For God's sake, I promise I won't move an inch. If you'll just let me talk to you. I can . . ."

"You can stand up, walk around the table to the other side. Place your hands flat down so I can see them. Then talk."

He did as he was told.

She was a tall girl, five-six or -seven, and the high slim polished boots gave her another three inches. White silk cossack blouse over a chocolate brown corduroy skirt. He let his eyes come up to her face. There was no light in the room, but he guessed the hair was nearly the color of the corduroy skirt. So were the eyes. The make-up was precise, perfectly blended, designed for drama but not overdone. A blusher had been applied to throw the cheekbones into high relief, narrowing the lower half of the face to give a lush, luminescent significance to the mouth. Her hands were long and slim and competent. The Special didn't look out of place.

"Well, say what you have to say."

Say what, for God's sake? "I've got proof of my identity in my . . . ," he began.

"I don't care *who* you are. I want to know *what* you are."

He relaxed. "O.K. You win. Do what the hell you like. I'm here because I was a friend of Walt's and because I found his body. I guess I don't really know why I'm here, except . . ."

"Except?" She came forward, the gun still steady in her hands.

"We talked. Nothing important, but we got to like each other I think. He asked me to eat with him Friday night. I couldn't raise him. I went around to the apartment the next day. He was dead."

"That doesn't explain anything." She moved to the table.

"Maybe that's why I'm here. If I could get . . ." His right hand lunged across the table and sent the Special spinning to

124

the floor. He swung across the tabletop, grabbed the girl's wrist and dragged her toward him. Her strength was remarkable; he could only contain her in the end by wrapping his arms around her from behind and crushing her into submission. He let out the pent-up air in his lungs. "That's better. My God, what are you—a lady wrestler?"

She squirmed again and he tightened the bear hug. "Look, damn you," he gasped, "will you promise to sit down and shut up? I don't know about you, baby, but I'm in no condition for unarmed combat. If you want to fight, go ahead. I've got just about enough strength left to poke you on the jaw. You want that, give me the sign."

She relaxed at once. He half carried her to a deep chair on the far side of the room, away from the fallen Special, and set her down in it. She fell back sullenly into its depths, crossed her arms and tested her shoulders with both hands. He picked up the gun, kicked the doors shut and flicked on the light. A tall table lamp behind her bathed her face with almost melodramatic blacklighting. Her hair was not brown. Not auburn either. It had the color he'd seen in Kentucky chestnuts raised to the peak of perfection for Derby Day. She glared back at him with brimming hostility.

"Now—can we start all over?" he asked gently. He sat on the table's edge, the gun behind him, out of reach. Her glare became unsteady. He stepped forward, reconsidered and returned to the table. "I came to help."

He picked up the gun and shoved it into the inner pocket of his fur-lined leather windbreaker, backed around the table to the door and surveyed the room. None of this fitted with the Walt Margolis he knew: the glib, dismissive old cynic, the chain-smoking toughie, the agent who dealt in expediency. John Roper Anson might have inhabited a room like this: soft dark leather, books, aging furniture polished more from habit than necessity. His eyes wandered down the shelves. Seneca, Cicero, Plautus, Ovid, Plato, Cato, Caesar's *Commentaries*. One whole section devoted to Roman history and mythology. So this was Walt's private passion, his anodyne for the chaotic freewheeling life he saw around him: the order and discipline of a dead world where gods made their compact with men to create order and sense. A man etched his personality, sent his roots deep, in a room like this, and death couldn't erase this image.

He looked at the girl. "You want to tell me why *you're* here?"

"I belong here. Walt was my father," she said bluntly.

"But I thought . . ." He stopped in time.

She sighed and returned to her mirror. "I came back last night. The police told me. I had a club date in Seattle."

Anson studied her. "Walt said you were a singer."

"My father sweated blood to keep me out of show business. Work of the devil, he said. He thought a girl should have a husband, kids and a checking account. His idea of independence outside of that was a night out at the PTA and church on Sunday."

"He could've been right."

"Not for me, he wasn't."

"I can see that."

She turned on him fiercely. "What d'you mean by that?"

"I mean you don't look like a nightclub singer." He added quickly, "I don't mean you look like PTA-and-church-on-Sunday either. You . . ." He returned to the table and sat down again.

The tip of her tongue appeared between her lips and she turned her head left and right, observing it in the mirror. "What do you think I look like, then?" She threw it out as if the conversation had to be maintained out of sheer politeness.

"You look like the kind of girl who gets her picture in the papers just stepping off an airplane."

She puckered her lips in the mirror. "I hope that's a compliment."

"So do I," he said. She raised her eyes wide to look at him. "I mean," he went on smoothly, confident now, "that I recognize you."

"Recognize . . . ?" There was sudden alarm.

"Right." He swung off the table and walked to where she stood in front of the bay window. The sun was probing the leaden cloud with occasional shafts of yellow light and, each time it pierced to the ground, the snow danced with the refracted light of a million diamonds. "I don't know a lot about nightclub singers but I'd put a year's pay on the fact that they don't handle a Special the way you do. Fact Two: That blouse is St. Laurent—old but good. Expensive. So's your taste. Like this room." He waved a hand around him. "Fact Three: Walt told me about you. Smith, a year at the Sorbonne. I'd say you were your father's daughter—tough, self-confident, independent. He gave you one sort of a life because that's what he wanted you to have and you chose another one—as far as you could go to the opposite end of the spectrum."

126

She snapped the makeup mirror shut. "Is class through for the day?"

"Yes." He bowed slightly. "I guess I've said enough."

"He must have told you a lot about me." She turned to the window.

"No. I think he mentioned you once and that was in passing. He was talking about his wife at the time." He clenched his fist in anger at the slip, but she said nothing. He went on, "Walt was like a concocted character. He left what was important to him back here, I guess."

"So he only talked to you about his work?"

He couldn't help staring at her hair. There were scarlet and gold fires in it where the light penetrated. "A little. He wasn't much of a talker. We talked about everything but it didn't add up to much."

She held her fingers up to the light. "But you knew about his work. You must have."

"You mean his memoirs? Sure, I knew about that. Did you?"

She turned toward him. Her face was serious. "How important do you think those memoirs were to Walt?" she asked.

He shrugged to conceal the excitement that slipped like an ice cube along his spine. "It was the last project of his career. It was important to him."

She laid a hand on his arm. "Important enough to die for?" He pulled his arm away roughly. She took a step closer to him. Her eyes had perfect triangles of green in the brown irises. "That's what you think too, isn't it? *Isn't it?*"

He clamped his mouth shut.

"I thought so." She watched him complete another tour of her face and when he realized she had caught him out, he stretched his mouth guiltily. She said, "He called me last week. We talked about you. He thought you were Prince Valiant and Captain Midnight wrapped in cloth of gold. He never spoke about anyone that way before. Did he tell you what he was doing? The research for his memoirs?"

Anson held his tongue in cheek. This was going too fast. "No. Not exactly. I knew the general outline."

"He didn't discuss any . . . specifics? Any names?"

Anson backed off again, this time to his baseline at the table. He said coolly, "I got the idea you and Walt didn't see much of each other. The way he talked, I thought you weren't . . . close. How much did he tell *you?*"

She raised her hands in a small show of despair and let

127

them fall again. "He didn't. He just hinted it was the biggest thing he'd ever touched. He thought it would blow half the Establishment sky-high if he played it the wrong way."

"Is that what he said?"

"He said, 'If I'm right, sweetheart, half the country'll wish me to hell and the rest will play deaf.'" She dropped into the chair as though suddenly exhausted. "He said nothing at all to you?"

"He said a lot of things that could mean that, I guess." Her face dropped and he experienced a ridiculous urge to comfort her. "I'd have to think about it."

"Will you? Will you really think about it?"

"If you promise to keep that look on your face." He had never been more serious in his life.

She bowed her head, then looked up again. There was the trace of a smile. "I spent last night looking through his den. Would you like to see his papers?"

At 12:30 it began to snow again. Anson looked up from the file he was reading, looked down again to the typewritten blue quarto sheet, then stopped. He should have called George Hyman. It was too late for that now, but tomorrow he'd need a damn good excuse for playing hooky for a whole day.

The sun was running out of the sky and it would be getting dark in a couple of hours. The drive back to Washington would be at best nightmarish. He closed the file reluctantly and got to his feet. Alice—it was her name, but he hadn't used it and neither had she—had left him alone in Walt's timbered den at ten o'clock. She had arranged the files on the brass-trimmed desk and left him to it. Walt had proved to be a copious researcher, an avid collector of disconnected Intelligence and a neat and orderly scribe. What he had failed to do was provide a key to his thoughts and his deductive processes—and that was hardly surprising; Walt, after all, knew what he was looking for. Give any persistent researcher the freedom to assimilate classified information and he can prove black is white and left is right. What Margolis had done, in fifteen linking files, was to kick history into a bucket. Fifteen years after the Warren Commission, Walt Margolis— the CIA's official Head of Liaison to Earl Warren's inquiry— had decided to absolve himself. In the course of the Commission's work, the federal agencies involved had been required to submit every scrap of information gleaned from their investigations into the assassination of John Kennedy, into

128

the backgrounds of Lee Harvey Oswald and Jack Ruby, their families, associates and connections. Margolis had meticulously listed numbered submissions made by the CIA to the Commission. He then listed facts he believed the Agency had withheld. Other files recorded areas of investigation concealed by the FBI and one itemized political findings hidden from Warren at the insistence of the White House.

It was a rhapsody in *déjà vu,* an eight-month stint in the confessional. At the end of it, Anson was convinced of only one fact: No one would have killed for this ragbag of innuendo and lovingly framed data. At least thirty books published in the sixties had set out to prove the conspiracy theory and most of them had done it with more cohesiveness, more articulation, than Walt Margolis. Walt's trouble was that he never seemed to finish any line of inquiry he started. His review of key witnesses at Dallas who died in the months following the assassination was a classic case; it was sketchy and incomplete. Much the same could be said for his system of recording conclusions. He seemed to tire of each specific thread of theory, passing on to another seemingly from sheer impatience.

Anson opened the last file wearily. His senses leaped to focus on the name:

John Roper Anson.

He read, feverishly at first, then returned to the first of the five loose pages and began again. Numbers, abbreviations, dates, obvious cover names: Tango, Otis, Billboard, Shrike. Meaningless—at least, meaningless right now, at this moment, with his eyes watering from too much reading and his head aching with frustration. He read through the pages again, but he could make no sense of it. The material had to be absorbed, weighed, solved like an obscure crossword puzzle.

Anson closed the file and went downstairs. Alice was in the sitting room, a book open on her lap. She got up at once. "Have you finished?"

"Yeah." Wearily. He didn't want to have to pacify her, make weak excuses for leaving.

"Does it ring any bells?" Her lips parted expectantly.

"Have you read any of that stuff?"

"A little. I don't understand it. There are too many abbreviations, too many initials and symbols. I couldn't follow it."

"I don't think it'll get us anywhere, frankly." He saw her shrink as if under a raised fist. "I'm sorry. I don't know what

129

he was trying to prove, but as far as I'm concerned he hasn't proved a thing. It's the usual Kennedy Conspiracy fantasy."

"But he said . . ."

"Sure. He said half the country'd wish him to hell and the rest would play deaf. Well—I guess that was wishful thinking. He just never got that far."

When she led him to the door a few minutes later, the life had gone out of her and he was in despair. They shook hands under the portico and he turned to trudge back down the drive.

"Harry!"

He stopped, unreasonably agitated at her use of his name, and looked back at her. "Yes?"

"You think he was . . . you think he was just an old fool wasting his time, don't you?"

"I didn't say that."

"Well, I don't think he was."

"He's your father."

"Was. Was my father."

"At least we share that."

Anson tried to tear his mind from the file he had just been reading. "I buried my father on Friday," he said, half to himself. Then, apologetically, "I'm sorry: I'm not trying to match your grief; that wasn't what I meant. I guess I'm just trying to come to terms with it."

"Have you?"

"I had." He shrugged. "I don't know why. My father and Walt Margolis seem to be scrambled up together right now."

"Harry . . ." Again the name moved tumblers to a lock he still hadn't found the key to. "Walt was reaching for something he'd taken a long long time to get near. I know it. Don't ask me how; I just *feel* it. Whatever it was, I owe him at least one try at finding what it was. . . ."

He knew only too well what she was trying to say, knew too the vacuum from which it sprang. The prodigal daughter, fabricating virtue to atone for past neglect. Too late, he wanted to tell her. We're both too late. Alice Margolis in Seattle, Harry Anson in Rome. The weekly phone call that became a monthly letter that became . . . silence.

"I can't help you, Alice," he said. He thought abstractedly, *Alice—the name doesn't fit her. Wrong again, Walt. Wrong name.*

She wrapped her arms around her body against the cold.

"Just do what you can. Please."

130

Something in his face he hadn't intended to be there must have reassured her.

"Thank you," she said simply. Before he could reply she turned and ran back into the house. From the gates at the end of the driveway he looked back. She was in the bay window of the sitting room, watching him. She waved. He waved back. He sat in the Porsche until the gushing heater brought the circulation back into his legs. In little more than an hour they had met, made their peace, explored emotions. He knew it wouldn't end there. She'd called him Harry. It sounded good, natural. That was a good sign.

He was back on the main road, concentrating on the icy road and the banked snow when another thought struck him: How had she learned his first name? She'd called him Harry. Could she really have remembered that from a telephone call her father had made a week ago?

And why?

When he had pushed through the gate, she went to the telephone and dialed a Washington number. Lucas Garfield was fighting a chest cold and in poor humor. She reported quickly and succinctly. At the end of her recital she said, "I think it would be simpler all around if we took him into our confidence."

"No." Garfield coughed and spluttered into a handkerchief. "He'll react better if he believes he's doing it for his own reasons. Good-bye."

MONDAY: 1430—ANSON

"State Department. I have a call for you." The girl's practiced singsong clipped short as she made the connection. Anson winced. It had to be George Hyman.

"Anson?"

"Sorry, George. I meant to call. Things got kind of, well . . ."

"What?"

"I should have told you where I was. I was planning to come in later."

"Nothing wrong, is there?"

"No. A few problems, nothing serious."

"Good. Listen, Harry, I have a message for you. It was passed through to my secretary and she didn't know where you were. Have you got yourself a secretary yet?"

"No."

"Well, it seems I got the job," said Hyman lightly. "Does the name Buffalo Morgan mean anything to you, or is it some kind of joke?"

"No joke, George. He's a friend of Walt Margolis."

"Poor old Walt. I heard about that. Heart attack. Couldn't believe it at first. Walt was granite. Anyway, the message is about the funeral."

"Funeral? No autopsy?"

"It's been done, I guess. They're burying him this afternoon."

"This afternoon!"

"Rock Creek. Three o'clock." Hyman sighed. "Found on Saturday, buried on Monday."

"Isn't that a little . . . premature?"

"It's the way they do things at Langley," said Hyman.

"So I gather. You say Buffalo Morgan called? I guess he'll be there. Will you?"

George Hyman breathed his unhappiness into the phone. "Nothing I'd like better, son, but they pulled a conference on me over at Justice just now. Have to be there."

Anson drove out New Hampshire Avenue to the cemetery on the northeast side, knowing he would be late. The snow was falling heavily and midafternoon traffic was sluggish. He bit back his impatience. He should have called the girl. He parked the Porsche inside the gates. Two hundred yards away a small group stood in the snow like black statues. Anson recognized Morgan's unmistakable bulk. Leo McCullen stood alone to one side. There were a half dozen others he didn't recognize. McCullen turned from the waist as Anson came up behind him.

"Dust to dust," said the priest. His fingers dug painfully into the rock-hard soil. He straightened and sprinkled the unyielding earth into the grave. A white coverlet of snowflakes was already draped over the coffin.

"Ashes to ashes." The priest tucked a hand inside his cassock for warmth. He read quickly from the Bible clutched in his trembling fingers.

"Amen."

"Amen," said Buffalo Morgan loudly.

The priest glanced around the company assembled at the graveside as if reluctant to appear too eager to retreat before the biting wind; then, lifting his robe clear of the snow, he walked away. Anson saw galoshes flapping beneath the flowing cassock. With his departure the others began to drift away, sweeping flakes of snow from their hair, banging cramped arms against their sides to restore circulation.

"So there was only a Company autopsy?" Anson said tightly.

"Did you expect anything else?"

Buffalo Morgan came from the lip of the grave and wrapped a hand warmly around Anson's. "I called you at the number you gave me," he said apologetically, "but some broad . . ."

"Thanks. I just got the message."

"When they took Walt away I asked them guys to let me know so I could arrange something. Flowers, that kind of thing. They never called. He could've been put away without no one knowing. So I called Langley. Told them his friends had a right to know."

"You called Langley!"

"That's where Walt worked, right? I got the number from the book. Said they had no right to keep him like that. Ain't decent. They might own a man's body but jeez, they didn't have no rights on his soul. They told me he was being buried today. Quick, ain't it?" He stared back at the grave. "Better than nothing." He glanced at Leo McCullen with a prize-fighter's eye, then his gaze lengthened and Anson turned to follow it. A black limousine was parked in the broad drive-way on the perimeter of the cemetery, partially obscured by a line of cypresses.

"Walt kept strange company, Louie," Buffalo Morgan said sadly. "What kind of a guy watches a funeral from a car?" He snorted his contempt. He eyed McCullen doubtfully. "I won't keep you, Louie. You know where I am if you need me."

He slouched off into the snow, the weight of him plunging his feet deep at each step. He stopped and turned his head, as if some profound thought had just found its expression. "Maybe they did own it, Louie," he called back. "Maybe they did own his soul after all." He shook his head once more, turned and walked away.

"Who in God's name . . ." began McCullen.

"A friend of Walt's," said Anson sharply. "A *real* friend. I thought maybe you'd met him."

McCullen hid his feelings well. "Once seen, never forgotten. No. I can't say I ever met him. Why does he call you Louie?"

"He calls everyone Louie. Makes life simpler."

"Quite a character."

The limousine in the driveway purred into life and slowly reversed to the gates.

"Do I have to guess?" asked Anson, nodding to it.

"Company," said McCullen. "They always turn up for funerals. That's Petersen."

"Petersen! He comes to Walt's funeral?"

"Walt got full honors."

"I hope he appreciates it."

"I know how you feel." McCullen lit a small cigar. "Walt was at your father's funeral Friday, wasn't he?"

Anson's anger overwhelmed him. "Listen, McCullen, there are a few things I want to get straight."

McCullen cut him short. "O.K., Harry. So you want to get things straight. Before you go any further, and before you get out of your depth, let me explain something. I don't respond to accusation. I don't like it." His voice had the texture of graveside gravel. "So let's just cut out the high moral outrage, shall we, and talk it through?" He paused. "Sorry, but I'm a little uptight myself."

Anson felt foolish and the initial flush of anger subsided.

"Come on," said McCullen, "let's have a drink."

McCullen led the way in his blue Ford to Grant Circle and turned into Illinois Avenue. They found a bar and downed a double bourbon apiece. The shot thawed them. McCullen was not an inveterate drinker; he blinked widely as the bourbon touched bottom.

"Another?" asked Anson. McCullen nodded reluctantly, and they moved to an alcove at the far end of the bar and faced each other. McCullen pushed his glass to one side and hunched on braced elbows. Anson kept his voice cool, pitched to a deliberate flatness.

"I don't know where you stand in this, Mc . . . Leo. I don't even know what *this* is. But something's going on here that stinks to high heaven. And Walt was right in the middle of it. If you don't want to talk, *can't* talk, O.K. We'll discuss the weather. But I'm going to take a gamble. I'm going to tell you what *I* think and put my head on the block if I'm wrong about you. Christ knows, I seem to have been wrong about almost everything else in this town."

McCullen was staring at a spot over Anson's shoulder, checking out the possibility that someone might be listening. Anson dropped his voice as if he had been slapped across the face. "Don't tell me there are spooks here too," he whispered.

McCullen finished his reconnaissance. "Go on."

Anson weighed his words. "First off—a question. Why did you turn up at Margolis's house right after they took Walt's body away?"

McCullen raised a single eyebrow. "You were there?"

"I was there."

"You really are into this, aren't you? O.K., I surrender. I went because Walt asked me to. He phoned the day before and we arranged a meeting. When I got there I didn't know he was dead. That answer your question?"

"Why did Margolis call you?"

"I don't know. I wish I did."

"And that was all. A call from Walt and you went to see him?"

"No more, no less. You believe me?"

"What if I said no?"

"I'd say you had a right. But I'd also say you were way off base. You wanted an answer. I gave it. If you don't believe me, why ask?"

It was Anson's turn to apologize. "All right, I accept that. You went to see Margolis because he asked you to. But you must have had *some* idea why!"

McCullen eyed him steadily. "Walt always had a notion he was being followed. Maybe he wanted to talk about it."

"You don't believe that?"

"About his being followed? Could be. About that being why he called, no."

"So why?"

"You talked to him. You tell me."

"I was due to eat with him the night before. I couldn't make it and I couldn't get him on the phone. But he phoned *you*. Next thing he's dead. I'd say there was a connection, wouldn't you? I thought we were going to level with each other!" Anson leaned back into the seat and shut his eyes. When he opened them again, McCullen was studying the bar as if deliberating whether to leave.

Anson gestured his resignation. "O.K., Leo. So be it. I quit. I've had a gutful. It's all yours. Tomorrow I ask for a transfer back to Rome. They can't stop me." He got up to leave, but McCullen stretched out a hand and clamped it firmly on his shoulder, pushing him gently back into the seat.

"You can't do that, Harry. There's too much here to walk away from."

"Then tell me what the hell *is* going on. All I know is I've been to the funeral of a guy who started out being black-mailed and ended up dead."

135

"Blackmailed?" The word came softly, wrapped in suspicion. McCullen's face creased. "Where's you get that?"

"From your boss, Milton Abrams. Doesn't he talk to you? He gave me the first straight answer I got since I flew in from Rome. Walt Margolis was a fag, Leo. He was being used to ferry classified documents to someone who wanted to put a finger on a big wheel . . . someone big enough to kill him *and* get the Company to draw a curtain around his death. Why d'you think Petersen was at the cemetery? To pay his last respects? Not on your life. Walt Margolis had something on a favorite son. One way or the other, the CIA covered up."

"Abrams said that?"

"Of course he didn't. He told me about Walt. The background. You don't have to be Ironside to work out the rest."

"Jesus." McCullen pinched his nose as if waking from sleep. Real shock etched his face, too deep to be fabricated.

"You don't know any of this?" Anson asked sarcastically.

"No. None of it. No reason why I should. It's not true, Harry. Abrams was lying."

"Who says?"

"It was a lie. Margolis was an obsessive man, sure, but he was no homosexual. And he wouldn't stand still for blackmail. You have my word on it."

"Then why did Abrams . . . ?"

"That," said McCullen, "is what I intend to find out."

"You think Abrams knew who killed Margolis? Is that what you're saying?"

McCullen leaned closer, his voice low. "Listen, Harry, things have changed so I want your word that none of this gets back. I talked out of turn there, but what you've just told me changes everything. Bear with me. I'll tell you when the time's right. Just believe me, O.K.? And do what I ask. I want to know—" He stopped abruptly.

"Want to know?"

"Who else talked to you since Walt died?"

"His daughter. She has your appetite for melodrama, Leo. She thinks her father was killed because he knew something. She wants me to find out what it was. You want me to bear with you. All right—what are you looking for? What was Margolis looking for? What did he find?"

McCullen remained tight-lipped. He drew his topcoat around him. "I've got a meeting, Harry. It's important I be there." He flicked up his watch and peered along the bar to the street. "You ask too many questions, Harry. Too many.

Maybe it's better we don't meet for a while. Wait till I contact you."

"Just like that?" said Anson. "You toss me a grenade and walk away with the pin?"

"It has to be that way, believe me. Meantime, stick by the girl. She may need you."

"Wait a minute . . ."

McCullen squeezed from behind the table and walked out of the bar. Anson stared at the depression in the plastic of his empty seat. He thought of following but decided against it. The girl. He should have called her. The least he could have done was tell her they were burying her father.

MONDAY: 1630—McCULLEN

They met like secret lovers, drifting together with calculated aimlessness until they were shoulder to shoulder on a small bridge spanning the winding thread of water. Neither of them spoke at first.

He had been leaning on the parapet staring out over the sprawl of the zoo and beyond to Connecticut Avenue and the dome of the Naval Observatory. He turned, as though surprised at her coming, and set his back to the railing. Less than a mile away in a direct line he could see Rock Creek Cemetery and the Soldiers' Home. He nodded into the whirling snow. "They buried Margolis an hour ago. Anson was there. I didn't expect to see him."

The girl turned up the collar of her wolfskin coat and blew a crystal flake from her nose. "Did he say anything?"

"Enough."

"You mean he remembered something? Walt told him something?"

"No. He doesn't know a thing, I'd swear to that. Garfield's clutching at straws. No—something else . . ." He linked arms with her. "C'mon, let's make this look real—if you can play the part from memory." Her face tightened and relaxed again. They walked to a small shelter beyond the bridge. He put his arm around her shoulders as they sat on the wooden bench. "Sorry about this."

She smiled brightly. "Don't apologize. I liked it, remember."

"Ironic, isn't it?" His laugh was forced and he lapsed into

silence. She drew her head back to study his face in the flat hard light; it was taut, gray, as if the snow had robbed it of feeling and life.

"God, Leo, you look like death."

"Only that bad? In that case it's not too serious."

She was angered by his flippancy, genuinely upset. She snuggled closer to him. "What's wrong? This isn't your style."

McCullen followed the swell of the white carpet away down to the creek. It was unbroken, undisturbed by the clumsy contamination of human or animal footprints; pure. He said: "Anson just turned over a stone. I was ready for it."

"What did he say?"

"He went calling at Langley. Saw Abrams; faced him out. Told him point-blank he thought Margolis was killed and demanded an autopsy. Jesus—can you imagine it! Abrams was sweetness and light but he said it couldn't be done. He told Anson Walt was a fag who'd been under surveillance and was up to his ears in homosexual blackmail."

"He what!"

"It gets better. His opinion was Walt probably committed suicide because of what was hanging over him."

"*Abrams* said that!"

"Anson believed him, on the surface anyhow. I can't pretend I know what goes on in that skull of his, but he seems to believe it. Why shouldn't he?"

"Abrams!" She slumped back in the seat.

"Garfield was right. That's one of 'em Anson turned up and with no help from anyone. If I know Abrams, he isn't alone. Goddamn it—I should have nosed him out. I should have seen."

She shivered, but not from the wind. "What happens to Anson now?"

"He goes on, what else? On two counts he's useful: he wants to know why Walt died and why he kept a file on his father. He won't drop out; he's got guts, that kid. Anyway, Garfield has some idea his father may have told him something. Something he may have forgotten. It'll come out in time."

"You believe that?"

"I'd believe pretty well anything right now. Why in hell can't he level with Anson? The kid's walking into a mine field and I'm telling you I don't think we can stay close enough to pull him out when the time comes."

"You know he can't be told." The sound of her own voice terrified her. She swallowed hard. "He wouldn't have gone straight to Abrams if Garfield had briefed him, would he?"

McCullen retrieved his arm round her shoulder. "Walt might have known. If I'd gone to his apartment when he called . . . It was stupid. Stupid!"

She grabbed his arm and imprisoned it firmly in hers. "It could also have been nothing. If he'd gotten something, something big, he'd have left a note, a message. Something. You know Walt; he believed in writing things down."

"Do you think Anson found something?"

"No, the place was sanitized. I saw it myself. Abrams doesn't do things by halves. The technicians turned the place over. Even the dust was fresh."

"Have you told Garfield about Abrams?"

He shook his head. "I have that pleasure to come. Baby— have I blown it!"

"Nobody's blown anything yet. We're even ahead of the game. We know about Abrams. We've got a target now, a trace. And The Matrix has moved, as Garfield said they would. They're in the open. You haven't blown a thing, Leo."

McCullen didn't seem to be listening. "Garfield's up to something, Lee. Something he's not telling me about. I can smell it." He twisted his head to look at her directly. "You hear that stuff about Nixon?"

"So? It's crazy."

McCullen scuffed the toe of his shoe in the snow. "He's up to something," he repeated tonelessly.

"Don't get side-tracked, Leo," she warned. "Stick to what you know. You've got to concentrate on Anson."

"No!" The sharpness surprised her. "You do. From here on in, I'm benched. Anson's all yours. He has to be."

"Oh, come on, Leo . . ." She had to get him out of that damned depression.

"I haven't told you everything." He tightened the scarf at his throat, sealing out the cold as a gust of wind set up a miniature whirlwind of flakes around their legs. "When I got through talking to Anson, I called Tom Massey in Technical Services. He owes me a few. I told him I was working on the Margolis surveillance for Abrams and what was the way-in we used on his apartment, technically."

"But you said it was a phone bug. You knew that. You bypassed it, didn't you?"

"I fixed the phone bug, yes, so he could call in an
139

emergency. Seems my idea of technique went out with the Ark. Massey says the phone was a decoy; it was there to be found. The real tap was a sound sensor located on the wall. It doesn't respond to a sweep so I had no hope of finding it. They're used in foreign embassies. Foolproof, Massey says. Last Friday, when Walt called, every word he spoke went down on record. Along with my replies."

"Did you say anything?" She caught at her throat.

"I didn't have to say much. Abrams has had me leaning on Walt for months. He called me again only last week and said to chase Walt some more, on a personal level. And I still didn't make the connection. Jesus—the first Matrix man we finger and I've been helping him flush out anyone on his tail." He rubbed snow from his brow with the back of his glove. "That call blew my part, Lee. If they had any doubts, they won't after Walt's funeral. Petersen and Abrams were there. They saw me with Anson."

He got up and paced away, turned and paced back, banging his hands to restore circulation. "I'd better be going, Lee."

She could think of nothing to say. In her mind's eye she saw the figure of the man crucified under the blasted door at the Statler. "You'll be all right, won't you? You want me to . . . ?"

"Stay close to Anson." He dropped his hands on her shoulders and stared searchingly into her face. "You won't find that too disagreeable, now will you?"

She blushed. "Leo, I . . ."

"I know," he said. He tried for a grin but it froze at birth. "Some things are better left unsaid. Now go."

He brushed his glove along her cheek and plowed off through the snow toward the creek.

TUESDAY: 0930—PETERSEN

Donald Petersen slipped a number 3 iron from the bag strapped to his bright yellow golf cart and made three exploratory swings. He had fallen short of the dogleg turn by thirty yards, and a belt of trees now lay between his ball and an approach shot to the green. Milton Abrams watched him coolly from a relaxed sprawl on the driving seat. He was a par golfer on this course and was already six strokes up on

140

his partner. He said evenly, "You're not giving yourself a chance there, Don. I'd go up an iron."

"Save it!" Petersen snapped irritably. It was not in his character to accept the possibility of defeat, and he considered it personally demeaning to lose to an inferior. He chided himself again for allowing Abrams to talk him into meeting here at all. The fellow never missed an opportunity to go one up. He fell into his stance, shuffled his feet to achieve perfect balance and direction. Left elbow straight this time. *Straight*. He brought the clubface slowly to the ball. It would have to be high and to the right to clear those trees and win enough ground to guarantee his approach shot's reaching the green. Easy. Backswing. Now!

The ball exploded from a nest of snow and grass and mud, rose like a lark and curled left, left, left. Petersen unwound the club from his follow-through and hammered it into the snow. "The devil fuck it," he swore. Abrams watched the ball disappear into a tree and rattle through its branches to the leaf-strewn ground inside the copse. He swung his legs behind the driving wheel and waited for Petersen to join him. The cart wobbled across the fairway and came to a halt under the offending tree. Petersen looked at the thickly growing young saplings and the piled leaves. "I'll take a new ball," he said flatly.

"Er—O.K., Don. Where d'you want to drop it? Here?"

Petersen dug a ball from the side pocket of his bag. "You think I'm going to drop it in this, you can go fuck yourself. Anyway, it's quiet here. Let's talk." He took a flat case from the inside pocket of his thick padded jacket and carefully selected a cigar. Abrams watched him but was pointedly ignored.

"What've we got here now?" Petersen said at last, his cigar billowing its grandeur in Abrams's face.

"A mess, to call it what it is," Abrams retorted coldly. "We should have gotten the Faber situation right the first time, and that Margolis sanction was stupid. Whoever . . ."

Petersen stared him hard in the face. "The stupidity, as you call it, was mine. The rank bad judgment that made it necessary was yours."

"I had Margolis . . ."

"Walking all over you," Petersen flared. "My God, man, what does it take nowadays to guarantee efficiency in this organization? I told you the first time you reported Margolis that I wanted him bottled up. Tight."

"I had him bottled. And tight. I knew everything he touched: every file, every transcript, every microfilm. At least give me credit for that. There was no call to . . ."

"He was within an ace of blowing the whole thing sky-high." Petersen leaned on every word.

"We don't know that."

"*I* know that."

Abrams held his breath. "If you had information I didn't know about . . ."

"I had the common intelligence," Petersen spat, "to do what you should have seen to yourself. I had him bugged. He made a call on Friday that left nothing to the imagination. There was a simple choice. Ride it out and hope—or kill him."

Abrams blew on his hands to warm them. He never wore gloves, even the grip glove. "I still say it was a mistake—in the context of the Company, if nothing else. It'll take a hell of a lot of bullshit to avoid an investigation."

"Leave that problem to me."

"O.K. What happens over the Nixon thing?"

Petersen contemplated the new ball he had taken from the bag. He turned it in his fingers, looked up and measured the fairway against the fluttering flag a hundred yards away on the green. He stepped out of the cart, drew back his arm and hurled the ball high in the air. It fell in a perfect position on a direct line with the flag. He took the cigar from his mouth and gloated crookedly at Abrams.

"That O.K. with you, Milt?"

Abrams blew a ghost of frosted breath. "Yeah. I guess that'll do fine, Don."

Petersen slipped back into the cart. "This Nixon deal needs a lot of thought."

"Hey, just a minute, Don." Abrams covered his alarm with brash humor. "You're not thinking we take *him* out?"

"I said *thought*." Petersen blew on the end of his cigar until it glowed. "We've spent too much time on this project to blow it now. We watched that security vault in Atlanta for two years. Two years, and we still came away empty-handed. If we'd got organized when I said so—when we canceled out the guy who locked that goddamn merchandise away and picked up his papers . . ." He paused. "You have those papers safe?"

Abrams nodded.

Petersen spat into the snow. "I told Arizona years ago he should've given me a free hand with that bastard Anson. If anyone started this it was him."

Abrams lost some of the glow in his lamp tan. "You can't be sure of that. That's a one-in-fifty longshot."

Petersen glared at him. "Why should you care?"

"His son came to my office."

"He did what?"

Abrams cleared his throat nervously. "It was about Margolis. He wanted the Company to run an autopsy."

"Mother of Christ!"

"He just happened along, Don. There's no connection. Believe me, no connection. He just . . ."

"And what the hell were you doing keeping that information to yourself? Jesus! Anson's son and there's no connection, he says. What the hell was Margolis doing those last coupla days?"

The wind whirled at them across the fairway and tore burning ash from Petersen's cigar. It whipped across Abrams's face. "He was at Justice first, then he drove over to Allentown; a retirement complex. Talked with a guy called Kaplan."

"Why?"

"Seemed to be running off on a tangent. At Justice he went over the Jaworski period on Watergate. You know, the attempt to subpoena the Nixon tapes. He pinned down one particular day; April 14, 1973. It's all on paper, you want to see?"

Petersen studied the flag on the faraway green with the practiced eye of the golfer who knows his limitations. "What was on the tape?"

"He didn't want the tape. It was a White House three-way conversation: Nixon, Haldeman, Ehrlichman. Nothing that connects with this, though. That part's all on public record."

"Tell me about Kaplan."

"He worked around Justice. Came into Watergate when the cover-up started. He's a technician."

"Tapes?" Petersen had closed his eyes.

Abrams caught his breath in his teeth. "Yeah, tapes."

A cart rattled out of the trees far ahead of them and plowed across the fairway and through a dip in the rolling rough. Its tracks lay black in its wake. Petersen spoke so softly Abrams had to bend his head to catch the words.

"Margolis goes looking for tapes and talks to a tape technician who played Watergate. The Atlanta vault gives up a tape. Nixon hits Bradley with a tape." He swiveled in his seat. "You want to run that scenario through again?"

"The tape Margolis looked at was public record," Abrams protested. "Nixon, Haldeman, Ehr . . ."

"What do you use for a brain, Milt? Jello? An experienced Company officer goes looking at a Nixon tape that everyone knows about. Why?" He sucked on the cigar. "Because the timing of the conversation was important, maybe. Or it told him where certain people were. Or . . ." The cigar billowed smoke. "Or he had an idea that something else should be on the tape. Something that went before or after. Something that wasn't scheduled. So . . . what do we have? Proposition: Nixon has a piece of tape carrying a conversation about the Kennedy thing and somebody used Margolis to check it out." He turned away to stare as the wind whistled through the trees, dislodging snow from the lower branches. "What's your reading, Milt?"

"I don't buy it. The Nixon tapes must have been played a million times. And on the Kennedy thing . . . the House Assassinations Committee sat for three years without coming up with one name to lock into their conspiracy theory. The civil hearing before Sirica in '77, nothing. A lot of speculation and no proof. Bradley's clean on that side."

Petersen leaned into the corner of the cart and eyed him with chilling objectivity. "Is he? I hope your confidence keeps you warm, Milt. Nixon wasn't playing when he hit Bradley with that story of his. A lot of technique went into that approach. A lot of resources. That's why LaCroix and I decided to hit back the way we did; challenge the bastard, face him out. That's why the election rumor went the rounds in Washington. We put it there."

"Nixon'll deny it," snapped Abrams, clutching at a winning point.

"Sure he will," Petersen breathed complacently. "But I'm ready to put a lot of money on the fact that Nixon is being handled by the same guy who used Margolis. And my money says he'll push Nixon all the way down the line. He's playing for keeps. He's got style, too, whoever he is." He pulled himself into an upright position in the seat. "There're too many loose ends in this. I don't like it. They need tying down."

"I don't see that . . ."

"Margolis was a loose end, Milt."

Abrams flexed his fingers into a fist. They were beginning to feel the chill. "You want to put that into plain language, Don?"

"In plain language," Petersen's breath steamed in the freezing air. "You seal off all unproductive channels. Perma-

144

ently." He watched the effect of his words on the younger man's face.

"I thought the idea was to keep the whole thing clean. No wet jobs."

"Politician's crap. You win or you lose." The blue cigar smoke laid trails across Abrams's eyes. "We're already wet; wringing wet. Faber. Margolis. That's why we can't afford any mistakes. We need follow-through. Margolis had a daughter. He might've talked to her; sent her papers. How can we be sure? And this guy who was at Justice; Kaplan. More loose ends, Milt. They need tying. And Anson's son. The guy who just happened along. I don't want that name cropping up on my bulletin board again, O.K.?"

Abrams tried to mirror his chief's sarcasm. "You want me to start a pogrom, Don? Anyone Margolis talked to over the age of twelve?"

Petersen clamped the cigar in his mouth and swung to the ground. He selected a number 3 iron from his bag and made a couple of practice sweeps. Abrams got out to join him. Petersen addressed the ball, cigar jumping in his lips as he psyched himself for the shot. He slicked into his stance, eye on the ball.

"Arizona can be left to handle Bradley...me and Arizona. But first we need to know the score. The *real* score." He raised his face. "Four strokes ahead, aren't you?"

"Six—up to that slice you made back there. You owe me a stroke."

Petersen's teeth showed yellow. He froze, gauged the distance one last time, coiled into his backswing, poised and brought the club down in a perfectly timed stroke. They both saw the puff of snow where the ball landed. "Ten feet from the pin? Would you say ten feet?" Petersen was delighted.

"Maybe ten. More likely fifteen, twenty," growled Abrams. He locked into his position, raised the club, uncoiled and ...

"Something else, Milt."

Abrams's ball scythed low to the right and cracked in among the black trees. He snapped his teeth shut on the oath that rose instinctively to his tongue.

"Bad luck." Petersen grinned wolfishly. "That was bad luck."

"You said there was something else."

Petersen strolled back to the cart and got in. He waited for Abrams to join him. "Yeah. That call Margolis made the night before we ... before he died. I want to know how deep they were playing, Margolis and his little friend. Listen to the tape of the call."

"You recognize him?"

Petersen laughed. He set the cart in motion. "You know the last place you look to find a rotten smell? Under your nose, partner. Slap bang under your goddamn nose."

TUESDAY: 1130—ANSON

Anson put down the phone on Tom Pringle. It had been an unsatisfactory conversation. Pringle laid claim to being a lifelong friend of John Roper Anson but it turned out to be a friendship that lay no deeper than any lawyer-client relationship. Pringle had been patently confused by Anson's line of questions about his father's political affiliations and beliefs. The old man had none, the lawyer insisted. Diplomacy was not just his trade, it was the hallmark of his character. He had served his country on the basis of constitutional ethic, not party politics.

The boxlike office at State offered no source of inspiration. He brooded. The file on John Roper at Hutton's Farm was irrelevant; another example of Walt's capacity for woolgathering. Or was its existence implication enough?

Anson pulled on his coat and went down to the car. The wind bit into him like a circular saw as he walked the lines of the parking lot and he ran the last twenty yards to the Porsche. He headed across town.

He parked a block down from the apartment house and trudged, head down, into the flying snow. What he could use right now was the company of a long pale J & B and a warm bed, but the image shattered on further reflection. The warm bed would lead inevitably to a hot Grazia, a long night and one giant step nearer captivity. Christ, he had to get her out of there. The thought of them entwined in John Roper's bed was more than he could deal with on an empty stomach.

He hammered on Buffalo Morgan's blistered door and there was a scutter of sound from the landing above and a plaintive mewing. The kitten, more raddled and torn even than on their first meeting, jinked nimbly down the stairs and sat a cautious two yards from his toecaps.

"Louie!"

Buffalo Morgan was a beaming blaze of tropical color. His bald head projected from a robe that fell clean to the ground, hiding his feet. It had a bright saffron background overprinted with white magnolias and generous bottle-green leaves. His initials were woven over the pocket in spidery script. He looked down at the kitten, which edged a foot nearer the door in expectation of attention. He bent down and scooped it up.

"You made it with the cat, huh?" He held the scruffy animal as if it were a child. "Good cat. Good cat." He looked up at his visitor with a start. "Hey, come on in here, son. Here I am, treating you like some doorstep salesman. Come on in."

The apartment required only a roped canvas ring to complete it. On the floor below the window lay barbells and weights and a half dozen Indian clubs of varying sizes. At one side of the room, a rowing machine was bolted to the floor and opposite it was a wall-mounted, spring-loaded developer of the kind that guaranteed no one would ever again kick sand in your face. The walls were littered with framed photographs of pugilists frozen in classic aggressive poses and posters advertising main events and supporting bouts across the country, but Buffalo's name seemed to figure in none of them.

The old man tickled the kitten behind the ears. He gestured to an array of bottled soft drinks on a table by the window. "Help yourself, Louie."

Anson poured a thick orange liquid, tasted it, shuddered as its sugar-free syrup rolled into his digestive system, and set the glass down on the table.

"Will you look at this?" The kitten was sprawled in Buffalo's arms, purring like an air-conditioner. "This is a first, Louie. You got good vibes. This here cat ain't no social climber, lemme tell you. Never crossed that threshold in all the time I bin feeding it. Leave the chow outside and he comes and eats or he don't eat. Independent, see? That's his style."

He held the cat at arm's length. Anson took the animal, one-handed. His finger swung the small brass identification tube hooked on the kitten's collar. "You said Walt didn't have a name for the cat, right?"

"Name?" Buffalo screwed up his eyes. "Right. Never had no name. Walt had this idea cats were special, see? Don't belong to no one in particular, you get my meaning. Walt was big on cats." He warmed to his subject. "He gave me this book once. Cats, it was about. Just cats. And emperors and stuff. I didn't read much. I'm not much on books."

Anson wasn't listening. Walt's library at Hutton's Farm. Shelves of books. Roman history, politics, philosophy, war.

Rome. In the little park he'd passed near the Spanish Steps on his way to the embassy each morning there was a statue of a woman holding some kind of broken sceptre. She had a cat at her feet. The old Roman symbol of liberty, the enemy of restraint.

"Why would Walt give it a name tag if it didn't have a name?" he asked.

He took the slim cartridge in his fingers, felt it move. It was in two parts; meant to unscrew. He unrolled the two ends.

The slim scrap of paper was still clean. New. He handed the kitten to Buffalo and took the paper to the table. He sat down; unrolled it carefully. The names and numbers were written with a fine cartographer's pen. Bradley. Petersen. Clegg. Colborne. Torrance. Denton. Sanforth. Keale. Engstrom. Bolton. Halliwell. Kragen. Polticians, administrators, businessmen, academics, writers. Big men in their fields, all of them. No first names. No initials. No addresses.

Below, another list:

H 127

CWC 301

S 24

It ran on to the back of the paper. In the bottom right hand corner was a scrawled cross and a question mark. And one word.

Nixon?

Another question mark.

"What you got there, son?" Buffalo Morgan peered over Anson's shoulder.

He held it up to him. "Mean anything to you?"

The old man studied it, his lips moving perceptibly. He shook his head. "Beats me. That belong to Walt, you reckon?"

Anson slipped his notebook from an inner pocket and copied the names, numbers and symbols. He furled the scrap of paper again and screwed it back into the kitten's identity cartridge.

He stood up. "A favor, Buffalo. If anyone asks—anyone at all—you didn't see this, okay?"

Morgan's face was a punchball of disingenuity. "What'd I see, Louie? I see the cat come for his chow. That's all I see."

Anson put a hand on the wide floppy shoulder. "Not even

148

that, Buff. You never heard of the cat. Walt never had a cat. He hated cats."

Morgan's jaw dropped, then closed tight, giving birth to a slow-burning smile of recognition. "Sure, he hated cats. Walt climbed walls to get away from cats."

Anson had gone to the door and Morgan shuffled after him. "You going son? You only just got here."

"Do me another favor?" Anson looked down at the wretched animal in Buffalo Morgan's arms.

"You just name it."

"Pour that cat a bowl of cream, will you? Put it on my tab."

TUESDAY: 2100—McCULLEN

Leo McCullen rolled a sheet of plain notepaper into the Olivetti portable and in the top right-hand corner typed the date, the time and his initials.

He had spent the whole day sifting through his own files, long-dead documents, reports, notes and clippings, looking for anything that might link him and Walt Margolis with Lucas Garfield. In the end he piled all of them into a box, soaked it with kerosene and burned it in the backyard barbecue pit. He scattered the ashes on the snow-covered rose beds.

He sipped the scalding coffee, perched the mug on top of the bureau and massaged the back of his neck. "O.K. Here we go," he told the typewriter.

"First," he wrote, "the bad news. My cover is blown. On two counts. One, some form of infinity transmitter was wired, without my knowledge, in Margolis's apartment. On Friday night—it must have been an emergency—Walt called me. Don't blame him for breaking silence; it should have been safe."

McCullen raised the typewriter bar and read what he had written. He underscored the word "should."

"The call was tapped through the infinity transmitter and presumably taped.

"Two, in a conversation with Harry Anson, I learned that Milton Abrams met with him at Langley Sunday morning and fed him a line about Margolis that was designed to allay any suspicions he might have about the old man's death. It was a cover-up, and a pretty desperate one at that. Abrams and

149

Petersen were at Margolis's funeral at Rock Creek yesterday. They weren't there to pay their respects. I believe they wanted to see if I would be there. I was. That clinched something for them.

"Take a deep breath. Abrams—I'm not sure about Petersen yet—is linked in some way with Margolis's death. This being so, we have our first Matrix link with the Company. That's my reading of it, anyway.

"This evening, I heard that Alex Kaplan, who used to work for Justice before he retired, had been killed in what they're calling 'a domestic accident.' A power drill he was using suddenly got live. Accidents happen—except that it comes five days after Walt Margolis drove out to see him in Allentown to talk about the Watergate tapes. Kaplan, you'll remember, made some kind of a technical appraisal of the tapes in 1973. Quite coincidentally, two Langley veterans also died today. 'Naturally.' George Beattie, who worked with Walt's Warren Commission liaison team, and Clyde Landstrom, a voice pattern expert living in Montreal. Walt called both of them a couple of times last week. He told me.

"Natural causes, of course. So clean, even the insurance companies will pay up. If all this sounds like the preliminary to a paranoiac brainstorm let me remind you what happened to Rose Cheramie. Rose worked with Jack Ruby and had stated countless times under questioning that the Kennedy killing "was common knowledge" before it happened. She said she recognized Oswald. Rose Cheramie was killed in a hit and run in 1965. And Dorothy Kilgallen, too—the only reporter to get an interview with Jack Ruby. She claimed she had enough to blow the whole thing wide open but she never got the chance. She was found dead: barbiturate poisoning. There were others we both know: Gary Underhill, a Company man, was shot through the head. Karen Kupcinet, a friend of Ruby's, was found murdered. One hundred and twelve other possible witnesses never got the chance to testify in the months after Dallas. They all died, 116 of them. I'm not telling you something you don't know, just reminding you of history we can't afford to forget.

"I won't bore you with any more of this, except to say that if I'm right and Abrams is mixed up in the Margolis killing, then he was also involved in the hit on Faber and, possibly, the deaths of Beattie and Landstrom and Kaplan. If I'm right, it's only a matter of time before another name is added to the list: mine."

He sipped his coffee. It was not what might be termed a
150

dispassionate report, but there was no reason to make Garfield read between the lines. There might not be another chance. Anyway, it was therapy. He began to type again.

"I suggest I drop out of the picture right away. Any connection I may now have with Anson can only endanger him. The girl is clean and has established rapport. I've talked with her and instructed her to stay with him.

"That's all. I have good reason, I'm sure you understand, for not trusting the phone anymore. If you wish, contact me through the girl. We have an exchange system worked out—*if it is vital.* I have destroyed all my documents. There is nothing that could form a chain.

"Whatever you decide I'll go along with."

He pulled the sheet from the typewriter and, without reading it, folded it and sealed the envelope. He typed Garfield's private address. He slipped from the house and dropped it into the box at the end of the street.

He turned back to the house along the deserted street, his shoes squelching in the gray slush of the sidewalk. He reached for a cigar and lit it, drew deeply on the smoke, felt its stimulus, comforting. He was twenty yards from the house before he saw the figure on the porch. A boost of adrenaline tightened his muscles. Nowhere to go now. Keep moving. The figure turned as he reached the pathway. "Is that you, Leo?" Harry Anson peered out at him. "Look, I have to talk to you."

Leo McCullen's den was as masculine as a truck driver's cab, as idiosyncratic as an anchorite's cave and as determinedly misogynistic as a Mount Athos cell. The rich odor of his cigars impregnated the fabric of chairs and carpet, heavy as incense and, to sensitive nostrils, vaguely nauseating. Stuffed heads of antelope, buck, bear and wildcat grinned from a ghoulish frieze, their teeth yellow, eyes button-black, dust in their hair. A jagged stump of wood hung from a bracket between an American red fox and a bay lynx. Burned into it with a hot iron were the words "Antwerp. SS. *Vienna.* Struck by lightning, June 1, 1914."

McCullen fixed drinks and Anson ran his eyes over the studied clutter of the room. A framed newspaper clipping of two unrecognizable people posing beside a huge conger eel hoisted on a crane; a rack lined with black and silver Turkish pipes, an old English green briar and a Dutch meerschaum with the face of Van Dyck; tattered, but genuine, posters from Pamplona, a good twenty years old; a surgeon's glass

151

model of an eye; three ancient Mannlicher pistols coated with grease in a box lined with faded red velvet. Most interesting of all, a framed hand-lettered copy of the "Desiderata" with a note scrawled at the bottom in red ink: "From Lee. With thoughts."

"... speak your truth quietly and clearly and listen to others, even the dull and ignorant; they too have their story ... keep peace with your soul ... be careful ..."

For no reason he could understand, Anson looked away guiltily as McCullen came into the room with a tray and picked up the first thing that his hand chanced to fall on.

"Scrimshaw," said McCullen.

Anson was holding a tooth some seven inches long and etched with a whaling scene in black filigree.

McCullen put down the tray. "Prisoners made them in England and France during the Napoleonic wars. Scratched their pictures on a whale's tooth. Nowadays, no whales, no romantic prisoners, but they still keep turning up. Quite an industry. That one's genuine."

Anson weighed it in his hand and replaced it carefully.

"Quite a den, Leo," he said.

"Yeah. You ever read Huysmans? No? Neither did I till some guy told me this room looked like it came out of one of his books. I read it. *Au Rebours.*" He splashed bourbon into a glass with the caution of the infrequent drinker. "This guy builds a house like you've never seen. Each room to suit a different mood. One like a church with pulpit, stalls, what have you; another draped in black like a funeral parlor; another like a ship's cabin. His name was Des Essenties. He was off his head. I got the message."

Anson took the glass and set it down on the window ledge. For a moment the two men regarded each other like chess players approaching a possible stalemate, each waiting for the other to decide whether the game should be artificially prolonged or brought to an end.

McCullen shrugged. "O.K., Harry. It's late. You haven't come by to watch the midnight movie."

"I should have called ...," Anson began.

McCullen cut him off with a tight humorless smile. "What is it?" Then, almost as an afterthought, "Anyone see you come here? Anyone know you came?"

"No, not that I know of. Why? Aren't you allowed visitors?"

McCullen disregarded the barb and dropped into a chair,

eyes half-closed, drink cupped in both hands. He flapped a hand wearily. "So, go on."

"I've got some more questions. You said later, remember? Maybe I should be asking them somewhere else."

McCullen shook his head. "If you thought that, you wouldn't be here." He jerked his head at the frame behind Anson. "I saw you reading it. 'Exercise caution in your business affairs, for the world is full of trickery.' That's what it says. That why you're here?"

Anson retrieved his glass and took a long slug of Old Granddad, McCullen hadn't touched his.

"Yes. Maybe it is. For one thing, I want you to tell me what these names do for you: Bradley, Petersen, Clegg, Colborne, Torrance. There are more."

McCullen shrugged, hiding a stab of interest. "Bradley everybody knows. Petersen, director at Langley. The rest . . . Isn't Torrance something in steel? The rest, well . . ."

"Not *who* they are, Leo. What do they mean together? Some of the names on the list, Walt Margolis also had files on. He had a file on my father. Why? And why Nixon scrawled on the bottom of a piece of paper? Bradley—Nixon. You read those rumors about Nixon?"

"Eyewash. He's said he'll deny it publicly. Anyway, what the hell is this 'list' you keep talking about?"

"It was inside a cat's collar. Friend of Walt Margolis's."

"A cat?"

"Cat's collar. In ancient Rome the cat was a symbol of liberty. The goddess of liberty was always shown holding a cup in one hand, a broken sceptre in the other and with a cat at her feet. Quote: 'No animal is so great an enemy to all constraint as a cat.' End quote."

McCullen shook his head. "Ancient Rome, cat's collars . . ."

"Margolis had something he wanted to hide. Something he knew people would move heaven and earth to get. He knew when they came looking they'd turn over everything till they found it. The cat was never in his apartment, but it was always around where he could find it."

McCullen sat upright. He placed the glass, still untouched, between his feet and gazed at Anson.

"You're asking *me* to make sense of all that?"

"Don't fence, Leo, for chrissake. Don't give me any more of that." Anson slammed down the Old Granddad. "Half of what you know is roughly twice what I'm being allowed to find out. Don't you think I can see that? Get me straight. I don't care about Company infighting. I don't care about lists and you can keep Walt Margolis's secrets. But I do care about finding my father's name in all this crap. So if you know why, level with me. Please. Just on that score. Then I'll go away and you can get on with the war."

Leo McCullen grunted out of his chair and contemplated the artificial whiskers of a stuffed gray-sided jackrabbit. He loosened the collar of his shirt and massaged his neck.

"Harry, I'm not trying to be smart. I'm not even sure I have the *right* to be smart anymore."

"You're smart enough to make some pretty good guesses," persisted Anson.

McCullen shook his head. He saw Anson's jaw muscles tighten. "O.K., Harry. Yes, there *is* something going on. Company infighting you called it. That'll do. You're right to keep out of it. At Langley they play with lasers, not paper darts. As for your father, maybe he *was* involved in something. I just don't know. Does it matter now? He's dead. Let him rest in peace."

Anson's face was a mask. "We didn't have much contact, John Roper and I. Distance, work—the usual excuses. Maybe I never knew him at all, Leo. But I want to know him now."

McCullen tested the line for breaking strength and put the last of the bait on the hook. "Your father's reputation is intact. Keep it that way."

The leather-smocked figure swung back on hinged hips and crashed a tiny mallet against the brass bell. Leo McCullen eyed the ancient Bavarian clock from the depths of the chair in which he had been drifting on the edge of sleep. He was alone. Anson had left half an hour ago, his mind questing and braced for action. It had been a lousy trick to pull, but Garfield's last instruction had been to set him on course. Anson was now on course.

McCullen's mouth tasted of tar paper; he realized he had drunk a full glass of bourbon, a normal month's consumption. He didn't drink for pleasure. He ran tongue over teeth, grimacing at the coating that had formed between them, and walked to the kitchen. Tomorrow he would drive out to Kentucky. Check in somewhere quiet. Wait till Garfield, in his infinite wisdom, decided his next step. He splashed a full glass of soda water. No, not Kentucky, New Mexico. That's what he needed right now.

154

Like a hole in the head.

He swished the empty glass under the tap. For the first time in a year he thought, in a purely domestic sense, of his wife. Ex-wife. Ex marks the error. Unwashed glasses used to drive her wild. Full ashtrays, clothes left draped over chairs, loose change scattered on dressing tables. He reached for the drying towel.

A puff of air bunched the venetian blind above the kitchen sink as if a poking finger had jabbed at it through the glass from outside. He started to dry the glass, but his hand traveled no distance. The glass toppled from his hand and smashed to the floor.

Leo McCullen never heard it break.

TUESDAY: 2345—GARFIELD

Garfield lunged into the book-lined room and slammed the door on the driving snow. He spared Fletcher and Goldman a brittle flicker of greeting and perched on the edge of his customary chair, huddled behind the Persian lamb collar of his black coat, gloved hands deep in his pockets.

He said to Fletcher, "What's so important it couldn't wait till morning? You look terrible."

Fletcher's mouth angled at one corner. "I'll survive. Will you?"

Garfield raised an eyebrow quizzically. "I take it that's meant as a shaft of your celebrated idiosyntaxery, is it?" Fletcher bowed his head. Garfield sighed. "You have the air of men who feel they should be washing their hands."

Goldman said, "What're you talking about, Luke?"

"Pontius Pilate," Fletcher murmured softly. "He knows why we're here."

"Well, who's for crucifixion, Fred?" Garfield tried a smile, but his bloodless cheeks offered no cooperation; only his mouth twisted. He felt cold inside and inexpressibly old.

Goldman scraped back his chair, stood up and let his weight fall forward on his hands. "I called this meeting, Luke. Not Fletch. He just agreed to go along with it."

"This isn't a seminary for girls of slender means, Fred," Garfield chided. "You don't have to excuse Fletch. He'll defend himself if he thinks it's necessary."

Goldman threw his hands in the air in a passionate gesture of resignation and turned to Fletcher in angry appeal. "Jesus,

Fletch! Jesus!" He threw himself back into the chair. "What the hell am I supposed to say to that?"

"Don't you think we should get down to what this meeting is all about, Fred?" Garfield remonstrated mildly.

"That's what this fucking meeting *is* about, Luke! It's about the way you run the store. It's about the way you play it so close to your goddamned chest me and Fletch are forced to double-guess you all the way. It's the way you just played your goddamned entrance—as though you're here on sufferance."

"Well." Garfield disinterred his pipe from a coat pocket and lit the blackened tobacco. "You seem to have it all worked out. You want to go into detail?"

"Just watch me . . . ," Goldman began but Fletcher touched his shoulder paternally.

"Easy, Fred. Let's not go off half-cocked." He dropped a gloved hand to the table. "Luke?" He paused, studying the older man's face intently. "How important are we to you?"

"That's a damn fool question. You know the answer to that."

"Oh, sure . . . ," began Goldman.

Again, Fletcher touched his shoulder, this time with firmness. "Good. As I understand it when you recruited me, our brief was to monitor all undercover agencies and contain them within the limits of their given codes. No more Edgar Hoover-type machinations at FBI. No more invisible government status at CIA. No more dirty tricks specialists blowing up foreign heads of state because some joker somewhere decided it was the thing to do. Right, so far?"

Garfield took his pipe from his teeth. "This recitation going to last long?"

Fletcher's smile was ice-capped. "Bear with me, Luke, there's a good fellow." The condescension was perfectly timed. Garfield clamped his teeth savagely on the pipe stem.

"The whole idea was naive. Crazy—but it works. Three Men in a Boat—wasn't that Kissinger's expression? Three men they wanted—three men they got. Small is beautiful; small is secure. You pulled me in because a deputy director of the National Security Agency has to be a useful ally. I came equipped with extra muscle. Besides, I'm clean and that's no small miracle these days. Then you looked for Number Three. More difficult than you thought. No one in the CIA you could trust. Someone who had the rank, a clean bill of health and hadn't gotten himself tarnished between Bay of Pigs and Watergate. So Langley was out, and so was

FBI and the Secret Service and a thousand elected law officers. Then you found Alfred Goldman. The new director of Army Intelligence. You saw a lot of yourself in Fred."

Garfield's smile was lazy but acquiescent.

Fletcher sighed. "Together, you said, we'd have total authority, the right to dip into the barrel at any point, any level. We had a need-to-know rating that was universal and infinite. Since we were both active in the security community, me and Fred, you elected to build and run your own working structure underground. So, occasionally, we've asked you questions. Occasionally we've gotten nosy—but all things considered, we gave you free range, Luke. Free range."

He massaged his gloved hands together painfully.

"Now, we're not stupid, Luke. Or blind. We recognized right off that you'd have to build that organization at active service level . . . street level . . . because that's where information breaks and that's where it has to be checked. We knew you'd have to recruit men in the Company, in the Bureau— yes, even in Fred's province and my own. We also knew that was dangerous. An agent who owes his allegiance to one outfit and moonlights parttime for another is never going to be 100 percent horn-blowing Archangel Gabriel. That was the extreme of our concern: that the Cleaners might get themselves sold out one day by one of your doubles going for the triple."

Garfield snapped his ancient Zippo to the pipe bowl. "You think I've slipped up?"

"Slipped *up?*" snorted Goldman.

"Like I said, Luke," Fletcher droned on, "we were concerned. You appointed your street-level agents and you hoped they'd play it straight. Well, we decided between us that was too naive for comfort. You have no resources to check out your bets. We had. We used them."

Garfield said coldly, "Like Fred's surveillance on Walt Margolis?"

Fletcher nodded. "Only because we came on Margolis by chance, sniffing around in the old conspiracy trash can. He made himself too obvious to ignore. You should've told us he was one of yours."

"Pity your interest didn't keep him alive." Sarcastically.

"I called it off when Margolis figured the tail," Goldman interrupted. "When you *told* me he'd figured the tail, Luke."

"So?" Garfield pulled out his fob watch.

"You took Margolis's death without a murmur, Luke," Fletcher hissed. "No explanation. You found him, used him, let him die. No—wait a minute!" He raised a hand to quell Garfield's protest. "Then you calmly told us you'd dropped another man into his shoes." His lips twisted. "The son of an old friend, as I recall. All right—tell him, Fred."

Goldman's teeth flashed in a vicious parody of amusement. "McCullen is dead. Killed. Murdered."

Garfield's face revealed nothing. He took the pipe from his mouth and nursed it in both hands. "McCullen?"

"We have our uses," said Fletcher coldly.

"In his own home. A .22, high-velocity, front of the head."

"Who told you?" Garfield's voice was level, unruffled.

"No one told me," snarled Goldman. "You didn't listen to a word Fletch was saying, did you? We ran a tail on Margolis, and Margolis gave us McCullen. We've been on him for five days. I had a stake out down from his house. They decided to take a look."

Garfield flamed the tobacco again.

"You have nothing to say, Luke?" asked Fletcher.

"Should I?"

"All right. You want to know who was with McCullen before he died?"

"You're at the wheel, Fletch."

"Young man. Caucasian. Six feet. 190 pounds. European clothes. Drives a Porsche, green, Washington plates. Ring any bells?"

"I know a lot of people, Fletch."

"Hah!" Goldman exploded again. "A lot of people! That's the question, Luke. Who *don't* you know?"

"You're making this very difficult, Luke."

"And you make it remarkably boring, Fletch," said Garfield. "Have you considered the possibility of getting to the point?"

"Very well. As I've said, Luke—we do have resources. Today they paid off and we're not sure anymore what to do about you. The young man at McCullen's, we discover, is Harold Roper Anson. Diplomat. Arrived in Washington last week from Rome. Son of the late John Roper Anson. Anson was scheduled to fly back to Rome Sunday morning. He didn't. The Army attaché at the embassy in Rome says he's been detached temporarily to unspecified duty at State. Someone in Washington is pulling strings."

"To quote you," Goldman cut in, "you put another man into Margolis's shoes. The son of an old friend. A man who coincidentally was the last to talk to a senior CIA administra-

158

tor before he died with a .22 high-velocity slug in his head." `

"And that tells you what?"

"That tells us every fucking thing!" stormed Goldman.

"Does it, indeed?" Garfield's face was a mask. He settled back comfortably in the severe wooden chair. "I think you're both to be congratulated," he looked from one to the other, his face relaxed. "I recruited you because you were the best. And from the best you get the best of all worlds—good and bad, useful and obstructive." He paused. "Conviction and well-intentioned stupidity." He watched their faces. "I've never pretended the brief we were given as a committee was orthodox or simple to apply. It isn't. Nor is it something as clear-cut and apple-pie-American as the Presidency might want to believe. We're watchdogs, yes. But as often as we've vetoed undercover exercises—in the name of moral decency and the rest of it—we've also encouraged others that raised the same kind of ethical stink in our noses. Tell me why?" He looked at them again in turn, but they said nothing.

"Because," he said softly, his elbows on the table, "when the chips are down and we've got nothing left to play, the last call is expediency. The security and well-being of the majority."

"The majority, in this case, being defined by you," Goldman snarled.

"You accepted my word, a few days ago, that Bradley had to be stopped. You showed the loyalty I've expected of you." He puffed at the pipe and raised a dense cloud of smoke. "I imagine you now think you hold a monopoly on moral indignation. Don't fool yourselves that much. You'll regret it." He placed the smoking pipe on the table in front of him. "I didn't know about Leo and I'm glad you mounted that tail on him, Fred, but I'd like to know the purpose of it if it wasn't to protect him. No—" He waved Goldman into silence. "No accusations. He's dead. Neither of us can do anything about that. Just give me credit for having feelings. I liked Leo. Liked him a lot. He would've sat where you're sitting some day. I was proud to find him; I had a lot of faith in him. . . ."

"You'll presumably accept responsibility, then, for the fact he was uncovered and killed?" grated Fletcher. "I go back to what I said. You had no right to leave us in the dark. You had a responsibility to . . ."

"That's enough, Fletch!" Garfield's glare was a high-

159

tension warning. He collected himself. "You've made your point. I respect your honesty. Well, then—I'd better take you completely into my confidence, hadn't I?"

WEDNESDAY: 0045—ANSON

It was a quarter to one in the morning when Anson crossed into Virginia. By the time he reached the Margolis house, he figured, it would be too late to convince a well-brought-up young woman that his intentions were purely academic. If he could have convinced himself, it would have helped.

When he left McCullen, Anson had driven back to the apartment. He had even got as far as ringing for the elevator, but then Grazia came out of the back of his head, rattling chains and handcuffs. The elevator doors opened, he went in, turned, came out and pushed the indicator for the penthouse floor. Then he left. It was a little like playing hooky from school. Up there in the apartment was warmth and comfort and identity—but also up there was authority and admonition and restrictive practices designed to break his will. Besides, Alice Margolis was a priority. Leo McCullen had thought so too.

He ran the Porsche as far down the snow-drifted track as he dared, then took the flashlight and plowed on to the double wrought iron gates. There was a slash of light showing between the drapes on the ground floor. He reached the portico and hammered at the door. The snow began to fall again, as if the knocking had released a valve in the clouds.

She pulled open the drape in the window alongside the door and flashed a light in his face. He winced and raised a hand to shield his eyes. She unbolted and unlocked the door and held it wide. In the light of the hallway the reason for his increasing nether discomfort became obvious: His pants were soaked to the waist and clogged with unmelted snow. He plucked tentatively at one sodden leg and a shower of flakes fell to the carpet.

He grimaced. "I guess it'd be kinder to the furnishings if I stood in a bucket for a while and defrosted."

She smiled. "Try the fire. It's quicker." She tugged him by the arm and opened the sliding doors to the living room where she had held him at gunpoint two days earlier. A vast blaze crackled in the old stone fireplace. Two deep armchairs

160

faced one another across a sheepskin rug; one with a tall standard lamp positioned above it had an open book straddled across its arm. She snapped it shut and gestured him to the fire.

"Look, this is kind of ridiculous . . .," he began. But she was already at the door. "Walt didn't leave much of a wardrobe, and the police took most of that; I've got a bathrobe of his, though. You just thaw quietly."

She came back holding a shapeless Royal Stuart tartan robe with a shiny black silk collar.

"Here, it should suit you."

"I bet you say that to all the half-drowned travelers."

"Not all. Some I point guns at, some I wrestle with. You know, the usual kind of thing . . ." She laughed again. The chestnut hair bounced in kindergarten bunches at the nape of her neck. The dark brown full-length velour robe she was wearing was held in place by a single thin silken cord tied at her waist, studied simplicity.

"A drink?"

"First I guess I owe you some kind of . . . , I got to thinking about those files . . ."

She handed him a whiskey and splashed a thimbleful of water into it. "And here's me thinking it was my magnetic charm, scintillating conversation and friendly personality. Files. Ah, well . . ."

He grinned and took a draft of the whiskey. "You didn't let me finish. I said I was thinking about the files, and I thought: to hell with the files, what I need is to talk to someone with magnetic charm, scintillating conversation . . ."

She narrowed her eyes in mock scrutiny. "You know, that's what I thought you were going to say. Now, are you going to stand there all night filling the place with steam or are you going to put on that robe? I warn you, if you get pneumonia, one thing I'm not is Florence Nightingale."

The banter was light, flippant, but beneath it there was something more. The invitation to stay could not have been put more elliptically, but it charged the air with a force field of implication. She turned her back to him dramatically. "You have two minutes. Starting now."

He slipped off the pants quickly, debated about the shirt and pulled that off too, drawing the robe around him. It reached just below his knees. The shoes and socks contributed an air of high farce. He kicked them off.

"You ready?"

He rolled the socks into the waterlogged shoes. "Ready."

When she turned to face him he had assumed the classic stance of an old-time pugilist. "How do I look?"

"Fantastic. It's the only word." She laughed. He looked pained; smoothed the robe over his chest.

"I thought it was pretty good myself."

She came to him rearranged a twisted lapel. "It looked better on Mar . . . Walt."

A blush skimmed her face. She hid it behind her drink. She placed her glass on the coffee table and stood in front of him, her face serious now.

"You really did come for those files of his, didn't you? They concern you that much?"

"I don't know. In some ways, yes. Ask me why, I couldn't properly tell you."

"You think they mean something?"

"I don't know."

"But they *might*," she insisted.

He held his hands wide. "Might."

She was very close.

"Might is sometimes right." Her voice was a whisper.

He nodded slowly. Their talk had become no more than a preparation of the atmosphere growing between them.

He tugged gently on the cord at her waist and she stood unmoving as the robe parted, her lids suddenly heavy as if with sleep. Beneath them the eyes were hungry, predatory. She was naked under the robe, as he had known from the first minute she must be. Not a fragile, exposed nakedness. Not vulnerable. Arrogant. Confident.

Her body said, *I do not give; I give and take.*

He pulled her to him.

Took.

Gave.

He rolled two more logs on the fire; the dying flames received them with a hiss of pleasure and a crackling hunger. Anson fell back on the sheepskin rug and she snuggled into his arms, her cheek pillowed on his chest.

He said lazily, "Why'd you cry?"

"Did I?" Suspicious.

He bit his lip; he had to remember she wasn't Grazia. "Was it me?" he probed.

She snuggled closer. "Do you always hold an autopsy afterwards?"

"Only if the outcome is unsatisfactory."

162

He felt her stiffen in his arms. Her face angled up to his. "Was it?"

He stared into the flames. "Was it what?"

She grinned and pulled him close. "The tears had nothing to do with you."

"Who, then?"

"It doesn't matter."

"To you or to me?"

She kissed the skin at his throat. "I was thinking about Walt."

He held his peace, watched the bounding flames curl darting tongues around the new logs. "How close were you?"

She closed her eyes and buried her face in his shoulder. "Nothing to do with that. It wasn't a . . . an agony thing. Just kind of sentimental. You know, dreamy. You and me here. The fire. The snow outside. And a million years ago, maybe, Walt had the same thing with his wife . . ."

"Your mother?"

Pause. "Yes."

He held her tightly. "I don't think I get the drift of that one."

"You wouldn't. You're not a woman."

"John Roper said women were just men with imaginations."

She raised her head. "John Roper?"

"My father."

She sank back to his chest. "I don't think he knew women too well, either. It's a little more complex than that."

"The seat of creative pain."

"You're very good at labels."

"You're not a man. You wouldn't understand." He kissed her tenderly and plumbed the dark eyes. "How d'you react to the theory that there's no form of communication possible between men and women except the physical?"

Her mouth formed the words on his chest. "I'll check it out with Betty Friedan, but . . ." She gripped him with sudden strength and rolled him on his back. She looked down at him hungrily.

". . . I guess I ought to give you the chance to prove it, first . . ."

Cakes and ale. She produced some cookies and a can of beer for him, made hot chocolate for herself. They sat facing one another on the sheepskin, their nakedness forgotten. She stared at him for a long time, like the new owner of a

163

priceless clockwork toy looking for outward signs of the sophisticated mechanism inside. He liked it; her eyes were level, and there was a candor in them that appealed. He had never felt Grazia's eyes on him this way, never sensed in her a passion for honesty and oneness.

He said lightly, "If Leo could see me now . . ."

She raised the mug of chocolate to her lips, burying her face. "Who's Leo? The family wolfhound?"

He chuckled. "He'd like that."

"Who is he?"

"I just left him. Leo's with the Company. Walt reported to him the last few years he was on the active list. They were friends. Leo knew about the research Walt was doing."

She leaned forward, one hand on his knee. "Did you tell him about . . . you know, the files upstairs?"

"Yeah."

She studied his face hard. "That doesn't sound too bright."

He took her hand. "What are you talking about?"

"Walt's dead!" she flashed. "And I talked with his doctor in Washington yesterday. Walt had *no* cardiac problems. His blood pressure was *fine*—below normal for his age. If anything he was as fit as a four-minute miler. Think about something—what if Walt was killed? Tell me that? And ask yourself—who knew him best?" Her voice was breaking. "The Company knew him best. People he worked with knew him best of all."

He set down the can of beer and drew her to him. "Relax. Relax." He smoothed hair from her face. "Walt told me himself I could trust Leo McCullen. He's clean." He thought guiltily, *Who says? Who laid hands on Leo McCullen and blessed him with integrity?*

"I'm sorry." She took his hands in hers and kissed them. "I can't stand weeping women—can you?" She handed him the can of beer. He drank deeply. "All right." She squared her shoulders resolutely. "What does this Leo feel about what happened?"

"Have you read all those files . . . in Walt's den?"

She shook her head. "I looked at a couple. I told you that. I couldn't make head or tail of anything. He seemed to have worked out some kind of shorthand."

Anson nodded. "Shorthand is close enough. There's more to it than that, though. At first I thought Walt had gotten himself into something big. It began to add up. But when I looked closer, there was . . ." He held his arms wide. "It's garbage. Third-rate, speculative garbage."

The muscles of her jaw tightened. "Walt was never third-rate," she said militantly. "If he had something on his mind, he did what he did because there was no other way."

He took a belt from the can. He had a burning need to use her name, but he still couldn't make his mouth frame it. Alice. Alice. It sat unhappily on the girl. "He was a trained operator," he said impulsively. "He was trained to think logically, sequentially. He was trained to put it on paper and close every loophole." He jerked a thumb upward, over his shoulder. "Read that stuff and you'll see what I mean. It's a million pieces of nothing going nowhere."

"Then he wasn't *writing* a report. Maybe . . ." She cupped her hands around her mouth. "Maybe it was some kind of mental exercise. You know, you write down on a piece of paper the fundamentals of a problem you have to solve. You put them down because just *looking* at them makes the wheels turn up here." She tapped her forehead.

He shook his head. "If you follow that argument through, you don't end up with a series of files. On that principle, once you've worked out the fundamentals and got the wheels turning, you throw away the pieces of paper because they're irrelevant."

"Not if you're a trained *agent*," she said triumphantly. "Not if you know a day's coming when you'll have to put it all on paper." She crossed her legs under her and rocked back on her heels. "Walt wouldn't throw anything away. He was a *hoarder*. And besides, his memoirs were important to him—you said so yourself."

"Did I?" He had genuinely forgotten that. He couldn't even be sure it was true.

"That's what you said." She drank more chocolate. "I think there's something else. I asked you, pleaded with you when you came here that first time, to find what Walt was looking for. Perhaps I shouldn't have said that. It's none of your business. You didn't *want* to get involved, did you? You said 'yes' at the time because it was the only thing you could say, I guess." She bowed her head.

He threw another log on the fire. "O.K. So I didn't want to get involved. But not for the reasons you think." He emptied the beer can and crushed it, one-handed.

"What other reasons are there?"

"Personal ones." He spat it out, glad to be free of the secret.

The outburst that followed threw him completely. "Damn you!"

"Now wait a minute . . ."

"No—you wait." She swallowed her rage. "It wasn't too personal to come out here tonight . . . to screw me in my father's house. What've you told *her*—this personal reason? That you had to go see a man about a bitch?" She pulled herself to her knees, swung the bathrobe around her shoulders and over her breasts and stomach. *"Personal* reason! I hope she's making out with . . . some bastard right now. In your bed."

In spite of himself, he grinned, leaned forward and wrapped her in a bear hug. She struggled and he tightened his grip. This time there was no resistance. "It matters that much to you?"

"Wouldn't you just like to believe it!" she snapped.

"I've got nothing personal in *that* department," he said. "But if you want it on the line—O.K. There *is* a girl. She's back in Washington—and if she's making out in my bed right now, fine. Maybe that'll get her out of my hair and into someone else's."

"Will you let me go?" Her voice was calm now.

He kept her in the bear hug. "No! You stay there till you hear me out. Her name is Grazia, if you really want to know. She belongs to my time in Rome. She followed me here when I came back for my father's funeral. I didn't ask her to come. I don't want her to stay."

"But you *let* her stay." Flat accusation.

"Well . . ."

"You let her *stay*."

"It isn't that simple."

"No?"

"I don't feel a goddamned thing for her."

"No?"

"I'll get her out of there . . ."

"Is she good? In bed, I mean?"

He closed his eyes tight shut.

"Is she?"

He pushed her away, got to his feet and began to dress. His pants were hot and stiff as overdone toast. She made a production of straightening her robe, tying the belt and smoothing the collar. She checked herself in the mirror, fluffed up her hair and ran the middle finger of her right hand around the outline of her lips. When he pulled on his jacket and turned to look for his coat, she stood in front of him and touched his arm. "I'm sorry. That was . . . childish."

He grasped the opportunity. "You got me wrong. Honestly. When I said there were personal reasons . . ."

"It doesn't matter." She raised her eyes to him. "I had no right to say any of that. When you came here tonight, I . . . wanted you. Answer to a prayer. That's all. I don't have Walt's sense of priorities. I don't have his strength, either. I wanted and I took and I thought I could . . ." She touched the lapel of his jacket. "Will you come back?"

He pulled her head to his shoulder and folded his arms around her. "I couldn't touch those files again after that first time because I didn't want to know. That's what I meant by personal. There's something in there that . . ."

Her face craned up at him, surprised. "But . . . ?"

"My father. There's a file up there on my father. I don't know what the hell it means or why Walt had to open it. I told myself he was out of his mind. Reaching in the dark. Do you know what those files are supposed to be about?"

She threaded her arms around his neck. "You said it was . . ."

"Walt was working some screwball theory about the Kennedy assassination into another conspiracy thesis. Well, McCullen's chief, Milt Abrams, told me Walt was in some kind of trouble, said he'd lost touch with reality. He implied Walt was a . . ." The word refused to leave his tongue.

She stiffened. "A what?"

He held her to him. "Security risk. Yeah, I know. That's baloney. McCullen thought so, too."

She touched his face. "So what does that make Abrams?"

He released her and shrugged on his coat. "A liar for sure. Maybe something else."

"Like what?"

He dug into his coat pocket and withdrew the envelope on which he had scribbled the names and numbers he'd found in the kitten's identity cartridge. He told her how he had discovered it. She studied the envelope closely. "Is the Bradley here supposed to be Ambrose Bradley?"

"I don't know. I assume so."

She peered again. "Why 'Nixon'?"

"I don't know that either. But if Walt decided it was important enough to hide, it's important enough to follow through."

He slipped the envelope into his pocket and placed his hands on her shoulders. "I've got a confession to make."

"This is the night for it."

"I've been game playing with you." He caught the look in her eye and said quickly, "No, for God's sake! Not *that* way. I mean I've been holding back. I wanted you to tell me everything you knew before I volunteered anything more."

"Because you didn't trust me."

"Because I didn't *know* you." He kissed her once, lightly, on the lips. Her eyes filled with reproach. He protested, "I had to be sure that . . ."

"Do you trust me now?" The words were an effort.

"Only a billion percent."

She smiled weakly. "So what now?"

He kissed her again. "Home, I guess, and . . ."

"Grazia?"

"Who's Grazia?"

"Change the subject. What do you intend to do about your father?"

"Find out why Walt was so interested in him—if he had a reason at all. My father was a . . ." He stopped. "I won't let this thing go. I can promise you that much because I've made the same promise to myself. I have to know what got my father's name into Walt's head." He looked at his watch. "I have to get back. I want to see McCullen in the morning and a couple of other guys who might help." He took her hand and they walked into the hall. They embraced and he kissed her long and hard. Her pelvis ground into his. He pulled away.

"Don't tempt me." He held her hands tight in his.

"You need temptation?"

"Not anymore."

"When will I see you?"

"Tomorrow?"

She reached up and kissed him. "Now go before I throw you into bed."

He stepped out into the night. A huge moon hung low over the silver-washed land. There was no wind, no sound. He turned to her for one last look.

She said, "Did you mean it? About . . . Grazia?"

"Getting her out, you mean?"

"Yes."

"Every word."

She shivered.

"Get back inside. You'll freeze to death."

She stepped back under the portico. "You really mean it?"

"Of course I mean it, idiot."

She beamed triumphantly. "Good. Then leave it to me."

168

He blinked. "What are you . . . ?"

"Second thoughts?"

"No, goddamnit!"

"Good. That's all I wanted to hear. Drive carefully. And . . ." She ran a slim finger from the bridge of her nose to her lips. "Don't worry. Women know how to handle these things."

She watched him trudge through the gates and disappear into the lane. She went inside, lit a cigarette and sat down at a rolltop desk. She found a piece of paper and a pencil and wrote down as many of the names and numbers as she had been able to memorize from Anson's list.

Then she dialed Leo's home number. The receiver clicked from its cradle and she heard a buzz of background conversation, scrapings and shufflings; bangs.

Then a voice she didn't recognize said, "Hullo? Who's this?"

She put down the phone at once, waited a full minute and dialed the number again. Same voice, same background clutter. She replaced the receiver, walked to the fire, knelt on the sheepskin and sat back on her heels. She blew cigarette smoke into the leaping flames.

'Do you trust me now?'

'Only a billion per cent.'

Why did it have to be him?

WEDNESDAY: 0800—ABRAMS

Petersen's rage was only tempered by disbelief.

"What d'you mean . . . gone? A locked drawer, locked office, inside Langley. Look again."

"I looked ten times. Everywhere. It was in that goddamn drawer." Abrams was glad they weren't face to face.

"You checked out your secretary?"

"Right away. She didn't know it was there. No one came into that office except messengers. They never got past her desk."

"Fucking stupid place to keep it. You should've burned it."

"You think I wanted that thing in my desk? Jesus Christ, Don, I held it on your instructions."

"You didn't lose it on my instructions."

"I haven't lost it! Some bastard got in here and jimmied the

169

locks on the door and the desk. Don't ask me how. They're supposed to be foolproof. What I'm trying to get across to you . . ." he was stiff with rage himself now, "is it had to be æ pro. Someone on the inside. You know what that means?"

"Margolis." Petersen's voice had lost its domineering tone.

"He said he'd gotten something big."

Petersen didn't speak for several seconds, then he came on hard. "Listen to me, Milt. Listen hard. I want to know who took that file, who has it, who's read it. And then I want it back. Fast. You do what you have to, understand? But leave me out of it."

"How the fuck am I supposed to . . ."

The phone crashed down at the other end. It sounded in Abrams's ear like a descending guillotine.

WEDNESDAY: 1000—NIXON

Somebody had bounced back the ball.

Washington was alive with the rumor that Richard Nixon intended entering the White House race. So far, it had achieved only limited space in the newspapers, and television had treated it with lofty contempt. It was, after all, a ridiculous proposition, outrageous, distasteful. But the rumors wouldn't go away. It was only a matter of time before the media would be forced to scratch the itch.

Nixon was slowly being dragged into the open. Garfield could feel it and knew he had to act fast. The rope the incumbent President had given him could turn into a noose if he thought Nixon was muddying the waters. Garfield had decided on a straight denial. One that would placate the President, lay low the press and yet somehow convince the Bradley camp they were not yet out of the woods. It would have to be a masterpiece of controlled ambiguity, its surface reflecting whatever people chose to see. Most would take it at face value. But it wouldn't bring Bradley any respite.

Garfield had worked on the speech himself. Nixon had taken it well, adding only a few minor "Nixonisms." He agreed to go along with it. The venue, he had insisted, though, would be the La Costa Hotel. Situated strategically close to San Clemente, the opulent La Costa complex, with its saunas and swimming pools, had been a favorite watering hole for Ehrlichman, Haldeman, Dean and all his other

170

acolytes and their wives when they visited the Western White House in more halcyon days.

It was, said Garfield, vaguely provocative, but he let it ride.

The motorcycle outriders, headlights blazing, swung with perfect timing into the hotel driveway, and four of them peeled away to take up their positions. The car rolled to a halt outside the hotel.

"Just follow me, sir," urged the Secret Service man as he opened the rear door for Nixon. "Stay close and—please—don't shake any hands." Nixon nodded. He stepped from the car and there was a doubtful ripple of applause, then a more confident shout of welcome, then a spontaneous burst of clapping that grew and pursued him as he passed through the crowd. Black-jacketed police lay back, arms linked, against the bodies. The applause gathered strength.

"Sock it to 'em, Dick!" shouted a woman's voice idiotically. The people roared. A pathetic old man stuck a thin hand through the police wall and a Secret Service man smashed down on it—but not before Nixon had managed to shake it.

The security man came up on his shoulder. "Keep moving, sir, please," he said with a note of suppressed irritation.

"I've done this before, son," beamed Nixon amiably.

A shrill falsetto screamed from their right, "Give us a sign, Dick!"

They reached the double glass doors behind which the reception party waited, red-faced and proud of themselves. There was a barrage of camera flashes and the excitement communicated itself. From high on the building's upper escarpment, willing hands showered ticker tape, and on the central lawn a band oompahed bravely into "Old Glory."

"We have men in every occupied room down here," the Secret Service man whispered comfortingly.

"Yours or mine?" grinned Nixon. "Relax, son. We're among friends."

"A sign, Dick!" screeched the falsetto again, voice breaking. Nixon paused as the glass doors opened. He turned to face the pressing crowds and stumbled as the momentum was checked to give him turning space. He straightened his dark blue tie, flicked unnecessarily at the immaculate lapels of his dark blue suit, raised his head and smiled in all directions.

"Sir!" hissed the security man urgently.

171

Nixon waved a finger of reassurance at him and raised his arms above his head in the famous victory sign. The crowd sank into a moment of expectant silence, acute as an indrawn breath. Nixon moved his raised hands with a theatrical flourish. The roar of delight rolled over him. It was still in his ears as he strode into the hotel lobby.

They were his.

The boy wore the medals of a Vietnam veteran, and he balanced uncertainly on his remaining leg, as though the crutches were new to him. His deformity cut no ice with the cop at the door. "Sorry, kid," he said. "This is a tickets only function. Maybe you'll get to see him on his way out."

The youngster had been pushed to the front by clutching hands. As Nixon moved inside to join the privileged, the crowd's character had grown more volatile. At first they turned in on themselves to generate new enthusiasm by singing and shouting catchwords and slogans, but when the young man swung, storklike, to the perimeter, they centered their attention on him.

"Wait a minute, officer," protested a diminutive gray crew cut in a Hawaiian shirt. "This boy here's a veteran." He jabbed at the medals crudely pinned across the kid's cheap sport shirt. "I'd say he earned his ticket. What do you say?" The crowd roared its approbation.

"Forget it," repeated the cop uneasily.

"Hey!" shouted the crew cut, conquering the empty stage. "We got a Vietnam veteran here who lost a leg. And they got no time for him. They don't want him in there. A guy who done his duty?"

The cop braced hands on hips wearily. "I got my orders," he said. "No tickets, no seat."

"What kinda orders are they?" screeched the falsetto who had been looking for a sign. She pushed herself against the cop's belly bulge, flaming red-dyed hair bristling under his chin.

"Look, ma . . . ," began the beleaguered policeman. His words were drowned in a cackle of protest. He raised an arm and two black-jacketed colleagues forced their way through the crowd to stand at his shoulders.

"Please—forget it," said the boy with the medals. "I don't want to cause no trouble."

"Trouble!" screeched the red-haired harridan.

"For chrissakes, what is this? Russia?"

"What army were *you* in, cop?"

172

"Give the kid a break, Dwayne."

The door guard glanced unhappily at his colleagues. The crowd surged forward menacingly. Cameras whirred. "What the hell am I supposed to do now?" he moaned to the man on his right. "Where's the chief?"

"Inside. You won't get him out here, Dwayne."

"Aw, shit. Let the poor bastard in. O.K.?" The embattled Dwayne took a quick vote. The three cops stood aside and Dwayne put a hand on the boy's back. He swung through on his black steel crutches, ugly in his broken youth. The red-haired harridan wriggled up and planted a kiss on Dwayne's ample jowl. "That's what life's about, son," she yelled.

Richard Nixon took up the glass of water and allowed them the impression that he was drinking. Their silence was respectful, controlled; there were no nervous coughs, no shuffling, no whispers. He knew when he had an audience. He replaced the glass and they watched him as if monitoring a particularly dexterous conjuring trick.

The raised rostrum was without decoration; no bunting, no flowers. At its center stood a lectern sprouting radio and TV microphones. Cables snaked down to the floor of the hall and along the aisle to the sound equipment and cameras strung out along the back wall.

Nixon touched a sparkling white handkerchief to his lips and pushed it down into his breast pocket, feeding the tension.

"So now . . . ladies and gentlemen, to the . . ." he paused to run his eyes mischievously along the first row of faces, ". . . to the disappointing part of this . . . of my address to you today."

The faces became charged with curiosity. There were murmurs. They didn't want to be disappointed.

"I made myself a promise some . . . years ago. No more political speeches." The murmur rose and tiptoed across the audience. He calmed them with a wide boyish smile. "But today I find I have to break that vow to some degree. It's not of my own choosing. I think . . . most of you," he favored the second row of faces with a penetrating examination, "will understand why. Over the past few days, rumors have been circulating in Washington and elsewhere that I am . . ." He made a pretense of searching for the right word, "*flirting* with the idea of involving myself in the coming elections."

The crowd broke its trust with him. "You bet!" yelled a man's voice midway down the hall. "Bless you, Dick!"

173

shouted a woman. He pulled a face that was neither friendl|
nor disputatious.

"Friends." He knew they were that all right. "I can onl|
guess at the source of that story. I can only guess at th|
motives for putting it before the public. But let me tell yo|
this: when—if—Richard Nixon ever decides to stand befor|
the people of America again in any poltical context . . .'
They were paralyzed with anticipation. He held them tha|
way, glaring at them until he judged it time to let the ol|
warming smile flower. "On that day, you won't hear about |
in whispers." He planted his hands firmly on his hips. "I'|
come straight out and tell you loud and clear."

The applause swept from back to front of the hall like |
tidal wave, drowning his attempt to add piquancy to th|
point. He grasped the lectern with both hands and let thei|
pent up frustrations swirl around him, engulf him. When the|
showed signs of wavering he held up both hands, palm|
wide.

"So for the benefit of these good people here from radio
and television . . ." The laughter was intoxicating. "Who, as
each and every one of us knows . . ." They waited for him,
mouths open; ". . . has a job to do . . ." The rest was lost again
in rapturous applause and hoots of derision directed at the
line up of technicians along the wall. "I want to say . . ." He
was finding it hard to speak. ". . . I want to say: For this year
at least, the campaign line is not Nixon for President."

There were a few catcalls mingled with jeers, but he knew
they were not aimed at him.

"On the other hand, let's be crystal clear on one point. If
the time ever comes when Richard Nixon is needed, don't
doubt for one second that he'll be there."

The cheering in the room was deafening. He raised his
hands high to quiet them.

"And one more thing . . ."

He stopped. His left hand slapped over a spot on his right
shoulder and he rolled back, right hand gripping the lectern
for support. His face, suddenly ashen and uncomprehending,
turned down to the Secret Service men standing below the
rostrum. His knees buckled. One of the security men leapt
upwards in a standing jump onto the rostrum but he was too
late. Nixon crumpled to the carpet-covered stage, his face
twisted.

A woman screamed, then another. There was a surge of
alarm that rippled through the audience like wind over a
sheltered pool. Only the television men remained unmoved,

their cameras sweeping the rows of shocked faces and pursuing police and security men as they raced to the stage to form a protective ring around the former President.

A piercing shriek from the back of the hall cut through the shouting. Under the very noses of the camera crews, three men and a woman rolled, thrashing and punching, into the aisle.

A young man in a brightly colored sport shirt fought savagely beneath them. He had only one leg. Trapped across his chest as he struggled was an automatic pistol.

WEDNESDAY: 1100—GARFIELD

Cornball padded into the den, saw Garfield and whimpered a greeting. The old man held out a hand of welcome and the yellow dog came to the desk and reared up to drop its forepaws on the worked leather. Garfield massaged the bands of fat around its neck.

Milt Abrams had briefed the Commissioner of Police on McCullen's status and once more invoked the Agency's right to administer its own investigation. The Commissioner had notified Munro Fletcher at once and Fletcher had called Garfield. The temptation to advise the Commissioner to veto Abrams's claim had been considerable, but Garfield finally dismissed it. McCullen's body was already in the Agency's downtown morgue, had been there since shortly after Fred Goldman's stakeout team put through an anonymous call to the duty officer at the CIA's Domestic Affairs Division last night. Garfield knew all he had to know about the manner of McCullen's death; it had been silent, swift, remote, efficient and premeditated. The intention had been to label it a Mafia hit, right down to the close-quarters strike with a high-velocity .22 caliber handgun. The FBI had a case list of more than thirty "executions" by such means in the last four years, and statistics could build fine circumstantial theories.

Let them have their theories.

He looked at the grandfather clock ticking loudly in the corner. He picked up the remote control switch from the desk beside him and pressed the button. The TV set in the corner blinked.

". . . time ever comes when Richard Nixon is needed, don't doubt for one second that he'll be there."

The cameras panned over the applauding, waving audience. Garfield watched them with satisfaction.

The cameras closed on Nixon. He raised his hands. "And one more thing. . . ."

Garfield tensed in his chair. As Nixon recoiled, a blank expression, half-questioning, half-pained, on his face, Garfield got to his feet. As Nixon fell and someone leaped up on to the rostrum, he strode close to the set, bent down to stare.

A commentator was· babbling something about a heart attack—reminding viewers of Nixon's mild stroke of last fall. There were screams and the audience boiled into the aisles.

The phone shrilled from the desk behind him. He stood uncertainly for a moment then went to pick it up, his eyes still on the screen.

"Goldman!" rasped the voice at the other end. "Did you see it?"

"It's running now," Garfield snapped. "I had some work to do. I was recording it on videotape. What the hell's happening?"

"Someone took a shot at him. High on the shoulder. He was two or three minutes into the speech."

"Is he alive?"

"Yeah. Just a scratch, they say."

"Who?"

"Some nut with a pistol."

"Goddamn it!" Garfield beat his hand on the desktop. "Have you talked to your people down there?"

"Yes. They got him backstage and found a doctor. He'll make it. More shock than anything else."

"I told you, Fred, this had to be watertight. I said he had to be covered every yard of the way. Every second."

Goldman flared. "We could only go as far as he'd let us. He thinks the world's in love with him. Hell, Luke, they did what they could."

"Never mind. What's happening now?"

"They've got the flesh wound cleaned and treated. The doctor gave him an injection. They're getting him back to San Clemente by helicopter."

"He can travel?"

"The doc says yes."

"Then I want him covered all the way. And make sure your people stay with him. How did a man with a gun . . . ?"

"We don't know. We'll check that out."

"You should have checked it before it happened!"

"We should have done a lot of things. We should have anticipated. I told you from the start this was a damn fool idea. Any madman. . . ."

176

"Keep me posted." Garfield slammed down the phone.

He killed the TV screen and went out into the hall. Cornball was instantly at his heels.

"Polly!"

She replied faintly from the back of the house.

"Pack me a bag, will you? I have to take a trip."

WEDNESDAY: 1210—ANSON

Anson was the last man in State to hear—at least, that was the impression George Hyman left him with. "Christ, son. You can't get anyone in Justice, the Bureau or Langley. They're all out building alibis. Every man, woman and bureaucrat on the Hill's glued to a TV set somewhere, watching repeats of the action."

"It was on TV?" Anson's tone implied it was a monstrous incongruity to broadcast assassination attempts on the public airwaves.

"Every move."

"Have you seen it?"

"Yeah. I saw it ten minutes back. That was the fifth or sixth time they've run it in an hour."

Anson stared at the far wall of his tiny office. Nixon.

"Who did it?"

Hyman spread his hands and shrugged. "What does it matter who did it? Some punk, I guess—another hyped-up junkie. It could just as easily have been a fifty-eight-year-old grandma with flowers in her hat or a Supreme Court judge."

"But why?"

Hyman perched on the corner of Anson's desk. "Where've you been, son? This election was shaping up to be a good clean fight. Big lineup for the primaries and some fine men playing it by the book. Oh, I've got no time for politicians—but I've seen plenty worse than this bunch. I'd say the President was right behind the eight ball and, if I was a betting man, my dollar would've been on Jerry Brown to run a close second to Ambrose Bradley. Then, the game goes crazy. The talk is Nixon wants to stick his nose in. You still want to ask me why?"

Hyman rambled off to find another victim. Anson put in a call to McCullen at Langley. A secretary answered. Would he care to leave a message? Mr. McCullen was not available just now. He said no thank you, but the girl persisted. Didn't she recognize his voice, sir? He put the phone down quickly and called McCullen's house. No answer. He leaned back in his chair.

He was dog tired. He had reached John Roper's apartment at 3:30 A.M. to find Grazia waiting under the explosive influence of a half bottle of J&B. She was a specialist in cross-examination and had pursued him from living room to bathroom to dressing room to bed, hounding, provoking, screeching, raging. At 4:15 he had forced her clawing hands out of range of his face and swung a backhander to the angle of her jaw. She went out like a fused bulb and the half bottle of J&B kept her that way. Anson had left her sleeping. She still hadn't called.

He turned his mind to Walt Margolis's memorandum from the grave. McCullen would wrap that up if anyone could.

But now Nixon. An attempted assassination. Rumors of his candidacy. A denial.

And, of course, Ambrose Bradley. Both names were on Walt's sheet of paper. What was the link? *Was* there a link? And where did John Roper Anson fit into the scenario?

His office door swung open without a heralding knock and George Hyman loomed large, his face this time creased with concern. He said, "You seen this?" and waved a sheet of yellow paper.

"What is it?"

"Read it." Hyman shoved it under Anson's nose and dropped into a chair.

The form was headed Department of Justice, Incident Report, Classified Personnel Only. It had been filed to Washington, D.C., by the FBI office in Seattle and carried an over-stamped request for "Closed circulation to qualified sources."

"At 0455 hours, this date, the body of a woman—Caucasian, 116 pounds, blond hair, blue eyes—was found on the sidewalk outside an apartment house. The body appears to have fallen from a window on the eighth floor. Death was caused by cerebral compression resulting from multiple fractures of the skull. Papers found in the apartment confirm the woman is Alice Margolis, twenty-seven, dancer and singer, last seen alive at 0225 when she left her place of employment, the Golden Goose Club. She lived alone. Letters found among the deceased's belongings led Seattle P.D. officers to advise this office. Preliminary checks indicate her relationship to former Agent Walt Margolis. Advise if further local action required."

178

The P.D.P.—the postdeath Polaroid—showed a round-faced woman of no great beauty. Her hair was yellow.

Anson had had few moments of genuine terror in his life, and in the quarter hour it took him to shake off George Hyman and get down to the parking lot, he tested the rawness of the experience. The outward signs were visible enough: His mouth was dry, his movements clumsy and erratic; there was a boulder of steel wool in his chest and his voice resonated in the back of his head. The agony reached his lips and he knew they were moving in sympathy.

There was a forest of waving placards along the railings outside the White House, and a motorcycle cop signaled the Porsche to a halt as a ruckus broke out between a black police sergeant and a bunch of protesters in fur-lined Afghan coats. The signs they carried read Who's Running America? and Nixon Out! Anson spared them only a cursory glance. A riot wagon hissed to a stop diagonally across the traffic lanes and a dozen cops in visored helmets and flak jackets tumbled out. They fell into a V formation and charged the demonstrators halfway along their ragged crocodile. The leading group was pinned to the railings; the tail was rounded up and herded across to the far sidewalk. Three more black-and-whites arrived. It was all over.

The waiting traffic was waved on and Anson accelerated away. McCullen would know. He had to find McCullen. Once and for all, he had to dump this whole crazy mess in McCullen's lap and go back where he belonged. Rome. McCullen could have it all—the Alice who terminated on a Seattle sidewalk, the Alice who wasn't Alice, Hyman, the files. Everything.

He raised howls of protest from the Porsche's tires as he pulled into the parking space with John Roper's nameplate on it. The name did nothing to restore his sense of perspective. It was no longer a device by which he recognized his father; it was an accusation, a threat.

He took the elevator. The door of the apartment was ajar, propped open by a black Gucci suitcase. There were two more immediately inside and a half dozen matching miniatures littering chairs and tables in the living room. Grazia's voice came from the bedroom: "Quickly, quickly, please, or I'll miss my plane."

He heard the phone jangle as she hung it up and shouted, "Grazia? Hey—what's happening here?"

She was at her best, her most beautiful, her most cosmic.

All black, head to foot, with a glint of gold at her wrist and at the heels of her patent leather boots. At her neck, one breathtaking splash of color, an emerald green silk scarf caught at the throat by a gold butterfly with emerald wing-spots. She leaned against the frame of the bedroom door and examined him from head to foot.

She said at last, "You really want to know what's happening here? I tell you, *tesoro*. Betrayal is happening. You know what that is?"

He strode forward and grabbed her black-gloved hands. "Don't give me that speechless innocent crap, Grazia. Why . . . ?"

She tore her hands from his, the smile on her lips warning of violence, tears, rejection or impending suicide. "Innocence! He tells me . . . *innocence!*" She touched an index finger to her lips and blew a kiss designed to poison on impact. "I trust you. Before all the men in my life I put Harry Anson first for complete trust. If I . . ."

He broke in violently, "Will you cut out the pidgin English, goddamn you! If you expect me to listen to this . . ."

She came off the door frame and pushed past him into the room, checked the small black boxlike handcases and locked one with a tiny gold key. She straightened. "All right, Harry. Have it your way. I don't owe you a word of explanation, but . . ." Her eyes blazed. "I'll explain because I want to watch you squirm." She waved a hand through the air, a circus ringmaster introducing a star act. "Mister Harry Anson, Gentleman. Man of the world. *Tough* Harry Anson. Seen everything, done everything. Easy come, easy go. Bigger than Casanova and quicker on his feet."

"I'm still waiting to squirm."

She put her hands on her hips and, not for the first time, Anson witnessed the magical reversion to type; somewhere under that supergloss was a Neapolitan fishwife screaming and clawing to get out. "So *manly!* So . . ." She choked. ". . . *masculine!* You dare not say it. You have to run away and hide and let *her* do it for you. Oh . . . you're such a *man!*" She turned from him in disgust.

"What the hell are you talking about?"

"I wouldn't stay with you now, if you . . ."

He flushed angrily. "I'm not *asking* you to stay. I said what the hell are you talking about?"

"Fuck you, Anson!" Her hands came up in front of her face, fingers clawlike. He backed off a step; he had felt these talons in his flesh often enough, usually in his sleep. She

180

froze, then let her hands fall to her sides. She said almost plaintively, "Why couldn't you tell me? Do you really believe it would have made any difference? You know everything there is to know about me. Why couldn't you have told me in Rome?"

"Told you *what!*"

Her anger mounted, contorted her face, died. She seemed to wilt. "Your wife was here, Harry. She came by two hours ago with her luggage. She expected to find *you,* not me. How'd you think it was for her finding me here? 'I'm terribly sorry. I'm your husband's mistress. I am just passing through.'"

Anson's jaw dropped. "What d'you mean . . . my *wife?*"

"Does it give you a kick? A little-boy kick?" she taunted. "Is it the sex thing that turns you on—or running from bed to bed, living dangerously? Maybe it's all in your head, Harry. When you're making love to her, do you make believe it's me?"

He was still reeling. "When did . . . ?"

"Oh, you'll have trouble there, Harry. Big trouble." She turned her wrist and checked the gold bracelet watch. "She's a real baby, isn't she? Girl next door. Is that what she was? Harry in haste, repents at leisure. She won't get over it. Ever. She couldn't talk for five minutes. I sat here comforting her. *Me!* Then she went to pieces and ran away."

There was a discreet tap at the half-open door and the janitor put his head around it, greatly daring. "You called a cab, Mrs. Anson?"

"I called a cab," agreed Grazia, flashing the hemlock smile, "but Mrs. Anson already left." The janitor peered at her through eyes bunched tight with confusion. Grazia patted the thinning hair of his skull with an elegant hand. "Take the bags down, there's a darling little man." The janitor withdrew, still grappling with his incomprehension.

"One thing you've got to promise me," she said slowly.

"I'll check it with my accountant," he snarled.

"Next time you're in Rome, call me." She showed her teeth. "I'll get such a kick out of telling you to go fuck yourself."

He hung halfway out of the window to watch her step into the cab. She looked up once. He pulled back and went inside. Then he began chasing McCullen again.

The same girl at Langley answered his phone and insisted she remembered Anson's voice—this time, he thought, with some truth. Mr. McCullen was still unobtainable. He tried the house number. No answer. With more trepidation than hope, he dialed Walt's house in Virginia. As the ringing blurted in his ear, he remembered the girl's parting words of the night before: "Women know how to handle these things. Leave it to me. Promise?"

Surely to God she hadn't marched into the apartment and played the tearful wife?

He stifled the thought. The ringing continued. He hung up. He walked through to the bedroom; it had the air of a rifled warehouse. Grazia had packed with a venom all her own. None of his clothes had escaped her private gesture of farewell. He began picking up scattered underwear, shirts, pants and jackets, discovered the lipsticked outlines like badges of rank on the collar ends of one shirt and realized she had left the same evocative stamp on all of them. He piled the clothes into a laundry bag and tossed it in the service chute. That would give the staff downstairs enough for a second installment on the Anson Saga.

He poured himself a tall J&B and slumped into a chair. A pair of Grazia's panty hose lay draped, forgotten, on the arm. He held the fine mesh in his hands.

Assume the girl came to the apartment and blitzed Grazia with the unsuspecting wife routine. O.K. That had some element of crazy logic in it—if he was stupid enough to believe she had done it to free him of Grazia. But that was only the surface motive, wasn't it? What was the real one?

Dead end.

Try another angle. If the woman who had taken the dive in Seattle *was* Alice Margolis, who was the girl with the chestnut hair who lost her heart to strangers coming in out of the snow? More important, who was using her?

Milton Abrams. The name drilled into the back of his skull with such force that he felt actual pain.

Abrams already had a track record in this game. He had deliberately set out to blacken Walt Margolis's name. Why? To deflect Anson from inquiring further into the work Walt was doing before he died. Abrams was powerful, powerful enough to appoint a girl to play Margolis's daughter, an agent whose job it was to scratch the Anson irritation and pass on any information.

He got up and poured himself another J&B.

He called State and asked for George Hyman. Mr. Hyman had been called to a meeting over at Justice. Would he care to leave a number for Mr. Hyman's return?

He hung up. Outside, snow glided in huge feathery flakes on the windless air. So, Abrams installed the girl in Walt's house. What then?

He sanctioned the real Alice Margolis.

Anson touched his forehead. It was beaded with sweat. He raised an arm and swept the perspiration into his hairline. He sanctioned her the same way he had sanctioned Walt Margolis. Accidental fatality. The thought ran feelers down his spine. That really must be crazy. Abrams was Company. Official. A pro. As a Company soldier he needed motive, opportunity and commitment. An arbitrary kill orgy was inconceivable. He would have to use outside help, presumably, and that meant laying his identity, his job and his neck on the line. He would have to use the Company's administrative structure to cover up facts and damp down police investigation. And all for what? To keep out of circulation yet another conspiracy theory on the death of Kennedy? Garbage!

No. The girl had pushed Walt's files at him from the first moment he stepped inside the house. She had *volunteered* them. Conclusion? He threw the last of the J&B down his throat. Conclusion: They had no idea what Walt's files meant either, but they were desperate to find out.

Why not burn them? Destroy Margolis, destroy his work. He pondered that one for a long time. Answer? Who knows. Maybe Walt wasn't alone in this.

He stiffened with reflexive shock. *McCullen*. Margolis and McCullen!

WEDNESDAY: 1200—PETERSEN

Donald Petersen had never made the covers of *Time* or *Newsweek*, an omission he shared with several other unsung Americans, but in his case it represented a singular achievement. From the moment he ascended to the Directorship of the Company, he had refused all interviews and press photosessions, had rejected all invitations to address public bodies and reduced his personal profile to a level that ensured his name would trigger no automatic responses.

It hadn't been easy, but as he hacked away at the dense undergrowth of the CIA's overgrown network, he realized the day of his emergence could only be postponed. His forceful control of the demoralized organization was raising far too many questions on the Hill and among the Washington press corps. He had recently allowed himself to be drawn into friendly circles at government level; small private parties, social gatherings of senators and congressmen; occasional carefully-vetted soirées for leading businessmen and service chiefs. He had also let it be known that the old Hoover cliché now applied to him and his officers: "The door is always open." In effect it was true, but as the FBI staffers had found with Hoover, so the Company men found with Petersen: the door to the office was wide enough, but the man himself was rarely behind it.

His office was empty again, but this time the business that took him away from it was an irritant. LaCroix had insisted. "We can't afford to allow Bradley to wriggle out of the net. This is the moment. It might be too late by tonight or tomorrow." Soothe his outraged sense of morality or pin him with his own sense of guilt? That would be up to Bradley. Petersen didn't care which way it broke.

"Don?"

Ambrose Bradley stepped uncertainly into the gloom of the little bar, spotted Petersen in a corner alcove and approached cautiously. He glanced around him at the empty benches and tables, slipped onto the seat opposite and automatically checked his watch. "Snow's playing hell with traffic. My driver had trouble finding the place." He stared around him again.

Petersen grinned easily. "Had trouble finding it myself, Ambrose. Sorry. I thought we ought to find somewhere ... quiet."

Bradley's eyes narrowed. "Neutral ground?"

"Could be. Clears the mind."

The bartender moved in their direction but Petersen waved a dismissive hand and the man retired to his perch on a stool.

"Well?" Bradley's eyes had not left Petersen's face.

"Big question, Ambrose. Be specific."

"Don't fence with me, damn you! LaCroix. Have you talked with him?"

"I talked with him. He was anxious that you and I get together."

"I don't think we have any common ground, Don. We won't be getting together on anything. Get that clear."

Petersen shifted in his seat. "Specifics, Ambrose."

"All right, specifics. You were the first man to mention the

184

Statler incident. Somebody else has talked about it. It involved the killing of . . ."

Petersen purred: "You'd believe Nixon?"

Bradley stopped. "You know about that?"

"I said I talked with LaCroix."

"He had no right . . ."

"He has *every* right."

"I insist you tell me! What was the *incident?*"

Petersen leaned forward on his elbows, bridging the gap between them. "Don't push me, Ambrose. The Statler affair was Agency business. A man was killed. One of my men. He was doing his job. That's all."

Bradley sighed heavily. "All right. We'll let that ride for the moment. Now tell me about the Kennedys; Martin Luther King."

"What the hell am I supposed to say to a question like that!"

Bradley said bitterly: "You're a credit to your profession, Don. You wouldn't recognize the truth if it came at you with a gun. Very well. Nixon said he knew about your *Agency* incident at the Statler and it seems he was right. He also knew about The Matrix. He knew John Roper Anson was a member. He said Anson had acquired a tape recording that links me, all of us, with the killing of the Kennedys and King. Now I'm only certain of one thing so far: I personally had nothing to do with any of those things, but . . ." He hunched forward, bringing his face within inches of Petersen's, ". . . if I thought for one moment that any of it—any single scrap of it—were true, I'd break The Matrix and you and LaCroix and I'd do it from the floor of the Senate. Don't have any doubts in that direction, Don. I'd crucify myself in public if I thought it was true."

Petersen pushed himself back into his seat. He said softly: "Back off, Senator. For your own sake."

"You have a lot in common with LaCroix." Bradley tried to close the distance between them again. "When the facts are unpalatable you resort to threats. Well, you've got the wrong man. I don't have a thing to lose."

"I'd check that out with my conscience first if I were you, Senator." Petersen kept his grin easy and his clenched hands hidden below the table.

"My conscience brought me here." The old man seemed near tears. "Dear God. I believed in Aaron LaCroix; I thought he was misguided at times, confused; but I never

185

doubted he was a man of God. I never doubted you were a man of principle. Yet, in days—hours even—you've destroyed . . ." He couldn't go on.

Petersen slipped a cigarette from a slim leatherbound case and lit it. He breathed the smoke deep into his lungs. "You really believe you can stand up in front of the whole country and play the innocent, Senator?" He let the smoke dribble from his mouth up into his nose. "You believe I'm so dumb I'd allow that to happen?"

"There's nothing you can say. Don't try. When I leave here I'm going to . . ."

"Keep your mouth shut!" Petersen flared. He relaxed at once. "Insurance, Senator. Everyone needs insurance, like the ads say. The Matrix needs a lot of insurance; I saw that right from the beginning. People with influence who get together to build Jerusalem in their own backyard end up serving their own goddamn interests. Always have. Always will. The nearer to God they climb, the thinner the air gets. People with immortal passions get worried; the mortal sweat of reaching up begins to offend their sensitivities. I didn't want to find The Matrix in a situation where individual members suddenly started coming up with second thoughts about the way it was going. Insurance, Senator."

"Blackmail," Bradley spat.

"You're the man of words, Senator. Call it what you want. I prefer insurance."

"There's nothing to say. Keep your insurance."

"I have. I have, Senator. I've kept it very carefully. For years. It's all on paper, suitably witnessed. There are people who saw you, listened to your views and opinions, voted with you—on all the issues The Matrix dealt with. All done democratically, Senator. Including the . . . arrangements for the Kennedys and Martin Luther King. I even have letters written in your own hand urging us to adopt a tougher line with Kennedy. I'll show you the letters if you like. You couldn't deny it was your hand."

"I've never . . ." The attempt at a second offensive was weak and despairing. Bradley was crushed.

"Don't tell me what you did or didn't do, Ambrose," Petersen whispered. "Go tell the Senate. Remember? Crucify yourself in public?"

Bradley's head sagged. "I deserve that." He looked up at Petersen and this time the tears were brimming at the lids. "Don't you have any feeling at all? You've taken away everything I ever held to be of value. You've finished me, you and LaCroix."

Petersen slipped from the table and stood up. He shrugged on his gray overcoat. "Cheer up, Ambrose. One man dies, another man steps from the ashes. The Senator's dead, long live the President." He slapped a hand on Bradley's bent shoulders. "We're almost there. The primaries, the convention . . . you don't have a thing to worry about . . . Mister President."

He crossed the bar, threading through the small tables toward the door but a thought stopped him. "Stay as long as you like, Ambrose," he said lightly. "You won't have any problems here. I booked the place for the day. The bartender's one of mine. He'll give you anything you want . . . except hemlock."

WEDNESDAY: 1740—NIXON

"No threats, no pleas, no nothing! I want no more of that. You remember what Averell Harriman said? Anyone who ran for President ought to have his head examined. He was goddamned right! If you've got a head left to examine."

Richard Nixon had been in full flight for five minutes, ranging freely up and down the chromatic scale from anger to self-denial, benign disgust to venomous attack. Lucas Garfield rode it as patiently as a buoy in a Pacific gale. They sat in the overstuffed study of Casa Pacifica, onetime holiday home, onetime Western White House. Shock alone would have laid low most men half his age, thought Garfield, but the man facing him, arm in sling, had the raw vitality of a Heidelberg duelist. It was a good sign, better than he had hoped for. It was also a salutary lesson in gamesmanship; no matter how well he might have thought he had Nixon's measure, the man was equipped with a formidable gallery of shifting character traits.

"I can only repeat what I said when I arrived, Mr. President. Thank God. I'm amazed you're not under sedation."

Nixon shrugged and the gesture twitched his bound arm. "Don't be so damned condescending. An inch or so the wrong way and you'd be dealing with a corpse." He drew a finger from the center of the wound across his chest to his heart.

187

"You're lucky you got yourself a live Richard Nixon. Because some hairy-assed ex-PFC couldn't shoot straight! That's the truth of what happened today, Mister."

"I regret deeply what happened today and . . ."

Nixon snorted his disbelief. "O.K. I'll accept that. Against my better . . . But don't ride on it." Nixon picked up the internal phone. "Have you got a rundown on that son of a bitch yet?" He listened. "Never mind the crap; who is he?" He allowed the speaker no more than a half dozen words. "Forget it." He slammed down the phone. "Secret Service they call themselves. Watch television and you have a better idea what's going on. You know, I sometimes think—and I hate to say it—but Hoover was a great loss to this country. This thing was political, right? You know anything I don't?"

"No, sir. Not yet."

"I can believe that." He eased one leg off the footrest and tested it. "I guess I have to believe it." He massaged the knee and cautiously swung the other foot to the floor. He stood up. Behind him the window looked out on to the roll of the Pacific.

Garfield got to his feet. "You're right, sir. This went badly wrong. I think it's gone far enough. My schedule didn't include setting you up for a shooting. I miscalculated."

Nixon turned from the window with a theatrical grimace. "You mean the Pope *is* fallible?"

"Something like that."

"I like a man who can admit his mistakes, Garfield. You know what I mean?" He turned his back again and looked out on to the gardens.

Garfield said casually, "I had no idea, the . . . ah . . . resentment . . . ran so deeply."

Nixon's head cocked.

"Of course," Garfield went on quickly, "there was always a danger, the chance that Bradley's group might do something crazy. But it *was* remote. The last thing they need right now is to act irrationally. That way they draw attention to themselves. My whole strategy was based on that. The other thing . . . well . . ."

Nixon's voice was artificially steady. "What other thing, Garfield? I want to be sure we understand one another completely."

"There was always a chance that . . . it doesn't really matter now . . ."

"Everything matters now!"

Garfield chose his words. "The facts of life have to be
188

faced in a freak situation like this. Truth is, there was always a chance someone would be personally motivated. That was the wild card. The possibility . . . I have to say this . . . that the aftermath of Watergate would catch up with you. I'm speaking very frankly now and, well . . ." He walked to the window and stood alongside Nixon. "I don't know any way of putting this politely. I'm not a politician."

Nixon threw him a sidelong glance that dissolved into a puckish grin. "How do politicians talk?"

"That's what makes it difficult." Garfield's face set. "My belief was that your personal safety wouldn't be a major factor. In the last few days it's been the *image* of Richard Nixon that was on trial. That alone. That bullet tells me I'm wrong. So, if you'll excuse me . . ." He stepped back.

Nixon's eyes followed him suspiciously. The grin had become an austere smile. "When did I first meet you, Garfield? Not over this. When? Kissinger and his plans for your committee? That was the first. But I knew about you. Yes—long time before that. The man who could walk the horizon at sunset and stay invisible—somebody once described you that way. All this doesn't do you justice. Or maybe it does in a way. You're a . . . formidable man. I like that. In some ways a voice, you know, tells me I could have used you. But you wouldn't have liked that. Not being *used*, eh? We share that feeling. Not wanting to be used. We have that in common."

Nixon lowered himself into his chair and idly pressed the selector of the automatic dialing machine by the telephone. It spun an array of names. "I don't even have a number listed for you, you know that? Everybody who's nobody is on this thing nowadays." He watched it spin, then snapped to attention. "O.K. The talking's over." He eased his arm to a more comfortable position in the sling. "I don't think I'm going to accept anything you've said here today, and I'll tell you why. You're working up to walk out on the deal we had—*your* deal, not mine. I set myself up, Garfield. I did it for decent motives, but I don't like being used. Now then . . ." He set his jaw doggedly. "I've been thinking this thing out. You handed me a stick of dynamite to scare up a reaction from Bradley. It didn't work. But I still have that dynamite, Garfield. I still have the motive. Suppose I use it my own way?"

"How would you propose to do that?" Garfield raised an eyebrow.

"Don't let's kid ourselves. I got a lot of good reaction at LaCosta. I felt it, you know? Maybe the straightforward simple way to break Bradley is to do as you suggested. Not

189

bluff. For real. Let's see what the people *really* feel about Richard Nixon. What do you say?"

"I've thought about it. They liked you at LaCosta. They also tried to kill you. They were supposed to applaud, not shoot."

Nixon stared at him for what seemed like an age. He said, "You're a son of a bitch, Garfield, you know that?"

"I have to deal in realities, sir."

"You're walking out, then?"

"I'm walking out on nothing, sir. Without you, I have no hand to play. If you pull out, Bradley's home free."

The ex-President eased his wounded arm and grinned. "Then don't think you can run the show all your own way, okay? We both have a lot tied up in this. If it doesn't work for you, maybe it'll work for me."

Garfield rode the waiting golf cart, complete with chauffeur, the quarter mile short cut across the private golf course to his car. As was his habit, he had mentally filed and cross-indexed his objectives before his meeting with Nixon and now he reassessed them.

They were in good shape. So was the man. Maybe Nixon's good spirits were too good and his ambition just a shade too sharp-edged for comfort; but the house of cards had withstood the storm and was still intact. There was no logical reason for his unease, he assured himself; none that a good night's sleep back home in Washington couldn't cure.

WEDNESDAY: 2355—ANSON

Anson stretched out on the bed, hands clasped behind his head. Grazia's pervasive musk was everywhere—clothes, sheets, blankets, carpets. She must have sprayed the room with a full hundred-dollar bottle of perfume. It was enough to lure a priest from the confessional. Still, it was cheap at the price. She was out of his life, wasn't she?

He felt the cramp gathering in the back of his legs, a sure sign his brain didn't intend to let him sleep tonight. A brain full of names: Walt Margolis, the girl (no name for her now), Leo McCullen, Milton Abrams, John Roper Anson. Especially John Roper, who had always been bigger than life; now, in death, he seemed bigger than that, too.

Those damned files of Margolis's—what were they? He'd

reached this stage a half-dozen times and the temptation to write the files off to the garbage dump grew more urgent each time. But still he persisted. He had agonized over it all afternoon at State; driven home to agonize some more; spent four hours in John Roper's apartment, running the evidence through his head; but it still made no sense.

In the dream he was knee-deep in snow thick as shaving foam, held rigid while a visible blue wind snatched puffballs from the creamy surface and hurled them against his chest and thighs like tumbleweed. He tried to pull a leg free; it wouldn't move. In the distance the white creamy blanket began to whirl, sucking the lathery spume into a black hole. He tried to run away, but the snow had risen to his waist. Then he was falling backward, arms wide, sinking deeper. Unexpected warmth spread around him and he was buried alive. He came awake, the sheets wrapped around him tight as a shroud. The telephone by the bed buzzed anxiously. He picked it up.

"Uh, Anson." He shook his head to clear it and peered blearily at his watch.

"Is that you, Harry?" demanded the voice.

"I think so. Yeah, this is Anson." He ran his tongue over his teeth. Dry. Grazia's perfume came off the pillow like stale gin.

"Milt Abrams. You awake?"

Good old Milt. Anson flopped back, exhausted, against the headboard. "You know what time it is?"

"Shape up, Anson. This is important." Abrams appeared to be recovering from a major throat operation. "Are you alone?"

"Sure, except for a couple of passing karate experts. They just dropped by for a workout on the back of my neck."

"Are you drunk?" Suspiciously.

"Sober as a spook. Now it's your turn."

"Are you sure you're O.K.?"

"I was till you called. What do you want?"

"I want to see you. Won't wait."

"What won't wait?"

"I can't talk over the phone."

"Is that what you called to tell me? That you can't talk on the phone?"

"You want to make it tough on yourself, go right ahead. When you hear what I have to say you'll realize what kind of a prick you are."

191

"What kind is that?" He sat up squarely in the bed. Abrams's voice had a note of urgency in it that was completely out of character with the personality he had projected so carefully at Langley.

"Something came up. It's about your father. Look—all that stuff I gave you Sunday about Margolis—it's crap. Far as I knew, you were just some creep from State sticking his nose in Company business. I've been checking out a few things since we talked. They just clicked into place."

"What about my father?"

"I've overshot my time, Anson. I said we couldn't talk on the phone. Listen. You know the Frederick Douglass Bridge? On the south side of the river there's a pumphouse where the road runs out around a headland. I'll meet you there in twenty minutes. Be there—on the dot. If you don't turn up you're a bigger fool than your father was." The line went dead.

Anson went to the bathroom and splashed cold water on his face. He pulled on a pair of faded jeans, a sweater and a pair of sneakers. Panic, or something approaching it, didn't come naturally to a computer like Abrams, but there had been more than subtle hints of it in his call. What did he mean by "a bigger fool than your father was"? And why the B-movie location for their meet? He pulled on his leather jacket and went down to the car.

Anson followed the signs to Anacostia Park, crossed the 11th Street Bridge and looped under the freeway past the Naval Annex and the Botanic Garden Nursery. His watch glowed quarter past midnight. The road blindly hugged the contours of the river, which was lit by a pale glow from the city. Scattered along its verges a few black-fingered trees crouched in the snow, branches groping forlornly at the sky. It was a night for only the lustiest lovers, the most dedicated muggers. He turned the heat up to maximum. Maybe in summer, people brought kids to picnic under those trees. Tonight they were as alluring as gibbets strung along the Via Dolorosa.

He checked the D.C. street map. Abrams had chosen his spot well. No factories, no houses, no cars, no people. Anson's mind turned speculatively on the inanity that the Company had bought up stretches of barren Washington real estate like this for the express purpose of mounting clandestine meetings. After all, back in 1963 hadn't they bought off a developer who planned to build high-rise apartments in Saddle Lane near the CIA offices? He wound down the window.

The wind slapped his cheek. The road was pockmarked with neglect, as if it had lost faith in itself. Up ahead, the thin ridge of brick marking its curb wavered and petered out disconsolately in a flurry of shale and mud. He turned off the road. The Porsche's wheels rasped unhappily, its lights bouncing. An answering beam flashed away over to his left as a car crossed the Frederick Douglass Bridge and disappeared over Potomac Avenue.

On the far side of the river the sprawl of the Navy Yard twinkled with light against an indistinct skyline of cranes and derricks. He braked uncertainly. Another car flashed across the bridge and, on his right, he made out the roof of a small, square building at the river's edge, half-hidden by the upper slope of the snow-covered bank. He eased the Porsche forward. The pumphouse stood on a platform of concrete, doors and windows barred and padlocked. It had the look of a medieval waterfront prison. Between the road and the bank lay a no-man's-land fifteen feet wide, crisscrossed with the treads of construction vehicles and punctured with puddles of frozen water. He pulled the Porsche gingerly onto the slope. The ground was as unyielding as permafrost. He cut the engine and doused the lights, half expecting Abrams to step from the locked pumphouse. But if Abrams was already there he wasn't ready to reveal himself. Not yet, anyway.

Ten minutes. Fifteen. Anson switched on the engine but it had cooled and what little warmth it supplied was no match for the deadly chill of the river. A dog came out of the darkness and stared at him, then began foraging in a pile of old cans and cartons at the river's edge. Humpbacked with hunger, it moved closer to the Porsche, trembling between fear and an irresistible curiosity. Anson clicked his tongue. The mutt bared yellow teeth and slithered away out of sight.

Twenty minutes. Still no sign of Abrams. The cramp returned to Anson's legs and recollections of the warm, seductively empty bed tugged obsessively at the corners of his mind. He jabbed the button of his watch. It was 12:56. He had left—when?—forty minutes ago. Abrams had been insistent on the timing. Twenty minutes on the dot.

He twisted the hand brake violently and pumped the gas. He checked the rearview mirror—and his hand froze on the gearshift. The big rig loomed blacker than the night less than ten yards behind him, its engine suddenly roaring with life. He swung in the seat and wound down the window. He angled his head through it. "Is that you, Abrams?" he yelled.

The rig hissed compressed air. Four blinding shafts of light

193

stabbed from above and below the cab, and Anson clutched his eyes as the dazzle exploded like orange balloons in his head. "Abrams! For chrissake!"

The rig lunged forward off the road and hurled itself down the bank. It struck the rear fender of the Porsche and crushed it instantly; metal screamed obscenely in a shower of sparks. Anson's left hand grabbed blindly at the wheel, but the whiplash effect snapped his head back on the rest and a curtain of blood surged behind his eyes. The rig plowed forward, urging the Porsche irresistibly down the slope. The little car scraped its belly on the stonework of the river's retaining wall, poised, and somersaulted into the water.

Anson's shoulder was wedged in the open window, one hand outside, clutching water. In a spasm of shock, he jerked upright, his arms rigid as the terrible cold paralyzed him, swallowed him whole. The car dived, nose first, and the anesthetic chill spread through his body. Then he erupted with terror. He lashed out wildly with both feet and threw his weight against the door. His free hand clamped on the outside handle and battered it savagely. The Porsche sighed down, its air bubble breaking into the river. Anson could see nothing, feel nothing. He touched his right leg and choked with relief; it was moving. He was moving. *Please keep moving. Don't stop now.* The orange balloons were growing inside his skull, billowing and bursting, splitting his head apart. He gagged as water seeped into his mouth and throat. The current caught the car in its arms, thrusting from beneath like a supporting hand. The door gave and he was floating up. His lungs convulsed, forcing his mouth to open. He gave in, sucked air. Air.

The lights of the Navy Yard winked as he rolled, gasping, on the surface. He thrashed the water in a frantic dog paddle and reached the stone of the river bank. He tore at the icicles of grass, found leverage and swung up and out. He collapsed on the snow, retching into it. The wind scourged him and numbness engulfed hands and feet. He knew he had to move. At the fourth attempt he managed to stand, his knees jack-knifing under him like a vaudeville comedian's, threatening to pitch him back into the river.

Run.

Jog.

Stagger.

Move if you want to live. Move!

The scavenging dog snarled out of the darkness. Anson stumbled forward, teeth chattering, mind focusing, half-

194

delirious, half-elated. "Fuck off!" he stuttered. He stumbled over the animal and it yelped and backed away, the snarl deteriorating to a submissive whimper. "Good dog," he said idiotically. "Race you home."

He lurched into a jerky trot toward the lights of the Frederick Douglass Bridge.

THURSDAY: 0145—ANSON

Anson ran the shower as hot as he could bear it until the pins and needles in his feet and hands told him the blood was circulating at last. He let it play over him for another ten minutes; then wrapped in a robe and a couple of towels, he poured three fingers of brandy into a tall glass of hot milk and turned up the heat to its limit.

He felt curiously fit, his skin tingling with that almost tortured prickling of health which comes at the end of punishing athletic endeavor. The tastes of brandy and milk were precise, magnified on his tongue, and his nostrils flared to catch the subtle distinctions of soap, steam, hot air and the lingering ghosts of Grazia's perfume around him. He flexed the muscles of his left arm and found an almost juvenile satisfaction in the firmness of the bulging bicep.

The euphoria faded when he considered what he had to do next. How do you tell Hertz that $20,000 worth of Porsche is lying at the bottom of the Anacostia River? How understanding would they be in the matter of loss as a result of attempted murder? The cabdriver who picked him up on the Navy Yard side of Frederick Douglass Bridge had peered at Anson's soaking clothes but kept his curiosity to himself. Tomorrow, if asked, he would spout like a fountain.

And what about Abrams? It *had* to be Abrams. Would he sit tight now and wait for Anson to make the next move? Or would he come back for a second hit? Anson took a long slug of the brandied milk. The chances were that Abrams—or his hit men—hadn't waited around to see him escape from the submerged car. Abrams had every right to expect that anyone bulldozed into the river in a closed car at night in sub-zero temperatures wouldn't climb out again. He grinned to himself and took another draft of the hot drink. Either he was light-headed with shock and getting feebleminded drunk . . . or he was actually enjoying this.

He reached for the waterlogged wreck of his jacket and

195

thumbed the black address book from the inside pocket. The pages were pulp. This was one book guaranteed to keep its secrets forever. He tossed it aside and took the telephone into his lap.

Buffalo Morgan's initials, according to the information operator, were C. W. Z. Anson called the number she gave him.

Morgan came on at once, characteristically avoiding unnecessary preliminaries. "Who wants him?" he grunted.

He mellowed at once when Anson identified himself. "I bin meaning to ask you about that cat necklace thing. I told myself, that thing has to be goddamn important if Walt gotta put messages inside. You know what I mean?"

Anson ignored the invitation.

"Can you come out to Walt's house in Virginia tonight, Buff?"

There was a pause at the other end. Morgan said slowly, "You mean, like now?"

"Have you got a car?"

"Sure, I got a car. You wouldn't rent it street space alongside that thing you drive, but it's O.K., I guess."

"Can you pick me up here?" He gave the address of the apartment. Another pause as Morgan wrote it down.

"Er . . . you wanna tell me something, Louie?"

"I'll tell you everything when we're on the way."

"You're sure you wanna do this?"

"If you want to pull out, you just have to say."

"Who said anything about pulling out? I just thought we oughta talk about it is all. What are we looking for?"

"We're looking," Anson said crisply, "for the way out."

There were no lights visible in the house this time and no cars in the driveway. The three-quarter moon lent them sufficient light to slog through the banked snow to the portico without falling on their faces. Buffalo leaned on the door and it groaned inward. He raised a thumb. "O.K.?"

"Never seen it done better."

Morgan expanded with modest pleasure.

They went inside. Anson turned on the lights in the living room. The fire was laid with logs. He set a match to them.

Buffalo stripped off his hooded parka. "You want to get right down to it?"

"You wait here. I'll bring the files down from Walt's den," Anson instructed. "Better not have too many lighted win-

196

dows. I wouldn't know what the hell to say if the local law came pounding on the door."

The files were where he had left them: four neat stacks of blue with a single pale green cover topping the second stack where Walt had clipped together a bunch of eight-by-ten black and white photographs. He touched the cover, taking its pulse; frowned at the empty chair behind Walt's desk. What had gone through his mind as he sat there, shuffling and dealing his collected paperwork?

A funeral cortege of names winding back to Dallas. Yesterday handcuffed to tomorrow. He slid one finger down the stack nearest him and let it stop on the file cover he knew carried the label John Roper Anson. He took it out and flicked the half-dozen quarto pages. Biography: birth, education, marriage, career, all in the most truncated shorthand. The birth of a son, Harold Roper Anson; nothing more on that line. John Roper's appointments, from China to Singapore to Colombia to Sweden to Italy to Germany to England. Meaningless Arabic numerology—1–7–37 (N–P 15864)—alongside a reference to an appointment as third secretary to the embassy in Shanghai. No accusative names anywhere in John Roper's file.

He gathered the four stacks into one and made a cautious return downstairs. In the hallway, his face all but obscured by the teetering column, he heard Buffalo's nervous throat-clearing cough and wondered fleetingly if he had ever been invited here before. Anson tapped the door with the toe of one shoe and it opened inward. He came over the threshold and said, as he advanced on the long polished table, "Make yourself at home, Buffalo. Nobody's going to . . ."

"Harry!"

He whirled on his heel. The files swayed drunkenly and tumbled to the floor. She was possibly more surprised than he; her eyes were wide with disbelief, her mouth open. But the Special in her hand was firm and unwavering and ready for immediate surgery. He found himself unable to tear his eyes from the tension lines where her right index finger cuddled the trigger. *Don't pull—squeeeeeze.* The lines relaxed.

"Why didn't you tell me you planned to come by tonight?" she breathed. She was wearing the velour housecoat. She let the gun fall to her side but did not move her fingers from the trigger guard. "I was in bed. I heard noises and . . ."

Buffalo spoke from across the room by the fire. "She came up on me, Louie. I didn't get to hear till she . . ."

"Louie?" Her eyebrows lifted and her right hand massaged the gun butt, puzzled.

"Everybody's Louie to Buffalo."

She started a smile. Anson pruned it before it had a chance to blossom.

"But, then, I should think you know all there is to know about all-purpose names, *Alice*."

The name gave him a preposterous kick of pleasure. He had known she couldn't be an Alice.

"Alice?" Buffalo Morgan took a step forward. "Are you Walt's little girl?"

The .38 swung to point at his stomach, stopping him in midstride. The girl looked across at Anson. Her face displayed a mixture of alarm and defiance, like a schoolgirl caught smoking in the bathroom. Except there was nothing of the schoolgirl in the way she readjusted her grip on the gun.

"What do you mean, Harry?"

"You know what I mean. If you didn't, you'd have no need to point that piece."

"We have to talk," she said suddenly. "Alone."

"In that case you have a decision to make. Either you talk in front of Buffalo here or we don't talk at all. You could lock him in a room somewhere, I guess . . ." He turned to measure Buffalo's giant frame appreciatively. "But I doubt if you've got a room that would hold him for long. And I'm not going to stick around all night."

She faced him squarely, the .38 bouncing in her palm. Then she raised it deliberately and clicked on the safety catch. She put the revolver down on the table and stood stiffly beside it.

"All right, Harry. On your terms."

Morgan whoofed a sigh of relief. "I don't get this, Louie. Is she Walt's kid or ain't she?"

"No," said Anson softly, his eyes locked on the girl's, "she ain't."

He pulled out a chair from the table and motioned her to sit down. He walked around and sat facing her. "Are we going to be allowed the pleasure of knowing exactly *who* you are?"

She threaded her long slim fingers together and studied them. "It's not that easy."

"You surprise me."

Her face tightened. The anger flashed—sudden, brutal. Then her eyes began to brim with tears.

Anson rested an elbow on the table and shook a finger.

"No. It won't work. Though you do it well enough for drama school. What's the secret: an onion? Garlic clove?" The sarcasm was ponderous, but Anson knew it was the safest substitute for the rage he wasn't sure he could control.

She brought her hands up to her face. Her voice trembled. Anson felt like snatching them away, bringing the whole sickening charade to an end. Buffalo could sense what he was feeling. "Louie . . . Louie . . . the kid's upset. Them's real tears . . ."

Anson shook his head. "Buffalo, if this girl were real, like she says she's real, she'd be in a morgue in Seattle." She parted her hands in genuine shock. Her lips moved but no sound came.

"Alice Margolis is dead," said Anson flatly. "She was found on the sidewalk outside her apartment building. Did she jump or was she pushed? It doesn't really matter now. Not to her."

"Oh, my God!" The tears began again.

Anson waited patiently, aware of Buffalo Morgan hovering like a shackled knight on a white charger, his instincts telling him to comfort the girl, the warning glances from Anson rooting him where he stood. The girl's face came up to level with his. And, for the first time, Anson began to have doubts. Maybe she really was . . .

She said with frightening precision, "Leo's dead."

It was Anson's turn to stare. "Leo? McCullen? What the hell d'you know about Leo?"

"He's dead, Harry. I know that."

"You're crazy!" Anson realized he was shouting. "I saw him last night, I . . ."

"What time?" she interrupted.

"Time?" He ran a hand through his hair. "About a quarter of ten, maybe later. I don't know exactly. Right before I came here."

"And you left . . . ?"

"10:30, something like that. Look, quit playing games, all right?"

"The coroner's report put the time of death between 10:30 and 11:00." She was defiant through her tears. Anson spun from the chair in disgust.

"There's a telephone over there, Harry. Pick it up. Find out."

He lowered his head slowly until their eyes met. She wasn't lying.

"How do you know?"

"It doesn't matter how."

"It matters to me, goddamnit. Do you know what you're saying?" He jabbed a finger at her accusingly. "He was alive when I left him and you'd better believe it!"

Buffalo Morgan was now in total confusion. His eyes darted between Anson and the girl with the regularity of a metronome. "Look—if you kids are having some kinda spat, fine. You wanna play games, that's fine too. But I ain't so quick. All I know is that Walt and me were like that." He twisted two pudgy fingers of his right hand together until the joints cracked. "And that gives me some kind of rights. You want help—tell me. You want I should get lost—tell me that too. But sure as hell, one of you gotta open this thing up or I walk outta here right now!" His chin wobbled with indignation.

The girl looked across at him. "That's the first nice thing I've heard tonight, Mr. Morgan. Yes. Please stay. I need someone." She switched her glance to Anson.

He shook his head in defeat. "As God is my witness, if you're playing me for a sucker again ..." He caught Morgan's stare. "Oh, to hell with it! O.K. How is it you know about Leo and I don't?"

She swallowed hard. "Leo was working with Walt Margolis. They worked together now three years. Leo ..."

Anson brought his fist down onto the table with a crash. "Will you answer the goddamn question!"

"Leave her be, son." Buffalo came along the table and rested a plump hand on the girl's shoulder. "Let her tell it the way she has to."

She thanked him with her eyes. "It started two years after Watergate. Leo realized things were happening at Langley that were outside the Company's brief ..."

"Blinding revelations on the road to Damascus!"

"Hold it down, son," rumbled Buffalo. He took her hand and squeezed it encouragingly. She clung to it.

"It wasn't like that. Leo was clean and decent, but he wasn't naive. He lived with the idea of the State's right to double-deal and he went along with it while the motives were right."

"Oh, come on ..."

"Go ahead, kid," urged Buffalo.

"Sometimes the motives *were* right," she persisted. "Anyway, he thought so. But around spring of '76 it all began to go sour. Everywhere he turned the Company seemed to have skeletons locked away. Watergate stirred up a lot of dirt and, the way Leo saw it, they couldn't find any more space under the mat to sweep it."

Anson turned sideways on his chair, his face averted.

She hesitated. "What do you want me to say, Harry? That Leo was stupid? You think he should have told himself *everyone* was corrupt, *everything* was corruptible?"

Anson swung on her. "I think Leo should have stayed out of the kitchen if he couldn't stand the heat. But I've got a nasty suspicious nature, so I don't see Leo with a ring of light around his skull. Leo was like everyone else in this town—he was ready to get down in the gutter to scrape up a piece of the action. He had a suit for every day of the week and a moral blind spot for every hour of the day." He stopped. He didn't mean any of that but he needed to vent his rage at the senselessness of the man's death.

She understood. She caught his eye and tested his anger. "He said about you that you were too honest ever to make a good diplomat."

"In two weeks he plumbed my soul." The sarcasm was bitter.

Buffalo squeezed her shoulder. She nodded. "Leo and Walt began to check out ... certain things. What they found that first year—'76—was dynamite. Leo took it to Capitol Hill and ... well, that was Step One. Step Two was the convening of the House Assassinations Committee. There was a lot more and Leo passed it through the same channels. He believed that had to be the way. In '77, the Senate Intelligence Committee was set up. Leo knew what that meant—he gave them a spy-hole right into the core at Langley. He named the files they needed to see, the dates and names and ... oh, all of it. The day they subpoenaed Richard Helms, Leo knew he'd passed the point of no return. He'd stripped Langley of everything; he'd sold them out and he knew they wouldn't just lie back and take it. He did everything he could to protect Walt ..."

Anson interrupted abruptly, "Those files of Walt's ..." He jerked his head at the litter on the floor by the door. "Are they for real or was it part of setting me up?"

She shook her head violently. "Nobody set you up!"

"I just happened to stray onto the field of play?" Acidly.

"In one way—yes. But ..."

He leaned forward. "The file on my father. If you're about to tell me Walt used that to hook me into this ..." He left the threat unspoken.

"That was part of Walt's investigation. He died before he

201

could tell Leo what he was following up. He called Leo the night he died. He said he'd found something . . . somone. But . . ."

"What's that got to do with my father?"

She watched him keenly. "I don't know."

Anson pushed himself to his feet and went over to stand by the fire. "So now you expect me to believe all this and say I'm sorry I made you cry?"

"You can do what you like."

"O.K. Go back to the beginning. I asked you a question. Who are you?"

She looked at him, her jaw firm, challenging. "My name is Lee Ritchie."

Right! Lee. That fits, he thought. She was never an Alice but she could never be anything less than a Lee.

"Can you prove that?"

"In my bag. There's a driver's license, credit cards . . ."

"We got the lady's word on it—right, Louie?" Buffalo Morgan didn't leave Anson much choice.

"Sure, Buffalo, we have the lady's word. One little thing, though. How come Langley told me on the phone today that Leo was not available, but they tell *you* he's dead? And they even turn up the coroner's report for you. Why would they do that?"

Lee Ritchie raked the Kentucky-chestnut curtain of hair from her face and raised her eyes to meet his. The pink tip of her tongue slipped over her lips.

"They had to," she said calmly. "I was Leo's wife."

Buffalo hung around for fifteen minutes, then pleaded old age and infirmity and went upstairs to Walt's room to catch up on his sleep, already deferred once tonight.

"A good fight I can referee," he told them, "but there ain't a single damn thing I can do for you guys you can't do better yourselves."

He collected the files and stacked them neatly before he left. When he'd gone, they sat face to face in the fireside chairs. Memories lay smouldering between them, entwined on the sheepskin rug.

Anson said guiltily: "Did Leo know about . . . ?"

She touched a hand to her brow, half shielding her eyes. "He knew, but not about . . . that. Just that we were . . . close."

"You could have fooled me." Anson draped a leg over the arm of the chair. "How much closer can you get than

202

marriage? You did drop by the apartment and hit Grazia with that stuff about being my wife, didn't you?"

"You said you were having problems. I just . . ."

"Yeah."

"I'm sorry if I spoiled it for you," she said acidly.

He chuckled. "I'm surprised you came out of it in one piece. Grazia has a habit of getting physical when she's aroused."

"I can handle myself." It was not boastful.

"Leo must have thought so. But then he knew, didn't he?"

She said defensively: "We broke up six years ago. Maybe longer. We didn't celebrate the anniversary, but we didn't cry a lot either. We came to the end so we stopped living together. There was no way of making it work."

"You don't owe me explanations," he retorted gruffly.

"I'm not trying. You asked. I'm telling you."

He fidgeted in the chair. Why the hell should he feel jealous, for chrissakes? "You broke up but you didn't break up, right?"

She watched his face for a moment. She seemed to find something there she was hoping for. "Six years ago I also worked for the Company." She drew satisfaction from his jerk of surprise. "That's where we met. Langley." She raised her eyes to the ceiling at the recollection. "In the canteen. With that kind of a start, how could a marriage fail!" She caught the empty ring finger in her right hand and worried away at it. "We tried. Leo tried a lot, but suddenly we realized how hard we were trying and how pathetic that made . . . everything. So we called it a day. A few months later, I left the Company. It seemed a little sick, living together at work when we couldn't live together at home. Anyway, I thought so."

"And then Leo came calling again?"

"Not right away. Two, three years ago. He needed someone he could trust; someone who wouldn't ask questions. He needed someone to carry the ball when he had to stay in line with the Company. It's not a unique situation."

"And when I came along, he needed bait and you were the natural candidate?"

"That's not fair!" Her face was flushed. She deflated. "Leo wouldn't have asked that of me in a billion years. And I wouldn't have done it. Not even for him."

"Your conscience didn't balk at playing me for a sucker . . . with everything you had."

Her fists clenched, knuckles white.

"I didn't make love to you because of Leo. Or because of Walt or the Company or a bunch of damned files or . . ." She was half out of the chair. "I *wanted* to. For *me*. Is that too much for you to grasp? I *wanted* you. The reasons didn't seem important at the time."

He waited for her to go on, but she sank deep into the chair, eyes closed. He said gently: "I'm not psychic, you know. Why should I trust you? Leo never told me anything that amounted to anything. He . . ."

"He trusted you. He knew Walt trusted you, too. He always believed Walt would pass something on to you. He said so."

"He did. The cat's identity tag. I *told* Leo."

"The night he died. *Minutes* before they killed him."

"So . . ."

"So he didn't have time to make use of it. He couldn't pass it on. You're still the only one who knows."

He studied her. "There's you. And Buffalo."

She sighed. "You don't have to worry about me. I'm no threat; not with Leo. . . ." The challenging smile returned. "I don't think Buffalo's going to ruin anyone's sleep, either."

He nodded slowly, filling in time. "Buffalo'll keep."

She reached to the back of her neck and massaged the muscles at the base of the skull. She felt his gaze on her. "I guess we ought to get some sleep."

He pushed himself to his feet and went around the back of her chair. He pushed her hands aside and began to knead the taut muscles of her neck and shoulders.

"Know what you need?" he said matter-of-factly.

"No. What?" She was off guard.

He bent, slipped one arm under her knees and swung her up into his arms. "You need a candle to light you to bed."

THURSDAY: 0315—ANSON

The fire burned low and he got up from the sheepskin reluctantly. Her hand clutched his shoulder as he rose, slipped along his arm, arrested his wrist. He bent and kissed her. "The fire's going out," he said. She giggled helplessly, and he caught the implication and choked on his unwitting pun. She slipped into her robe while he built fresh logs over the ashes of the old and coaxed life back into the fire. She left the room and returned five minutes later with hot chocolate. They sat together on the rug, back to back, supporting each other.

She said seriously, "What now?"

"Us? Or . . . ?"

"You know what I mean."

He poured hot chocolate onto his tongue. "I want you out of this," he said firmly. "If anyone's going to get hurt . . ."

"No deal." She spoke quietly. He didn't bother to fight her.

"O.K. So tell me now—what do you make of Walt's files?"

She reached a hand over her shoulder and ruffled his hair. "I don't—that part was true, too. I guess I told you what I really thought the second time you came here. Walt was working his way through the undergrowth, dismissing some things, holding onto others. There's no kind of methodical system about the files. They read like someone thinking out loud. The parts he left out are what count."

"Leo never talked to you about them?"

"No—except he said once that Walt was using the cover of his memoirs to get high-grade information from official files. It was a way of nosing around without exciting suspicion."

"You think Walt was killed?" Anson asked her gently.

"Leo said so."

"The autopsy said it was a heart attack."

"They made it *look* like a heart attack."

This confirmation of his own first reaction made him shudder. "They must have been out of their minds."

She leaned her head into his back. "They were. Panic, not insanity."

"We keep saying 'they.' Who?"

"Leo said it was political but with a lot of extra muscle. Some of it was Langley. He didn't say too much. He . . ."

He reached behind him and took her hand. "I know. He didn't want you to get hurt."

She turned, knelt behind him and rested her chin on his shoulder. "You have most of it—at least that's the way it seems to me. You have Walt's list. You have his files. There has to be a link."

He shook his head. "We already guessed Walt left out the things he considered important. That list includes a half dozen of the most influential men in America. We may not know everything there is to know about them but, my God, they're not killers."

205

"Then what are they?"

"A couple of them played polo once—but not for the same club. Three were corporation presidents—but in different industries. They could have met, but on paper they have nothing in common. There's an Assistant Secretary of State and the Director of the CIA—but their careers don't overlap, nor do their interests or social activities. Yeah, they could be friends, but so what?"

"And what about the wild card?"

"The what?"

"The name Walt scribbled on your list, Nixon. Why that? What made him write it?"

"There's nothing on him in Walt's files. But that means . . . ," he shrugged, "means anything. Nothing. I don't know. Bradley—Nixon. I ran it through with Leo, but it meant nothing to him, either. At least he *said* it meant nothing. I'm beginning to wonder if anyone in this goddamn town is capable of stringing three words together that aren't open to five different meanings."

She watched him silently for a moment. Harry Anson hid a natural strength beneath a veneer of diffidence. The veneer was beginning to wear thin. And what might be revealed underneath was the only thing she was unsure of about him. She said, "All this. Your *involvement*. It's not Walt's death, is it? It's your father."

"What?"

"Your father," she persisted. "You cared a lot for him, didn't you? It shows."

Anson grunted.

"Did you share much?"

"Share? Share how?" He began to feel the old unease.

"You know. Fathers and sons. Fishing, shooting—that kind of thing. I'd like to know."

"We did the usual things. Later, he got so's he didn't have the time. I was studying."

"Do you remember him well?"

"I'm not sure."

"But what was he *like?* I mean, was he stern? Did he talk to you? Was he a doting father? I only read about him. I can't picture him."

"He was a father. What should fathers be like?"

"Well, what kind of friends did he have? You must have met them, even when you were little? I mean did he throw parties? Did he . . . ?" Too fast, too far. She didn't need the puzzled expression on his face to tell her that. She broke it up

206

before he could, rose, settled into a chair and shook her hair over her shoulders with a toss of the head. "My father wouldn't let me date till I was eighteen. Can you imagine that?" She arched an eyebrow. "See what a good girl it made me?" She held out her hand and waited for him to clasp it.

Anson's frown evaporated. He tried to pull her to her feet, but she tugged him off balance and he fell in a heap beside her, laughing. He got to his knees and cupped her face in his hands.

"Your father was a good guy," he said. "Let's go to bed."

THURSDAY: 0455—ANSON

It took Anson half an hour to sink into fitful sleep. He lay in the darkness, body satiated and at ease, mind in tumult, doggedly rejecting the seductive waves of exhaustion. The nightmare realities of the Anacostia River came back to haunt him: the scream of metal as the rig crushed the Porsche, the anesthetic dive under the black water, the ice-cold descent . . .

He fell, at last, into the void, leaving Leo McCullen, Walt Margolis and John Roper Anson standing silent and accusing on the edge of his consciousness. He never hit bottom. He woke, uncertain if he had slept five minutes or five hours. All he knew was that something was resolving itself, had begun to surface in his sleep, something he didn't fully understand as yet. He looked at Lee; she lay motionless, one hand under her cheek, breathing steadily. He slipped from the bed, threw Walt's plaid robe around him and went downstairs to the living room. The files were still stacked on the table. He flicked through the top one, trying not to think too deeply, letting his mind drift as it chose.

Inside the file, a photograph of Ambrose Bradley smiled up at him. The picture had been taken several years earlier. It was not the face of the craggy white-haired gospeler Anson had seen on TV newsreels. The man looking at him had been in his prime; unshakable self-assurance was molded in every line, intelligence, strength, conviction. Birth and privilege could create that, of course, but the face had more to it than the stamp of inherited arrogance. Bradley had a visionary awareness of himself that obviously satisfied him. Not one to tolerate weakness in others any more than he would tolerate it in himself. Too complex and too considered to be simply a bigot, though that was an accusation he was bound to invite. He looked too . . . good to be true?

He would be equally at home defining justice in the Supreme Court as he was exchanging homilies on the porch of some hick-town drugstore. A man for all seasons. If they ever made a film around Ambrose Bradley they'd have to resurrect Spencer Tracy.

Anson reached for his jacket and took the slip of paper from it. He smoothed it out on the table alongside the files. What in God's name was Margolis trying to tell him?

He stared again at the letters and numbers.

The files weren't numbered, so there was no connection there. Anyway, if the files were that important, would Margolis have left them around to be found? No, whatever he'd learned he'd locked into this damn slip of paper. Maybe he hadn't even left it in the cat's collar for someone else to find. It could be his own *aide-memoire*. A reminder. Why would he need to remind himself of something he already knew? Because it was complicated or . . . or because he'd chosen a code at random.

He was looking around the room as he thought and his eyes stopped at the bookcase. A book code? He took the paper to the shelves and studied the volumes.

CWC 301.

It jumped out at him. He almost cried out as he saw the title on the faded leather binding: Caesar's War Commentaries. The sheet of paper was imprisoned between pages 300 and 301.

S 24. That was harder. It took him three minutes to trace it to Seneca, page 24.

He worked methodically down the list: Cicero, Plato, Thucydides, Heraclitus. One by one, the sages gave up their secrets. When he was through, he had collected thirteen sheets. He arranged them in numbered order and began to read.

Walt hadn't compiled the document; the style was wrong and there were penciled notes in the margins that were too neat to be his. It reminded Anson of a police report. It was also an investigative triumph and a damning one. It was an astounding denunciation of what Anson could only assume was an organization, a confederation of some kind. It wasn't named. But there *were* names: Bradley, Clegg, Torrance . . . All the names Margolis had written on that scrap of paper. Lines had been drawn linking them into some kind of

208

hierarchy but the notes were too cryptic to divine what precise purpose they served or what common denominators the names shared. His father's name was mentioned twice, but only in passing:

"J. R. Anson told . . ."

". . . and confirmed with J. R. Anson."

Nixon was mentioned once. Again the restrictive style obscured the context, but implied his indirect association with "the property."

The last sheet was a biography of someone Anson had never heard of, whose name was not even mentioned in the list or the files. Aaron LaCroix. The dates stopped with his death twenty years ago. But there was a link.

Anson pushed it aside and pulled Margolis's file on Ambrose Bradley across the table to check. The biography was sketchy.

"Son of Homer J. Bradley; landowner, rancher, industrialist, engineer, businessman; who inherited, in turn, from his father, a panhandler who struck it lucky on the Comstock Lode in 1859 . . ." Anson skipped down the page. "Homer Bradley's mining interests were sold out in 1934 (bad timing); reinvested in land. Ambrose Bradley born Turtleback, Arizona, and lived there until . . ."

Turtleback, Arizona. He glanced down again at the biographical sheet on Aaron LaCroix. Turtleback, Arizona. Minister of the church. He'd established a pastoral group in Turtleback in the early fifties.

The memory floated to the surface as if freed from a tangled weedbed. He was a young boy—no more than twelve—sitting with his mother in the back seat of the big black Pontiac John Roper drove, on their way to what his father had described as "an adventure." It had been rare for them to travel so far together in an automobile. John Roper had preferred airplanes or trains, as a rule, because the State Department were great worriers, he said, and feared for his valued neck when he took to the road alone.

The trip was a mixture of business and pleasure; business for his father, pleasure for him and his mother. They registered at a small boardinghouse calling itself a hotel, although no one would deny it was by far the grandest establishment in that curious little desert town. John Roper had pointed out the names of the towns as they came up on the signposts: Carefree, Sunflower, Granite Mountain, Cave Creek. His father went away in the car, leaving Harry and his mother in the care of a half-caste guide who took them each day on a

209

new "adventure." After three days, John Roper returned and they drove home to Washington.

Anson turned off the light and crept back up to the bedroom. He slipped into bed beside Lee Ritchie and allowed his mind to carry him off again to a town called Turtle-back.

BOOK THREE CHRONICLES

. . . And they conspired against him and stoned him with stones . . . .
2 CHRONICLES, 24:21

Garfield's underground walk to the White House was more depressing than usual. He could have delayed the visit, but he had already overstepped the acceptable limit. It was too early in the day to hope for measured judgments and worldly pragmatism.

The first fifteen minutes were taken up with Garfield's account of events since their last meeting. It sounded like a prelude to the Apocalypse. He finished with a selective account of his conversation at San Clemente. He reached for his pipe—a nervous reflex—but remembered in time the President's no-smoking rule and rammed it back into his jacket pocket. They faced each other in silence. The President picked up a silver letter opener and bounced it experimentally on his desk blotter.

"You have any doubts about what I'm going to say, Luke?" he ventured quietly.

Garfield let the breath flow through his nose. "I don't expect medals, sir."

"You won't get them." He studied the old man's face. "You must have known when you decided to come here what my reaction would be. How'd you intend to defend yourself?"

"With respect, sir, I don't think I need a defense. The information I've given you is privileged. There's no legal process involved here yet. Anything I've done was subject to one criterion: the security of the state. I'm satisfied on that aspect."

"Satisfied." The President considered the word. "All right, Luke, let's take a look at what we have so far. You've perverted the outcome of a Presidential election. A senior—a respected—figure in my own Party with a long record of public service and *no known criminal association* is being manipulated into a position of withdrawal. A former President of the United States—no, forget his background—is being forced to act against his will, against the will of the people, to support *your* private contention. You tell me an assassination attempt against him was an unscheduled *accident*—but in the course of six days you've lost two senior security officers. You've exposed yourself and your committee. You've put me in a position where I have to back into a

213

corner and hope nobody's going to ask me straight questions." He paused. "You want me to go on?"

Garfield shook his head. "I know the situation, sir. I'm not proud of it and I couldn't defend it morally. But, then, I wouldn't try. The threat is a practical one. It has to be dealt with practically." He opened his blue eyes wide. "If I recall, that *was* your advice when we talked last week?"

The President lay back in his chair. "Don't bargain with me, Luke. You're holding the wrong hand."

"No bargaining intended," Garfield said easily, "but I know the strength of my hand." He waited.

"Go ahead."

"The tape. It's . . . everything the letter said."

"I told you, Luke, I'm not ready to have it made public."

Garfield raised his hands expressively. "I'm not suggesting we should."

"Good. What do you figure would happen if it got out?"

"It'd set a match to a short fuse with a constitutional bomb at the end of it."

"You want to explain that in words an impeachment tribunal could understand?"

Garfield's mouth performed a brief stretching movement. "I have a list of names. Members of The Matrix. I'd say my list represents a small percentage of the total—maybe 20 percent. The names I have represent something else: the fabric of this country."

"I don't want names, Luke." Warningly.

"I won't embarrass you with names. But you asked and I'm . . . explaining. There's an Assistant Secretary of State on that list. There're two senior executive officers of the CIA—and God only knows how many underlings *their* names conceal. There're three of the country's top industrialists—two of 'em identified with your campaign in '76, incidentally, and one who held office in the late sixties. There are writers, churchmen, diplomats, scientists, bankers."

"The Matrix! The Matrix!" The President shook his head until a lock of hair fell across his forehead. "That's all I hear. You tell me yourself what kind of men they are. They don't sound like conspirators to me. What's so wrong, anyway, with a group of guys getting together in some kind of . . . secret society. The country's riddled with 'em. Orders of the Pine Lodge, Sons of America, Masons, Rosicrucians—you name it, we got it. To my mind it's part of what democracy's all about. But you think differently. O.K., I read Anson's letter and maybe there is something more . . . maybe. But maybe you're chasing something that fits a pattern someone has designed to mislead you?"

"I'd like to think so, sir. *That* would resolve a lot of things. But we both know it isn't like that. Yes, I believe the bulk of The Matrix is genuine. Yes, of course, they have the right to come together. But not if that organization is corrupted to the detriment of the nation. Not if it aims to undermine the democracy you're talking about. Have you ever heard of the orange armadillo?"

"Spare me your allegories, Luke."

"This one's appropriate. The orange armadillo is a native of South America. Hasn't got the speed, the strength or the drive to hunt, so it survives by scavenging. In the desert there are plenty of scavengers. There's no guarantee the armadillo gets a place at the carcass. So it operates covertly. When an animal dies, the armadillo tunnels under it and comes up into the carcass from below. Lives in the flesh. Eats its way out."

The President sniffed. "Well?"

"We have an orange armadillo situation here, except it's eating away at living flesh. The Matrix is the carcass and its flesh and blood are power and influence. When it's finished with The Matrix, this armadillo intends to move on to a bigger carcass—the Presidency."

The President brought a hand to his face, brushed the hair from his forehead. The grin began small, then widened. "You know the worst thing that could happen to me this year, Luke?"

"Sir?"

"You could decide to run for office yourself."

THURSDAY: 0615—ANSON

She woke and he was gone.

Lee Ritchie slammed one hand angrily across the empty sheet. "You stupid, stupid bitch." She punched the pillow and sank back in fuming exasperation, her mouth set hard. The house was silent, his clothes gone from the basket-weave chair in the corner. "Stupid cow!" she added for good measure.

His face bobbed up from the foot of the bed and peered at her over the rumpled sheets. He blew a low, provocative whistle. She sat bolt upright, eyes owl wide, the covers falling unnoticed from her breasts. Anson eyed them appreciatively. "Stupid for what?" he said. "Last night?"

She closed her eyes for a full fifteen seconds. When she blinked them open, he shot her another amused glance. "O.K. now? Or still stupid?"

She scowled to hide her confusion, but made no attempt to pull the sheets across her body. He liked that. "What are you doing on your hands and knees?" She flicked back her hair and held it behind her head.

"Looking for my socks. And, you know, that's your only giveaway."

"Giveaway?" She reached for the sheet.

"Fiddling with your hair like that. It's called a displacement activity. Means you're trying to cover up something you really need to say."

"You any relation to Margaret Mead?"

"Konrad Lorenz." He sat back on the floor, back propped against the wall, and lit a cigarette. "You want to do or say something," he explained, mock seriously, "but you hold back because this inner voice is telling you to button up. That's a conflict situation. Unbearable. So you do something neutral. Covers up by making you behave as if everything's dandy. Like fiddling with your hair. Displacement activity." He dribbled smoke from his nose. "Three years of psychology lectures and that's all I remember. I was a keen student of displacement gags."

She pursed her lips, turned her head to one side. "Like smoking cigarettes?"

He stared at her blankly.

"Displacement activity, Professor."

He winced and turned it into a grin. "You talk dirty." He sucked deep on the cigarette and practiced a smoke ring. "What brought on the self-denunciation when you woke up just now?"

"Why? Does it worry you?"

"It occurred to me you might have been regretting last night."

She leaned forward, elbows on knees. "I thought you'd flown the coop."

"And that would be the end of the world?"

"It would mean I was wrong about you."

He stretched and yawned hugely. "And you'd blame yourself for that?"

"Some men take you for a ride and you know it's going to

216

happen the moment you meet them. All you have to guess is when. With others it's different."

He pushed himself to his feet. "I'm sorry, Lee. I have to go."

"Have to or want to? I like to be precise about these things."

"Have to."

"You have five minutes and the floor's yours."

He debated the wisdom of it, remembered last night and felt terrible. "I think I know why Walt died."

She said nothing.

"The files are meaningless. So much junk. But there was another one. I found it last night, while you were asleep. Pure luck."

"How?"

"Walt's magic numbers. The scribble in the cat's collar."

She inched forward on the bed. "Can I see it?"

"No."

"Just no?"

"Look," he paced away from the bed, turned on her sharply. "Somebody tried to kill me last night. You know what that means in simple everyday terms? I'll tell you; it sets a clock ticking in your guts with repeaters all over your system. You get sick all the time wondering if it'll happen again. You wonder if anyone around you will suffer because . . ."

"I'm not asking for protection. I just said: let me look at the file."

"No. What you don't know can't hurt you."

"Tell that to Leo."

"Leo died, baby, because they thought he knew too much."

His anger lasted only seconds. She stared him down. "You said you have to go. Where?"

"Buffalo's getting the car. We're going into town, then we part company. He's out of this one too."

"And that's the way it ends, is it? So long. That's it. Good-bye?"

He hung his head. "I'm going back to Rome. Where I belong."

"Bullshit! O.K., keep your file. But spare me the garbage about crawling back to Rome. You tell me you know why Walt was killed and the next minute you're packing your bags for Rome? Try harder, Harry. I was picking the bones out of fairy tales that transparent when I was two years old."

He propped himself against the wall facing the bed. "You finished?"

"I haven't even *begun*. Short of tying me to a chair, you aren't going to move a step out of this house without me. I can run, too, you know. Of course, if you really left me behind, I might foul up the whole thing by trailing around looking for you. That would be kind of messy. You wouldn't like that."

He pushed himself off the wall and studied her face for a long moment. "O.K. You can see the file, but later. If you're coming with us you come now, or . . ." He looked at his watch. "In exactly twelve minutes. Because that's when we pull out of here."

She leaped to the floor at once, ran across to the bathroom and turned on the shower. Steam rose and rolled out into the room.

She tied on a robe and pulled a shower cap over her hair. "About that file . . . ?" she shouted.

"Names, dates, people. Some I recognize. Others don't make much sense. One thing, though, looks pretty important. Ambrose Bradley was born in a place called Turtleback. It's in Arizona. My father took me there once when I was a kid. There's another name tied up with the place, too. I found it in the file. I . . ." His voice changed. "Look . . . do we have to scream at each other over the shower? I'll be back in a couple of minutes. Get dressed. You now have ten and a half minutes."

"Wait a minute!" She poked her head out from the shower. "Where are we going?"

"There's a TWA flight taking off at 7:00 A.M. from Washington. Gets into Phoenix at a quarter of one. We stop over for an hour in Chicago."

"I adore Chicago."

"Ten minutes flat."

"I'm there!"

She gave him thirty seconds, then sped into the room, dripping water and soap. He had left the file on the chair where he'd hung his jacket. She flipped it open, dabbing at drops of water with a towel. A name, he'd said. Another name tied up with Turtleback. She riffled through the sheets; too much, far too much. It would take an hour to read and digest. Name, name, name . . . Turtleback jumped out at her. Bradley and . . .

She went to the phone by the bed, slipped it under a tent of

218

sheet and blankets to suppress any possible sound, and dialed.

Garfield was incapable of letting a phone go unanswered. He picked it up on the third ring.

She whispered under the tent of bedclothes: "I've got something. A name. Get it down. I don't have any time."

"Where are you?"

"The farm. I've just . . ."

"Call me back from outside." His irritation was mild but measurable.

"There isn't any *time*. Will you listen. Please!"

"I'm listening."

"Aaron LaCroix. Two As and the French for cross. That's all. Anson found another file here. The name was in it. I think it's Matrix. He says it might link with . . ."

She heard his foot on the stairs and killed the phone instantly. She put it back on the bedside table and ran silently back to the shower.

"One minute, Harry!" she shouted as the hot water hit her.

THURSDAY: 0730—PETERSEN

As Harry Anson and Lee Ritchie checked in at the TWA desk for flight TW 237 to Phoenix, a Boeing 727 on charter to the U.S. Central Intelligence Agency lifted smoothly from the main runway into the pewter gray cloud above Washington. At 32,000 feet, in the sunshot ice blue of open sky, it leveled out and headed southwest. The pilot's instructions had been to prepare a flight plan Washington-Phoenix-Washington. There were eight passengers, one of whom, Senator Ambrose Bradley, would leave the plane at Phoenix.

The aircraft was unmarked. Its interior resembled the smoking room of a desert resort hotel: pine-colored fabric on the bulkheads; royal blue carpeting; low, circular teak tables and deep leather swivel chairs. The flight deck was sealed off and, at the rear, a door led to a rest room, air-to-ground communications room, toilets, kitchen and shower.

The passengers fitted the setting. They wore their anonymous, expensive clothes with an indifference born of long experience. Only one wore his hair in the longer, modern fashion, but sober horn-rimmed glasses and a cultivated air of authority robbed the fashion of any raffish element. Three of them were smoking pipes, three others cigars. The atmosphere was complete: a select club, the membership of which was closed.

Donald Petersen surveyed them critically. Ambrose Bradley was in conversation at the forward table with Luther Torrance. They shared a passion for Mozart and cattle raising, Torrance in the dilettante style of a man who furnishes his life with "interests" as he furnishes his homes with antiques. Petersen was indifferent to him as a colleague but he held him personally in contempt. Torrance's strength was his status, his inherited name, his homes, his personal covenant with Providence. He indulged himself with moral integrity as a junkie does with speed. He also indulged a covenant with God, as though He, too, were a member of the club.

Richard Kragen and Peter Bolton were less well endowed by heaven, but they'd lost no time in remedying the shortfall. Both had achieved fame before they were thirty years old: Kragen as Director of a space research project, Bolton as a hustling Dean of Faculty at a midwestern university. They were both now in their early forties and counted their blessings in strict, competitive terms: *Time* and *Newsweek* cover stories, TV punditry, Special-Adviser status to Presidents. Kragen wrote prolifically on a range of subjects from astrophysics to space law. He had been described once, in an acid review in *Nature,* as "one of a breed of contemporary scientists who writes books to identify the gaps in his own knowledge."

Bolton had helped fuel the youth explosion of the sixties, had shrunk from the monster he created and turned his coat to ensure its demise. He had armed himself with the mute anger of the silent majority and defended the bloodletting at Kent State. They were both opportunists and their god was ambition.

Douglas Engstrom was the most formidable asset of his own banking corporation. Alert, sophisticated, shrewd, he clung to the belief that people were the building blocks of society, but, in his view of social architecture, the human element emerged clothed in concrete and steel. Engstrom claimed Swedish descent, but Petersen had uncovered the reality of his German roots. He had also uncovered Engstrom's collusion in a German–South African diamond cartel during World War Two. Petersen was still sitting on that one. Engstrom sat alone, pipe in teeth, watching the cloudscape through a window.

Across the cabin, also alone, Roy Sanforth perched with an open briefcase on his lap, brow furrowed, juggling paperwork. He was in his early fifties: ascetic, dull, intense, brilliant. His empire was vast, varied, complex. He had started life as an engineer, discovered in himself a facility for financial maneuvering and carried it to Wall Street. He was a Vice-President of the World Bank, a Senior Adviser to the International Monetary Fund and progenitor of banking and finance houses throughout Europe and the Middle East. No single company or corporation bore Roy Sanforth's name, but his genius put cereals on a million tables, jet engines into a thousand airliners, steel by the million tons into ships and industrial construction, chemicals into a vast array of drugs. Sanforth was unmarried, unloved and untouched by the experience of living. If it ever became necessary to prove he was also vulnerable, Petersen was equipped to do that, too. Sanforth had indulged an appetite for pre-teen girls. Petersen's file was exemplary.

Milton Abrams sat at Petersen's left hand. They had discussed the disappearance of the file only once since their telephone conversation and Petersen had left no doubts in his mind that it had become a short fuse with a bomb at the end of its run. The operation to counteract that potential explosion had been set in motion. Abrams had planned and coordinated every step himself; it now occupied his mind to the exclusion of all else.

Petersen beckoned to the steward and whispered in his ear. The man ducked his head respectfully, retired to the end of the cabin and passed through into the galley, closing the door behind him.

"Gentlemen." Petersen raised a hand, calling them to order. Roy Sanforth blinked over his rimless glasses, puckered his mouth irritably and snapped his case shut.

"We have a little over an hour to Phoenix," Petersen said firmly. "Let's try not to waste it." He stuck his hands on his hips and surveyed them challengingly. They could only be taken by storm. Not too much detail, either. Get involved in detail and the whole thing would become a debating match. He gestured around them airily. "I guess you'll want to know why you're here."

Sanforth jabbed a finger across the space at Abrams. "That man hijacked me from my own bed!"

Petersen pretended pain. "That's a little strong, I'd say, Roy. Not hijacked. But it was urgent that you get here on time. I apologize for any inconvenience, gentlemen. You're here because you happened to be in Washington."

"Don't give me that, Don." Luther Torrance grunted forward in his swivel chair. "I was asked to fly in last night. You think I'd come all this way in the middle of the week when . . . ?"

"Me, too," snapped Engstrom. He turned puzzled eyes on Torrance; their discomfort flowed and blended. "I haven't got time for this. I told him. I needed to be in New York."

Petersen colored; irritation on the long march to anger. "Luther, Doug—I needed you in town for something else. It just worked out this way."

Pete Bolton assumed the TV pundit's knowing smile. "That's a very interesting proposition, Don. Me and Dick here kind of got the impression you railroaded us, too. Unless the message my secretary took yesterday was a practical joke. Is that a possibility, you think?" He looked around for support and approbation. No one contributed.

Sanforth shook his thin head until his glassees bounced on the lower slopes of his nose. "I think it's absolutely unforgivable. I won't let it drop, either. I'm a senior member of this group and I deem it my privilege and my right to—"

Petersen brought the flat of his hand down on the table beside him with thunderclap effect. "All *right!* That's all you care about is it? Your stiff-necked fucking pride. Fine. Well, that's fine with me. You want it straight, I'll be happy to oblige. Just do me a favor and cut out your goddamn whining."

Kragen tried to stand, but the aircraft lurched over a thermal and tipped him back in his seat. He stretched a clutching hand at Bradley, but the Senator turned away.

Torrance snapped: "Ambrose. For God's sake, man, ask him what the hell this is all about. If he thinks he can talk to me like . . ."

Bradley fixed on the unlit cigar in his hand.

"What is this, Bradley?" Sanforth snapped. His eyes flickered from Bradley to Petersen and back again.

Torrance tried again. "All right, Petersen. What's going on here?"

Petersen took up his glass of bourbon and sipped it. He set it down again, composing himself.

"O.K. I'll tell you what it is, Luther. It's Judgment Day."

"Now, look here, Don . . ." Richard Kragen began with a half smile on his face.

"Shut it, Dick, there's a good boy. Now . . . I thought this could've been a nice civilized little gathering and no harm done to anybody's big fat ego. You could've kept your hands clean." He shot a look down at Bradley. It was not returned.

222

"I should've known you were too *important* to have it the easy way."

"What's he talking about?" Roy Sanforth worried at Bradley's sleeve. The Senator was apparently mesmerized by a spot on the carpet at his feet.

"Right." Petersen's lip curled. From here on in he was going to enjoy it. "Let's run a few flags up the pole. One: Nixon." That got their attention; even the set of Bradley's lowered face showed he was at least listening. "We started that Nixon rumor." Four of them began to remonstrate at once. "Quiet!", he thundered. They bit off their attacks. "We had to. Last Friday night, Nixon had a face-to-face with the Senator here." There was another attempted interruption but he quelled it with a slice of his hand. "We didn't choose it. Nixon did. He had a message for Ambrose; for all of us."

"The Matrix?" Kragen's voice wavered. "How would he know about The Matrix? I mean . . ."

"He knew. Like I said, he had a message. Bradley quits the race or Nixon goes public with information he has about . . ."

"I heard those rumors," Torrance cut in harshly. "They're crap, take my word for it." He glared around the others. "What the hell has this got to do with anything?" He leveled his finger, arm at full stretch, at Petersen. "I want you to know something, Don. I don't like you; never have. Better—I don't trust you. You're too rare for my blood."

Petersen turned with a crooked smile to the hunched figure of Ambrose Bradley. "They don't seem to want to listen, Ambrose. What do you suggest I do?"

Bradley looked up momentarily, opened his mouth; snapped it shut and swung away to the window beside him.

"The Senator isn't quite himself today, gentlemen," Petersen purred comfortingly. "So I guess you'll just have to listen to me. And this time keep your mouths shut, will you? I'll say it once. That's all."

"Nobody talks to me that way," Sanforth stormed.

"You know, Roy, you've got a head full of shit."

"Bradley!" Sanforth tugged again at the Senator's sleeve. "Do you intend to sit there and . . . ?"

Petersen lowered himself into his seat and sipped at his bourbon. It left the floor vacant. Bradley's voice, when it came, was only just audible over the subdued hiss of the air-conditioning and the animal purr of the engines.

"Listen to him. All of you. There's nothing else you can do."

"Ambrose! What the hell are you talking about?" Torrance protested.

"Listen!" Bradley said again. He turned back to the cloud-scape beyond the window.

"Good. Thanks, Senator." Petersen got to his feet again and beamed at them. His sense of well-being was quite genuine. He had waited a long time for this moment. "Right. Nixon has a piece of tape. I knew it existed . . . at least, I knew there was something in a safe deposit vault in Atlanta. It was put there by one of our old friends, an ex-member. Doesn't matter who. He's dead. That safe deposit was opened a few days back. A package, the tape, was taken out. We tried to intercept the delivery and . . ." He pouted at the memory. ". . . we failed. Now, I guess I don't have to tell you anything about Nixon and tapes. This one, if my guess is right, was recorded during his Presidency. The conversation is about The Matrix." He swung a pointing finger from face to face. "About you and me."

Torrance rapped: "We know about Nixon and tapes, all right. So does every man, woman and child in the country. What does it matter? The Matrix has nothing to lose. Some of us might even prefer it that way."

"You all think that?" Petersen's smile was wolfish.

"Well . . ." began Bolton uncomfortably.

"See what I mean, Luther? You can't speak for everybody because you don't know your friends, do you? You don't know yourself, either, for that matter."

Roy Sanforth's glasses glittered with outrage. "I've had enough of this."

"The door's over there, Sanforth!" Petersen snarled. "It's a long way down, but you might just live. That's the easy way out. This tape is something you wouldn't survive. Any of you." He glanced down again at Bradley.

"Facts!" hissed Torrance on the edge of his seat.

"O.K. Facts. What do you think we've been doing all these years, Luther? Think about it. The Senator's on the road to the White House. How d'you think we put him there? By sitting around batting principles back and forth? Talking philosophy? Oh, sure—all together, you pack a lot of muscle and that was important. And you have money. Money's the thing, isn't it? But do you think that buys you the right to put a man on Pennsylvania Avenue? Not quite, gentlemen. Not quite. Your money bought action. *My* action. Me and Abrams here and a few others made the decisions; pushed the action along. Your money, your influence..." He paused significantly. "Your *information* and our action."

Bolton put on a brave front. "If this is some kind of confession, Don ..."

"Call it group therapy, Pete. More in your line. Since 1958, The Matrix has been building for the Presidency. We didn't advertise it. Even for your benefit. We were prepared for a long haul but that was necessary. Plan, conserve, consolidate. But we couldn't wait forever; leave history to take its turn and you wait a lifetime for the kind of opportunity we were in business for. History needed a push in the right direction. We gave it that in 1963."

Bradley whirled in his seat. "Tell them!"

Petersen measured him coolly. "Sure, Ambrose. I'll tell them. The Kennedys were shaping a dynasty. They were also running this country into the ground. We couldn't let that happen." He studied their faces; they were trying to convince themselves they were not about to hear what they expected. "It was a bad time. Martin Luther King came on the scene, too, and his kind of dynasty was something else. He also picked up bits and pieces about us: The Matrix, the membership. He had things going with Kennedy we couldn't turn our backs on. Not if we hoped to survive." He gave them what they knew was coming. "We had to deal with them."

"Are you saying ... ?" Torrance began.

Bradley almost shouted. "They killed them."

Bolton rocked back in his seat as if he'd been punched in the face. "Killed? They ... ?"

"John Kennedy. Bobby. King. They killed all of them."

"You?" thundered Torrance at Petersen. Sanforth groped in his jacket pocket and came up with a silver pillbox. He slipped two pink tablets into his palm and tossed them down his throat.

"And *you*, Luther!" said Petersen equably. "You and the Senator and Sanforth and Kragen and Bolton, all of you. You want specifics? You gave us the lead into the King situation, Bolton."

"That's a damn lie!"

Petersen shrugged. "It's on record, friend. Think what you like. You supplied the information. You *all* supplied information; pieces of the jigsaw. Every scrap of evidence you passed on ..."

"I passed on nothing!" shouted Engstrom violently.

"Talked about then, Doug. Every scrap of information you

225

talked about is on record. You weren't exactly fond of the Kennedy administration, were you? You could've kept a tighter curb on your tongue."

"You're not telling me Nixon has all ... *that* on tape!" Sanforth developed a blue green tinge to his cheeks.

"Good practical thinking, Roy," Petersen applauded. "Let's take it from there. We're guessing this tape's too hot to play publicly and, anyway, it's a pretty good bet Nixon's being handled by somebody we don't know about yet. If they really wanted to air the tape they'd have done it days ago." He flipped a cigar from his case and lit it. "They figure to blackmail Ambrose here ... all of us. O.K. The Iowa Caucus is ten days off and then we're into New Hampshire. We can't afford to have Ambrose tied into a scandal. So we have a week to find that tape and destroy it." He glared down pointedly at Abrams. "Whoever's running Nixon has maybe infiltrated The Matrix, too. We'll know about that soon. A couple of days."

"Dear God!" Engstrom slapped his hands to his face. "You weren't responsible for the Nixon shooting ... ?"

Petersen's brow clouded. "Don't be a damn fool, Doug. You think I'd entertain a dumb play like that?"

"But his denial."

"He had to deny. We called their bluff. They couldn't hold up a scenario that thin for long. So, as I said, we have a week."

"You'll get no help from me," roared Torrance. "Not a damn thing."

"We'll need your money and your connections, Luther," Petersen said levelly. "You'll contribute with your usual goodwill. You all have a role to play, too, in locating that tape. We'll discuss that later."

"What makes you think ... ?" Torrance was red-faced.

"I said we kept records, Luther. Tapes, everything. You're in this up to your eyebrows. Your virtuous, principled eyebrows." He dropped back into his seat. "You've all reaped your own benefits from the group over the years. You've all used it for your own advantage. Fine. That was part of the deal. Cooperation among equals. Well, now you start paying interest."

"And what if I go straight to the President?" flared Sanforth.

"Go right ahead," drawled Petersen. "But check with the Senator first and the rest of your friends here and the other forty-two members of the group. Some people don't take kindly to public confession. And examine your own motives too, Roy. I can sew you up tighter than anyone."

"That goes double for you, Petersen," Kragen said bitterly.

Petersen grinned at him without animosity. "You go ahead and do what you have to do, Dick. But take my advice: do it to me before I do it to you."

He looked around at the rest. "Anyone else?" There were no offers. "Good." He tossed the rest of the bourbon into his mouth. "Just a reminder then: too much pressure on the brake just now and this whole thing goes into a skid. You won't come out of it alive, any one of you. I'll promise you that. So . . . no one's a passenger anymore. No one's just along for the ride." He looked over at Bradley. "Anything to add, Ambrose?"

Bradley shook his head.

"Good. I like people to know the score. We're all in this together and we're all traveling the same way. Right?" They accorded him no agreement. "So let's get down to what you're going to be . . . contributing over the next few days."

Petersen made his call on the radio-telephone link installed in the communications room at the rear of the plane. The line was good.

LaCroix was sepulchrally cool. "How did they react?"

"As you'd expect."

"Specifically."

"They won't be running to the FBI. They'll do as they're told. They know how much they stand to lose."

"Were there any . . . difficulties?"

"Some. But they dropped out."

"And Bradley?"

"Good as gold. He's going through his dark-night-of-the-soul phase. It'll pass. He'll play."

"Are you sure? If he were to renege . . ."

"He's a politician, isn't he? He'll turn his guilt into a virtue overnight. He's a natural for it. But if you want, I'll have another talk with him."

"No. Leave him to me."

"We set down in Phoenix around a quarter of ten. I'll have him call you before noon."

"This is . . ."

"Senator! Petersen said you'd be calling." Aaron LaCroix lifted the receiver from its amplifier cradle and put it to his ear. "I gather the . . . conference went well. Are you at The Springs?"

"I'm at the airport." His voice was artificially soft. "That was quite a performance Petersen put on this morning. Do you think they're going to cooperate?"

"You were there, Senator. Your judgment's always sound. What would you say?"

Bradley began a sentence but nipped it off. He paused. "I'm trying to keep this conversation civilized, LaCroix. Petersen was . . ."

"Acting on my instructions. You feel he was a little heavy-handed, I take it?"

"He left them with *nothing!*" Bradley's voice rose to a shout on the last word. "You claim to be a student of human nature. You accept the principle that a man should be given an escape route, an opportunity to salve his conscience in a situation where there's no alternative. Well, you've given them no escape. Me either, for that matter. They have their backs to the wall, everything to lose. Consider the implications. They're not entirely without resources. If one of them, just one of them, finds enough backbone to talk . . ."

"They won't. Each one of them was carefully selected, for his power and for his . . . shall we say, inadequacies. If any one of them talks he knows he will pay with his professional and social reputation. Not one of them is in a position to afford that kind of indulgence. Not one of them."

"They could have been left in ignorance."

LaCroix clicked his tongue in irritation. "Oh, come now, Senator. You know the weakness of that argument at a time like this. Petersen armed them with the facts of life. They'll go away and brood on them and by tonight each one of them will have built a wall of expedient justification around his acceptance of the inevitable. It is inevitable, you see."

"If any one of them were to make a deal with . . . well, with Nixon or whoever's putting him up to this . . ."

"Illogical, irrational and invalid. Unless Petersen made a very poor job of it, they understand perfectly well that

228

they're totally vulnerable, no matter what the circumstances. Confession is no answer to their predicament."

"Nor is cooperation."

"True. But cooperation is quite unavoidable."

"You had no right to involve them."

"I had no choice. To retrieve that tape, to discover precisely who is manipulating Nixon, calls for a very considerable logistic operation. It calls for cash money on a scale neither you nor I could produce without arousing curiosity. It calls for contacts, infiltration. We need the help of powerful *committed* associates, Ambrose. You've just been present at the initiation of their commitment."

"You can't believe they're going to stand still for all this."

"Curiously enough, I think they believe they have more to fear than you. Stupid of them, of course. You've a great deal to lose. Everything perhaps. I thank you, I mean this sincerely, for submitting as you did. Knowing I have your support, the rest of them will come to . . ."

"Support! I would have taken my *life* rather than support what you did. If the reality of this ever takes hold of those men—God help you."

"My actions were your actions. And theirs. Collective responsibility, Ambrose. You must accept that."

"Spare me your goddamn hypocrisy."

"Not hypocrisy, Ambrose. Calculation, the servant of vision. Cathedrals are built on vision. Whole religions. But behind the vision there has to be calculation. Cathedrals grow from an exercise of muscle and sweat; the physical submission of the people to the vision. A faith need only be half understood by its disciples to win their devotion, but their continuing commitment to it must at times be reinforced. Fear is an honored tradition of religion, Ambrose. Crude, perhaps, but I think you'll agree that the cruder the faith, the stronger its influence. Too much knowledge breeds contempt, doubt. What we have to achieve is *acceptance*, total acceptance. Men have died for what they believe, however ill-conceived. The Church is built on blood, Ambrose. The blood of the Lamb. The blood of Man."

"Damn your blasphemy!" Bradley's hand shook with rage and his voice with it. "Do you really believe you can crush every decent man, every decent feeling, with that lunatic's mumbo-jumbo? What do you . . . ?"

LaCroix was not moved. "I think you've overdone things, Ambrose," he said gently. "You've had a series of unpleasant shocks. I suggest you get back to The Springs for a few days and concentrate on the campaign."

"I can't leave things . . . like this. I insist we meet."

"Very well. Saturday at noon. Here. Does that satisfy you?"

"I'll be there."

"And remember, Ambrose: *Die fortioribus adesse.* The Gods are on the side of the strongest. Be strong."

Ambrose Bradley paused. "My Latin isn't as good as yours, Aaron, but I think you might recognize it. *Quos Deus vult perdere, prius dementat.*"

There was silence from the other end.

Bradley persisted. "Whom God would destroy, He first makes mad."

He put down the receiver.

THURSDAY: 1240—ANSON

The plane wheeled over the suburbs of Phoenix and they gazed out on the angled world. The desert rippled in the noon sun, interrupted only by the thin gray threads of highway. On the convex rim of the window lay a distortion of mountains.

"First cousin to the moon," said Anson over Lee's shoulder. "That's what some English writer called it." He craned his neck. "He was being unfair. To the moon."

At the airport, they rented a Ford in Lee's name and bought a map of the area. Lee circled Turtleback with her eyeliner pencil.

"Heard of it," said the man behind the Hertz desk. "Nothing much to it. You with Bradley's people?"

"Bradley?" asked Lee innocently.

"Senator Ambrose Bradley. Born in Turtleback. You never heard of him?"

"Of course," said Anson.

"Does he come here much?" she asked.

The clerk stared openly at the tight curve of her sweater. "Nope. Busy man these days."

"You've just met Phoenix's cultural attaché," whispered Lee as they walked to the car.

"I don't *want* to treat you like a child," Anson hissed, bundling her into the passenger seat. "But will you kindly keep your damn fool questions to yourself? He's not going to forget you, if he's asked. It won't help."

230

She sat stiffly as he smoothed open the map on his lap and checked the route for Turtleback. He handed her the map and turned on the ignition.

"Did you talk to *her* like that?" she said. "Grazia. You don't have to say anything if you think it'll incriminate you."

"We didn't talk, period. You don't talk to people like Grazia; you recharge your batteries on silence. Look, there's a turnoff about twenty-five miles out of Phoenix. If we miss it, chances are we finish up in the Grand Canyon." He gestured to the map. "Watch the route and sing out when you see a sign."

She kept her silence for exactly twenty minutes. Then, "Do you expect to see her again?"

"What?"

"Grazia. I don't suppose you cut yourself off completely."

"Jesus Christ!"

She drew down the corners of her mouth in a parody of his temper. "Sorry." She stifled a smile, but he caught it out of the corner of his eye and did a double take.

"What's the matter with you? I say something?"

"Nooo."

"So?"

"You look so defensive, crouched over the wheel like that. All bent and intense. Like one of those private eyes in a forties movie. You know, peering through the lashing rain, he hurtled to the rescue of the millionaire's daughter."

"Thanks." Anson snorted, relaxed his shoulders, leaned back. "Here's looking at you, kid."

She laughed. "I like it when you relax."

"You don't do much of that yourself."

"No."

"Why? Is this really that important to you?"

She shook her head, hesitated. "Yes, I guess it is. It's important to you."

"I wish I could believe . . ."

She gave a small squeak and jabbed a hand across his face to the left. "There, quick!"

He swung the Ford off the highway onto a secondary road. Lee Ritchie read another sign: Carefree. She looked down at the map. "It's the only town before Turtleback. The only anything as far as I can see."

"Let's hope it lives up to its name."

He tried to relax again but it didn't come easy. Not for the first time since they left Washington, he regretted his weakness in allowing her to come with him. Another pair of hands, another head, he had deluded himself, as long as the hands were steady and the head clear. He toyed with the idea of leaving her at Carefree, but he knew she wouldn't accept that, short of being bundled out of the car bodily.

"New River Mountains," she said.

He glanced away into the distance at the wind-blasted rocks, jagged as coral. He recalled the name immediately and, from across a vacuum of twenty-five years, heard his father's voice.

"It's not far from here," he said. They had been driving for almost forty minutes.

"Just follow the sand," she joked.

They passed through Carefree in the blinking of a blinded eye and the desert tightened its grip with each mile beyond. Twice she offered to drive; Anson refused. Turtleback coalesced out of a dancing haze, and Anson lifted his foot and reduced speed.

Welcome, said the new sign, to Turtleback—birthplace of Senator Ambrose J. Bradley.

"The Town That Made Arizona Famous," said Anson. They cruised down Main Street and pulled into a gas station.

"Does Bradley *live* here?" asked Lee. "Here?"

"He's got a big spread a few miles outside of town. The Springs, it's called. I read something in *Time* about it. Exactly where, I don't know. It doesn't usually encourage visitors." He hit the horn, but there was no response from inside the gas station. He pulled the car away from the pump and parked in front of the building. "We better get out." He swung the door wide and the heat came in.

Lee got out. "It's not that bad," she said, looking around. "In fact, it's really rather quaint. Bigger than I thought."

It was, indeed, bigger than Anson remembered it. Main Street was lined with bright modern single-story buildings and, at the far end, Spanish-style villas set in desert gardens. They left the car and began to walk.

"They must be expecting us," said Lee Ritchie.

"How come?"

"Nobody's giving us a second glance. Two city slickers blow into a place this size and they don't even look twice."

"Don't kid yourself. We hadn't moved a yard over the city limits before the jungle drums were beating like crazy. In two hours there won't be a citizen within twenty miles who couldn't paint a picture of us down to the last button.

Curiosity isn't a pastime in a place like this. It's an art. That's our problem."

"Bradley?"

"Could be." He craned his neck to read a sign over a store window."

"What are you looking for?"

"The newspaper. The one place asking questions is acceptable. I want to know exactly where Bradley's place is. It's not on any of the maps. The newspaper here is called the *Oracle*. Fount of all wisdom. I hope."

They turned off Main Street and wandered hopefully down the block. The *Oracle* office was sandwiched between a grocery store and a lumberyard. A matchstick of a man was sitting on a bench outside it, watching them as they approached; he seemed to have no doubt in his mind they were bound his way. He got up as they neared him. He was about five feet two in his boots.

"Howdy, folks. You'll be from back East." He offered his hand. "New Yorkers, are you?"

"Hullo." Lee shook his hand warmly, her smile wide.

"Wilbur Bisbee Shumway." He angled a thumb up at the *Oracle*'s shingle. "Proprietor and editor. King of all I survey. You want to come inside?" He led the way into a cool jumbled office, went to his desk, opened a drawer and took a folder from a pile. "I guess this is what you want, huh?"

They looked at each other in surprise, but Anson took the folder at once. "Well, thanks, Mr. . . . er . . ."

"Shumway."

"Mr. Shumway, I think I ought to explain."

"No need. Spotted you the second you turned off Main. Newspapermen, I said. Right off. What do they call you, son?"

"Hamilton," Lee interjected from across the room. She had gone to browse the racks of faded bound copies of the paper. "Bob Hamilton. I'm Jean Harris."

"Ain't the first. Won't be the last," said Mr. Shumway. "Anyhow, you'll find everything you need to know about Ambrose Bradley in there." He indicated the folder in Anson's hands. "Had 'em printed up. Saves time. Ever since the Senator got himself talked about for the White House, you newspaper people been coming here in droves. And I have to say I'm kinda proud it's happening to the town. Fine man, the Senator."

Lee Ritchie returned from her reconnaissance of the files.

233

"You can't fool an old news hound, Mr. Shumway." She flashed a smile. "Bob and I are with Press International Features. We're here for a couple of days to put together a background release on the Senator. Bob, here, was rather hoping for a chance to talk with him."

Mr. Shumway shook his head firmly. "Won't get that. Likes his privacy when he's down here. Place to get him is up in Washington. Wouldn't want him to think I sent you two up there to The Springs." He looked worried.

Lee touched his arm reassuringly. "Don't worry, Mr. Shumway. We didn't really think there was a chance. We're not about to antagonize Ambrose Bradley in the year he makes it to the White House."

"That's mighty understanding of you, young lady. You can see how tough it is running a paper in a small town. You have to run with the pack, right?"

"Yes." She shook her head and he leaned forward, concerned. "I was just thinking . . ."

"Thinking?"

"Would it be O.K. if we kind of took a long shot of The Springs? You know, from say a few miles away. Just to give some idea of the setting, that kind of thing."

Mr. Shumway rubbed the stubble on his chin. "Like I said, the Senator likes his privacy, and this town likes the Senator. Ask anyone here to direct you to The Springs and they wouldn't give you the time of day. That's how deep the respect goes."

"He's a good man, that's why," Lee said quickly. "Respect like that can take a man all the way to the Presidency. I don't want to intrude, you understand. Just . . ."

The little man scrubbed away again at his jaw, still looking doubtful. Then he nodded, obviously having come to an important decision. "All righty, then. I trust you. Between professionals. Here . . ." He hunched over a piece of paper and drew a crude map with the town of Turtleback as the starting point. When he finished he handed it to Anson. "That's the highway. You follow it down to here, fork right and . . ."

"That's marvelous, Mr. Shumway." Lee pecked his cheek. "You don't know how much time you've saved us. You really don't."

Neither of them spoke until they had lost the town in the dust tail rising behind the car. Then Lee said: "Back to Phoenix?"

234

Anson nodded.

"Why not . . . ?"

"Bradley can wait," Anson interrupted. "We split up here."

"What do you mean, split up? We're a team, aren't we?"

"I don't want you around," he said impetuously. "No. I don't mean that. I want you out of this." He laid a hand on her shoulder but she shook it off.

"I've come this far," she snapped.

"And I'm grateful. But for a couple of days at least, I figure we should cool things down. Running as a pair is a fine way to draw attention."

"If you're really intent on a lonely bed . . ." she tried. It was a lame attempt and she regretted it. He ignored her.

"We passed a motel on the way out here. It's not far from the airport. You check in there. I'll be at this place." He handed her a printed card he had picked up from a stack on the Hertz desk. "Phone me if you have to, but we'll stick to your pseudonyms. Hamilton and Harris."

"I want to be with you," she said impulsively. "I don't want to spend days sitting by a phone."

"I said we split up, Lee. Accept it this time, will you. I'm not kidding."

He refused to talk for the rest of the journey, and when he pulled up in front of the motel, she swung open the door and marched briskly to the glass fronted office.

"You can have the car," he yelled after her. She didn't look back. "Lee!" She disappeared into the office. He got out, hesitated for a moment, then walked quickly into town.

THURSDAY: 0310—ANSON

Anson picked out a sand-colored jeep. He followed the Avis clerk back to the office and headed toward the row of pay phones. He flicked through the book and found Ambrose Bradley's number.

"The Springs. Senator Ambrose Bradley's residence." Ronald Colman English.

Anson dropped his voice an octave and gave it what he hoped was an overlay of arrogant insistence. "Give me the Senator."

"Aaaaah—the Senator is not here right now, sir."

"Where is he?"

"I couldn't say, sir." The ground frost of loyalty rimed every word.

"Find out, then. And fast. Tell whoever's in charge there that Abrams is on the phone. Got that?"

"Yes, sir. If you'll just wait . . . ?"

The voice came on again in seconds. "I'm extremely sorry, sir, I didn't connect the name with—er . . ."

"Well, where is he?"

"He went out a while ago, sir. We expect him back in an hour, maybe. If it's urgent, I could . . ." The man was warming to the task of proving himself the perfect servant.

"I'll call him later. Thanks." Anson killed the phone.

He signed the papers and, on his way to the jeep, paused again at the pay phone. If he called Lee, she'd want to join him. No. Leave her to sulk.

Five miles beyond Turtleback, a dirt road wound up into a cluster of spiky hills. Anson took it, following the map drawn by Shumway. The track was barely wide enough for two vehicles to pass, but it showed evidence of being carefully and continuously repaired. As he drove into the narrow canyon where the track began its climb into the hills, he saw a miniature earth mover parked under a shelf of sandstone. Beside it was a tin shack, a rockpile and a heap of red sand. Bradley was either a responsible landowner or the state of the road was important to him for other reasons.

The track twisted and writhed through pillared bluffs, skirted precipitous rockfalls and amplified the jeep's throaty roar for five miles; then it crested the summit with a suddenness that was almost theatrical. Anson braked and killed the engine. The track slid away to the left across the face of the hill and reappeared on the valley floor as a trickle of old gold in a mottled rash of mesquite and brush. Seven or eight miles away, more hills rose, blue and black and shadowy as the sun began its run for the horizon. Between, and parallel with, the two lines of hills ran a river, sluggish brown and slow but full. It was a landscape of desolation, of stunted growth and lifelessness—but where God had failed, Ambrose Bradley had breathed sufficiency. At the heart of the valley, sandwiching the river for two miles on either side of its banks and perhaps four miles of its length, the desert bloomed in verdant apple green. Fields had been laid out, plowed, sown and watered. Trees stood sentinel around the perimeter, daring the desert to encroach any further; a small plantation lent its shade to a sun-dappled lake and a group of modern buildings. The house itself, or as much of it as Anson could see through the trees, was single-story white stucco, robbed of its intended Spanish influence by a roof of green tiles. On either side of it, clustered at the lake's edge, were smaller buildings, also green-tiled, maybe six or seven in all. Men moved about the living area. It was a compound, surrounded by a ten- or twelve-foot chain-link fence, with only one gate leading out to the main road. There didn't seem to be any guards—why should there be? As Anson watched, a helicopter rose from a space beyond the central copse of trees and clung to the air, delicate as a dragonfly, before peeling away to the east.

Anson crouched down against the rock wall instinctively. He had not really worked out the mechanics of approaching Bradley once he had him pinned down. Now he considered his position and regretted his total lack of strategy. What Bradley had down there was a fortress designed to protect him against uninvited guests. He went back to the jeep and climbed aboard. He turned it around and drove back a half mile to a gully he had noticed on his way up. It siphoned off to the left. He reversed the buggy into the cleft and edged it back as far as its width would allow. When he halted and switched off, the main track was invisible. He lay back in the seat and closed his eyes. It would be only slightly less hazardous in darkness, but he couldn't go back now.

Anson left the jeep 150 yards from the perimeter of trees, behind a patch of scrub that would screen its shape from any observer patrolling the fence. He bent low and dodged Indian-style until he reached the cover of the tree line. The compound was bright with the glow of arc lights mounted on fence posts and buildings. The Garden of Eden image of that afternoon had been replaced by an overwhelming atmosphere of prison security. The arcs shot their beams into the trees and conjured up humpbacked dwarfs from their shadows. Anson took a firm grip on his imagination.

There was still movement in the compound and the subdued rattle of men's voices as they wandered from place to place, building to building. One of the larger constructions seemed to be a bunkhouse; Anson could see figures moving in silhouette behind its shaded windows. It was 10:40. He had decided to give them time for supper and maybe a little drinking, and hoped the influence of their master would lead them to bed at a respectable hour.

His plan was to test the fence for electrical current, climb it if it wasn't live and enter the compound. He'd had four hours to deliberate what he would do if he ran into opposition, and the only weapons in his armory were his fitness, a few half-remembered lessons from a judo course he'd never finished and the jackhandle he found in the back of the jeep. It was four feet long and cold smooth. It felt substantial, but he knew his limitations; when the time came to use it over the occipital bone of a human skull or on the bowed vertebrae of a man's neck there would be no time for moral debate. He had considered the idea practically: jackhandle raised overhead, savage downward stroke, crunch of bone, splitting flesh . . . blood. In the middle of it he remembered, with vomitous shock, a day in his eleventh year when his mother, shopping with him in New York, had slipped into the back of a cab and reached out to pull the door shut. An overzealous doorman beat her to it; he slammed the door with a flourish—and the door crushed her thumb. He remembered the shock—so great she couldn't cry out; he remembered the pain that sucked the color from her face and left her palpitating, the bloodied member ragged and terrible held in front of her as though it belonged to somebody else. The memory made his skin crawl. That's what he was committed to, just that.

But he brought the jackhandle along anyway.

At 10:30 the lights began to wink out. The bunkhouse fell dark and the voices died. A few minutes later, a silhouette with a shotgun in the crook of its arm strolled within fifteen yards of where Anson crouched under a hanging branch. The man was whistling under his breath, his eyes on the arc-lighted bunkhouse where, no doubt, he would much prefer to be.

At 10:50 a lance of light spilled across the veranda of the main building and a man stood in the doorway, a pipe flowering in his mouth. From among the trees a voice shouted a challenge and the man on the veranda replied. He stretched, arms high above his head, then ambled down the steps and, hands in the pockets of his jacket, made for the southern perimeter of the fence. Anson strained his eyes. Bradley? He checked his bearings and set off on a crablike run to his right, keeping pace with the figure in the compound. The man stopped at the fence, swung a keychain from his pocket and clinked steel against steel. An inset gate, which Anson had not noticed before, swung open, and he stepped through it and locked it behind him.

Anson backed away from the trees and tried to judge his position. Maybe a half mile from the river. From the fence exit, the man had a wide choice of directions. All around him were cropped fields where, at sundown, sprinklers had furnished man-made rain. The soil smelled clean, rich, fruitful. The man strolled on and Anson followed, keeping low.

Anson heard the barked command with frightening clarity. A shadow bounced from a clump of bushes in the stroller's path, shotgun leveled. "Hold it!"

The stroller stopped. "It's me, Buck. Couldn't sleep. Thought I'd take a turn down to the river and get some air."

"Shhhheeeeewwwww, Senator! I guess I'm kinda jumpy. Sorry."

"S'okay. Night, Buck."

Ambrose Bradley clapped the man on the chest and walked on. Anson stepped to the tree line and made his way toward the river. From time to time he stopped to peer into the darkness. Bradley's white head moved along the field path, his pipe trailing smoke. Anson judged a diagonal course through the trees to keep him apace of the nightwalker and bring him closer. When Bradley reached the river, Anson was twenty-five yards to his right.

The field path opened out onto a paved landing. A fifteen-foot boat with an outboard motor on its stern lapped under the bank. Bradley stood above it, puffing at his pipe, and stared out over the slow-flowing water. Anson knew he would never have a better chance. He came closer, fifteen . . . ten . . . five yards.

Ambrose Bradley said conversationally, "I wouldn't do anything stupid, my friend. There are guards all around the estate. They have guns and they don't ask questions first." He didn't turn his head.

Anson came up out of his crouch. "Thank you," he said, stupidly.

Bradley turned slowly. He took the pipe from his mouth. "There's nothing here for you to steal." He peered closer. "Who sent you, son?" Doubtfully.

"No one sent me, Senator. I'm not a thief."

Bradley blew air through his nose with intended humor. "Just out for a stroll, huh? Well, boy, you're a long way off your route. Main road's seven miles the other side of those hills. You walk it?"

"No. I've got a car back there," Anson waved over his shoulder.

"Only one reason to take this road. There's only me at the end of it."

Anson walked to the river's edge and looked down at the boat. "I came to see you, sir."

"We're pretty up-to-date here at The Springs, son. We have telephones."

"I couldn't be sure you'd talk to me."

"So you thought you'd make sure by breaking into the place."

"I had it in mind."

Bradley stuck the pipe back between his teeth. "It's a fine night. A man takes account of the time he lies abed when he gets to my age." He assessed Anson with shrewd eyes. "What do you say we take the boat upriver for a spell? Get some air?"

Anson checked the river banks left and right of him. "Anything you say, Senator."

Bradley came close and slapped his big hands on Anson's jacket, patted pockets, waist and under the arms. He stepped back. "Sorry. Just a precaution."

They climbed down into the skiff and Bradley primed the engine and tugged the starter cord. The engine whirred energetically and they turned out into the river, headed upstream, the motor revving low. They sat in silence for ten minutes. Then Bradley switched off the engine and allowed the boat to drift with the current. The lights of the compound sat like a green dome over the land, dimmed now by a million sapphire stars in the greater dome of the sky. There was no moon, but Anson could identify the outline of the hills left and right and the pass which carried the track back to the Turtleback road.

Bradley set a match to his pipe. "Twenty-six years, son." He flicked the match far away into the river. "That's how long it takes to water the desert, make it green, raise crops, win a hand against nature. I reckon that's close on as long as you've lived."

"Not quite, Senator."

"Near enough. Less'n half my lifetime, though. When I started out, it seemed like The Springs was more important than anything I'd set my hand to. That's man's supreme egotism, son. Not content with being made in God's image. Has to prove he's all-powerful, too. Didn't hit me till I'd got the place springing up green all over—if the Almighty took away the water He gave me, if He turned up the sun a mite hotter one summer, this place goes back to what it was. The way I see it, I did nothing."

Anson pried into the gloom around the burning pipe bowl. "Did the Almighty tell you to run for President, Senator?"

Silence. Then, "You sure nobody sent you, son?"

"Nobody."

"You have a name?"

"The name is Anson. Harold Roper Anson."

The teeth clicked on the pipe stem. "Good name."

"Familiar name?"

"You're sharp. Your father was sharper than a sackful of nails."

"My father's dead."

"I know that, son. I . . . know."

The pause was a long one. From both banks, a chorus of insect ticking noises rose and grew in volume.

"What did he have going with you, Senator?"

"We had common . . . ideals, son. Old-fashioned word. We thought we could do something about them." His voice grew almost inaudible. "It didn't work out."

"He never dabbled in politics!" Anson made it an accusation.

"That's right enough. He didn't. There are higher aspirations. We joined together with . . . others . . ." His voice trailed away painfully. "What do you want, son? You come all the way out here to talk about your father?"

Anson sat straight in the seat, gathering strength for the assault. "I came out here to talk about him, yes. And about you, Senator. And Torrance and Bolton and Petersen and Beale and Engstrom and . . . Aaron LaCroix." He could remember no more of the names.

Bradley's hand snaked out and gripped his knee tightly. "What are you talking about, boy!" The voice was sharp, strong, commanding. Anson swallowed hard.

"I'm talking about my father's association with his friends, Senator. I'm talking about your candidacy. I'm talking about an old man called Walt Margolis. About a guy named Leo McCullen. They got themselves killed . . ." He let the anger hang in the cool desert air. "I'm talking maybe about Richard Nixon."

Bradley's hand on his knee became a vise. "What about him?"

"I'd like to hear it from you, Senator."

The deep orange glow of Bradley's pipe guttered and died. He removed it and knocked its dead ash into the river. The embers drifted across the reflected stars like a flock of

migrating birds. He watched them fly, lost in som
private thought. He looked up. "Nixon is my business, boy
So are the rest of 'em. You're playing around wit
something you don't understand. Forget the names. Forge
Nixon."

"I can't just let it go like that. I can't do that."

Bradley stared into his dead pipe. "You know, boy, we ha
a dream, your father and me. We gave shape to it, invested i
it. Gave ourselves up to it like I gave myself up to Th
Springs here."

The boat had drifted a third of the distance back to th
compound. "I guess you could say we were all setting out t
water the desert in the beginning. At least that's what i
seemed and...," his voice grew resonant with memory
"... by the Lord God Almighty, it was worth all our time an
all our energies. Oh, we were idealists, sure enough. But w
were practical men, too. I reckon you'd agree your pa was
practical man."

Anson said nothing.

"We came together because we pulled a lot of weight
Started in '56. Small. A couple of years later it was bigge
than we thought it'd ever be. We decided our influence or
national affairs could be turned to...good effect. A long
haul, we knew that, so we worked in secret, in our own small
corners, if you like. One day, we figured we'd be in a positio
to..." He let his hand trail in the water beside him. "Mean
time, we could check events, if not change them. Your pa wa
a supreme example of that. I read the *New York Times*
obituary the other day. If they knew what he'd *really*
achieved for this nation..."

Bradley looked down at his trailing hand. "He was a good
man. He was..." He stopped again. "I had an idea you were
with the State Department. Didn't John Roper tell me you
were in Europe somewhere?"

"Rome."

"Rome." He brought his hand from the water and tapped it
across his brow. "How'd you get yourself into this?"

"A man died. At least it looked like he died, but I think he
was murdered. Walt Margolis. I met up with him a few days
before he died. He knew my father. He was with the CIA.
He'd been investigating the background to the assassination
of John Kennedy and..."

Bradley stiffened in his seat and pointed the pipe stem at
Anson's chest. "I don't want to hear any more of that, son. I
want you to give me your word, here and now, that you'll get

242

out of here quick as you can. Get yourself back where you came from. Rome."

Anson shook his head doggedly. "No, sir. I said I can't do that. I came here half expecting you to laugh me right off your property. Instead, everything you've said tells me I'm right."

"You damn fool kid! Can't you see it could be the last thing you do? You're into something you don't understand. Leave it to people who do. Leave it to me."

Anson gritted his teeth. "You and ... the rest? Leave you to bury it ... like you buried Margolis and his daughter? Like you ..."

"Before God, I swear I have had nothing to do with anyone dying."

"Neither did Pontius Pilate."

Bradley swung his arm, backhanded, and the blow caught Anson high on the side of his head. Tears of pain distorted his vision. Bradley's hand reached forward at once and gripped his wrist. "Forgive me, son. I'm sorry. I didn't mean to do that. You got me so upset ..."

They were almost level with the green mushroom of light over the compound. Bradley turned to the outboard, ripped it into life and headed the boat in to the mooring. They tied her up and stepped out onto the paved landing.

Bradley moved off along the river bank, away from the compound, and Anson followed him, his head still ringing. He said, "Did my father do ... anything wrong? Criminal, I mean?"

Bradley halted in midstride. He clamped his hands on Anson's arms above the elbows. "I don't give a damn what you think about me, son, but I'll bust your head if you walk away from here thinking ill of your pa. John Roper Anson was the finest man I ever met in a lifetime of looking. He had a right to expect your faith in his goodness because he poured everything he had to offer into creating a reputation you could be proud of."

He turned then and trudged away along the bank. They walked in silence until they reached a second field path running at right angles from the river to the compound. Bradley waited for Anson to catch up, dropped a hand on his shoulder. "I'm taking this path back to the house," he said. "You go back to your car, wherever you left it, and remember what I told you. Get out of this and stay out. You want to contribute something—you just go do half as much for the human race as your pa did."

243

"That's not good enough. I told you—I can't leave it at that."

Bradley raised a finger in front of his face. "I said we *tried*—me and your father. We tried and we failed because we had too much vision and too little sense. Well, that's a debt on my conscience and I don't intend to live the rest of my life with it. There's nothing you can do for John Roper or me or anyone else. But there's plenty I can do, and I don't aim to have you falling around my feet while I'm doing it. Go home, boy, and don't come back here again. You understand me?"

His hand strayed to his lapel, to a tiny gold cross, just visible in the darkness. He smoothed a finger over its outline, turned abruptly and walked away. He didn't look back.

THURSDAY: 2000—LEE RITCHIE

By eight o'clock she needed Harry Anson, but not in any way Lucas Garfield would understand. That was an exciting revelation: She could care without strings. It hadn't happened for a long time. She allowed the need to draw her to his motel.

The clerk, an apologetic pimple of a man who looked ready to burst, told her Mr. Hamilton had checked in around three o'clock, dropped his bags and walked right on out again in minutes. No, he didn't say where he was going or when he'd be back, and there were no messages. She drove back to her own plastic room near the airport and clutched her frustration to her like a comforter. She felt sick, too full for anger, but in the course of the next half hour she diluted the yearning for Harry Anson with cold logic. He'd planned this from the beginning, never intended to wait for her call. He'd managed to sneak off to see Bradley without her. How stupid could she be?

She dialed Lucas Garfield in Washington.

"Phoenix?" he repeated when she told him where she was. "Aaah, of course."

"You were right," she said, irritated by his manner. "Harry was the key. He didn't know it, but he was. He remembered a connection between his father and Bradley from . . ."

"Quite," said Garfield dismissively. "Where's Anson now?"

"He's . . ." She clutched nervously at a trailing lock of hair.

244

"We were supposed to meet this evening. When we left Turtleback he insisted we split up. Different motels. I've just checked at his. He hasn't been back since this afternoon. I think he's gone to see Bradley."

"Of course he's gone to see Bradley!" She heard his pipe clunk against the receiver.

"He remembered the town, Turtleback. His father brought him down here when he was a boy. It's Bradley's . . ."

"He was born there. Yes, I know that."

Her anger overflowed. "And what do you know about Nixon?"

Silence. Several seconds. Then: "What's that got to do with anything?"

"His name was on the list Margolis left behind. And it's in the file Anson found at Hutton's Farm. I didn't get time to read it before we left Washington. Just the name I gave you, LaCroix, and Nixon several times."

"I don't see the point."

"You saw Nixon on television? The shooting?"

"Forget about Nixon. Concentrate on Anson. That's your job. He *has* gone to Bradley."

"How do you know that for sure?"

"You don't imagine I allowed the two of you to run wild, do you? I had Anson followed to the farm last night. We tailed you to the airport this morning and picked you up in Phoenix."

"And you still have a tail on him?" She didn't know whether to feel relieved or even angrier.

"No. Surveillance stops short of The Springs. I can't permit it to interfere with the natural course of events." He yielded at last to the strain in her voice. "I told you from the outset: this exercise is too important for shallow emotional responses. I didn't *want* to use Anson. I *had* to."

"Like you had to use Leo?"

Garfield's tone was level. "I can't give you back what you've lost, Lee. I'm sorry."

"Then don't let me lose Harry Anson."

"If you stay calm and do as you're told, no one will get lost. Is this thing between you and Anson . . . personal?"

"Personal! How could it be *personal?*" She swallowed hard, trying to knit together the cracks in her voice. "First I lied to him. Then I made love to him. Then I lied some more. Then I let him take me to bed to make him believe another set of lies. How could it be personal?"

"He'll be all right."

"He's gone to see Bradley!"

"Bradley won't harm him. He's not that kind."

"What about the rest of them? Abrams?"

"Bradley won't call in Abrams or anyone else. He'll go to the fountainhead. He has to. We've lost Abrams temporarily, but don't worry, we'll find him. Just sit tight. I'll be out there myself tomorrow. Give me the name of your motel." She spelled it out. "Good. Now don't leave there. Don't budge. And leave Anson alone. Totally alone. Understand me?"

"Wait a minute!" She gripped the receiver hard. "I gave you that name this morning. The one connected with Turtleback. Aaron LaCroix. Does he check out?"

Garfield's pipe clanked again on the receiver. "Aaron LaCroix checked out a long time ago, Lee. He's history. He's been dead for twenty years. If we're looking for anyone, it's his successor. Goodnight to you."

The line went dead.

She stared at the instrument for a full half-minute, weighed it in her hand, then pressed the cradle down with her fingers and held it there. She knew she couldn't leave it at that. Garfield could rule all he liked against "shallow emotional responses" but that was because he had none. Harry Anson would be allowed to survive or not survive on the basis of pure mathematical chance. It made no difference to Garfield as long as his survival or death led to a turning point and a successful conclusion.

She didn't trust him. Couldn't trust him.

Then who could she trust?

No one.

The voice inside her responded at once: Yes, there was someone. Not necessarily someone she could trust with the truth, but a man who would offer straightforward, old fashioned, no-questions-asked help.

There was Buffalo Morgan.

She took her hand from the cradle and rummaged in her bag. She came up with a small address book. She dialed the Washington area code and Morgan's number. The receiver came off the hook at the other end, but for a moment there was no reply.

"Mr. Morgan?" No answer. She tried again. "Mr. Morgan? This is Lee Ritchie. Harry's friend. Are you there?"

There was a fumbling noise, as if the receiver had slipped from hands unfamiliar with it. Then, "Buffalo Morgan. Who's there?" His voice had more distance than she expected. Perhaps he was holding the phone at arm's length.

246

"Harry Anson's friend, Lee," she repeated.

"Yes?"

"Buffalo, I'm calling from Phoenix. You know—Arizona? Harry is with...He needs help, Buffalo. You remember...?"

A violent burst of coughing exploded in her ear, followed by what sounded like a bronchitic apology. She raised her voice despairingly. "You remember? You said if he ever needed you to call? Well, if the offer's still open..."

"Remember," choked Buffalo Morgan. "Yeah. Got you."

"Are you all right? You sound...not too well."

Pause.

"I'm fine, miss. Cold, is all."

"Are you well enough to come down here? *Will* you come?"

"Come down there?"

"To Phoenix. Harry wants you to come here. He needs your help, Buffalo." Her fist clenched, willing him to agree. "Can you hear me?"

"I hear you. Phoenix, are you saying? Arizona?" She wondered in passing if he had drugged himself to beat off the cold. He spoke as if the phone he held were a dozing rattlesnake about to wake.

"Buffalo? *Buffalo!*"

"I'm here, miss. Still here. Where's Harry?"

"I'll explain when you get here. Now go to the TWA desk at the airport and I'll fix the ticket from this end. There's a flight at 8:00 A.M. tomorrow, the same one we took this morning, remember?"

"Where's Harry?"

"He's here, Buffalo. Not right now, not this minute, but he's here."

"Phoenix?"

Lee Ritchie closed her eyes. It was like talking to a child. "Phoenix. The flight goes to Chicago first. You'll be here about a quarter of one. Now—can you manage that?"

The coughing erupted again and a hand covered the phone. She waited. "I'll be there, miss."

She breathed an audible sigh of relief.

"Where are you?" he said indistinctly.

"I'm..." She stopped. He was hopeless. Maybe he'd never even flown before. "I'll explain tomorrow. I'll meet you at the airport. At 12:45. O.K.?" She paused again. "And Buffalo?"

Silence.

"Buffalo!"

"Yes, miss?"

"Don't breathe a word to anyone. Just come."

She dropped the receiver on its rest and tried to imagine his relief at coming to the end of his electronic ordeal. She lay back on the bed and stared up at the crack in the ceiling. So much for a helping hand. To hell with Lucas Garfield.

Milton Abrams plucked the phone from Morgan's hand. He traced the lead to its wall connection, wound the cable around his fist and ripped it free. He glanced back at the two men ranged on either side of the fat man and hooked a thumb at one of them. "I want a Company plane scheduled for tomorrow morning. No job specification, no complement report, no flight record. That clear? If you run into any snags, check with me."

He turned to Buffalo Morgan and poked him playfully in his rounded gut. "And as for you, Fat Man, you did a good job. Get a good night's sleep and you'll be about ready for the next round."

FRIDAY: 0530—GARFIELD

The only light in the sky was a reflection of the city's illumination. They arrived at the Chapter House in shadowy succession: Garfield first, shivering with cold and impatience; Goldman second; Fletcher last by fifteen minutes, grayer and more hollow than ever and bowed over two stout walking sticks. The room crackled with cold, the door as they opened it, the polished floorboards as they crossed them, the leather of the chairs as they sat. There was no light.

Garfield told them about the Ritchie call and about Anson. His teeth chattered in spite of the heavy greatcoat, the coiled wool scarf and an incongruous wolfskin flapped cap. Fletcher's face remained impassive throughout and even Fred Goldman held his peace. When he had finished, Lucas Garfield got to his feet and made two shuddering circumnavigations of the table to restore his circulation, his hands buffing at speed as if trying to produce a spark.

Goldman broke the silence first. "I think you're crazy." He blew on his hands without removing his gloves.

"Is that a comment on matters in general?" Garfield

248

prowled behind the Army man's chair on another circuit of the table.

"Going to Phoenix. That's crazy."

"Its where it'll end . . . if it's going to end."

"You'll be on your own. Up front. Visible. I don't care what's happening out there. It's not worth stepping out of cover for."

Garfield came to roost in his chair. "I'm not thinking of leading a cavalry charge, Fred. Just watching things from closer in. Anson is the key. I've brought him too far to drop him now."

"You aim to watch his head roll?" Fletcher winced.

"Don't be so damn cussed, Fletch. You know better than that."

"We know what you tell us, Luke. No more," snapped Goldman. "You set us up too. You let us believe Anson was a pro. You didn't say anything about using him blind. If he comes out of this dead your name'll be on the death certificate, far as I'm concerned."

Garfield withdrew into the folds of his wool scarf. "I also told you I'd assume complete responsibility for running this operation as I saw fit—if it was necessary. It *was* necessary."

"So you didn't feel you had to consult me and Fletch?"

"You've both up-to-date now," Garfield said gruffly.

"Are we? Are we really up-to-date?" Fletcher's delivery made Garfield's neck hair rise. "If I called a meeting of the National Security Council right now, could you talk your way out of it? All the ends neatly tied?" His skin had the glaze shine of white china. "Is the President aware of what's really going on? Does he know about Anson? Does he even know about the Nixon deal?"

Garfield shuddered again in the barrel of his coat. "I didn't call you here for a discussion on group conscience."

"Nice to know there's a reason," growled Goldman. He lit a long thin black cheroot. "But why 5:30 in the morning?"

"I have a plane to catch at 7:30. For Phoenix. You'll be traveling too, Fred."

"Oh?"

"San Clemente."

They both leaned forward at once. "Another *fait accompli?*" Goldman said acidly.

"I talked to Nixon a couple of days ago. I told him to prepare to record a TV statement on the tape."

249

"You did what!" shouted Goldman.

"Madness! Absolute madness!" Fletcher burst out. "Look, I think it's time we called a halt to this whole ridiculous exercise, Luke. Bradley's been hammered from every side and he still hasn't shown a sign of cracking. We've tried pressure and it just isn't worrying him. We agreed from the beginning there's no way we can ever hope to use that tape publicly. Now you waltz in here and announce that you've decided to put Nixon on the air with . . ."

"I said I told Nixon to prepare to record a statement. That's all. You're right. We can't use the tape and we still haven't accomplished what we set out to do. One: put Bradley out of the race. Two: squeeze The Matrix and finger the force behind it. No inquiries. No Senate investigations. No fuss. No blood."

"No blood!" Goldman's guffaw was hollow.

"No *more* blood," countered Garfield irritably. "But you're wrong about one thing, Fletch. Bradley isn't taking this on the chin. He's cracking all right. He's got Nixon on one side of him and young Anson whipping away at his heels. And he's got another problem to live with. Himself. He's got to be a very lonely troubled man, just about now. We've already accomplished a lot. We've reached the point where he must know he's been manipulated all these years. I'm sure of that. They couldn't hold him after the Nixon thing unless they turned the heat on him. So he knows. That's a big point on our side. With a little help, he might be prepared to break out."

"What's that got to do with my going to San Clemente?" prompted Goldman.

"Another nudge, Fred. The one that might push Bradley over the edge. I said Nixon will be set to *record* a TV statement. I didn't say it would go on the air. But a private showing of that recording, for Bradley's benefit, just might convince him we're prepared to go the whole way and to hell with the consequences. In Phoenix or San Clemente, one or the other, we're going to break The Matrix in the next couple of days."

"But why do I have to go to . . . ?" began Goldman.

"Trust me, Fred. Your plane's at 8:15. You're booked into a suite at the Balboa Bay Club. You'll be carrying the tape when you fly down. You, Fletch: you stay here. If things go bad on us I'll be counting on you to come up with a smart explanation." He smiled into Fletcher's scowl. "Fred and I may be putting more on the line than our careers."

250

Garfield watched them from the door; Goldman's squared shoulders betraying his frustration, Fletcher's disintegration evident in every grunting step. Garfield reflected, with genuine pain, that he might have to replace Fletcher before the winter was out. He had little time left.

Their cars sprouted headlights on the far wall of the courtyard and glided forward to meet them. Goldman handed Fletch into his black Lincoln and stayed, head bent, for a few seconds. Garfield guessed they were talking about him. It was only natural. Goldman straightened and strode briskly to his own faceless Chevy.

When their winking taillights pulled through the arch, Garfield turned back into the room and crossed the creaking floor to the phone. There was one thing more.

The death of Faber had shown, if nothing else, that the manipulator of The Matrix was a man prepared to fight on more than one front, and the Nixon leak underscored his capacity for thinking on his feet. He wouldn't be at a loss for long, not where Bradley was concerned. He could control Bradley; he'd used Nixon with real flair. And in addition to monitoring Bradley's every move, he would be dogging Nixon's footsteps. That was the crunchpoint: Nixon.

Garfield had put a team on it three days ago when the intuition, the suspicion, the itch in back of his skull came up with its simple proposition. Whoever this man was, in the context of the game they played he would be Garfield's mirror image, and he too would be looking for a manipulator: the force manipulating Nixon. Could he have infiltrated Nixon's well-guarded camp?

In the past three days, the whole staff at San Clemente had been, in the jargon of the trade, spin-dried. It had not been a difficult exercise; the flaws showed up on Day Two but last evening it was made child's play for them. The suspect had placed a call to a man he referred to as Tony. It was a report. They didn't have to look further.

Now came the difficult part.

Garfield waited a couple of minutes while the operator put him through.

"Good morning, sir," he said pleasantly, when Nixon came on.

"Morning! You know what time it is?"

"Sorry, sir. I have a plane to catch and I want you to handle a pretty sensitive job, if you will. I had to call."

"O.K. What is it?"

"You have a young man on your staff. Name of Jake Henry."

"Jake? Yeah."

"Does he know about the arrangements we've made for the TV recording?"

"Nobody knows. That's the way you wanted it. Nobody knows."

"That's fine, sir. But now we'll make an exception. I want Jake Henry to know, and I want him to learn about it in the next few minutes. It'll have to be subtle and indirect. It can't come from you, of course."

"How's a man supposed to be subtle in the middle of the night, Garfield?"

"It's essential, sir. Absolutely critical."

The sigh was a heavy one and wrapped in static. "O.K. Leave it to me; but what's going on?"

"Jake Henry's been passing information to Bradley, or someone in the Bradley camp. I want this passed on, too."

"My head's on the block, Garfield. You thought of that?"

"I've thought of everything, sir. My colleague Fred Goldman will be on the eight o'clock plane out of here. Let Henry hear about him, too. Particularly about Goldman. You might add that he's checking in at the Balboa Bay Club."

FRIDAY: 1230—LEE RITCHIE

Caution. She tasted the word as she moved toward the airport's glass doors. A 707 had landed minutes earlier and a stream of passengers was discharging from the main lobby.

The stream became a torrent where it hit the cab rank and exploded into a maelstrom of chaotic militancy. She fought for a way through the emerging crowds, but the bodies crushed in on her, paralyzing her. She screamed, "Let me through. Damn you, let me through!" but no one was listening. Lee was off balance, being held upright by the crowd, when she felt a supporting hand at her elbow. He was the football type, maybe fifteen pounds heavier than his original gridiron weight but still slim in the right places. He had a strong grip on her arm. In his other hand was a smart alligator briefcase with a light raincoat draped across it.

"Stick with me," he yelled. "Stay close." He grasped her around the waist then and dropped one shoulder expertly to ram forward in a line-out lunge. She hesitated fractionally,

252

then fell in behind him. The crowd gave; thoughtless self-interest was one thing, but they were no match for power-driven thuggery. "My!" he said with mock propriety when they were safely in the clear. "They surely don't know how to treat a lady." He smiled. It took ten years off his age.

"Thanks," she said, smiling back. "I guess I'm not built for that kind of thing."

He ran a measuring eye from the toes of her sandals to the bulge of her breasts under the light blue cotton tunic. "You're surely not, ma'am," he drawled softly. "Surely, you are not."

She crinkled another brief smile. "Well, thanks, anyway," she began. "I think . . ."

He held up his free hand, palm forward. "Wouldn't hear of you going back into that mess. No *sir*. My car's waiting over there. You see it?"

It was a powder blue Cadillac, its blackened windows reflecting the scene.

"Look, it's all right, really . . ." She was torn between irrational negatives: the knowledge that she had to brush off this incarnation of Playboy Man and a fear of missing Buffalo's incoming plane.

"It's got air conditioning."

"Fine, but . . ."

"Quadraphonic tape deck."

"I bet."

"Its own bar. I play a mean cocktail shaker, ma'am.

She laughed in spite of herself. He was only trying to be friendly. Well, yes, that as well, but she could deal with that. It was important to get inside. Distract him. Play along. "O.K., Samaritan. But I think I ought to tell you . . ."

He threw back his head and laughed. The sound had qualities she associated with Boulder Dam. "I know, ma'am. All you ladies are married with four of the most beautiful little kids ever born. I'll tell you something, shall I? Me too, and so darn proud of it you couldn't guess. You keep me hanging around here much longer and I'll show you their pictures."

Before she could stop him, he took her arm firmly and led her across the road to the Cadillac. "Here you are, ma'am." He took the handle of the rear door and made a little bow, his body momentarily shielding her from the crowd. In that instant, he swung open the door, pressed down on her shoulders and flipped her bodily inside. He was beside her at once. The door slammed and the limousine eased away.

"What the hell ... ?" She got no further. The rest of the sentence was superfluous. Her eyes ran around the stolid faces of the other three men in the cushioned gray opulence of the interior and she recognized their make, mark and registration.

"What is this?" she snapped. But there was a tremor in her voice that had no right to be there. None of the men replied. Not one of them even turned to look at her.

"Look, if you want to know who I am, all you have to do is check with ..." She swung on her erstwhile savior. "You have no right to pick me off the street and ..." He wasn't looking at her but he turned his head even more to stare out the window.

The collar at the back of his neck showed a smudge of sweat.

The Cadillac crossed town, left it behind. She was aware of flattened, single-story suburban homes, then a break, then the prefabricated concrete gray and khaki brown of small factories and workshops, acres of them. Maybe not acres. The driver, without any spoken commands, made more than two dozen turns in the space of minutes. He seemed to be turning arbitrarily, backtracking and recrossing his tracks, right and left, left and right. She had taken care to memorize as far as she could the first part of the trip through town, but even with the sunlit world open to her beyond the windows she was soon lost. At last the driver grunted and the man beside him nodded stiffly.

The building showed no windows and, at ground level, no doors either. At one end a green-painted steel stairway led up to a second-floor balcony which ran the length of the concrete facade. At the top of the stairway was a green steel door. The man waiting at the foot of the stairs wore a black coverall and a camouflaged combat hat. He said nothing to the men in the car, nor they to him. Halfway to the balcony, with the man's hand firmly on her elbow, she heard the car pull away and glanced back. None of her four kidnappers had gotten out.

The boiler suit pulled back the door with obvious effort and signaled her in. She stepped over a foot-high threshold and the door thundered shut behind her. Two reflexes met head-on in her nervous system: the shock of the stench in her nostrils and the boom of the door at her back. She leaped to her right and cracked her shoulder against an echoing clang of metal. It was dark, totally black. Instinctively she fell to her knees, reducing profile, minimizing target area. The boom of the door was still rolling around the invisible shell.

The air settled into silence. She reached out and her fingers touched metal: steel, tubular steel. She ran her hand left and right. Metal supports. An upper and a lower horizontal rail. A fence of some kind. A safety rail? She froze. She lay full length on the concrete floor and touched the door, raised herself and found the outer edge. No handle. No lock.

She climbed to her feet cautiously, one hand above her head to avoid further painful contact with metal. She inched to her left. The rail ran on, seemingly to infinity.

The light stabbed the darkness with explosive intensity and caught her full in the face. The shock of it was monumental; she heard her heart pound in her head before she heard her own involuntary squeak of terror. She clasped the rail double-handed, eyes closed, and waited. When the beam moved she opened her eyes. On her far right, the safety rail turned to follow the wall; halfway along its length, a bulb burned in a suspended light fixture. Below it was a bench. On the bench sat a figure in black. He had no face. One hand beckoned her, idly, almost nonchalantly. She obeyed its instruction. As she rounded the right-angled turn, she felt the relief flood through her. He was wearing a mask, an ugly black rubber thing with huge circular eye plates and a concertinaed breathing tube that disappeared into a black plastic casing clipped to his belt.

When she reached the bench, a gloved hand pointed silently to a small white transistor pack. She picked it up nervously and turned it over in her hands. It was a simple battery transceiver set, a refined version of the old walkie-talkie. She pressed the transmit button.

"Where is this?" It was genuinely the first thing she wanted to know.

She released the button and the voice crackled out of the white plastic box, flat and featureless and unidentifiable. "You're a very practical person, Miss Ritchie." The printed circuit had probably been doctored to achieve that very special shapeless sound. Anonymity. She clung to the idea, joyously. A man who concealed his identity was probably not planning to kill. A killer had no reason to hide.

"What am I doing here?"

"Now that's a little more human, Miss Ritchie. Not much, but some. I have to say I expected more than that little scream back there. You have good control. Good agent."

Agent. "What d'you mean, agent?" It was childish, but then

freaks who worked in the dark behind gas masks didn't inspire maturity. *Gas mask.* The stench was now so great she had to cup a hand around her nose.

The transistor picked up interference, which she interpreted as laughter. "Sorry, Miss Ritchie. No time for the intricacies of verbal fencing. I've traveled hard and long and I'm not blessed with a sense of fair play. I have schedules. I'm afraid I'm going to have to be very practical about keeping them. So let's get down to it."

He came off the bench, studied her for a moment, then crooked a finger. He walked to the far corner of the catwalk, turned left and switched on another hanging light. She followed. Twenty yards farther along the catwalk he switched on a third light and pointed downward. The stench was overpowering.

The vat was thirty feet across and maybe twenty deep. It was full, its surface erupting gently and continuously with a foul gray froth, broken at intervals by a curve of dark, substantial material. The burgeoning fumes were unclassifiable. She reeled back to the security of the wall, both hands over her face.

"Now then," the receiver blurted thinly, "this is it in a nutshell. A body—a living body, that is—lowered into that—whatever—would survive . . . well, how long would you say?"

Lee lay her head against the coarse concrete of the wall and closed her eyes. *Where in the name of God are you, Garfield?*

"Too technical? You're right. Well, let's say a body would survive for a minimum functional period contingent with its capacity to breathe, head down, in a liquid composite heated to 186 degrees Fahrenheit. Now, you're a jargon person. That conform with Company standards?"

She didn't reply. "Aaaah! The purist. That . . . mess is some kind of acid—or maybe I mean alkali—or maybe I've got it mixed up with something else. Anyhow, the floating stuff—that's cowhide right off the hoof. Some day it'll be shoes and gloves and handbags and suitcases . . . you know, leather. What the hell they do with it at this stage I couldn't say, but if that human body we were talking about dropped smack in there . . . ," he made a swallow-dive motion with one hand, ". . . I don't think anyone'd know the difference, do you?"

"Go to hell."

"That's Company, sure enough. But like I said, we don't have time—even for displays of tight-lipped courage. You think I got you up here to trade *your* life for what I need to

256

know? No marks, Ritchie. You're pro and pros take time to break. So, let me offer you a small demonstration. It won't take two minutes of your time."

He moved to his right and uncoiled a length of hanging chain from a wall-mounted cleat. He pulled on the chain, hand over hand, and Lee heard a block-and-pulley system clicking high in the unlit gloom above her head. The man's pulling slowed and he laid into the chain, using his body weight to develop momentum.

In the blackness of the catwalk, five or six feet beyond the chain, Lee saw a rustle of movement, then an angling up of a bulky mass from the floor. The man in the mask heaved with more deliberation and the weight rose and swung free. Lee flattened herself to the wall as it gained momentum, stroking the air like a pendulum. When it reached a height of three feet above the safety rail, the masked man relaxed, judged the disposition of the weight, then reached up on the wall and turned a ratchet handle. The chain inched forward over the vat, carried by a wheeled block high in the ceiling. When it was an arm's length from the rail, the man reached out and tugged at the black sheeting enclosing the weight. It came away without difficulty. Lee Ritchie stared at the upside-down face.

For a moment, the shock flooded her, destroying sensation. The man hung above the vat. Head first, above the vat. She twisted her head, strained her eyes in the poor light and . . .

"Yes." The transistorized tormentor was pleased with his stage effects. "His name is Morgan. Buffalo, I think he calls himself. Buffalo Morgan. So there he is, Miss Ritchie. To put the whole thing beyond any possible margin of confusion: I want to know where I can find a Mr. Harry Anson. Simple matter of communication. You tell me. I tell my friends in the car . . . ," he nodded at the transistor in her hand, ". . . they fetch old Harry, you and Morgan here go play together and everything ends sensibly. Alternative: Morgan goes for a swim. Head first. Inch by inch. At 186 degrees Fahrenheit."

She opened her mouth. The figure raised a hand. "No, Miss Ritchie. This is real. Really real. No alternative happy endings. Believe me. Ten seconds, girlie. Now—where's Harry?"

FRIDAY: 1340—ANSON

Harry Anson crawled up out of the tube of sleep and remembered vaguely beginning the same painful ascent just minutes before. This time his eyes were finding it difficult to perform the normal opening function. It had been that way last time he tried. He hadn't reached the motel until 2:00 A.M. and he had been dead on his feet. The upper half of his brain seemed to have taken over the function of his nose. He had the thought-smell strong, locked up in the cerebellum. That's where it was.

The eyes nearly opened that time. God—he felt terrible. What time was it? Shards of dancing gold, shattered yet complete, joined at the center, yes, that's it—like a window shattered by a bullet.

No. It was a hanging light. Feeble, not too bright. Steel mesh guard under the bowl to protect the bulb. Then he remembered. There was no light with a steel mesh cage shining in his eyes last time he woke at the motel. No smell in his mind. He'd been in bed. He'd heard the door and he came to and saw a shadow on the wall, fixed by the flooding sun. Lee? He had been lying on the bed on his face; he had pushed up and back on his elbows. Then, a hand pressed something in his nose, on his mouth . . . sweet, beguiling, drowning . . . and he had fallen down the tube of sleep again.

Now . . . faces. One face and . . . He blinked his eyes.

Another face swam like a visual computer image, flowing left and right, up and down. It coalesced and he grasped at familiar features: hair, eyes, mouth. Her. Lee. The face zoomed in close to his as she knelt beside him on the catwalk.

"Harry?"

A flat metallic voice came from a hundred miles away. No—it came from her hand. It said, "Good afternoon, Harry. It's a lovely day. Rise and shine, sonny boy."

He saw the face—Lee—raise a white box to her mouth. "What did they do to him?"

"Ether. Would you believe ether? Just a smidgeon. Nothing serious. Get him on his feet. He'll be fine."

He felt her arm crook in his and was surprised at the strength in her. There was a bench on the catwalk and it swam around as he came upright. So did the hanging light

258

with the mesh guard and the demon—no, a mask of some kind. *Shake me and I'll wake up.*

"Harry? Are you all right? Can you stand?" She meant it. No playacting this time in her voice.

"I'll be O.K. Just let me sit down somewhere."

The bench came up to meet his backside and he fell squarely on it. His sight was coming back at last.

"And then there were two." The voice from the box in Lee Ritchie's hand was not a voice, but he knew it was being transmitted from behind that mask. Gas mask. Distortion. All done by distortion—the essence of magic. Who said that?

"You able to talk now, Harry?" rasped the box.

"Yeah." He wanted this over with. He wanted sunlight and air . . . what the hell was that smell?

"Bring him along, Ritchie. This way, please."

She grabbed his arm again and slung it around her shoulders, taking his full weight on her hip and thigh. Why had he never noticed she was so strong? He said to her, "Tell the creep to go fuck himself," but she carried on, ignoring him. They rounded a corner and in the faded light ahead he saw a taut chain slung from the darkened ceiling, the weight at its end, the vat below, the fumes rising from it. He raised a hand to his nose. Ten paces from the hanging chain Anson realized the weight was a man. At six paces his eyes told him what his brain wouldn't accept: The pendulum was Buffalo Morgan.

"That's Buffalo," he told her stupidly. She propped him against the wall like a drunk. The man in the mask took up a position next to the rail and motioned Lee Ritchie farther along the wall, back to it, wrists flat to the concrete where he could see her hands. Anson couldn't tear his eyes from Buffalo's inverted face. It looked all wrong: The flesh rolls hung against their natural fall line, the veins in his forehead and smooth skull and neck were thick as tug hawsers. No sound came from him, no breathing action, no pulse in the throat. His skin was dark—he couldn't make out the color in this light—and that was wrong too because Buffalo Morgan wore a perpetual troglodyte tan the shade of cream cheese.

"All righty," said the box in Lee's left hand. "Talking time, Harry. Go ahead, Ritchie. Turn him on like a good girl."

"Turn him on yourself."

If the gun had been in the man's hand before, Anson hadn't registered it. It was small, matt black with a silencer. It made a tiny sucking sound like a badly aimed kiss on a damp cheek and the concrete kicked six inches from Lee's head and pellets of debris whined off along the catwalk into the darkness. "We agreed, Ritchie. So little time, remember? Talk to the guy. Tell him."

Lee held her eyes steady on the little automatic. She said, "I had to tell them where you were, Harry. He was going to drop Buffalo into *that* . . ." She couldn't elaborate.

Anson's tangled brain cells ignored the words; they had been trying to process a thought, a memory, fragments of elusive detail. It came together out of nowhere. He said impulsively, "That's a .22 silencer automatic. They killed Leo that way."

"That's enough, Anson! Tell him some more, Ritchie. Just tell him."

He was two arm lengths from Lee, but he felt her body tense. The voice coming from the white box in her hand became almost human—a mixture of frustration and annoyance. "He wants to know who Leo worked for. He knows a lot but he doesn't know that. He says . . ."

"I said, Harry," broke in the box, "that neither of you knew enough on your own. Together you know what I need to know. Now, I credit you with a brain, Harry, and I credit this lady here with a high degree of professional acumen, so I'll tell you what I'm going to do. She's too well-trained to talk to save *your* hide, and you're not about to throw your life away on a bit of tail who's played you for a dummy. So, the object up for auction here is your mutual friend, Mr. Morgan. Now, I know Ritchie here accepts my offer—information or Buffalo takes the plunge. How about you?"

Anson could see no movement behind the mask. If lips were moving behind the black rubber, if a jaw was rising and falling, he couldn't see it. The white plastic box was doing the talking and he wasn't afraid of white plastic boxes. On the other hand, that .22 talked big. His head was clearing. It began to ache at once. "Get him back in here," he croaked.

"Sorry, Harry. You know how it is. Facts first."

He pulled himself together. "I don't know what you want. I'm not working for anyone. I . . . I started in on this because . . . I wanted to be sure my father . . ."

"History, Harry, and sheer poetry, but that's not what I'm buying. You tied in with Walt Margolis. Leo McCullen was running you. Why?" The box hissed for a space of seconds. Then it addressed Lee. "O.K. Ladies first. Now you could maybe explain away Anson's death, but you'd find it goddamn difficult to paper over Mr. Morgan, Ritchie. You'd have some public explaining to do and, at this stage of the game, explanations hurt, don't they? Sure they do. So—one name,

Ritchie. Just one little name, and a couple of other pieces of information. It's up to you. Think before you answer because the next word you speak could kill the man."

Lee swung her eyes guiltily at Morgan's dangling form. His chest and legs were encased in a blanket. The chain had been wound over each shoulder, around his barrel chest and stomach, between his legs and around his ankles. If only she could see some flicker of life . . .

Anson broke in quickly. "You don't have to tell him anything . . . Alice." She shot a look of complete surprise at him. He widened his eyes fractionally. He angled his head toward Buffalo. "The bastards have already killed him. Look at his face. The color of his face."

The box snapped, "What's he talking about, Ritchie?"

Anson swung to face her, his eyes wide in appeal. Surely she understood. She stared back, her eyes hard, without depth. His stomach whirled in hurricane circles and hurled updrafts into his chest.

She pointed upward. "That's what he means. Look at him. He quit the ring because of a heart murmur. You killed him when you put him up there. You haven't got an auction any more."

The man in the mask swung to check Buffalo's face, then back again in a fraction of a second. "He's O.K. And, if he isn't, old Harry here can take his place on the . . ."

Lee Ritchie put the white box on the catwalk, turned to the chain curled on its cleat, found the backhaul and began to pull.

The .22 developed a nervous sweeping motion. "Enough, Ritchie. What the hell're you doing?"

"I told you. . ." She hauled Buffalo in, inch by inch to the rail; his bared skull was three feet above the upper horizontal. "He's dead. Can't you understand? How long have you had him up here? How long d'you think a diseased heart holds out if you hang it upside down over *that* . . ." A violent gesture of her hand downward.

"Wait a minute!" The man in the mask, unable to hear her, stepped two paces forward along the rail. She ignored him. When Buffalo was suspended just inside the catwalk, safe from the ghastly gray bubbling detritus of the vat, she dropped the chain. She took the great shiny skull in her arms and pulled it to her, as if trying to warm it back to life.

"Will you get away from him," spat the box.

"Forget it." She came round Morgan, putting her body

261

between him and his tormentor. She took the weight of him tenderly in her arms and leaned into the suspended body.

"Anson!" snapped the box on the catwalk. "Pick up that transmitter."

He bent automatically. The circular eye plates followed him every inch of the way. Lee Ritchie, her weight angled into the pendulum of Buffalo's body, forced it away from her again: one pace, two paces, three. The chain was still taut to the ceiling pulley but it angled out now, fifteen or twenty degrees from the perpendicular.

Anson engaged the transmit button. "Well?"

"That's better. Ritchie. Get yourself back against that wall or, so help me, I'll kill you."

Buffalo Morgan's weight was colossal. She could hold it now for no more than seconds. She swung her head to look back over her shoulder at the masked man. He took a threatening step forward, his free hand palm flat over the automatic, cowboy style, his left leg and hip flush with the safety rail.

Anson glared at her, wide-eyed. "Let him go—do what he says, will you?"

She sidestepped with lightning speed and Buffalo swung like a bucket of steel, downward to the nadir of the chain's perpendicular, upward with the impetus of his own weight. The flat plane of his armored skull caught the man in the mask a deflecting blow in the middle of his chest. In the time it took Anson to transfer his eyes from Lee to the farthest limit of Buffalo's first arc, the masked tormentor had disappeared. Anson, confused, looked right, left, right again. Then his brain computed the only possible equation and he stepped unsteadily to the rail.

The vat simmered in its ominous gray scum. He waited. In the very center of the huge cauldron a shiny black head appeared. It turned with the ponderous thrust of the rising heat and burst like a tar bubble. The face of Milton Abrams glittered up at him, eyes wide, mouth slack, then sank. The black overalls performed a slow roll, chest first, then stomach, thighs, knees, feet. And disappeared.

FRIDAY: 1340—GOLDMAN

Alfred Goldman dropped his bag in the living room of his suite at the Balboa Bay Club in Newport Beach. The clock in his head told him he was too old to pack more than twenty-four hours into a day. His flight had gained him three more. He loathed travel. He equated it with active service, and active service with the man he had once been and was now too stiff-jointed, too slow, too physically fearful ever to be again. He had traveled through one entire life being someone, something, whose existence was now a myth. He had replaced that myth with a set of well-pressed dark suits, handsewn shoes, conservative ties and a body clock that rang alarm bells several times a day. Alarm bells needed a wife and secretaries on hand to keep the score and arrange essential servicing requirements. Travel made a mess of all that.

He checked the flowers on the center table. *Welcome, Mr. Murray*, said the manager's card. *Please call if I can be of service*. He checked out the room, unscrewed the phone for concealed mikes, reversed the watercolor prints on the walls, followed phone and electric light cords to their source, inspected the air conditioning. The kitchen was primed for use and the refrigerator was stacked with food he would never eat. He made a cup of coffee and examined the bathroom minutely. When he was satisfied, he unzipped the bag, located a pair of binoculars and took them out onto the living room balcony.

It overlooked the yacht club and the bay. He held the coffee with one hand and set the binoculars to his eyes with the other. Two-thirds of the boats he could see were huge power-driven gin palaces. There was little sign of life aboard any of them.

He went back inside and rummaged further into the bag. The black dispatch case lay under a covering of shirts. He snapped it open; the circular tape canister lay in its molded green baize bed. He touched it; it didn't burn his fingers. He closed the case, zipped the bag shut and carried it through to the bedroom. When he came back, he touched the black case again. Reassurance.

The phone took him by surprise; it started a little pulse in his throat.

"Murray."

"Murray?" The young voice paused nervously. "Er . . . oh gosh, sure. I'm sorry, Mr. Goldman, I had the name in my head when I picked up the phone but . . ."

"Who is this?"

"Jake Henry, sir. Mr. Nixon's staff at San Clemente. It's his wish I call you right away, sir. He'd be glad—appreciate it if you came out this way as soon as you've settled in at the Beach."

Goldman closed his eyes. "Look—I've got people here just now. The manager. Understand? What did you say your number is?" He memorized it. "O.K. Call you back. Coupla minutes." He killed the phone and took a black Gucci notebook from his hip pocket. He checked a list of numbers, bunched his lips in mute confirmation and snapped the book shut. He dialed the number Henry had given him.

"Casa Pacifica, San Clemente."

"Give me Jake Henry, please. My name's Murray." Henry's voice came on the line. "That you, Mr. Goldman?"

Goldman bared his teeth at the mouthpiece. "You have any idea the trouble and expense I went to to be plain Mr. Murray?"

"Gosh—I'm sorry. I hope I haven't . . ."

"Forget it. What's the problem?"

"No problem, sir. Mr. Nixon asks me to say he's sending a limo over to the Beach to pick you up. Should be there in five, ten minutes."

"The schedule says I come out to the house at 3:30," Goldman said tersely. "Nobody's told me about any changes."

"Mr. Nixon wants to talk with you, sir. A few points cropped up, I believe."

Goldman allowed one hand to fall away to waist height and pulled a stool away from the leather-clad bar. He perched on it. "Let me talk to Mr. Nixon," he ordered.

"I can't do that, sir, I'm afraid," Henry answered patiently. "He's getting ready for the recording right now. He kind of has it in mind you'll be there before the cameras roll."

"What about the chauffeur?"

"Name of Tony Javallo, sir. He's dark, about 200 pounds, brown eyes, around six-two and . . ."

"He's just a chauffeur?"

"No, sir. One of Mr. Nixon's men. Handpicked. He'll have a Secret Service ID wallet. You better ask him for that, sir."

"You sure this is necessary?"

Henry coughed diplomatically. "The—er—*case* is necessary, sir. For the recording. Mr. Nixon's going to introduce it as evidence, and he's planning to play it right there in front of the cameras so people can see it."

"All right. I get the picture. But I don't like being hustled."

"I'm sure Mr. Nixon will explain everything to your satisfaction, Mr. G—Mr. Murray," Jake Henry said soothingly.

Tony Javallo was nearer 220 pounds than 200 and his handclasp was a gloved vise. He belonged to that small subspecies of the human order who electrify any first meeting with unspoken aggression; Goldman felt it as he opened the door of the suite to him. Javallo flashed his ID, raised the big dark glasses from his face, replaced them and presented his wrist, from which hung a chain attached to a security wristband. Goldsmith declined the offer. He tucked the tape case casually under his arm and they went down to the waiting black Cadillac.

They ran the course of the freeway in silence, and Goldman, who had insisted on taking the front passenger seat, had time to examine his companion. Javallo's slate gray uniform jacket bulged ominously and his jaws worked mechanically under the reflecting sunglasses on a ball of gum. He had long muscular hands, carefully manicured, but he shaved sloppily. He seemed uncomfortable in the peaked cap.

Javallo eased the limousine off the freeway onto a minor road and dropped his speed to a stately forty-five. The land flattened down to the beach, and the beach to the sea, and both sea and sky met in a shimmering heat dance. Goldman was reminded again of his body clock. It would have been easy enough to doze off in the car. He adjusted the air conditioning. About 200 yards offshore a flash of reflected light caught his eye; he turned to focus in the seaward glare. The motor yacht was long, sleek, beautifully streamlined, sixty or seventy feet at least. She was at anchor, securely bottomed out fore and aft. He could understand why; some decaying roué out there, he thought wistfully: gutful of expensive booze, deckful of assorted broads, flat on their backs and running with suntan oil. Fishing, maybe, or just plain lazing. Javallo followed his eye and made a clicking sound with his tongue from the side of his mouth. "That's living, huh?" he growled.

"Living," agreed Goldman with feeling.

The house was a typical Spanish-style villa, penned around with a chain-link fence and embraced by gardens rich with tropical flowers and shrubs and lawns on which the sprinklers never slept. There was no one at the main gate, but at the door a couple of well-cut dark suits with bulges came out to greet him. It was a serious ceremony without benefit of

265

welcoming smiles. One of the men took the car and Javallo tossed his cap onto the seat. "This way," he said, nudging Goldman ahead of him, his eye on the black case.

They came into a marble-floored lobby. Sunbeams streamed down in myriad colors through a modern stained glass window and cascaded over white stucco walls. A young man emerged from a door to their right, a smile squatting defiantly on his face. "You here for the recording?" he asked brightly.

Javallo spoke from behind Goldman's back. "The boss here?"

"Yeah—he's inside. Are you . . . ?"

"This here's Alfred Goldman. That thing he's carrying is for the boss."

"Fine. I'll take it." The man approached Goldman with outstretched hand. Goldman sized him up; he'd have made a good shot-putter, he thought. Good shoulders. He didn't have to be so nice to people if he didn't want to. Why did he want to now?

Javallo came up quickly on Goldman's shoulder and held out a warning hand. "Hold it, buddy. That thing goes right into Mr. Nixon's hands and nowhere else. Right, Mr. Goldman?"

Goldman nodded. "Why don't you just take me inside, son. I'll talk to Mr. Nixon."

"Whatever you say, sir. But you'll have to wait a coupla minutes. They're making him up for the cameras, like I said." He opened the door behind him and ushered Goldman inside. Javallo cut in on his heels.

The room was built for lounging and drinking; stuffed leather stretched in all directions and a bar ran the length of the far wall. To the left there was a raised dais which presumably looked out through French windows to the ocean. The curtains were drawn against the offending natural light. There were eight men in the room and very little space for them to put their feet which wasn't already occupied by writhing cables and conduits. Eight floods burned mercilessly on stainless steel stands, and two cameras were positioned at an angle of sixty degrees from an empty armchair. A man in a fine tan suede jacket moved from camera to camera, microphone to arc light, arguing and gesticulating. The others appeared to ignore him. On the raised dais a man hunched in a swivel chair, a cloth draped ludicrously over his head like a peasant woman's shawl while the makeup man bent over him, an eyeliner brush poised expertly in one hand.

The young man gestured discreetly across the room to the figure under the cloth. "Mr. Nixon's nearly ready. Maybe you'd like to take a coupla seats over by the bar. Better not to interrupt. He's kinda . . ." He dropped his voice to a whisper. "He's kinda sensitive about the makeup thing. You know how it is."

The youngster winked and slipped back into the hallway, closing the door with mannered gentleness. Goldman took a step toward the bar, his mind fleetingly conjuring a picture of Richard Nixon seen from the makeup man's point of view.

Then the case was plucked cleanly from his hand.

Before he could complete his turn, Javallo's voice crooned softly in his ear. "Hold it there, friend." Something hard dug into Goldman's back. "Feel it?" Goldman nodded his head fractionally. "Keep it in mind." The clamor in the room hid Javallo's whispering; no one displayed the slightest interest in their presence.

"Just move across to your right, near the bar. Nice and slow. I'm holding a piece behind this case and if you look like you're gonna be brave, friend, I'll shoot first. No questions. I use a silencer. In here, they wouldn't know it till you were dead. O.K.?"

Goldman's neck stiffened and Javallo accepted it as a sign of acquiescence. "Go, baby, go," he whispered. Goldman hesitated, then flattened one foot in front of the other and dawdled across to the bar. When he reached it, he dropped onto a stool and looked back at Javallo. The chauffeur stood by the door, the case in his left hand, his right hidden behind it.

"All right. All right. *All right!*" shouted the man in the tan suede jacket. "Will you hold it down, please. Chuck, I want to check sound levels now. Quiet, please, QUIET!" The room froze. The silence was momentarily so complete that Goldman thought he could hear the grating of the makeup man's hand across Nixon's jaw.

"That's right. You heard what the man said. *Quiet!*" Javallo, his back square to the wall, brought the gun up from behind the case. It was a Luger and it wore a screw-on silencer. The first few seconds of inactivity were followed at once by rapid movement as bodies spun to face the stranger's voice, but Javallo called out, *"That's* enough. Not one more move out of any of you or you die where you stand." He waved the Luger at Goldman. "Tell 'em, Mr. Goldman. Go ahead. Tell 'em."

Goldman tightened his jaw, shedding embarrassment. "Do as he says. All of you. Do . . ."

"Right. You hear the man. Now I want every one of you . . ." He gestured with the Luger to the makeup man. "Yeah, you too, dimples. Every one of you face down on the floor. Go on. Faces down." He turned again to Goldman. "Except you, Mr. Goldman, and Mr. Nixon, of course."

Goldman said in a burst, "You'll never get out of here. If you make it out of the house, they'll pick you up before you can move a mile. And you can't kill us all . . ."

"Never mind what I can do. You just sit tight on your ass and keep your mouth shut. I got plans for you."

He addressed himself to the man in the makeup chair. "Well now, Mr. President, what d'you say?" Richard Nixon said nothing. His head and neck were shuddering with tension under the cloth. "Oh, come on now, Mr. President. You got something to say, haven't you? You always have something to say." He raised the end of the silencer and used it to adjust the dark glasses on the bridge of his nose. "These boys and girls here have a big investment wrapped up in you, Mr. President," he drawled. "Their lives."

Nixon stiffened in his chair and the figures prone on the floor turned their heads fearfully to look up at the gunman.

"Don't worry, Mr. President," Javallo said with a chuckle that was almost genuine. "They're fine as long as you cooperate. The faster you cooperate, the longer they live. You got that?"

Nixon's head nodded several times very quickly.

"Fine. We're getting along fine here. Now this is what you do. You get up outta that chair and you walk backward over here to me. You receiving me? *Backward*. You got three steps down from that raised part of the floor, then a lot of wires and stuff and then there's the end of a couch. When you reach that, then you can turn around. I don't want you to think I don't trust you."

Nixon rose stiffly to his feet, his shoulders bent. He sidestepped.

"Right. Right. Come on."

Nixon reached back with one foot, located the top step of the three and negotiated them awkwardly. He had no sense of balance at all and the makeup cloth over his skull was no help; he kept his hands clasped in front of his chest, elbows tight to his body. He reached the main floor area, trod unwisely and nearly fell over a cable connection. He recovered and one of the prostrate TV crewmen pulled the

268

bling out of his way. When the back of his leg touched the couch, Javallo said, "That's good. That's very good. Now I want you . . ."

Goldman protested, "For God's sake, man. Leave him alone. You don't think you can . . ."

Javallo whirled on him, the Luger circling hungrily. "Mr. Goldman . . ." His voice hummed with brimming violence. "One more word out of you and I'll kill you where you stand."

"I wouldn't advise it."

Goldman reacted as if he had been stabbed in the throat. The figure, round-shouldered and comic under its ridiculous headcloth, had turned to face Javallo, a squat black Magnum firm in its right hand.

Javallo's mouth gaped wide, his Luger still pointing at Goldman's chest.

Lucas Garfield tugged the makeup cloth from his head and let it fall to the ground. "Put the gun on the floor. Slowly."

Javallo didn't move. The muscles of his free left hand bulged and contorted. The TV team got to their feet.

"We're all armed. Put the gun down."

Javallo's eyes flicked from Garfield to Goldman and back, but his gun arm remained stiff and trained on Goldman. He backed off two paces until his shoulders met the wall. He hissed, "You want him to die?"

"I don't want anyone to die. But if you shoot him, I'll get you. I'd say that was a waste of two lives. That doesn't make sense . . . for a professional."

The TV crewmen formed an arc at Garfield's back.

Javallo said, "Come over here, Goldman. Walk slow."

"Stay where you are, Fred," rapped Garfield.

"You do what I tell you." Javallo seemed to grow another inch. His free hand was throbbing with independent muscular life. He raised the Luger on a line with Goldman's throat.

"I'm coming. O.K., I'm coming." Goldman took two paces forward. A third, fourth . . .

Javallo swung away, his right arm dropping to change trajectory, the Luger sweeping the room toward Garfield's face.

The roar of the Magnum was thunderous. Javallo splayed like a starfish against the wall, dropped a hand to the gaping hole in his stomach and collapsed.

Three of the TV crew were beside him at once. One took the Luger, another raised his head, the third felt vainly for the pulse in his throat.

269

Goldman let the breath out of his lungs. "What kind of a game do you call that?" he breathed.

Garfield handed the Magnum to one of the crewmen. "Did it bother you, Fred?"

"I thought you were headed for Phoenix."

"How many times do I have to tell you? I have a personal responsibility for this."

"Why couldn't you have told me this morning? Why do you have to play everything so damned deviously?"

"I knew they'd go for the tape. I knew they'd take a lot of precautions to make sure they had the *genuine* tape. That meant they'd have to come right in here and see it handed over to Nixon. So, I gave them you, Fred. You could have been a decoy, you could have been the real thing. They had to have someone walking on your heels to make sure. It worked out." He sucked comfortingly on his teeth. Then he looked down at Javallo's body. "I haven't done that before outside a firing range. Who is he?"

"Name's Javallo. That's all I know. And you'd better get your hands on a creep named Jake Henry."

"He's being well cared for," Garfield said equably. "He's been very useful, Mr. Henry." He dusted his hands across his chest. "I think I'd better leave the rest of this to you, Fred." He nodded at the technicians. "They're all aware of what's going on. They'll do the legwork."

"You going back to Washington right away?"

"Washington? Of course not. I told you this morning. I have to be in Phoenix. With a little luck I'll be there for dinner."

BOOK FOUR KINGS

*... for they were no
gods, but the work of
men's hands, wood and stone ....*
    —2 KINGS, 19:18

Lee Ritchie was dimly aware that she was no longer alone in the room, but she didn't look up from the bed. White lace curtains billowed and swooped in the open window, and from a long way away came the comforting sounds of an innocent world. The room was wide, airy, graceful, an unbridgeable gulf away from the depressing box of the motel room where she and Anson had brought Buffalo Morgan hours ago.

The presence in the room grew stronger. She kept her eyes on the floating curtains.

Anson leaned in the frame of the door. He said, "Are you O.K.?"

She turned on the bed and gestured, one-handed. "Well, are you coming in?"

"Are you going to answer my question?"

"What d'you want me to say? That I've never felt better in my life?" Her eyes fell to her bare feet.

He studied her in detail for a moment, then, "When I woke up in that . . . dump, back there, you know the first thing that came into my head?"

She made no attempt to answer.

"I said to myself: You crazy, pig-ignorant son of a bitch, you've done it again. She just has to say to you: Come step off this cliff, Harry, and you'll get this beautiful floating sensation. And off I step. Thunk!"

Her jaw jutted. "Are you coming in or aren't you? I was there too, remember?"

"Oh, yes—you were there too. Superwoman personified. You get a kick out of killing Abrams?"

She opened her mouth, shut it with a snap and turned away. He closed the door.

"Is this visit leading somewhere?" she snapped spitefully.

"Oh, come on, you know better than that. Anson doesn't lead anyone anywhere. He's the one you lead around in circles. Follow me, Harry, I know where I'm going. Isn't that the way you played it?"

"I said I was sorry about that. I told you . . ."

"You said a helluva lot, baby, but you keep changing the message. I got a little confused. First I have you straight in my mind, then you shuffle and deal again and I've got another Lee Ritchie."

273

"You're not exactly the Prince of Truth yourself."

"At least I have a conscience."

She colored.

He pressed home his advantage. "You should learn about conscience, Lee," he said. "Except professionals don't need confessionals, do they? You just wipe your guilt clean with a pure thought. I guess you'll wipe me clean too."

"When I was brought into this I didn't *know* you," she said imploringly.

His eyes found hers. "Do you get danger money for this kind of work? Shacking up with pigeons?"

"I had a job to . . ."

He ignored her. "Did I really fall for it *that* hard? God, it really was easy, wasn't it?" He pinched fingers and thumb together and shook them in front of his face. "You, or whoever runs you, picked me out of a perfectly ordinary life. You stepped in and switched the reality off and the fantasy on. And I didn't notice a damn thing. Not once. Even when . . ." He stared at the pinched fingers. "Even when you had me believing things about my father I knew had to be . . . *lies!*" He bellowed the last word; the venom in it struck her like a blow. "Am I especially stupid or do all your patsies act this way?"

She tried to speak but he locked her out. "I guess there's nothing much worse than knowing you're a fool, but I don't mind that so much as . . . as . . . How could I not *know?* You scare the shit out of me, I'll tell you that much. You and the rest. You make phone calls and people *die*. They *die*. You know what that means to someone like me?" He was breathing hard, the words tumbling unconsidered, uncontrollable. "I've been working on *security* duty for three, four years. And do you know something? The only dead man I ever saw fell under a Fiat in the Via Veneto. I was sick to my stomach." He swallowed hard.

"Don't be so damned naive!" she flared. "Oh, Harry, please —that's enough."

He leaned elbows on knees and dropped his head. "Whatever you say."

She came off the bed, crossed to him and fell on her knees. She put her arms around his shoulders, her cheek against his. "Don't. Everything you've said about me—it's true. I was part of it. I didn't like it, but I did it. I just wanted you safe."

He pushed her away. "I'm kinda tired."

She stood within touching distance of him, but without

274

touching, her fists clenched. "They'll be sending you back to Washington anytime now. We won't have . . . a chance to talk again."

He glanced at her once. "So what? We don't have anything left to say."

SATURDAY: 1000—GARFIELD

She allowed the floating lace at the window to hypnotize her and drifted uneasily between sleep and waking. The light was hard, brittle, and the breeze stirred the curtains with growing vigor. She touched her cheek to reassure herself she was awake, that what had passed between this wakening and the last was also real and not a dream. Something had woken her. She heard it again. "Who's that?" she called out.

"Can I come in? Garfield."

"Yes. All right, come in."

He was impeccable, as usual; his suit was lightweight silver gray. He wore his half glasses perched high on his forehead and carried a thick document file under one arm.

"I let you sleep as long as I could. You needed the rest."

She sat up on her elbows. "Is Harry . . . ?".

"He left a couple of hours ago." He sat down on the side of the bed. "He gave you a hard time last night."

She blinked heavily at him. There was an implication there she couldn't grasp. She chivied her listless senses. It clicked. "You mean you listened to . . . ?"

"Downstairs. This house belongs to Domestic Operations Division. You can bug a conversation anywhere, any room, just by flicking a switch."

"Thanks for telling me." She blushed.

"Not important. You handled a difficult situation very well."

"He walked out on me."

"I'm surprised he had the strength to walk. He has guts, that boy, but he has his father's philosophy. He's an ordinary man."

"That puts him a mile above our heads then," she snapped challengingly.

"Does it?" He was about to expand on the thought when the phone bleeped. He picked it up. "Yes?" He listened attentively. "Later. Get me a dozen men, four cars. And,

275

Sorrel—tell your stakeout cars I want them to stay well out of sight on Bradley's tail. I don't want him to change his mind."

He replaced the phone and got up. "Bradley's on the move. I'll bet you a blood orange to the Federal Reserve he's taking his troubles to the top. This is what I've been waiting for."

SATURDAY: 1000—BRADLEY

Aaron LaCroix whirled the electric wheelchair expertly as Ambrose Bradley entered the room through automated sliding doors. "Ah, Senator." He passed a glance at a sunburst clock over the mantel. "You're early." The chair squeaked across the polished wood floor to an antique rosewood cabinet. "You'd like some refreshment?" Bradley shook his head. LaCroix poured himself a tall iced soda. The Senator watched him test the drink.

"I apologize for the delay in seeing you," LaCroix said over his shoulder. He added more ice and brought the wheelchair around to face his guest. "There were matters I had to attend to personally. You understand." He waved airily, demonstrating the imperfections of delegation with a fluttering swallowtail flight of fingers. Bradley strolled to the huge sliding windows looking out on the paved terrace. A smooth concrete ramp swept down from the house and became a path that crossed the desert to a group of outbuildings a hundred yards to the left. It was cracked at regular intervals where the sun had baked it beyond endurance.

LaCroix seemed unsettled at Bradley's silence. "Your call on Thursday was inopportune. A degree thoughtless in the circumstances. If I was brusque I apologize. I had a great deal on my mind."

Bradley gave no evidence of having heard a word. He ran his fingers thoughtfully over the pillar-cut arches and flutes of a crystal vase on a small side table.

LaCroix continued testily, "I *am* limited in the time I have at my disposal, Senator."

Bradley flicked a finger at the vase and it rang true and pure. He looked up and held LaCroix in a firm stare. "I wouldn't want to waste your time, Aaron," he said softly.

"You gave me the impression the matter was urgent."

Bradley turned away and pushed open the window. Heat

276

flooded the room instantly, covered the floor and rose from it like vapor. The sigh of the air conditioning became an urgent hiss. LaCroix put down his glass. "What is this . . . Ambrose?" His use of the name was rare; they both noted it with a degree of embarrassment.

Bradley walked toward him and unknotted the brown silk neckerchief at his throat. He draped it across the back of a chair and came to stand behind LaCroix.

"Ambrose?"

Nothing in his tone could have been defined as fear or apprehension, but his frail upper body straightened in anticipation. Bradley disengaged the electrical controls on the chair, took the pushing handles and guided the vehicle through the window and onto the terrace. The temperature, magnified in the still air, was well over a hundred degrees. Bradley blinked, flinched visibly. LaCroix crushed the armrests in his narrow fists. "Ambrose! If I've upset you in any way I . . . Ambrose! You know I can't allow myself to be exposed to the sun. You must take me inside at once. This is childish."

Bradley ignored him and pushed the chair down the concrete ramp. He stopped halfway along the slope, the chair pulling against his fingers. LaCroix sensed the gravitational insecurity. He fought to keep his tone level. "If this is an attempt to prove your physical superiority, Ambrose, I'll be happy to concede the point. I . . ."

"Listen to me." Bradley's voice reflected his own physical discomfort in the merciless heat of the noon sun. "I heard from Washington this morning. Petersen. He told me Milton Abrams is dead."

"I know nothing about . . ."

"Be quiet, Aaron. Listen. Petersen's taking a plane to Europe; he's not quite sure where and I doubt if he knows what he'll do. I suppose Intelligence executives have a certain currency value anywhere in the world these days. He'll go to the highest bidder, I suppose—if he's alive to clinch the sale. He told me to run." He flapped a blue and white polka dot handkerchief from his pocket and dabbed the sweat from his face and hairline.

"Petersen's a fool! But you don't have to worry about . . ."

"That was his considered professional judgment. Run, he said. I thought you ought to know that, Aaron, because you don't run too well."

"Ambrose. Please. Be reasonable. I can't take this . . . heat.

277

You must let me go inside." There were already three or four irregular humps in the skin of his shaven scalp that had not been there minutes before. On the back of his neck a dark rash spread hungrily from behind the ears to the base of the skull.

"I told him," Bradley went on wearily, "that I was too old to run and, anyway, I had nowhere to go. You know what he said to that?"

"Ambrose! For God's sake!"

"No, not exactly that but you're close." Bradley stared out over the desert to the smudge of mountains on the horizon. "He said if we ran they'd leave us alone. He said they didn't want a scandal so they'd leave us alone. What do you think about that, Aaron?"

LaCroix sagged in his chair. The blisters on his skull were bigger now and fast developing nasty white hearts. There was no perspiration visible anywhere on his face or hands, no smudge of it on the black-edged green robe where it touched his body. Bradley looked down at him without compassion.

He flapped his handkerchief around his face again. He was beginning to feel giddy, couldn't adjust his eyes to the glare; he seemed to have lost all sensation below the knees. "You remember the day you told me the plans you had for me, Aaron? I remember it. Day like this. Hotter, maybe. Summer of '76. You decided I was going to run for President and I wasn't any too keen about it. But you talked me around, didn't you? Wham bang."

The voice gasped from a position head down in the green silk folds. "Ambrose. I beg you. Please . . ."

"You were good, Aaron, but you forgot to tell me then what you'd done for Christian decency. John Kennedy. Bobby. Martin Luther King. You left that to Petersen. He killed me that day, Aaron, finished me."

LaCroix groaned loudly.

"For a while I got pretty carried away with the idea of being President. Maybe that's what makes the office so open to hypocrisy. Once you're in it, it blinds you to everything you had to do to get there."

He gave in to the weight of the chair on his wrists and tottered almost to the end of the slope. He flapped the handkerchief again. "This is what you've been missing, Aaron. The heat of the day. The harsh bright light of experience. You know what it's saying? It's saying: Come on out here and try your luck; test your strength. And you know what it does if you lose? It eats you alive, Aaron. Bit by bit,

278

until you don't know how much of you is left and how much you've lost. Step too far out of the cool and you're alone in the wilderness and the only way back is all uphill."

He blew hot breath into hot air. "We both live in glass-houses on the edge of a desert. We both strayed too far and we're both cut off. No way back. No way . . ." He looked down as a thought struck him. "Do you still take the chloroquine?" He glanced back over his shoulder. "I suppose it's in the house. I'll go back and get it . . . when I feel better."

He had given up trying to focus. The bare light had taken over, and the patterns now glittered from behind his eyes; chartreuse and gold and opal. "You know what kept me going these last few days, Aaron? The thought that when I got to the White House I'd sure as hell make you and Petersen pay. I can do some good up there. That's what I said to myself. Come the day, they'll pay. That's quite a slogan, hey?"

He swayed unsteadily, his mind lifting clear of his skull, a tightening in his chest where the skin ran free with sweat.

LaCroix was bent like a stuffed toy, unmoving. His head was blotched white with dehydrated skin.

"The best and the brightest we were, Aaron. Somebody said that. Damn pity all that energy had to go to waste. I reckon you're the one to . . ."

The horizon performed a slow loop and hung across his vision on a diagonal, left to right. He tried to twist his body up to counteract the phenomenon, but it refused to move. He raised his hands to his face and the skin burned hot. The chair hissed down the last of the slope, leveled along the path and shot over its edge into the sand. He opened his fingers and through them saw LaCroix topple in slow motion to the ground. He turned toward the house, his own weight now massively beyond his strength to maneuver. The house also floated on a diagonal from left to right. He took three steps up the ramp, four . . . and his knees gave. He sank gratefully to the concrete, sat down, fell drunkenly on his back, opened his arms to the sun.

The doctor knelt swiftly at Bradley's side, bound both fists together with threaded fingers and smashed down at a point over the heart. "Get some shade over here," he yelled. "Anything." He pounded again and again at Bradley's chest, then stooped to listen. "I want a chopper here," he yelled at Garfield. "And if you want him to stay alive you better tell them to make it fast."

279

He wrapped his mouth around Bradley's and breathed air into his lungs, his hands splayed across the chest to expel it. The man beneath him shuddered, moaned. His face jumped with reaction.

Garfield came back from the radio car. "What about *him?*" He looked across to the pool of green silk in the sand.

The doctor looked up briefly, then returned again to his patient. "I concentrate on the ones I can save, mister," he snapped. "He's beyond any help of mine."

Garfield nodded. While they had fought for the life of Ambroke Bradley on the burning sand, he had gone into the house. The filing cabinets in the annex left no doubt of the man's identity.

Aaron LaCroix.

It was not the first time Lucas Garfield had tasted the gall of self-disgust; it wouldn't, he knew, be the last. Errors, blind alleys, wrong assumptions went hand in hand with luck, perception, experience.

Aaron LaCroix.

The mistake had been elementary. Because he had chosen to believe the evidence of his eyes, what was *on record.* Aaron LaCroix was dead and buried, the record said, and he *had believed!* And he, Lucas Garfield, had told the President that files, data, records, facts, were insubstantial things, unworthy of blind belief.

There were some dueling scars one could bear proudly. This wasn't one of them. Garfield looked down at the body, swollen by the heat. LaCroix had died long before they arrived. Now the lifeless eyes stared like black marbles into the sun.

"Get him out of here," said Garfield.

SUNDAY: 0500—PETERSEN

The *Washington Post* story was blurbed on page 1 and ran to thirty column inches on page 2. It was by-lined Carl Bernstein, and in it the sudden resignation of Donald Petersen, Director of the CIA, was treated acidly by the now veteran gadfly of the Company. It expanded on a theme he had first introduced in *Rolling Stone* some two years before.

The main story was headed SOMETHING ROTTEN IN THE

STATE? The query was a careful addition by an editor, much to the author's chagrin.

It began:

"The sudden, unheralded departure of the most powerful executive in the CIA would seem in itself no more than a natural extension of the policy of cosmetic surgery that has marked this Agency's recent history.

"With monotonous regularity, the pruning shears has lopped and lopped again at the topmost branches in a desperate attempt to curb unnatural growth. Whatever the motives for the latest paring, it can be said with certainty that, true to form, it is not for the reasons stated.

"In a short press release, Donald Petersen is said to have retired voluntarily for 'health reasons.' Now that may surprise the squash-playing companions with whom he has worked out at least two evenings a week over the last several years; it may even puzzle his buddies at the golf club where he regularly spent his Saturday mornings playing to a butch five handicap. It should not surprise Mr. Petersen's doctor; yet, in reply to my telephone call, this gentleman was at some pains to point out the legendary fitness of the Director. He was clearly embarrassed when I revealed to him the reason for his patient's resignation.

"And so, what can we assume from the demise of Donald Petersen?

"One thing only: that the sickness is a corporate one. That a cancer has spread through the Agency to a degree that requires far more than cosmetic surgery. But not even the next of kin are to be told how virulent the disease really is. We are, as always, to remain in ignorance.

"It is the story as before, except this time the disturbing side effects are impossible to hide. From inside the CIA, word comes that Petersen has been locked in a power battle with political figures who, one assumes, have some control over your destiny and mine. There are also unofficial reports that, during the past week, certain members of the Agency have either simply not turned up for duty or have been stricken with the same terminal forms of illness that would seem to plague Mr. Petersen. None of this, of course, can be verified. The CIA, for all its faults, can still be relied upon to lock all storm doors at the first sign of an approaching twister.

"The men who were left standing outside when the twister struck are unlikely to describe their experience. Men like Milton Abrams, Head of Classification, officially described to

281

me as being 'absent on leave until further notice.' Jerry Clay, Petersen's aide, 'reassigned.' Miles Dooley, Special Counsel to the Director, 'transferred.' Barney Keyhoe, CIA Domestic Operations, 'reassigned.' Among the lower echelons, too, desks are empty.

"But what kind of man, in an organization where personal commitment is only as strong as the next rung up the ladder, could inspire such loyalty and bring down so many? What secret do they share? And who had the power to shake the tree until they toppled?"

Despite the loaded questions, Bernstein's frustration at not being able to answer them was apparent in the next twenty paragraphs as he launched into a barbed, but predictable, attack on the Company's failings over the past ten years. Even so, the blow struck home. Next morning a sensationalized précis of his words hit every paper in America. The *London Evening Standard* interviewed him and *The Times*, under the headline WHOSE COMPANY? carried a lead page article analyzing the CIA's role in domestic politics.

It was a good story.

SUNDAY: 0528—THE PRESIDENT

Lucas Garfield hooked out the half-hunter. Two minutes to go. He knew the President was already in the Oval Office, but the Executive Protective Service Officer had volunteered no information and it would be unthinkable to ask him.

The President had called him a little after midnight; he'd barely set foot over the threshold on his return from Phoenix. Sleep first and a 5:30 start, the President said. He had called for a total situation report and listed it at the top of the Day Sheet. Garfield would be first in line.

The Sunday edition of the *Washington Post* had already turned the first spadeful of earth. Sunday readers loved spy stories and they hadn't been let down. The value of being one's own Deep Throat, Garfield reflected, was that you controlled not only the substance of the story but also its speculative direction. Petersen's departure and the hiatus at the CIA were occupying stage center. It would fizzle out within a week, but it had, incidentally, served to make Ambrose Bradley's heart attack a down-page "indisposition."

The two stories rubbed shoulders, but there was nothing to connect them.

The officer's monitoring device flashed and he got to his feet. He waited for Garfield to do the same. The officer opened the door, announced Garfield, ushered him in. The President was already on his feet and coming around the desk. "Luke!" They pumped hands. The President pulled up one of the blue chairs and gestured Garfield to sit. He dropped into another and inched it forward confidentially. "O.K., Luke. Tell me what this is all about."

Garfield talked for ten minutes without interruption. When he finished, he discovered he had the pipe in his hands. The President's smile was a controlled muscular spasm, caught midway and preserved in ice. He let it die when Garfield stopped talking.

"You want to tell me where that leaves us?"

Royal *us?* Garfield said, "I think if you leave matters in my hands for another forty-eight hours, sir . . ."

"Luke—I have no intention of handing over responsibility to you for another *second*. Get that straight in your head. I've had enough of sitting in the dark. The President has a right to know what's happening in his own backyard; I can't justify turning my face away again for the sake of expediency. Look at this. . . ." He waved a copy of the *Washington Post*. "It takes a guy and a typewriter to tell me what you won't. And they're damn close, aren't they?"

"As close as I permitted them to come."

"You leaked this stuff on Petersen?" He was incredulous.

"Yes, sir. It was unavoidable. Petersen flew to Europe yesterday. Someone was bound to report his flight."

"You mean he's on the loose?"

"He's under surveillance. I'll have him picked up if he does anything foolish but I don't think that's likely. He's hoping to stay out of sight for a while. North Germany. The Baltic coast."

"That's a useful stepping-off point if you're traveling East," the President drawled.

"Hmmmm. Moscow wouldn't have any attractions for Petersen. He'll kick his heels for a while and then he'll make an indirect approach. I'll see to the arrangements."

"For what?"

"He'll have to come back, sir. That means assuring him his freedom, an income; some vice-presidential niche in a small company somewhere. It'll look pretty convincing."

"You want me to hand him my job on a plate as well?"

Garfield bowed under the sarcasm. "I'm sorry. He's an important man to us and he knows it. We can't afford to lock

283

him out and we can't afford the luxury of bringing him to trial."

"What about Bradley? And Nixon! Dammit, Garfield, he tried to call me last night."

"Leave them to me, sir. I'll have a quiet word with each of them."

"I'm making no more concessions to you, Luke. I told you once before. No more card tricks."

"No, sir. No tricks. But I think there's a danger here if we leave Bradley or Nixon to their own devices."

"Spell that out."

Garfield shrugged. "I think Mr. Nixon has the bit between his teeth. I intend to convince him it would be unwise to seek further public . . . exposure."

"Where does that get you?"

"He has to recognize what he'd be up against if he decided to tell his side of the story. A full-blooded scandal, initiated by him, would backfire on him, no doubt of that. The media wouldn't let him get away with a reprise of Watergate, with him on the side of the angels this time. I think he's shrewd enough to see that. Besides, I'll have the tape and . . ."

"*I'll* have the tape, Luke," the President interjected swiftly. "I'll have it and I'll see it destroyed."

"As you wish, sir. But that's the way I see it."

The President pawed his chin. "What about Bradley?"

Garfield relaxed. "Different situation. Easier to handle. Bradley's at Walter Reed. I had him flown up with me last night. It's a heart attack, as I told you on the phone. Not massive, but a warning. Second he's had in a year. He can step down with perfect justification. It'll raise questions, of course. They'll talk about strange coincidences, but the doctors can fend off that kind of speculation. He's not a young man. The pressure of his campaign—so on and so forth."

"He's still culpable, Luke."

"Yes, sir. And he knows that. He's lying there in the hospital waiting for the ax to fall and that brings us right back to the situation we faced at the beginning. Exposing Bradley means exposing The Matrix, and that means a public outcry, official investigations. A lot of important men— innocent men, as it happens—would be out in the open. The media will howl for blood sacrifices, and every committee chairman on the Hill will be hustling for a piece of the action. I think we have to accept compromises: LaCroix is dead. Bradley's out for good. The Matrix—they can be controlled as individuals. A few private conversations here and there'll keep them in line."

"That doesn't sound to me like an organization we had any reason to fear in the first place."

"With respect, sir, we have no reason to fear any organization, large or small. It's the vital organs we have to worry about, the eyes and ears and heart and brain. LaCroix and Petersen—to some extent, Abrams—and in a very reluctant sense, Bradley, were those vital organs. But LaCroix and Petersen were the motivators. They used the others, developed the information, provided the drive. I suppose we'd call them crazy, looking back on what they did, but there's no insanity on either side. They used ritual murder the way politicians use television—to get the electorate primed. To prepare the way, eventually, for a hot gospeler riding in on a law-and-order, back-to-the-old-values ticket. You have to admit—they damn nearly made it."

"You say Bradley was reluctant? Couldn't be."

"Not at all, sir. He didn't want to play at first, but LaCroix pulled the rug out from under him. He told him what he'd done in the name of The Matrix. In Bradley's logic, that implicated him totally. His finger was on the trigger as surely as if he'd been on the mound in Deeley Plaza. I should think that at first he had some kind of sublime belief he could make it all work out once he had the Presidency. He's not the first man to put everything on a throw for the White House."

"What do we do with him?"

Garfield exhaled. "My advice, sir, is you leave him to me. I'll talk with him, I'll promise him protection from exposure . . . if he backs off. Retires from active politics."

"I have an idea you're not telling me everything, Luke. Not everything you know."

"I think the Presidency has to be protected, sir. I don't think the office can afford to be seen with dirty hands. Not this year." He jerked up the corner of his mouth.

"You're sure you can tie all this down to The Matrix?"

"It's nothing new. Been with us a long time—the need to group, regroup around a philosophy. The Anabaptists set out to establish the Kingdom of God on earth. They didn't approach the idea with the attack principle LaCroix had, but they were running in the same direction. Every movement has to sow the first seed. How the plant grows depends on the nature of the soil and the prevailing conditions. Mormons, Rosicrucians, Christian Scientists, Freemasons, American

285

Israelites . . . they grew to their soil. The Matrix had small beginnings. It started as a kind of missionary society, nobody very important in the ranks except Bradley, and he was only a circuit judge then. People identified. Important people. They joined. And I guess it was LaCroix who saw the potential and made The Matrix what it came to be—small, exclusive, elitist, right-wing, conservative, evangelical. His gospel was no better, no worse than a dozen fringe Fundamentalist faiths. The one had no contact with the other. LaCroix needed no justification for what he did. And, remember, he was unknown to the membership except for the few who made up the coordinating committee, Petersen, Abrams, mainly."

"That's facile logic, Luke, and you know it."

"The concept of fifty powerful men linking arms to form a solid wall around a religious despot is facile, taken in isolation, sir. It still happened. The Constitution may decree a separation of church and state, but you'd need a secret police system to enforce it."

"You're the man to talk about secret police methods." The President got up from the chair and paced across the Presidential Seal woven into the blue carpet. He looked back at Garfield warily. "All right, Luke. Bradley and LaCroix paid for the privilege. That leaves you, doesn't it?"

Garfield raised an eyebrow.

"You did what you thought you had to do in this, I don't deny that. But the way you did it makes you no better than LaCroix. You used a former President. You played with Bradley and pushed him into a hospital bed. You let two men, three men, die." He swung on his heel. "Or is it more?" He turned away again. "What do you think the people out there, the people who put me here, expect a President to be, Luke? You think I can go stand up and ask them to endorse me in a second term with *that* on my conscience? We both know the answer to that. No—there'll have to be an inquiry. I can't protect you from that, Luke. When the time comes, you'll have to . . ."

"There won't be an inquiry, Mr. President." Garfield stood up. "Nixon and Bradley . . . well, as I said, I think you can leave them to me. The Matrix needs one of two things. The fear of God in every individual belly or—something more sophisticated."

"Like?"

"Like . . . leadership. New direction, new ideas. A little fear, yes; they could use a little fear to prove how lucky they

286

are to be out of this with their skins intact. I'd like to think about that."

"You're playing it behind your back again."

"Sometimes that's the only way. I can't honestly see how we can avoid it in this situation. You don't close down the store because the manager runs off with the till." The President smiled wanly. Garfield was encouraged. He went on glibly, "More to the point, you don't parade your wife's infidelity up and down Pennsylvania Avenue unless you want to look like a fool." His mouth set hard. "Just forty-eight hours, Mr. President. Forty-eight hours."

"That's all I can give you. Not a second more."

"All I need, sir. I'll be back here Tuesday morning—with the tape."

The President offered his hand and they shook. He bunched his mouth. "You'd better be sure you are, Luke. Or I'll come looking for you myself."

SUNDAY: 1045—ANSON

It was a gray day, low clouds bleak with snow, a high wind, filtered light so weak that the airport was ablaze with neon at ten in the morning. George Hyman had insisted on driving him to the airport, but it was a gesture both of them privately resented. Hyman arrived at the apartment at nine, a whole half hour early, and they pretended it was a perfectly normal departure. The pretense grew horns and became a practical dilemma neither of them was equipped to deal with.

They made the run to the airport behind a slush-spattered windshield; the image fitted snugly into their private anguish. Hyman took him to the security office and arrangements were made to get Anson aboard without tedious legalities. Hyman tried to say something appropriate about John Roper's death, about his own unwilling involvement in the Margolis affair, but he made a mess of it and, at the first opening, begged a pressing engagement and ran for it.

Anson had a window seat in the first-class cabin, but immediately after takeoff he left it for the bar. He wedged himself into a corner and swapped drunk stories with the steward for a while, but he soon tired of the exchange and fell into moody reflection.

She hadn't phoned. Face it, he knew she wouldn't but he'd

traded on his innocence just enough to make believe she might. John Roper always said you had to write all women off to experience, even after you married them. They had the constancy of butterflies and the single-mindedness of lemmings. Never ask them to return what they'd stolen from you; they don't know the meaning of honesty when it comes to handling men. Right. But all she had to do was—just call. *Sorry, Harry—it was all in your mind. Necessary evil. Let's say we're both better off. 'Bye, Harry.*

Even that.

Back in Washington, all day yesterday he had tried to find a way back to her but they blocked him at every turn. Langley didn't want to know him; Langley was standing on its head. George Hyman didn't know her. No answer, of course, at the Margolis house. He even called Buffalo Morgan, but the phone company said the number was disconnected.

This morning, at 6:30, before he was properly awake, a man called Lucas Garfield arrived at the apartment and told him he had arranged the return to Rome. No delays. No embarrassments. Go now. "Don't get back to work right away. Enjoy yourself. Relax. Take a couple of weeks off somewhere." The *Post* had front-paged Ambrose Bradley's heart attack and constructed a tasteful obituary to his candidacy-that-never-was.

Then Hyman arrived at the doorstep this morning with the janitor on his heels, clutching the mail that Harry had neglected to collect the day before. Anson took it and went back to the kitchen to make coffee. He never made the coffee. Grazia's letter finished that.

"Tesoro," she wrote, "I see things better from here. When that woman turned up at the apartment and said she was your wife—can you blame me for what I did? But here in Rome, I think: *For one whole year we were together here, in love.* It was beautiful. And where was *she?"* The epithet was underlined three times. "She was not here. She was not in your heart. I would know if she had been. She was not in your thoughts. You could not love her, that woman. So, I went to our apartment and it was not changed and I think we could be together here. It could be beautiful again. But I will not be the one who makes it happen. You must come to me and, if you do, I promise to say nothing of that woman. I will ask no questions. We will forget her—together. Please come quickly."

There was a postscript. *"Tesoro*—there were many letters
288

but this one only I send. It has your father's name on it. You would want this, I know."

He read John Roper's letter several times; in the end he could have recited it from memory. It brought a lump to his throat and then his eyes flooded and his teeth drew blood from his lower lip. It was written four days before John Roper died. It must have arrived in Rome a day, perhaps even hours, after he left for Washington. If only he'd read that letter. If only . . .

It was a letter that anticipated death; in a gentle way, almost welcomed it. A confession, a preparation for that Judgment he believed was inevitable, unavoidable. The words were so redolent of his father's speech that he could hear the voice quite clearly. The fourth paragraph from the end came off the page like a hammer blow. It began:

"I have confessed at this length once already today in an attempt to achieve practical political, rather than spiritual, grace. But what I concealed in that first letter I will reveal to you. 'Reveal' is the word: it implies strict confidence and you must honor it. All else considered, it must strike you as bizarre, if not absurd, that I, of all people, chose to align myself with The Matrix. Zeal, commitment, a sense of belonging—all those elements had a hand in it, but it would be the final act of self-deception to allow you to think that was all. In the end, we act as we do to satisfy personal need: vanity, egocentricity, envy, hunger, greed. I plead guilty to all of them.

"So there it ends. I have to say that I intended nothing as serious as this in my last words to you. I always hoped it would be a somewhat lighter occasion—one of rejoicing; after all, heaven has been my goal all my adult life. I won't burden you with more sermonizing; I guess I did enough of that while you were a boy. If I failed to school you properly in those years when discipline and example were my privilege, I suppose I've lost the right to influence you now at all. But allow me two shafts.

"One: I've instructed the lawyers to continue handling the family's financial affairs, now in your name. Everything is yours, for what it's worth. Enjoy it, but not at all costs. Learn to stand on your own feet before you stand on mine. Whatever you do, avoid applying good intentions to money. The best intentions not only pave the road to hell, they disguise the path to happiness and self-fulfillment.

"Two: The mantle of the gay young dog sits awkwardly on you. You're too old to cling to it much longer. Marriage will be on you before you know it. Whoever the girl is, grace her with one private gift: faith. When your mother and I married we had little else. It bred everything—and at the end we had a great deal. It even bred you."

Faith.

In Grazia? *No, John Roper, you didn't mean Grazia.*

In Lee Ritchie, then? He ordered another scotch. The steward built him a double, compliments of Pan Am. The woman John Roper had in mind might be a butterfly, might be a lemming, might steal and never return—but she would have called. She would have written. She would have been there, sick with unhappiness and guilt and despair, but she would have been there.

Dear God, he couldn't even be sure her name was Lee Ritchie.

He half emptied the glass in one gulp. The heat it generated in his stomach radiated through his whole body. What the hell! Anything he'd felt for her had been born of deceit, manufactured to fit a particular set of circumstances. It would never have worked. Never. Think about Grazia. The worst deceit she was ever guilty of was feigning orgasm.

At least she did it to make him feel good.

The 747 bore down on Rome, treated the tourists on the starboard side to a lightning travelogue of St. Peter's Square, the Tiber, the Seven Hills and swept down to Fiumicino. This time there was no George Hyman to play escort. Anson trailed the crowd through immigration, collected his single bag from the revolving carousel, passed quickly through customs and began the walk to the concourse.

Decisions. State had talked to the ambassador, so he was free to take at least two weeks' vacation if he chose. Take a cab to the apartment, bath, shave, catnap for a couple of hours, then supper at Piero's. No, not Piero's. The place was on Grazia's regular patrol schedule and, if they met, his clean slate would be sullied forever. Bed, bodies, breakfast. From that moment on she wouldn't budge. Better steer clear of the apartment, too, in that case. The alternative was to go to the embassy, check in and check straight out again. His car was still in the parking lot there. Drive along the coast. Portofino would be perfect at this time of year. No people.

He didn't hear the announcement at first. The reprise stopped him in his tracks. "Would Mr. Harold Anson, a passenger on flight 429 from Washington, please come to the reception desk."

The message matched his train of thought so perfectly that he experienced real panic. Grazia! How the hell could she have known? Simple. She phoned the embassy, of course. She'd probably been calling every day. He glanced wildly around him, weighing possibilities. He could walk in the opposite direction and duck into the men's room for a while. Grazia wasn't the type to hang around for long.

The thought lingered long enough to expose its weaknesses. Dodge her here, maybe, but how long could he keep it up? No—she had to be faced. Told. No more, *tesoro*. All finished. He turned resolutely toward the reception desk and shouldered his way through the crowd.

From fifty yards he saw her and his heart lunged into his throat. She had her back to him. She looked different, somehow. The clothes, maybe.

She thought, *I can't go through with it.*

She dug into her shoulder bag, scooped out a compact and opened it. She pursed her lips, checked the outline of lipstick, the subtle strokes of blusher, the soft green shading on the eyes.

She angled the mirror and caught him in its circle, watched him push through the throng of travelers. There was a scowl on his face; determination, not anger. Well, maybe anger. God, what could she say? How were you supposed to breathe life into something that had died like they had died?

Twenty yards. He nearly fell over two tiny girls clinging like toy dogs to their mother's coattail. He stopped, touched their heads, smiled weakly at the mother. He was an ordinary man.

What could she say? What would he do?

Lucas Garfield had said, "You want him, you can have him. On my terms. I want him watched, taken care of, for at least a year, starting tomorrow. He may still be vulnerable. Meet him. Talk to him. If you think you can't handle it, tell me now."

Handle it!

I love you, Harry. Pick the lies out of that. Tell me it's true. Tell me you know I mean it this time. Tell me we're on our own now. Tell me I don't have to make that call to Garfield tonight. Any night . . .

She was following his approach in her compact mirror. He could almost hear her mental computer calculating events. She'd let him come right on up to her shoulder and then she'd turn in surprise and play the come-to-bed fluttering lashes gambit. *Tesoro!* Slanting eyes perfectly wide. Lips rounded.

She spun to face him when he was still ten yards away. He stopped dead. She tried to make words come, felt her lips working. No sound. His face was expressionless. Stone.

Lee! He stared blankly across the space between them. Lee. Smiling now. Walking toward him. Four paces. Two. He dropped his bag and grabbed her to him. They were both laughing suddenly. He wrapped her in a bearhug and the compact leaped from her hand and hit the ground.

She lay her head against his shoulder, tears flowing. On the ground at their feet the open compact winked up at her. The mirror was cracked from side to side.

But she could still see their reflection in it.

SUNDAY: 1200—BRADLEY

There was a sulfurous cloud of irony in the air, Garfield thought, as he followed the Marine lieutenant into the elevator at Walter Reed Hospital. They hit the sixth floor and the Marine led the way to Ambrose Bradley's door. There was no mistaking it; two Marine corporals stood in poker-straight severity on either side, polished leather holsters unbuttoned for possible emergencies. They snapped to attention as Garfield went inside. The door closed.

Bradley lay face up on the bed, arms at his sides. He looked weak, helpless, open to assault. The sunlight streaming through the window on his white hair caused a halo effect.

"Luke!" The voice was strong, no decline there. "Take a seat."

Garfield grinned good-naturedly. "How are they looking after you, Ambrose?"

"Oh, fine. They're good people here. The best."

Garfield came around the bed and sat at the foot. "You have any pain?"

"Can't complain. Wouldn't do any good, I guess." He stared vacantly above him, and Garfield searched for an opening that wouldn't embarrass them both.

"What do the doctors say?"

"Very little I can understand. And when I pretend to, they drop their voices so I can't hear. Terrible places, hospitals, Luke. You need to be healthy to survive in them."

Garfield missed the joke. "The President sends his warmest wishes for your recovery, Ambrose. He's told the hospital he wants to be kept informed."

"He does, does he?" Bradley drew his eyes down from the ceiling. "Good of him, but he can't be too unhappy, I guess. The nurse read me the papers this morning. You see that profile Woodward did? What was it he said about me?"

"The President we needed most."

Bradley's pallid cheeks flushed with pleasure. "Yeah. Hogwash." He was quiet for a moment. Then, "Luke?"

"Yes."

"LaCroix died, right?"

"Exposure, the doctor said. He had some sort of glandular abnormality. He couldn't . . ."

"I know." He closed his eyes wearily. "It was me, Luke. I did that to him. I took him out there, knowing the way he was in the heat. It was all over and I told myself I had to make good . . . something."

"We won't talk about that, Ambrose," Garfield purred. "Some other time."

"We have to talk sometime. You've got me here now. Captive audience."

Garfield shrugged. "What do you want me to say?"

"Nobody's said a word to me since I came to in the hospital in Phoenix. I asked the Marines out there if I'm going to be questioned. They don't know. What the hell's going on, Luke?"

Garfield rose, opened the door and studied the Marine guards. Their eyes did not waver from the forward position. He closed the door and returned to the bed. "Nothing's going on," he said quietly. "Nobody's waiting to question you."

"You're fooling me. Why would the President want to cover up for me?"

"He doesn't want to cover up for anyone. He was all for an open inquiry. Senate Investigation Committee, if necessary. I persuaded him to leave things in my hands."

"Why should he do that?"

"You're not that naive, Ambrose. The pool's still clear. I think it should stay that way, don't you? At least until January."

"New President," Bradley mused.

"Or the same President."

"Is he planning to use me as a vaulting horse into a second term, Luke? It won't work, you know."

"He's not that naive, either."

"Then why?"

"You're the politician. Work it out for yourself."

"No news is good news, huh?"

"Something like that."

Bradley stared at him fixedly. "Who opened all this up for you, Luke? Who started the hare?"

Garfield shook his head. "Don't look for whipping boys. It came out, that's all. Thank your stars you survived it."

"You heard anything about that young Anson kid?"

"What Anson kid?"

Bradley sighed heavily. "All right, Luke. Have it your way. But tell me one thing at least. You know about The Matrix, I guess. You planning to arraign any of them over this?"

"No. I'm not planning anything like that."

"No news is good news again?"

"I think so."

Bradley closed his eyes again, tightly. "I murdered La-Croix, Luke. No matter how fine you slice it, I murdered him just as surely as if I'd shot him down."

"Aaron LaCroix has been dead a long time, Ambrose. I looked for the man at the heart of The Matrix and found a dead man. It fooled me. It fooled a lot of people. It could have gone on that way . . ." His voice trailed away. "The sun killed Aaron LaCroix, Ambrose. Not you. I don't want to hear any more of that."

"Hmmmm." Bradley lay quiet for a long time. Then he said, "On the table. There, by the bed. There's a box. Open it, will you?"

Garfield reached over and took the small blue box, the kind in which a girl would expect to find her engagement ring. He flipped it open.

The tiny gold cross shimmered against a cushion of red silk.

Bradley suddenly found talking difficult. "Luke, *that's* The Matrix. When a man joined us he accepted that pin as he accepted our precepts. Not LaCroix's precepts either." He paused. "You tell me you won't act against the membership. I'll take your word for that. And let me tell you, you're right. The Matrix is purged. It's what it was twenty years ago. No, *better.* It's been through the furnace. It's clean." He looked up at the pin. "The Matrix is potentially a force for good in this country. But it needs new focus. We need new targets. New *drive.*" He paused on the word. "The Matrix needs a leader; a man capable of channeling real power for the good. It needs a man like you, Luke."

Garfield got to his feet and turned away to hide his satisfaction. He studied the tiny gold cross for a moment, then bent back his lapel, attached the pin and folded the cloth into place.

He had only to say yes.

But first, it would be proper to say no.

At least three times . . .

ABOUT THE AUTHOR

FRANK ROSS is a pseudonym for an author who has written extensively for magazines and newspapers. He has published two previous novels, *Dead Runner* and *Sleeping Dogs*.

WATCH FOR
THE "THRILLER OF THE MONTH"

Every month, beginning with FALSE FLAGS, Bantam will publish a highly acclaimed adventure thriller. They will be available wherever paperbacks are sold.

FALSE FLAGS by Noel Hynd

Six silicone chips from an American computer are found in a Soviet diplomat's apartment. These miniscule dots can be programmed to do anything—and yet they are blank. So why do the Russians want them? Ex-CIA agent Bill Mason is enlisted for a daring mission through a maze of intrigue and fallen bodies to find the answers.

THE DANCING DODO by John Gardner

A wrecked World War II plane is discovered in an English marsh containing six bodies all wearing dogtags of men very much alive. Who were they? What was their mission? Why have the crash investigators been stricken with a strange illness uncommon to England? The climax is a race to prevent a catastrophe.

MOSCOW 5000 by David Grant

July 1980—the 5000 meter race at the summer Olympics brings together the most spectacular and troubled field ever presented. And in the stands CIA agents use the games as a cover to rescue one of their men. The KGB is trying desperately to prevent disaster as a terrorist bomb threatens the entire stadium.

THE 65TH TAPE by Frank Ross

A deathbed confession forces our hero to find the whereabouts of one tape, made in Nixon's office, that proves a gigantic conspiracy by some top officials to run their own man for president and take over the country. Only two men can stop this—our hero and Richard M. Nixon. "Knife-edge suspense," says *Publishers Weekly*.

THE WATCHDOGS OF ABADDON by Ib Melchior

A page-turner about a retired Los Angeles cop and his son who stumble on a Nazi plot which, 33 years after Hitler's death, is within weeks of deadly fruition. Their investigations uncover a fiendish plan to set off a nuclear blast and start the Third Reich. By the author of *The Haigerloch Project*.

PARTY OF THE YEAR by John Crosby

Chosen by *The New York Times* as one of the best of the year, this fast-paced story centers on a wealthy woman who decides to give an elegant party for the international jet set in spite of terrorist warnings. An ex-CIA man tries to defuse the situation which could erupt in a shocking bloodbath.